Clean Skins, Teeth and White Bones

Clean Skins, Teeth and White Bones

George G. Kiefer

Copyright © 2005 by George G. Kiefer.

ISBN: 1-4134-5878-5

All rights reserved. No part of this book may be reproduced or transmitted in any form or by any means, electronic or mechanical, including photocopying, recording, or by any information storage and retrieval system, without permission in writing from the author.

This book was printed in the United States of America.

Contents

Acknowledgement	9
Introduction	11
The Canal	15
Haiku	21
Redemption and Two From Column B	22
Haiku	25
Song From Rabbit's Hutch	27
Three Boys Age Ten	33
Watering the Garden Thoughts	46
The Anniversary	50
Haiku	63
Echoes	65
The Boon	95
Monticello, Dove and The Cove	111
All That Live	115
The Summer of the Best Purple Seedless Grapes Ever	122
Haiku	124
Nightfall	126
Haiku	128
Don't Rain On My Charade	130
Edouard	135
Softshells and a Hard Row	141
Jerry, Johnny and My Season at Zatarain's	148
Merchant of the Eight Part Street	162
Beddy	166
LaClede	213
Above Timberline	237
When Words Fail	239
Upon Mine Altar	254
Haiku	260
Election Day	262
Evergreen	314

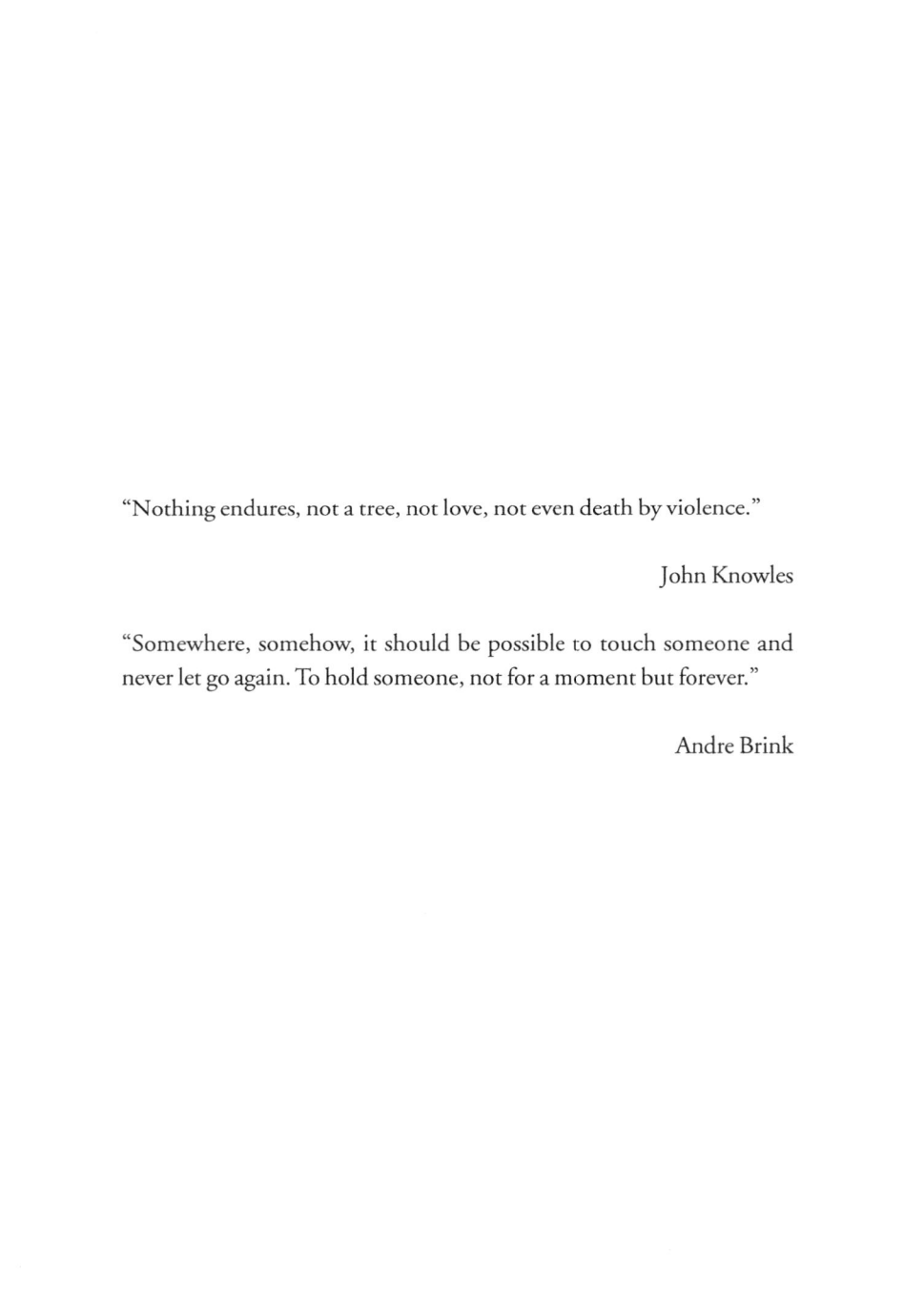

"Nothing endures, not a tree, not love, not even death by violence."

John Knowles

"Somewhere, somehow, it should be possible to touch someone and never let go again. To hold someone, not for a moment but forever."

Andre Brink

To Elaine, for letting me smile at Knowles' taunt and attain Brink's possibility

Acknowledgement

I wish to thank the following friends who edited, encourage and otherwise nursed this book into production: my wife Elaine, Thomas Ford, Charles Lacoste, Melanie James, Mildred Guichard and a special nod to Raymond Russell whose kind assistance when above and beyond.

Introduction

I remember New Orleans, that worn out, laid back, friendly whore of a city laying just north of where the Mississippi plays her last note but closer still to Europe in the way she smiled. I remember her when she was unique and had character, before she became a tourist theme park version of herself. The shadows of the years lengthen and selectively sifting through the tailing of what has gone before, I remember easiest the good times and the people who shared them. I remember New Orleans.

I remember the seductive movement of the French Quarter in nights so full they should have never ended and the muted light playing off the slate roof of the Cathedral moments before dawn. I remember summer afternoons and easy evenings touched by the heady mixture of oleander, hints of spilled bourbon and stale beer. Balconies, ancient frozen balconies, lined the streets on either side. Black painted or orange rusted wrought iron balconies stretched from Esplanade to Canal until they converged at the vanishing point and played out. Beyond those hard, cast metal vines and lovely flower-bedecked balconies waited soft young women with whom to share time. I remember too the sweaty black giant with arms of a fiddler crab. With one chiseled arm, shiny and ripped with muscle, the other withered and crippled, he'd watch my car parked behind the oyster shed where he worked while I played in the Quarter dives. After many of my nights of excess at Harry's, the Seven Seas and too much time trifling upon a bed, I'd return to the parking lot and we'd end the night, the black giant and I, pouring a bottle of Port and laughing at those few parts of the world which were common to us both.

I remember the unforgettable flavor of a Parkway Sandwich Shop roast beef, hurriedly put together by aproned, racetrack guys with boney, tattooed shoulders and cigarettes hanging from their lips. Lotus Street Bakery donuts, running over with sugar glaze, hot, straight from the dark and tumbling grease at midnight. Manuel's Tamales when you were hungry and half-loaded or the smell of Lucky Dogs on Bourbon Street after you blew all your cash. I remember too the love in my youth and soft nights along the lakefront lost in tenderness that crowned and then tormented. I remember the football, the drunken street fights, the politics and the pain.

    I remember all that. And I remember clearest all the ways New Orleans had of laughing when we were young.

The Canal

"Why do the young die? Why does anyone die, tell me?"
"I don't know."
*"What's the use of all your damn books? If they don't tell you that, what the hell
  do they tell you?"*
"They tell me about the agony of men who can't answer questions like yours."

(Dialogue from "Zorba the Greek")

In summer the rains came in the afternoon. The sun warmed the land and the air above it expanded, became lighter, and rose. Moist air from the Gulf was pulled in behind it and across the marshes and bayous it moved inland to form the thunderheads. Rain peppered the rooftops and streets, gathered in puddles and pools and then ran into the catch basins carrying bits of dust and debris into the storm drains. The rain cleaned the air and the black topped streets, mirrored with a coat of water, threw the sun's rays into your eyes when it reappeared. Beneath the streets small lines fed the rain water to larger lines and all the street water of the neighborhood gathered and merged into the square tunnel that ran beneath the length of Mirabeau. From the mouth of the tunnel the runoff and everything it carried emptied into the open canal on Peoples Avenue. Silt collected on the canal bottom and water plants grew in spring and lasted late into autumn. Minnows and crawfish moved with caution among the plants. Egrets hunted on the edge of the cement trough that formed the canal. Water snakes glided and hid beneath the overhanging sides. Pieces of trash floated by, pulled by the large pumps miles to the south.

Forty yards east and up a tree-covered embankment, railroad tracks ran parallel to the canal. In early morning before school, asleep but measuring time by the sounds of the house, I could hear the deep-throated steam whistle of the Southern Pacific alerting the yardmen of its arrival. That lovely haunting sound, so correctly identified in our collective psyches with lonely travel, lingers as the two-note overture to those dust covered boy-days spent around the canal, on the railroad tracks and in the woods beyond.

Warned by parents not to, we did jump the slowing trains and rode them a few hundreds yards before jumping off. We saw the men riding the boxcars in ragged coats looking at us with eyes that told of the dying of something inside. We caught snakes and crawfish, explored the tunnel, shot B-B guns and ambushed the Japanese from the trees near the tracks. Every winter, several days before the eve of the New Year, young men in woolen jackets from the Krupp family carried handsaws into the woods and returned with tree trunks for the fire. They shaped it like a large teepee and built it on a point of land to the side of the tunnel overlooking the canal. The neighborhood, parents and children alike, would gather near midnight, set off fireworks, sing Auld Lang Syne and greet the New Year warmed by the fire and a feeling of comfortable belonging.

The canal, the tracks and the woods were an unrestricted playground where boys were free to settle their disputes on their own. It was an unsupervised classroom where we learned how to make friends, to shoot, to catch snakes and explore even the forbidden. We smoked without inhaling cigarettes slipped out of unguarded packs. We looked at pictures in nudist magazines, the areas of real interests somehow smeared in the printing process so we never really understood. We released the snakes but sometimes, when we pleaded, our parents boiled the crawfish. Blackberries picked from along the railroad tracks were made into pies and Indians faced cowboys daily in the woods, locked forever in eternal combat in which no one died for more than a few minutes. Six shooters never needed reloading and you rode your pony legs with a galloping skip, slapping your hip to run faster, morphing into Tonto and the Masked Man rounding up cattle rustlers.

On the street intersecting Mirabeau just before Peoples Avenue and at its corner, Bill and Bird Nodier operated their small neighborhood grocery. In front of the store between the sidewalk and the street a sycamore, nearly forty feet high, shaded the ground where boys sat on summer days drinking sodas. Inside women, mothers most certainly, could find laundry items and bread. Occasionally a man, out of cigarettes, would be seen going in. Children bought candy and soft drinks when there was a nickel to be had. Stout Mr. Gauff, the silent German whose past and future was a question mark, stopped in every day after work. He spoke rarely but when he did so it was with a heavy accent without removing his curved black pipe. His house was half a street away resting on a small, weed covered lot. There were no weatherboards. He, his wife and children lived in a box-shaped shack covered with tarpaper that was barely visible through the trees and weeds. The back of their house faced the open canal separated from it by a rusted wire fence.

In winter their chimney gave out black smoke from a coal fire when no one else in the neighborhood used or had fireplaces. He was a garbage man. Hurrying home after work he carried himself with quick steps, but his eyes had no light in them. Treat the man with respect we were told. So we greeted him as we would any other adult.

"Afternoon Mr. Gauff."

"Ha-low" he'd say without lifting his eyes.

He wore dark clothes and heavy black boots. Usually he was in wrinkled black pants and a long sleeved shirt but in the summer he'd roll up the sleeves. In winter he wore a thick seaman's cap and a woolen muffler.

"Why doesn't he cut his grass or finish his house?"

"Look how he walks stooped over. He's too tried to do it after working all day."

"He works two shifts a day my father said."

"Nobody knows his kids either."

"They haven't been in the country very long. Maybe they want to stick to themselves for awhile. Maybe because of the war, they're afraid to talk to too many people."

"Maybe they're Nazis."

They were not seen at school or church either.

Mr. Leonard would occasionally go to the grocery to buy a can of motor oil or cleanser for his garage. With broad shoulders and thick powerful hands he'd ask me to walk with him and he would tell me of carburetors and crankshafts and push rods. I pretended to be interested because I liked him. He taught high school woodshop and was the neighborhood mechanic. He and his wife hosted one of the New Years Eve parties that made its way to the bonfire shortly before twelve each year. They lived across Mirabeau from us and they had the first TV set in the neighborhood. My brother and I watched the weekly Lone Ranger in their front room on the six-inch, rounded black and white screen.

Kids would run to Nodier's with a small list of items that had been forgotten when their parents shopped at the larger groceries. The neighborhood was known and the movement of its people, children and adults usually on foot, had a familiar pulse. In summer with doors and windows open you heard laughter and perhaps a dog barking. All else was quiet except for wind in the tall trees and the voices of children playing.

I recall those joyful innocent days first but as I pull up more and sift through the distant memories of the canal, the picture clears and widens and I see Zimmer and the paint can of kittens. He carried the three cats in his right hand, the can in his left and worked his way down the slope from the end of Mirabeau to the edge of the canal where two of us stood watching. There was some talk, some protest, but we were too small to do more. He placed the kittens in the gallon can together with a stone, punched holes in the top, tied a string to the bail and shoved it underwater. Frozen with cowardice I could only ask him why as the bubbles broke the surface. Minutes went by with painful slowness until he pulled up the can and opened the top. Not all of them were dead and he put them back into the brown water and we waited again. My anger grew but I could not act and I hated both of us because of it.

He held the three of them in his hand, ugly dead gray and white things dripping water, limp. Instinctively, even now, I do not like red-haired, freckle-faced boys. Perhaps it is because of my watching redheaded Zimmer that day. He laid them across one of the pipes that crossed the canal and beat their dead bodies with a stick. He crushed their skulls and one of the eyes came out of a socket and hanged down the side of the pipe connected to the kitten's head by only a few twisted strands. He was laughing. I left without an answer to my question but years later, Zimmer, at my hand, received the beating he earned that day.

I discovered one day the body of an animal that drifted in overnight and became lodged in the cattails. Over the years there would be more. It was badly decomposed; gasses distorted the stomach, floating it half out of the water. I picked up a dried cane from among the dead ragweed and turned the animal around to see its face. I pulled back from the smell. It was a black dog, its body bloated and malformed beyond recognition. The belly was pulled tight and the hair on his side no longer covered his skin. I freed the body with the cane and pushed it down the canal, away from where I was playing. And then I went home.

Flash forward to another warm month and my fourth grade classmates and I were at a daytime birthday party. Twelve-year-old Milton was drinking a soda beneath Mr. Nodier's sycamore. My brother, a year younger than Milton, was in our back yard, the length of a football field away from the store. My mother was inside cleaning the house. Overhead, a military aircraft, its crew and seven men returning from their tour in Korea were coming down.

Milton heard the engines sounding too close and too loud. He looked up as it cleared the rooftop across the street and just a moment before it clipped the top of the sycamore. My brother saw it above Mr. Leonard's house and he watched the right wing take a few feet off the rear of Nodier's just before it slammed into the top of the canal and the embankment of the railroad track. Milton and Hartley were the first to the plane. My brother, ignoring my mother's yells, was next.

My mother called the parent hosting the birthday party, told her what happened, and asked that she keep the neighborhood children there until the bodies of the dead were moved. She did that and led the party children in prayer for the soldiers. My mother told my brother not to tell me what he saw at the crash and I was told not to ask. But the story reached my ears from other children. The men were mangled. The pilot and co-pilot were broken red dolls dressed in olive uniforms embedded into the instrument panel, pinned by their seats. One man was decapitated. Hartley, older than both my brother and Milton by a few years, pulled open a door to help those who were alive inside. There were none but the three boys tried to find them anyway. There was blood and parts of human beings everywhere inside the plane.

Someone from the neighborhood placed two long planks across the canal and military men retrieved their comrades. They carried them in covered stretchers down the cement far side of the canal, across the makeshift bridge, and up the near side to waiting ambulances. The white cotton sheets over the bodies were soaked with blood. Someone slipped and a body fell off the stretcher and rolled into the canal. My brother did not sleep well that night. Nor did he for more than a week.

The next day most of the neighborhood gathered on the grass and cement opposite the crash site, sat down and watched as more military men climbed though the crash. All the bodies had been moved the previous afternoon and we were silent saying not much more than how unfair it seemed. I couldn't tell what kind of plane it had been. Far too small to be a C-47 but the tail was similar. Could they look that small after nosing in like that? Someone mentioned that the pilot was probably trying to make it to the small cornfield on the other side of the tracks. Others agreed.

Again in a summer month heavy rains came. Bird Nodier and the rest of the neighborhood knew the rain would cause some minor flooding. The children knew the canal would rise nearly twelve feet to the wide brim of the cement trough. Many, in spite of being forbidden, would swim when the rain stopped. The center of the canal moved swiftly when it flooded. A large volume of water was pulled by the pumps designed to empty the city. The children, the smaller ones, avoided the center. Bigger boys with strength enough to overcome the current swam with it downstream before pulling to the side. A small child, perhaps miscalculating or perhaps too young to understand, was taken and went under. Word and fear spread through the neighborhood and impromptu rescue teams of men were sent up the canal from Mirabeau to the pumps. The children stood on the bank, shivering with cold that wasn't there moments before. Then the police and firemen arrived. Mr. Gauff heard shortly after stepping from the bus that a child had drowned. Paying for a loaf of bread at Nodier's he told Bird Nodier, "Thank Got it vussant one uf mine." She began to cry and said, "Dear God Mr. Gauff, I believe it was one of yours." They found his child's body the next day on the grate in front of the big pumps.

In summer the rains came in the afternoon bathing the houses and streets of the neighborhood and made their way into the canal carrying with them the collected debris. The water flowed indifferently past the cattails, the egrets and a new group of playing boys. The gash in the woods and in the ground outlived several of the neighborhood's parents and a few of its children, including Milton and my brother. The cement that replaced the section crushed by the plane remained a whiter shade than the surrounding original cement. The mute memorial of white cement reminded some of us that while life could be unbelievably sweet, it could also end suddenly, cruelly and without regard to fairness or love. And it was best that the children knew this early on.

Silent night heron
balanced near the shadowed reeds
unmoving, unseen.

Redemption and Two From Column B

Most people are other people. Their thoughts are someone else's opinions, their lives a mimicry, their passions a quotation.

Oscar Wilde

Scanning a room of strangers, we linger on the unusual. The out of place, the oddity, demands not only our attention but also an explanation. With him, I suppose it was the tension in his body. He was leaning forward in his chair, his chest resting on the edge of the table with his hands clasped together between his knees. His head was lowered and his eyes looked into the face of the man seated across from him. His feet were pulled back under his chair, heels up with his toes poised on the floor. He wore a simple flannel shirt and khaki pants. His shoes, selected without regard for style, were dark and worn. There was more than a touch of gray in his hair and, although worn short, it needed a trim badly.

His age was a problem, between 42 and 52, I guessed. His face was lined but young and difficult to date. From my seat at the next table I was able to study him for brief moments without being noticed. He gazed into his companion's eyes with a look of both pain and expectation or perhaps a naive eagerness that hinted of a Rockwell painting. Either way, I was intrigued by his appearance.

His dining companion, in between spoons full of wonton soup, spoke quickly in deep tones with the assurance of one who knows, or at least, one who asks no new questions. He, in contrast to the younger man, was dressed in a dark suit and appeared to be in his sixties. He wore thick glasses and looked directly at the man opposite him. He had the air of religion about him; a somber grayness that seems to suck up light and joy like a black hole.

Something had happened to the younger man some years earlier. Judging by his speech patterns and vocabulary he had been educated beyond his apparent condition. He seemed at a loss to understand something; some answer, some key, had eluded him. His older associate offered platitudes and little else, an egg roll not withstanding.

He spoke of some event after which he was unemployed for two years. During this time he was involved, or rather consumed, he said, with the charismatic movement. He then found the Seventh Day Adventists more appropriate.

Overhearing him, I thought of my own religious shifting. I had not attended mass for years, but one Easter I returned to find the priest now facing the congregation and speaking English, traditional Latin having been discarded. Inexplicably some strange young man singing folk songs and beating a guitar had replaced the choir. It was like returning to the old family home, finding the furniture rearranged and that some of the folks have moved. Not that these superficial changes caused a theological upheaval, they merely underscored the changes that had already taken place in my ideas of religion. Still vague about the questions, I knew, at least, many of the answers were no longer here.

Eventually the younger man had found work in a hardware store and life and his understanding of it apparently was still difficult. He was assured by his companion that we must accept God's will. (An easy task provided He wills you well.)

The younger man lowered his eyes and began eating slowly; he was obviously thinking on his most profound level. I heard no details of the event that brought about his collapse, but its effect was obvious. This man was devastated. He sat there, eating, frozen in thought. His fork would move from his plate to his mouth so slowly and so painfully, I felt ashamed, an intruder on an extremely private moment. His eyes were fixed not on his food but on the center of the table. Neither man, it seemed, was reaching the other. The younger man's need for answers or reassurance or forgiveness was not fully understood and the other's superficial replies offered little. If there were words, this man did not know them. From where I sat, the younger man was either depressed or far too sane. Life requires a bit of madness, enough at least to give us the strength to laugh when the world falls gray.

After the long painful silence he spoke again and the words came only with effort: "I believe what happened to me had a purpose. I believe God wanted to use me as an example. Things like this don't happen without a reason." I heard in his voice the dead leaves of his life pushed along by the indifferent winds of hopelessness.

The older man spoke slowly. "God has a plan. In time it will be revealed to us and it will be clear."

What if they're both wrong? What if there is no plan, no reason, only the accident of life? Right now, at this moment, what difference would it make? Would his pain be any less? Perhaps. Perhaps, if he were more secure in his beliefs. Perhaps it's the belief itself that's important. Perhaps a belief in anything, if it were sure enough, would ease his pain. Perhaps even a belief in himself.

They finished their meal in silence for the most part. The younger man had lost interest and he ate and moved more by habit than design. The check came; he opened a fortune cookie, gazed at the message briefly and tossed it onto his plate. He leaned back in his chair and hooked his thumbs in his rear pockets. He stared ahead looking through his companion no longer hearing his words. The bill was divided, money placed on the tray, and he lifted and fingered the bit of paper again while trading small talk with his acquaintance. His friend continued to speak, and he studied the fortune again. He folded it carefully, placed it in his wallet and returned his wallet to his back pocket. He inhaled deeply, held the breath a beat and silently exhaled. He looked down at the table, unmindful of his companion's words. He gave a bit of a shrug to his shoulders and moved his head slightly from side to side.

In a moment, they rose and walked to the exit. The younger man felt for his wallet just before he stepped through the door.

Moonlight tinted trees,
Silver strokes on satin limbs.
Geese conduct the wind.

Song From Rabbit's Hutch

Wild things leave skins behind them, they leave clean
skins and teeth and white bones behind them
and these are tokens passed from one to
another, so that the fugitive kind can always follow their kind . . .

> Tennessee Williams, *Orpheus Descending*

Rabbit sure didn't look like a rabbit. Powerful shoulders and deep chested like Dad, but taller and with the hands and face of a boxer. Not cut and scarred, mind you, but massive and with the weathered character of a New England seacoast. In spite of his blue eyes, Rabbit was not a man to piddle with.

On most Friday nights in post-war New Orleans, our clan would gather at a small neighborhood restaurant for the traditional Catholic seafood blowout. Davises and Gallaghers, Richards and Kiefers, and food and laughter everywhere. Softshells and shrimp, flounder and french fries, trout and tartar sauce, boiled crabs, and oysters, both fried and raw. And beer. Lots of beer.

The kids, my cousins and I, would run and cavort, largely ignored by our usually stern parents. Friday nights, in my memory, were the resilient core of a great ball of happiness that was my childhood.

Uncle Bob, Rabbit, and his wife, my mother's cousin, Aunt Colette, were there most weekends, and when they moved into our neighborhood, the knot that binds a family tightened a hitch or two. Their two-bedroom bungalow was constructed on the front portion of two lots. Uncle Bob immediately planted citrus plants in the large side yard and in the rear of the house and along the fence he ran his vegetable garden.

Tomato plants, tied to supporting stakes, bore red-orange fruit rivaled only by pictures on seed packets. Okra, by summer's end, would be well over ten feet tall and still producing blooms. Eggplants sagged under the weight of huge purple-black produce. And corn. Tall and crowned regally with yellow tassels, they would sway with the slightest breeze. Bob, who did all of his cooking in the garage on an old Roper stove, would grab a few ears when Dad and I would drop by, plop them in some boiling and slightly salty water, crack open a couple of long necks and wait. Covered with melted butter, those yellow kernels tasted joyously and with an unforgettable aftertaste. In cooler months, however, his energy was focused on his *coup de grâce*, the cabbages. Large-leafed and confident, they hugged the soil like huge green stones, not shying from their fate, but inching towards it each day, eagerly, as if in some quiet green competition. The cabbages were so large and sweet, and when smothered with a bit of ham and bacon, you felt like crying for the Irish.

In later years, after my marriage, he shared the knowledge he had acquired over a lifetime of observation: the soil mixtures, the proper ratio of potassium, nitrogen and phosphate, the shade or sunlight requirement of each plant. The diseases, the sprays, the amount of water, and the care or neglect each required, were patiently shared with me, his neophyte. He fostered so much love and care on his garden that surely it would have produced fruit out of pure guilt, if nothing else.

"Those tomatoes love sun, but water them regularly. Too much or too little is no good. No fluctuations. Flood them for three or four days and you'll get end rot."

Sounded like good advice for loving a child, too.

* * *

When they were younger men, before I was born, Bob and Dad sang the marshes, hunting and fishing. I arrived late in my father's life, and by the time I was old enough, hunting was far in his past but we did some fishing.

The adventures that united the three of us in the brotherhood of the wilds was the recurrent springtime quest for crawfish. Crusaders turning to our personal Mecca, nets folded and slung over their shoulders, they led me through roadside ditches and wetlands in search of that most prime of all Louisiana delicacies. Avoid ponds where the water was too clear and where the duckweed grew thickly. Cloudy water a foot and-a-half deep with just the right arrangement of water plants was choice. Only melts were ever considered proper bait. Place the net on the end of your pole and run it out to a likely spot. Set it down easily, and gently press the center of the net down with the pole so the net would remain flat on the muddy bottom. Squeeze the bait later in the day to bring more blood to the surface. Respect the snakes. Clean up your mess. Wash the nets with clear water, and stand them open until sun-dried so they won't rot.

Returning home with our catch, we would purge the crawfish in salt water while the proper mixture of crab seasoning, garlic, onion, and lemon was brought to a boil. To the uninitiated, odors coming from Bob's garage were foul, no doubt. Pungent vapors of almost caustic nature: crab boil, fish fry, and his *nom de cuisine*, rabbit stew, tumbled and rolled down the drive, capturing the unexpected passerby like a sinister and spice ladened fog.

Perhaps the rabbits came from the hidden recesses of his huge chest freezer, or perhaps they were taken out of season or fell from the sky. I don't know, but they were in endless supply. Every other week, it seemed, Uncle Bob was stewing rabbit in the garage. On Friday or Saturday afternoons we would drive by, see the garage door open with Bob sitting on a chair in front of the stove, his mitt wrapped around a chilled bottle of Falstaff. The witches' brew of brown-gray sauce, peppery and offensive to my young nostrils, always seemed to need another splash of red wine. Dad would pull up a chair, grab a brew, and give the pot a few authoritative stirs before taking a seat. Standing on tiptoes, I would peer into the massive pot and see legs, backs, and rib cages of what used be little fur brown bunnies.

On special occasions, or when the mood would strike in those Roper-stove-days, Bob would drag over a step ladder to the center of the garage, ascend to a large shelf located in the ceiling, disappear from the waist up, root around, and after clunking a few bottles together, descend holding a dusty bottle of rare nectar—Cherry Bounce. Never did these occasions seem to fall more than twice in the same year. How many bottles were up there, only he and Dad knew. The precious fortified wine, dark and syrupy, would be poured into glasses the size of large thimbles. Vague references to its potency were tossed back and forth, as each of them took the smallest of sips, fearing to consume such a gift too hastily. I remember Bob, holding his glass at arms length, looking with pride through the liquid, back-lit by the afternoon sun. These bottles, at the time, were twelve years old, having been the last batch they put up. Their method was simple enough. They would spread out sheets beneath a black cherry tree and bump the tree with a car, dislodging the ripened cherries. Perhaps sensing that neither would bottle another vintage, they savored the last of the Cherry Bounce as they savored their days, with measured appreciation and lightheartedness.

Bob and Colette had no children, but drew their nieces and nephews into their warm circle. Assorted candies and goodies were always on hand awaiting our visits. Colette succumbed to one of the many rages of the fifties and purchase a parakeet she named Pretty-Boy. Pretty-Boy occupied his days in the kitchen, his cage located on the freezer chest, where Colette repeated his name with barely a pause until he learned to say it properly. That being done he quickly progressed to "Love ya momma." For a few weeks it was cute, but now the feathered chatterbox was a non-stop "Pretty-boy—Love ya momma" aggravation.

It was during this same time that Bob acquired a high-strung Doberman, regally named Baron. Hyperactive did not quite describe his relentless pacing and fidgeting. Back and forth, to and fro, he wore a deep, narrow trench, inches from the chain link fence and the prized vegetables.

On more than one of those rabbit afternoons, the back door would fly open, a female arm would swing bird, cage and all, into the backyard. As the door slammed shut and the cage bounded across the yard, the bird would let out a series of frightened squawks while Baron jumped, barked frantically and danced puppet-like on his hind legs. A muffled "son of a bitch" issued from behind the now secured kitchen door.

Bob lowered his blue eyes, stared deeply into his liquid amber refuge and proclaimed, "Got a neurotic dog, a neurotic wife, and now the bird."

Dad threw back his head, scrunched his nose and roared with laughter. I believe it was the first time I heard the word "neurotic" and when, years later, it was used to describe my generation, I could face that truth with a smile, thanks to that earliest encounter.

I remember cool nights with on-shore breezes when the lakefront, from East to West End, was a yellow-orange necklace of smudgepots against the dark crescent of the shore. Men and boys, the three of us among them, cracked clams with hammers and threw their broken bits and flesh into the then safe water of the lake.

Shrimp, attracted by the orange flames and the clams, were caught with cast nets thrown like large woven frisbees. Never in those days, was it difficult to catch a washtub of shrimp or a hamper of crabs. A dozen crab nets and a few chicken heads easily became a family boil any summer evening of your choosing.

During the week, my father was on the road, conducting his business in the other cities and towns of Louisiana, but he arranged his schedule to have Fridays to himself. Work was not the most important part of his life, living was. From around the state, he would return home laden with gifts of deer meat, French duck, pintail, geese, redfish and crates of vegetables.

These harvests from land, sea, and sky would find their way into Dad's or Bob's stew pots. Dad zeroed in on the gumbos and stewed *poule d'eau*—the man loved the gizzard—while Bob fashioned venison, rabbit, and the occasional squirrel into dishes I can still taste these forty years later.

Bob and Dad did not march to the beat of any drummer, different or otherwise. The music they heard was inside them, the way wind gets inside you at sunrise in a duck blind; the way rain gets inside you fishing in an open boat; the way seasons get inside you when those kinds of things are important.

Most of us desire a successful life, but few of us get around to deciding for ourselves what it is. Usually for most, it is measured in terms of possessions. Dad did not spring the materialism trap where possessions wind up owning you. He could not adopt someone else's idea of success as his own. His goal, his ambition, his *raison d'etre* was simple: contentment. He did not arrive at this conclusion through laziness, for he was not, nor through lack of ability, for he was capable. A modest home, a family where he felt loved, more than a few days in the outdoors, and a couple of brews on the weekend, that's all. A simple life can be truly enjoyed only by the simple or the enlightened; the bulk of us falling in between are cursed with insatiable restlessness that drives us to escape, rather than pleasure and illusion, rather than creed. Dad's contentment sprung not only from what he had, but from what he did not need. He had what he wanted; the rest was unimportant.

Years later, after he and Bob were long dead, I was hunting near the river's mouth. Out in that quiet predawn marsh the sound of thousands of wings high up, pushing air, was heard before their faint calls. Coming before and during the rising sun they flew, on and on, line after line of geese. From one edge of sky to the other, they made their way to some remote and sacred feeding ground. The golden morning, the chill of a winter wind, a patchwork of blue-white sky, band after band of geese and the rush of far-off, high-away wings. And in the holy sound of their distant voices, I could hear laughter and understand its meaning, laughter of two men who found endless joy in places such as this and times such as these.

In those post-war stoic days love was not spoken of among men, but I felt it, always. Occasionally, at high school football practices I would see Dad sitting in his car, watching. Knowing the embarrassment it would bring to me, he never made his presence obvious. The sudden silent hand on my shoulder as we walked, voiced unmistakable affection. Never, can I recall, did he reach for dessert until my brother and I had our fill and left the table. Only then would he sneak a piece of cake.

Only then.

*　*　*

Dad died when I was not quite twenty-four. Too soon for the both of us. He slipped into a coma, and during my lunch hour, I would ride the solemn streetcar down the mainline of town to visit. After work I would return with the rest of the family to be at his side, keeping death at bay with our frail weapons of hope and prayer.

It was during one of those midday visits that I was sitting on the air conditioning unit staring across the room without seeing. I glanced down at him and his weak and apparently unresponsive eyes were fixed on mine. He was breathing heavily. I moved my head to the side a few inches; his eyes did not follow. I diverted my attention a few moments and then looked back at him. Again, his eyes had found mine. In the long visual embrace that followed, we communicated those things we had known all along anyway, but it was time to feel and know them again, a final restatement of love.

* * *

For years I continued to crawfish and hunt, and I'm still inclined to plant a tomato or two. My wife stews the rabbits and I still make one hell of a gumbo. I do it because I enjoy it, and partially in remembrance of the fellows who taught me their art and more.

Some time after Dad passed away, I stopped by Uncle Bob's on a Friday. As expected, he was seated before his stove and stew pot. He shook my hand, offered some words of meaning knowing that there were none, and pulled out his ladder. Coming down from the attic-like shelf, his blue eyes gleaming, he brushed off some of the thicker dust. Taking down two shot glasses he poured us each a measured amount of purple-red memories. After we both took a small sip he added, "Good stuff, huh, kiddo?"

Looking out the garage window, over the Roper stove, past the cabbages, the crawfish, and over the crab and fish ladened lake, and into the heart of things, I replied, "It sure as hell is, Rabbit. It sure is."

Three Boys Age Ten

We are told that the America of the '50s was a time of simple innocence. Should history find the generation of that period less than perfect, then let it be noted, at least, that the times were.

*   *   *

Jeff stood by the window in the side room of his house and peered through an Official Cub Scout telescope. A light rain had just stopped, and he focused on a drop of water suspended on the tip of an azalea leaf. He turned the telescope around, pressed his eye to the larger end and was amazed by the diminution which took place. That morning he stayed home, feeling the need for a brief interlude from the rigors of grammar school. He held a thermometer under the hot water tap long enough to raise its reading to simulate a mild fever, and presented it to his mother along with the vague complaint of feeling none too well. Rarely did he use this ploy and, consequently, it was believed every time. His older brother had employed similar devices far too often to be believed and, of necessity, he would carry on for hours, finally winning his reprieve through the surrender of his opponent rather than guise. Far too much effort, Jeff concluded. His method was painless, he thought, and although not put into effect as often, it accomplished its end without ruining the day with a whining confrontation. The real trick, he thought, as he raised the telescope to spy on the neighbor's dog, was to time his recovery with school's dismissal. At one o'clock he informed his mother that he felt much better, and now, near three, the next phase of the gambit began. Again he took his temperature and this time he stayed in his mother's presence. Oddly enough, it read normal.

"I'm going to walk around the block and see if I still feel good. Okay?" He asked, flying boldly into the most hazardous aspect of the scheme.

"You should stay in," his mother said.

"But if my temperature is gone, doesn't that mean I'm okay?" he countered.

"If you go out too soon, you could have a relapse and I don't want you missing school tomorrow," she said.

"But how do I know I can go to school tomorrow if I don't go outside to see if I feel okay? I'll come right back if I start feeling bad."

It was hopeless. Check and mate.

"Okay," she said, "but stay away from the canal."

Too late; he was out the door and on his way to Leslie's. He rounded the street corner to see Leslie and his younger brother jump off their porch over a much-abused poinsettia. Their house was a shotgun double, the porch of which was divided by a square brickwork two feet high. They climbed this in order to jump over the plant which grew in front of, and was perhaps a foot taller than, the brickwork. Young agility occasionally failed and the poinsettia's limbs suffered for growing too tall.

"Hey," Les called out, "you missed school today."

"Yeah. Didn't feel well. I'm okay now."

"Let's get our bathing suits and the hose," Les said.

"No. I'm supposed to be sick. My mom wouldn't let me," he said with a shrug. "Do you have a dime?"

"What for?"

"If you have a dime, I'll show you how to get a lot of candy, if you promise to split it," Jeff replied.

Les' younger brother grew tired of jumping over the poinsettia and ran to the back of the house for some undisclosed purpose. A fortunate turn, as Jeff was reluctant to reveal his plan and only did so now because the gumball machine was at low tide and he was out of funds.

"I've got to go to Dreux Street to buy some stuff for my mom and she promised me a dime," said Les. "What do we do with it?"

"Come on, I'll ride with you and tell ya about it."

Les ran in to get his mother's list and came down the driveway on his bike. He stopped at the sidewalk and Jeff hopped on the rear fender, placing his feet on the pedals. Leslie pushed off and placed his feet on top of Jeff's, and as they double pumped down Eastern Street, Jeff unfolded his plan.

"The gumballs in Mr. Bill's machine are almost gone and half of what's in there are winners. For a dime we get five or six prize palls. I promise. I do it all the time."

Mr. Bill's. That treasure trove of Hershey bars and Snickers, Ju-Ju Bees and Whatnots. The corner grocery and candy outlet was operated by old Bill Nodier and his sister, Bird. On the right-hand counter, in front of the cash register, stood the gumball machine. Multicolored balls of chewing gum were crammed in and, along with them, red and yellow striped prize balls. The lucky kid who won one of these jewels was entitled to five cents' worth of candy. The prize balls were placed carefully by hand near the sides of the glass container, while the center portion of the display was filled with ordinary gum, so the prize balls appeared far more numerous than their actual count. The center of the display was dispensed first and, owing to this arrangement, a large number of prize balls were left with relatively few gum balls as the machine became nearly empty. Many months earlier, Jeff had noticed this phenomenon and would bide his time until a winning situation presented itself. On those days he would, unnoticed by the other children, descend upon the machine with a fist full of pennies and parlay his holdings into a considerable amount of candy. Not always did he have the necessary capital for this undertaking, however.

"Are you sure?" Les asked, his greed tempered with caution. Ten cents was no idle sum to be wasted on gumballs.

"Stand on your toes and look in the machine. You can see for yourself."

The pumping on the bike quickened and the boys rushed through the purchases of sewing items for Leslie's mom and returned home quickly for the dime.

Leaving the bike at Leslie's house, the two boys ran to Mr. Bill's across the street.

"Promise not to tell anyone," Jeff said.

"I won't."

They burst into the grocery, the screen door slamming noisily behind them. "Easy boys. Take it easy," Mr. Bill warned and continued waiting on Mrs. Southerlin. The friendly old counters of Mr. Bill's store were two large wooden affairs standing side by side. Their tops were worn smooth and slightly concave, polished by hands picking up change and goods over the years. High as a boy's chin, the counters were divided by an ancient mechanical cash register, engraved and lettered with intricate designs. The base of the counters pressed forward forming a curved frontispiece, and emblazoned thereon was the large and then familiar red circle logo of Lucky Strike cigarettes. Overhead, two large ceiling fans circulated the air silently. To the left of the counters and perpendicular to them stood the candy display. This shelved cabinet enclosed in glass held the desires of their small world and all for a nickel apiece.

Mrs. Southerlin, the neighborhood crone, glared down at the offending children and turned briskly to face the grocer. Using a pole device with flexible clamps operated at the lower level like a pistol grip, Mr. Bill grabbed a paper product from the top shelf. "You wanted some cheese, too, right?"

The boys ran to the gumball machine and on tiptoes peered in, their heads pressed together. As predicted, the machine was nearly empty and there were more prize balls than regular gum.

"Wow!"

"Shh!" said Jeff, afraid of being discovered by some unseen child.

"Get the pennies! Get the pennies!" said Jeff.

"Mr. Bill, I need some change," shouted Les, waving the dime above his head like a small silver flag.

"One minute boys. Mrs. Southerlin was here first. Bird. Bird, can you take care of the boys?"

Bill's sister appeared at the top of the four stairs that led from the grocery store to the living quarters they occupied in the rear. Slowly and carefully the gray-haired lady let herself down the steps.

"Hello, boys. Whatcha need?"

"Ten pennies!" cried the two in unison.

Bird hit the "No Sale" and fished out the coins. She handed the pennies to Leslie with one hand and at the same time took the dime with her other.

"Thanks, Miss Nodier," they said.

"The first one's mine," Les stated firmly while inserting a coin.

"Sure. That's all right. Hurry up."

Les gave the crank a turn and a ball fell in the covered receptacle. He opened it and retrieved a blue gumball.

"Do it again! Do it again!" said Jeff.

Again. And this time a red ball.

"One more time! Come on! You can't stop now!"

Blue again.

"Keep trying! I promise!"

The door opened and out rolled a prize ball into Leslie's anxious hand.

"What'd I tell you?" said Jeff with his pride intact, "Go again."

Another prize ball.

At the end of the dime they had four gumballs and six prize balls. Jeff was vindicated. His enterprise had brought them thirty-four cents worth of sweets. Two gumballs and three pieces of candy for each.

"Promise not to tell," Jeff said again as they walked toward the canal, peeling the first candy wrapper.

"I told you okay and I mean it," said Leslie.

Beneath the length of Mirabeau Avenue, from Elysian Fields to the Peoples' Canal, ran a storm drain, large enough for a man to stand in. The tunnel opening on the canal was cool and wide and formed a favorite retreat from the summer's sun on those pre-air conditioned days. Here the boys sat and ate their candy.

A pair of legs appeared above them in the tunnel entrance, bent and then jumped to the tunnel's floor.

"Hey," said Lenny, after landing with a thud which echoed down the cavern. "Whatcha doing?"

"Just sittin'," said Les, while he chewed on a chocolate bar.

* * *

For years the older neighborhood boys bragged of having walked the length of the tunnel all the way to Elysian Fields. Horrible tales of snakes and oozing slime, punctuated with hints of certain death by sewer gas, were told repeatedly whenever someone would mention the tunnel. Peering through the stretched out bowel of Gentilly, the children could see a flicker of sunlight at the far end. Remote and unreachable, that distant light drew Jeff like a lodestone.

"Let's do it," he had said, or one of them would say on more than one occasion.

"The sewer gas is only there sometimes."

"But ya can't smell it and what if it explodes?"

"What if we're halfway and it storms? The rain will fill up the tunnel before we can get out. We'll drown."

Several tentative assaults were made, usually on impulse, over a period of months without success. The further along their journey, the greater would become their fear and the safe opening on the canal would begin to close like a sphincter choking off the sunlight behind them.

After they endured the mounting tension for a block or two, a car somewhere overhead would roll over a manhole cover and the resulting thunder reverberated down the length of the cemented maw and sent the boys running back to the safety of the known and above-ground world.

Soon the invulnerability of youth, that protective cloth of confidence penetrated only by aging, would again propel them down the neighborhood dragon's lair.

This time with planning.

Three flashlights with fresh batteries were smuggled out of tool boxes and a B-B gun, purloined from Jeff's brother, was loaded and taken, just in case. No matches—the sewer gas would explode. Three root beers and a bottle opener completed their provisions.

The floor of the tunnel slanted inward from both sides toward the center, forcing the street run off to form a slow flowing sliver of water, perhaps a foot wide. On either side, eighteen inches of cement completed the trough of this dark, man-made cave. The angle was such that tennis shoes could hold for several steps and gravity would force the boys to either stop, or jump to the other side to continue onward.

Overhead, manholes were located at each street intersection along with multiple feeder lines which emptied into the tunnel halfway up the wall on either side. Iron rungs anchored in the cement led to the manholes, but provided little hope of escape as each cover weighed well over a hundred pounds.

Those smaller lines located closer to the opening and sunlight grew gardens of green slime and algae. Those further back produced only brown ooze and foul odors. Surely, evil crawly things lurked in these side culverts, just out of sight, waiting.

Onward they pressed, flashlights made constant sweeps, and they watched the ceiling and every scummy opening as they passed.

Were there snakes in the water? Or worse?

"What was that?"

"Something splashed in the water up ahead."

"Shine the light, quick!"

Nothing.

"How far have we come?"

"Jesus, the canal is far away. Look behind you."

"Is the gun cocked?"

"Yeah. Let's go."

"Do you smell that? Is it sewer gas?"

"You can't smell sewer gas. That's how it gets ya."

"Jeff, you have the gun. Go first," said Les.

"Here, Lenny, you're a better shot, take the gun," Jeff countered.

"Okay, but one of you hold my flashlight and root beer. And stay right behind me with all the lights on."

"Don't drop the gun if we have to run," said Jeff.

The air became damp and oppressive. The walls were wet and brown gunk draped the side and lay along the bottom. Rounded gas filled pockets formed and looked like bulbous neoplasms.

Years of street dirt washed into the tunnel and lingered there, silting the bottom so the watery slime was everywhere and their shoes became soaked with offensive goo. They spoke only rarely and then in whispers, each boy dealt with his fear quietly and alone where all battles are lost or won. Give in to the fear and the walls would crush you; floods would drown you, or worse, you would break and run.

Slow drops of water splattered in a rhythmic pulse, their volume magnified in the confining cave. The boys now trudged over muck and slop and broken bits of cement and stone scattered across the floor of the tomb-like cavern. Cars, both near and far, would strike the manhole plates and sent thunder down the corridor and fear to their deepest core.

Water dripped from the ceiling, fell in their hair and on their shoulders and caused a rush of goose flesh. Six blocks in and one of the flashlights inexplicably failed, but the boys held fast.

A large sewer rat, caught in the beam of one of the remaining flashlights, jumped into one of the smaller tunnels, its claws slipped and scratched noisily on cement as it scurried to the safety of darkness.

Once the rat was recognized, the fear it caused diminished. It was the unidentified, the unknown, that struck the deepest fear. The sound whose source could not be reasoned, the strange odors of uncertain potency, and the unseen and unfelt hands that clutched at their throats as they passed each side tunnel, these were the worst. The malevolent creatures of their imagination were far more frightening than the reality of a rat and the threat of sewer gas.

Was it harder to breathe? The air was heavy with vapor and the odor of filth. At block seven Lenny labored up the iron rungs to a manhole. He grasped the top rung with his left hand and pushed with his right. The cover did not budge. If the idea of retreat was felt by the three of them, it was not shared aloud.

The light source from Elysian Fields did not grow larger, but the tunnel opening to their rear grew smaller in the distance. Certainly they had come more than halfway. Something was not quite right.

It was Leslie who spoke first. "Look! It goes into a smaller pipe!"

There, at the end of eight blocks underground, the large tunnel stopped in a cemented wall with a culvert no larger than two feet in diameter in the center.

"Those bastards! They didn't walk through. Ya can't go any farther!"

They ran the few remaining yards to the wall, to the pipe, to feel what their eyes had seen, to confirm the hoax. Looking down the pipe, they could see the sunlight from Elysian Fields.

"Those lying yellow-bellies!" screamed Les. The boys now stood where their heroes never did. Surely the older boys had been drawn here just as they had, but just as surely their failed back there, not in the tunnel, but in the labyrinths of their own minds. Freed from the quest, the boys returned to the sunlight, not realizing the importance of the battle they had won. But they did know they were victorious over something and it felt good.

* * *

"Where'd ya get the candy?" Lenny asked his two friends.

"Nodier's."

"Oh," he said. He eyed the fist full of sweets and slid his back down the wall of the tunnel and squatted next to Jeff and opposite Leslie. "Is that a Powerhouse ya got?"

"Yeah," said Les.

"I was on my way to the store when I saw you two headed this way. Think I'll go back and get a Powerhouse, too."

"I'll sell you this one for a nickel," said Les. I haven't even opened it yet. Ya want it?"

"Did ya mush it?" asked Lenny.

"Naw. Like new. Just got it a minute ago."

The trade was made and the three boys sat in the cool shade of the mouth of the tunnel and munched their candies while Leslie fingered the nickel and smiled to himself. Jeff stared at Leslie. He did not know the word cunning, but he had just been given a demonstration of its meaning.

When the cement was laid for the tunnel, a small circular hole formed where crawfish now liked to hide. Lenny dug in the opening with a stick on the chance he could prod one of the creatures into view. Finding none he finished his candy bar and flipped the stick out into the canal.

"Y'all wanna catch crawfish? My dad did yesterday and I got four nets still baited," Lenny said.

"Yeah," shouted Les.

"Go get 'em!" said Jeff.

The three boys were up and moved in unison. Lenny lived near the canal across the street from Nodier's. He turned the corner of his fence and as he opened the gate, Les yelled, "I'm going to Nodier's. I'll meet you at the canal."

"Okay," shouted Lenny, without turning.

Jeff watched Leslie retrace their steps to Nodier's and the gum ball machine. It pained him to see this improvement, this modification of the gum ball scheme, played out before him by his recent trainee. "Wise guy," Jeff yelled.

Lenny reappeared holding four folded nets and a bucket.

"Carry the bucket," he said and placed it on the ground.

The two boys walked the few steps that led to the embankment and down the slanted cement sides of the canal. Soot and dirt collected by rainwater from the streets and gutters was deposited into the canal and here and there water plants grew forming habitat for crawfish and minnows. They placed the nets fifteen or twenty feet apart and sat on the bank. Les returned chewing on a candy bar and held out another to the two boys.

"Here," he said, "y'all split this."

The three boys lay back on the embankment, let time pass and stared at the clouds drifting overhead, occasionally finding a face or two. One looked like Mrs. Southerlin. A gentle breeze stirred and carried to them Mr. Bill's laughter from the store. Mr. Bill always laughed. Bill and his sister, Bird, made their meager profit by spending next to nothing on overhead. Regular customers were asked to bring their own grocery bags, and you could purchase ham only if you had placed your order a week beforehand.

Mr. Bill's outing, his weekend treat, was to spend seven cents on a bus ride to Audubon Park to watch the softball games and then spend another seven cents on the return trip. Every Sunday of those boyhood days, Bill Nodier would don his straw hat, grab his black walking cane, and ride in simple fashion to Audubon Park. Except for church, it was the only time one saw him outside this small, secure grocery. Should a child encounter him on the street, Mr. Bill would stop and stare at the child and, with a dopey smile, he would watch, caught up in the child's world and its wonder. The line separating the observer and subject faded, and Bill Nodier would become the child. He would gaze intently, his silver blue eyes accenting his white, white hair; and, by God, he was thrilled by what he saw. Children delighted him and often, when Jeff played, he would turn to see Mr. Bill, his straw hat and smile in place, staring in genuine awe of youth and its exuberance. And always in the Gentilly of those days, Mr. Bill's booming laughter lilted their lives.

"Let's go. It's time for a run," said Lenny.

"We need a stick!" Les said.

"Here's one," said Jeff as he grabbed a large stalk of dried ragweed.

"Me first," said Lenny, "They're my nets." He reached for the stick, and the reasonableness of the request and his huge size caused no hesitation in Jeff. He handed him the stick.

"Me next," Jeff said, "It's my stick."

Lenny hooked the first net and pulled it straight up, bending the stick dangerously. Four crawfish were inside feeding on the smelly bait.

"Get the bucket! Get the bucket!" he yelled to the others.

"Les left it. I got the stick. *He* should have brought the bucket!" said Jeff.

Leslie, in the excitement, had already begun to retrieve the bucket from the top of the embankment.

"Watch it! That one's getting out!" Jeff yelled.

"No he's not," Lenny said confidently as he tilted the net in the opposite direction. From the other side of the net, another crawfish fell to the ground and scampered back into the water.

"What'd I tell you? Les, hurry up," shouted Jeff.

The crawfish were quickly dumped in the bucket and the three boys looked in, their heads touching, and they watched the frightened creatures throw their claws up in a defensive and threatening stance.

"Where's the other one?" asked Les.

"Lenny let it get away," answered Jeff.

"It was your fault. You told me to watch the other one." And after a pause, Lenny added triumphantly, "Besides, they're my nets, anyway."

"They are not. They're your father's," said Jeff.

"Well, he said I could use them," said Lenny.

"Come one. Pick up the rest," said Leslie.

Within the hour the boys filled the pail with crawfish, and squatted around the bucket on their haunches, studying the shelled creatures.

"Who gets 'em?" asked Les.

"They're my nets," said Lenny one more time.

"You can have them, Lenny," said Jeff.

Lenny, after a pause said, "No, we ate the ones my dad caught yesterday. You two take 'em."

"My mom's already cooking paneed meat," Leslie said.

"We have beans and rice," Jeff said.

They squatted in silence, staring at the mudbugs moving slowly in the bucket. Lenny stuck a twig at one of the creature and watched it rear back and throw its claws up. After a discussion of selling them and realizing no one would buy them, the boys released them back into the canal. Eating was no fun, merely an unpleasant task one undertook to please one's parents. Catching things and looking at them, that was fun. Finding things, that was fun. But eating was a sheer waste of time, like sleeping and bathing.

Leslie's mother called from around the corner, and the three boys trudged up the embankment and down the street, each to their homes for supper.

Jeff lived the farthest from the canal. He passed the family garage and heard his brother's voice and that of another person. His brother was several years older than Jeff and weeks earlier he had built a one-room clubhouse on top of the cypress chicken coop behind the family garage. Jeff hear the sound of hammering and followed it to its source.

He walked into the hen house and saw a large square hole in the roof of the coop. A ladder was nailed to the wall and afforded entry into the clubhouse above. Through the hole he could see his brother's face.

"Whatcha doing?" he asked.

"Bobby and I built an escape hatch," the older boy answered.

"How you like it?" Bobby asked.

"Dad's gonna be mad," Jeff said.

"No he won't. He hasn't used this coop since the war. He wouldn't be mad. Watch."

His brother was a runaway, uncontrollable optimist but this time, for sure, Dad would be mad, thought Jeff.

"Whatcha making now?" Jeff asked, referring to the hammering which had not stopped.

"Trap door," said the brother.

"Does Ma know?" asked the younger boy.

"No, and don't tell, either."

"Let me up to see," Jeff asked.

"No. Wait till we're finished," said his brother.

"Jeff!" his mother called from the back porch.

"What?" he replied.

"Leslie called and said you could go over to his house after dinner and spend the night. Do you want to?"

"I don't know," said Jeff.

"Well, call him and let him know."

Inside, on the phone, Les explained how they could make a telephone using two cans and a piece of string.

"But it *will* work. My Dad says so," he said.

"Are you sure?" asked Jeff.

"Sure, I'm sure. Come over after dinner and I'll show you."

Jeff reluctantly gave up the security of his own bed for the promise of a new device; a device he doubted would work well, if at all. After dinner he called Leslie to say he would come over and Leslie offered to wait for him on the front porch. Not that the streets were unsafe then but one never knew about demons or perhaps madmen.

* * *

"Did you ever see a madman?"

"Yeah. A long time ago, by the railroad track past the show. It was late at night, and he said he had just gotten off the train, riding in boxcars. He was all dirty with a dirty old overcoat down to here and was sitting by a fire. He had three hot dogs wrapped in crinkled wax paper. He roasted them and tried to give us some. Poisoned probably. I got scared and left."

But that was before, before the tunnel, before the slime, before the reality of the cement wall far beneath the street. And now another voice is heard, a small voice at first, "He was probably just a hobo, a broken man who saw fright in a small boy's eyes, and extended a hand across the chasm of fear, a hand which held a hot dog."

* * *

"No, you don't have to wait. I'll be over in a few minutes."

Leslie opened the front door and held two tin cans and a ball of string.

"Hey, here's the stuff." They walked through the shotgun double past his parents' bedroom and into the children's room next to the kitchen. The room was small with a bunk bed on the far corner. Linoleum with various board games covered the floor. Checkers, Backgammon, Parcheesi, and other games formed the design of the flooring. A small desk was placed before the window overlooking the driveway. Leslie's parents and brother sat in the front room listening to the radio. Occasional laughter found it's way down the hall to their inattentive ears. They located a hammer and nail and Les began banging the nail into the base of the first can.

"Stop the noise, Les," Leslie's stern father spoke quietly.

"But, Dad, I'm making the holes in the tins," Leslie pleaded.

"Stop the noise, Les" his father repeated.

"Let's go to the back step," Les said.

Out back on the step, Leslie succeeded in making the holes in the center of each can. He passed one end of the string through the first can, knotted it and pulled the string forcing the knot into the hole. He unrolled about thirty feet of string and cut it with a kitchen knife. He repeated the procedure with the knot and handed the other can, string now attached, to Jeff.

"Here. Hold this, and when I talk, put the can to your ear like this." His hand shot up to his right ear, completely covering the ear with the open end of the can. "When it's your turn to talk, just put the opening by your mouth and talk. Stay here and I'll go in the front."

Bewildered, Jeff stood in the kitchen holding an empty tin can, from which dangled a limp piece of string. Seconds passed; the string drew taut.

"Here I go, put it to your ear," Les instructed and, after a pause, "Can you hear me?"

"Yeah, I can hear you," Jeff said.

"Is the can to your ear?" Les inquired.

"No, but I hear you anyway. You're just down the hall," Jeff said.

"Wait a minute!" said Les with sudden insight. He placed his two hands around the mouth of the tin, cupped his face in his hands, and he again spoke into the can. The string was stretched tight against the door frame of the kitchen, angled across the bedroom, and pulled tightly against the frame of the hall door, effectively cutting off all sound and vibration.

"Mmummph mumm," said Les.

"What?"

"Mmummph uuh mumm," came the reply.

"What?" Jeff asked again.

"Maybe we got the wrong kinda string," Leslie said in a loud voice. "Or maybe the wrong kinda cans," he added in a lower tone.

"Yeah," said Jeff, glad to be rid of the unworkable apparatus. "Let's play some checkers."

So the night went just as the day, boys doing boy things, exploring hidden treasures, the trading of secrets and sharing loyalties until at last it was time to rest. Fatigued from a day of play, they fell silently asleep, each clutching a tin can, each tied to the other by more than that string.

Time would end soon enough this idyllic boyhood. Time, pack ratting joy for pain, soon enough, would chill their spirit, but for now they slept, safe in that Gentilly of my youth.

Watering the Garden Thoughts

Maybe books have taught me
    something.
     Maybe I can separate wheat
from chaff
    but not the profound from the pertinent.
                            for instance:

I don't know
    why the rhythm of the world
    is so harmonious,
    the golden section
    so predictable,
    the season's pulse
    so tranquil,
    and human relationships
    so chaotic.

I don't know
    why free will causes
    such damage
    and the secret transcendent beauty of will
    remains
    a secret.

I don't know
>   why self-sacrifice is the hallmark
>   of love
>   when
>   so many lovers
>   would rather die
>   than sacrifice.

I don't know
>   why the Boss had to
>   off his son
>   to save us
>   when all he had to do
>   was
>   save us.

I don't know
>   why Gurdjieff had to invent
>   the bullshit
>   of Askokin
>   when all he had to say
>   was:
>   we die for reasons that have nothing to do with
>   God
>   or fairness
>   or eternal life.
>   randomly
>   we just die.

I don't know
>	why humility is now a vice.
>	why those who care, care mainly
>	to control.
>	why beauty is no longer a fit
>	subject for art.
>	why eyes that seek the inside
>	are considered crossed.
>	why paintings of flowers are more
>	important than flowers.
>	why little children grow up to
>	be just people.
>	why mothers wind up weeping
>	when governments are formed.

>	why it is so easy to see
>	beauty in nature
>	but not
>	in its sons or daughters.

Tanked-topped, beer-drinking,
loud-mouthed,
deadfromtheneckupsleepwalkingtube-
addicteddungheaps
(but
every now and then
one
>	of
>	>	them
creates a David.)

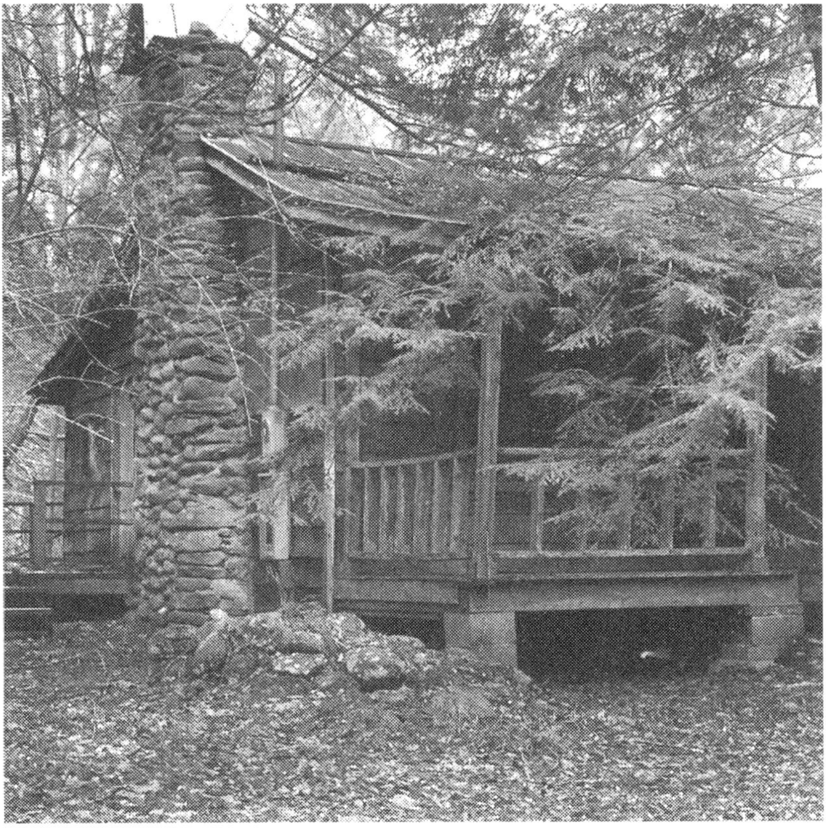

The Anniversary

The first rays of sunlight were just easing over Ledbetter Ridge when John awoke. He lay quietly on the bed for several minutes without moving letting his eyes adjust to the dimness in the room. He knew without looking that the calendar on the wall had today's date circled, the thirtieth of March. Outside the bedroom window he could see the old, twisted maple next to the barn. In the dim light of dawn he could see the twigs and branches covered with small red buds each bursting with spring. He quietly turned the quilt down over to his left and sat on the side of the bed. He turned to face his wife's side of the bed making sure he had not rearranged her covers. The chill of early spring filled the small home but it was time to begin his day. He stepped softly across the worn wooden floor into the kitchen and mindful of the quiet and the early hour, he closed the bedroom door with deliberate silence.

His Sunday pants were neatly folded over the back of one kitchen chair and his best shirt was open and hanged from the rear of another. His worn shoes were polished and a clean sock was placed in each one waiting for him to dress. He ran some water, cupped his hands and brought it up to his face. The chill of the water on his face had started his days as far back as he could remember. Before the power company brought the line into their valley, the kitchen had a hand pump but the water was just as cold and sweet back then. Maybe sweeter.

His father built the original house just a bit uphill from this spot in the early thirties when he was ten. Together they built this place in the forties just before he married Mary. It wasn't much back then. The indoor pump was the only luxury. No real plumbing or lighting except for the old kerosene lanterns. But the spring ran year round, clean and fresh. And the corn was sweet and his tobacco dried the darkest in the valley. It wasn't an easy life but it was better than most in these parts. Children would have made things easier for him and Mary but none ever came. Mary cried when the town doctor told her she couldn't have any. But it wasn't her fault, not his Mary's fault. He still felt he was the luckiest man in Dawson County because she chose him to marry.

Her family lived beyond the valley in Seaton where her daddy and brothers worked for the Seaton Lumber Company. She and her two sisters were the prettiest girls between here and Johnson City. He remembered when his friend, Morris Claypool, spent the summer of '38 in Seaton and came back with talk of the three prettiest girls in the world all belonging to the same family and living over in Seaton.

"John, when I seen those girls my knees got to shaking. Each one is purdier than tha other. You ain't gonna believe me no how 'til you see 'em fer yurself."

The next time his father took the wagon over to Seaton he insisted on going along to help unload the corn and bush beans. Things between him and Mary just seemed lucky from the start and it was luck that caused him to see the three sisters walking with their mother into the dry goods store as soon as he and his paw got into town. He also knew right off that Morris told the truth. But the prettiest was easy for John to pick out. She was shorter than her sisters by several inches and her gray-blue eyes danced with the excitement and joy of a child on her birthday. Her hair was long and curly and she wore it down but under a small bonnet. Her smile was natural and all ways in place as if caused by the happiness of some private and eternal holiday.

He returned to the valley and when he saw Morris the next day, John announced, matter of factly, he would marry one of those girls, the smallest one.

"You jest out of yer head, John Ledbetter. How you gonna even meet that girl much less marry up with her?" Morris asked.

"Well, I don't know jest yet but I'm a-telling you, I know the truth of what I'm a-feeling and I'm gonna marry that girl."

Morris just stared at him a moment not knowing if he was serious and again asked, "The small one? What's her name?"

John, with some of the wind taken from his sail, turned and walked away answering,

"Don't know that yet either but she's gonna be my wife. You watch Morris Campbell. Jest you watch."

Within a few weeks he applied for work at the Seaton Lumber Company. While he waited to hear about an opening, and when the chance or time permitted, he would walk or catch a ride into Seaton. Several times he would see the girl or her sisters and learned her name was Mary Thrasher. She was 13 and not allowed to court yet. Finally he received word that his application had been accepted and his first job with the company was hooking the large steel tongs into the fell logs to be dragged away by the overhead skidders. More than a few men were crushed or crippled by those logs slamming together or falling off a loaded flat car. It was hard and dangerous work but the pay was higher than anything else in Dawson County. On Sundays after services in summer the men and their families gathered for the company picnics. Children would run sack races and play hide and seek and games of all sorts. On those quiet days between hard work and tough times the women chatted while the men's baseball league played inning after inning. On John's team, one of Mary's brothers, Samuel, was the third baseman. John honestly liked Samuel and it wasn't long before they became friends and worked together on the same skidder. In their spare time, what little there was of it, they both enjoyed fishing in the high, cold mountain streams. John showed him how to match his trout bait to the insects found inside the belly of the first fish taken. It was a simple and sure way to catch all the brown trout a body could eat. Returning from one of their fishing trips, John was introduced to Mary and the rest of her family. He had already met her other brothers, Aaron and Seth, and her father, Malcolm, in the lumber field or in the mill yard. Her mother was more than pleased to meet the boy responsible for the fish Samuel had been bringing home and thanked him by asking him to stay for dinner. Wisely he begged off saying the hour was late but when she insisted, he agreed to stay if it wasn't too much trouble to set an extra plate. "Trouble," she repeated, "Ain't no trouble to set another plate seeing as how you caught most of these fish yourself. You stay and rest right here with Samuel. Won't take no time at'tall." Through out the meal he stole glances in Mary's direction and several times he felt sure he caught her staring at him. Later, as he sat with Samuel and Mary's father in the parlor, he could hear giggles from the girls upstairs. He heard Mary's voice saying, "I was not and you know it" quickly followed by the laughter of three girls.

By the time Mary was old enough to court everyone knew John would come to call and they were married shortly before the new house was finished. Not, however, before several magical nights were spent together beneath the stars and moon. On one of those nights when the jet-black sky blazed with diamond stars from one edge of the world to the other, Mary confessed she had noticed him every time he came to town. She had even remembered his first trip with his father. She would look for him on their outings to town and said she loved him the first time she laid eyes on him. Never, she said, had she seen a more handsome boy. If those hills held a happier man, it was not on that night, not when he heard Mary's words. They promised that night never to be apart again and decided to marry even before the house was finished. They planned the wedding for the next week at the end of March on the 31$^{st.}$ The roof was finished and the walls were up. They could bundle up against the cold until John finished the house but they figured they had already spent enough of their lives without each other. Her family didn't approve of such a quick announcement and was quietly worried that people would talk about how their daughter had to get married. After John spoke with Mary's father he went home leaving him to decide. Samuel spoke for the couple that night and the next day Mary's father gave them his blessing.

Before they celebrated their first anniversary the Second World War caught up with Dawson County and when John received his draft notice he reported to the induction center in Johnson City. When he left their cabin that morning, his young bride stood in the doorway, watched and waved as he walked across the field to take the woods trail to Seaton and the bus line. When the notice came, Mary waited a few minutes and walked to the springhouse and cried quietly to herself. John had never seen her cry and now wasn't the time to let him. Neither that night nor the next morning did she cry but when he reached the woods on the other side of the field, Mary sobbed loudly and openly, her head leaning against the doorway. Neither of them could find France or Germany on a map and now John was going there to get crippled or maybe killed. It wasn't fair. They hadn't been married a year and now he was gone. It just wasn't fair. Why should John fight in a country he never saw before or heard of or cared about?

On the long walk to Seaton John thought about the war and Mary and his country and duty. He thought about taking Mary and hiding out or claiming to be one of those conscientious objectors. But he couldn't do that. He couldn't live with himself nor could Mary if he did that. Other boys from Dawson County who had their notices, boys who John had grown up with or knew from church or school, were eager and proud to fight for their country. One boy at the bus stop had brought his Kentucky rifle with him and said, "I'll pick off that Hitler fella and be done with this war quick like." The half-day journey to Johnson City was noisy with the boys and the well wishers on the bus who joined in the party-like ride to the induction center. John was not happy to leave Mary but if his country needed him and boys like him, well, he would be proud to wear the uniform of his country. He knew Mary was a strong woman. She'd get the corn in and the hay bailed before it would rot in the field. He knew paw and her brothers would pitch in. He also knew her brothers, at least some of them, would be called up before this thing was over. He hoped Samuel would be left behind to watch over Mary for him. Between paw and Samuel, Mary would be just fine until he returned.

But luck ruled much of their lives and when the doctor told John something was wrong with his back, he didn't understand the meaning of the words other than he would be going home. God knew he didn't want to leave Mary but not to be taken was a disgrace. He would be the shame not only of the valley but of all Dawson County. 4F. He knew how people would talk behind his back and the shame he and Mary would have. Weakling. Cripple. Faker. Coward. And if other boys from the county were killed, the talk would be worse. The other boys at the center shied away from John as word spread about his being 4F. He asked the doctor to check him again to be sure and whether there was some branch that would take him anyway. After hearing the torment in his voice the other boys gathered around him in support after the doctor told John again he was sorry and there had been no mistake. John's back had some defect that he was born with and while it had caused him no difficulty, the government would not let him in uniform with that condition. None of the boys understood because John had been fit and strong as long as they knew him and he worked one of the hardest jobs at the lumber company without any problem. John understood least of all. He could run further and faster than these boys. He was a better woodsman, stronger and smarter than most of them. How could he be 4F? How could he explain this to his family and how could he ever explain it to Mary?

That night the other boys boarded a train to Knoxville and then on to an army base in North Carolina. They put John up in the YMCA that night and gave him a bus ticket back to Seaton for the next morning. He did not sleep worried about Mary and the shame he was bringing home to her. What would her paw say? And her brothers?

It was early afternoon when he cleared the woods and entered the field across from their house. He let out a shrill whistle and in a few moments Mary stood at the door wiping her hands on her apron. She studied John only briefly and took off running across the field, jumped into his arms and wrapped her legs around his back like a child. Crying with joy and disbelief her words poured out, "John, my dear John, is it for sure you? Oh how the Lord has answered my prayers! Sweet, sweet Jesus, are you home for good?" She kissed his cheek and held his hands, kissing them between her words.

"Yes Mary. I'm home." The words he rehearsed since last night wouldn't come. Now that he saw her face again, he didn't know how to start. He placed her on her feet and he blurted it out when Mary began asking him questions.

"How John? What happened? Was your notice a mistake?"

"No Mary, it wasn't a mistake. My back. I'm 4F. They don't want me."

"Your back? Are you ok? Will you be all right?"

"Yes, yes, I'm as fit as I was yesterday and the day before. It's just something they don't want in the army. They wouldn't take me."

"Thank God John. Oh thank God." Mary cried again. It was the first time he had seen her cry and he expected shame instead of her happiness.

"Mary, what will the people say? What will your family say?"

"About what? Your back?"

"About me being 4F."

"My family and your family will understand and so will our friends. The people? I don't care about the people. I care about you and I love you and you're home safe and that's all I care about."

Mary was John's world and if that's how Mary saw the rest of the world, well, that was good enough for him. If Mary still loved him, he was man enough to ignore the rest of it. In those few simple words she made things right for him. He may have doubted himself a time or two after that day but never Mary. There was talk all right and Samuel got into a fistfight with one of the Thorton boys, Tom, from Salt Lick when his cousin was killed in Normandy. And when Mary's brother Aaron was called up, John could feel some stares on the back of his neck. But they got through it and when the war was over in '45, it never mattered any more. Not to most anyway.

At the war's end John and Mary had been married for a few years and there had been no sign of children. They both were young and strong and John began to wonder if it had something to do with his back. When the talk in the family got to the questioning stage, John decided to go into Johnson City and see the doctor there. Mary came with him. He told his paw they'd be gone for a day or two into the big city and to keep an eye on the place. No one asked why they were going and no one had to. John tried to keep the trip light and told Mary about the thoughts he had when he reported to the induction center. Thoughts about running away to Canada with her or hiding in the barn or in a cave when they came to get him. She laughed and knew it was just crazy talk to avoid what was on both of their minds. They checked into a small room at the hotel and walked three streets over to the doctor's office. The doctor spoke with them both and asked Mary to leave the room so he could examine John. After the exam and some blood samples were taken, he again spoke with them both. He could find nothing wrong with John but some other tests could be preformed. He went on to say that before he'd run those test it would be better to examine Mary to make certain that the problem wasn't there.

Again in the room with both of them he told them that Mary had some tissue growing in her which prevented her from being pregnant and that nothing could be done to correct the condition. Hurriedly he told them not to worry, he was certain it was not cancerous and that Mary was fine. He told of other, similar cases where the wife was able to conceive and they should not give up hope. John could feel Mary's heart break. He looked at her as the doctor explained to them how to chart her fertile time and she betrayed not an emotion. Not a tear, not a frown, nothing although he knew she was in agony. Mary, strained to keep control, worried for John and the children they would never have. Who will carry his name and what evil thing have I done to bring this to him?

That night in the hotel they lied to each other saying how they were sure they would be one of the lucky ones and have a baby in spite of this and how doctors are wrong all the time. And then John took both her hands and looked into her eyes, those lovely blue-gray eyes. "Mary, I don't care. Do I want kids? Sure, but I want you more. Nothing matters to me in this whole world except you and you're all I want. You're all I ever wanted. Don't you know that? Don't you see me thanking God for every day we're together? The way you touch me and make me feel I'm more than I am. No one can do that except you. I've loved you since I first laid eyes on you and I'm gonna be at your side just as long as you'll let me."

"Oh John, I'm so sorry," she sobbed.

"I'm not. I'm the luckiest man alive because you're my wife and nothings gonna come between us. Not the war and not this. Nothing. We made a vow, remember? We'll never be apart."

The next March on their anniversary, John planted daffodils on a little knot of a hill just to the side of the barn where Mary could see them from the window in the kitchen. Over a period of time he later planted rhododendrons there for her as she was fond of them as well. Finding small ones growing wild in the woods he dug them up and planted them down the backside of the hill. Across the top of the hill he planted more of them in a half circle around the daffodils. The opening in the circle faced the kitchen window forming a background for the flowers in front. In spring the sun would strike that hill before it touch any other ground near their home and Mary said the sun lit up the daffodils like little yellow players on a green stage. Often in the cool of the summer evening or in the late afternoon they would climb the little rise and sit near the blooming shrubs. It was Mary's favorite place on the farm. During the heat of summer she would spend a moment or two in the cool of the springhouse but for thinking and talking, the tiny hill was her favorite.

Early one day in fall, while John walked behind the plow horse turning over sod for the winter, Mary's brothers with Samuel in the lead appeared at the far end of the field. John pulled up the horse and walked over to his water bucket and waited for them to cross over to him. He wiped the sweat from his forehead and lifted some water with the wooden cup. Samuel was surely agitated and his pace quickened as he neared John. Thinking the worse John asked before they drew very close, "Everything ok? Someone hurt?"

Samuel was still twenty feet away when he began. "It's them sons a bitches again, them Thortons. They talking about you and Mary all over Seaton. I guess Tom Thorton ain't learned his lesson the last time ah busted him up cause he's at it again." John could see the rage behind Samuel's eyes. Aaron was just as angry and the youngest brother, Seth, was holding a fist-sized rock.

"What's this about Mary?' John asked.

"Tom's wife, that skinny woman, she always was jealous of Mary. Well, she was at Sutton's hardware with Tom buying something or the other. She starts talking to Mrs. Sutton about her kids and how they do in school and help around the farm. Next thing you know she's saying what a shame it is for you and Mary to have no kids to help out with the chores and everything. Mrs. Sutton allows as how it has to be hard on you two and that skinny Thorton woman says Mary can't have any children cause she was touched by something evil when she got the devil to keep you out of the war. She turned to her husband, that Tom bastard, and says 'Ain't that right Tom?' And he says to Mrs. Sutton a conjure woman over in Salt Lick told him that."

John dipped the wooden cup into the water bucket again and drank slowly.

"Whatcha gonna do, John?" Samuel asked.

"We with you John. That Thorton family's got a lot of men folk. You can't handle them all," Aaron said.

"He's right John. That Tom's gone too far this time," Samuel added.

John placed the cup back in the bucket and wiped his forehead with his rag again and without much emotion he said, "I think I want to do some thinking on this. Don't want to go over there right now with the lot of you and get every body all shot up."

"But John," Samuel began before John cut him off.

"Now Samuel, let this cool down a bit. You ain't thinking right. We go over there now, the whole pack of them is up waiting for us. Now let me think on it and I'll see all of you tomorrow. Understand?"

He could tell Samuel wasn't pleased with having to sleep with his belly on fire but John was certain that all the men of the Thorton family were at Tom Thorton's house waiting for him and Mary's brothers. "And none of you say a word to your paw or Mary about this, ya hear?"

He walked the horse back to the barn and wiped him down after he gave him some water. He went to the shed, pulled out the riding saddle and placed it on the stall fence. He found an axe handle and leaned it across the saddle. He cleaned up in the wooden trough through which part of the stream ran and went into the house. Mary had dinner nearly ready and he told her he had to go into Seaton to meet with Morris Claypool. He said he heard Morris was having some hard times and wanted to see if there was something he could do to help his friend. He wasn't really telling a full lie. He would see Morris that night.

Childhood friendships formed in the valley lasted a lifetime and he knew Morris had a good head and could handle himself. John knew that afternoon that he couldn't talk Mary's brothers out of all of them going and if the Thortons saw the four of them at once, shooting would start for sure. For what he had in mind, one good man with a cool head was all he needed.

It was after dinner when John arrived at Morris' home. He knocked and when Morris came to the door, he asked him to step into the night so they might talk. Morris listened intently and told John he'd get his riding mare and gear and be out directly. It took the better part of two hours for them to reach the Thorton's home and they were still too early. They tied the horses up a quarter of a mile from the Thorton's gate and waited in the darkness for the moon to set. The house was dark when they pulled even with the garden. John figured the Thortons would get liquored up on shine and sleep early once no one showed to face them. Morris slipped off to the side as John walked straight up to the home stopping thirty yards in front. The dog started barking and John yelled, "Thorton! Tom Thorton, get your ass out here be ya man enough!" He could hear rough cursing from the men inside awakened from their drunken sleep. Stumbling in the dark house they knocked over tables and chairs that were in their way. The men poured onto the porch and two were holding rifles. Behind them some of their women folk stood and watched in silence.

Tom Thorton spoke once he could see it was John, "You must be crazy coming here at night by yourself. What's that you got there an axe handle? What ya gonna do with that boy?" Everyone on the porch laughed at John standing in the shadows armed with nothing but an axe handle against six men with two rifles. "Where them brothers-in-laws of yourin? I was a-hoping that Samuel bastard would be with you tonight."

"I figure they'll be home in bed about now. I don't need them for your kind," John answered.

"You watch your tongue boy. You ain't got no friends on this here porch and you might wind up going under tonight."

"I'm here to fight you fair and square Tom Thorton and iffin more than one of you come at me at a time, I'm gonna take someone's head off with this here axe handle before I go under."

There was no laughter this time and the six men moved off the porch toward John. When they were a good ten to fifteen yards from the house, Morris slipped around the corner to the front of the house. He fired the first barrel of his shotgun into the night air and dropped it at his feet. He now held a six shot revolver in each hand both trained on the Thorton men. In a voice as measured as John's he said, "Now you boys just drop those rifles so we can have us a fair fight. I ain't gonna miss either one of you from here and I ain't gonna be asking again." The guns fell to the ground and Morris then said, "Step away from them now and get over by that tree where I can see all of you. You women up there get over with them. Easy, all of you move real easy."

"Tom," John said, "Tom I come for you, you low life son of a cur. Get over here you coward, come out here and take your beating." John dropped the axe handle to the ground.

Stepping away from the other men Tom sneered at John. John was a fair sized man but Tom stood four inches taller and weighed some forty pounds heavier. "Your wife enter another pact with the devil to protect you tonight boy?" As he finished his words he ran at John, grabbed him and took him to the ground. They rolled and punched each other until John was finally able to get to his feet. John bled from around his eye and mouth. On the ground wrestling, John was no match for Tom and they both knew it. Tom again rushed at him from a crouched position but John sidestepped and slammed the bottom of his fist into Tom's back as he went past. Seething with anger

Tom turned, stood erect and again hurled himself full speed at John. Again John stepped to the side as Tom went past and he kicked his left foot out from under him. Tom fell hard onto his side. "Get up you son of a bitch. Get up and get what's a-coming to you." He tried deliberately to enrage Tom, to blind him with anger so he could continue to use his greater size against him. Again he ran at John like a wild bull. John dropped his right foot behind and to his left fully cocking his hips. As Tom went past he hit him just at the edge of his ribs, full and square in his liver. Tom let out a sick growl and fell heavily to the ground.

"Get up you tub of guts. Get up so as I can shut that mouth of yourin for good." Blinded by pain and rage Tom again ran full tilt against John. Again John cocked his hips but this time the blow was delivered to Tom's throat. He fell to the ground gasping, desperate for air. He clawed at the ground on all fours and tried to pull in enough air to stay conscious. His throat was smashed closed and he fought to force air through the small part that remained barely open. Finally he was able to breathe in painful spurts and he rolled on his back in agony. He threw up the moonshine and foul smelling vomit cascaded down his face and onto his shirt and ground.

John walked over to where he had placed the axe handle and turned to the other men. "Any of you other bastards want a try?" Morris walked over, collected the rifles and told the Thortons they could find them tomorrow at the bottom of the well on the old Tyson place. John walked over to where Tom Thorton lay on the ground and pushed him over onto his stomach with his foot. He slipped the axe handle under his throat and lifted his neck a few inches. In a voice loud enough to be heard by Thorton's wife and the others he said, "If you or any of you kin speak about my wife again, I'm gonna come back here and snap your neck like a twig. And then I'm gonna do the same to that chicken-faced woman of yourin. You hear me boy? You hear what I'm telling you and yourin?"

Tom still couldn't speak but he nodded his head without opening his eyes. John removed the axe handle from under Tom Thorton's throat and together he and Morris backed up to the fence and then turned and walked away once they reached the darkness. Nothing was heard coming from the Thorton house.

The years slipped by and he had no further trouble from Tom Thorton or his family. Mary and he lived quietly in their part of the valley. They harvested their crops, mended their tools and home, visited family and friends and worshiped their God. There were nephews and nieces and holidays spent with family and some alone together. In all the time they shared together, they were still the other's best company.

In time their parents took ill and passed on. John's father stayed with them until the end came for him. Mary cared for him as she would a child. She sat over him at night and fed him during the day. One night as they lay in bed she told John, "They done brought us into the world. The least we can do is help to ease them out of it." As they grew older and their needs grew less, the farm grew smaller. Not as many chickens were raised and the corn and hay fields were smaller as well.

As John slipped on his pants and shirt he looked at his frail, weathered hands and found it hard to believe they had been married for fifty years. He began to hurry for he knew Mary would be waiting for him to return. He put on his socks and shoes and guided the door closed so the spring wouldn't make it slam. He slid into the front seat of the rusted old Ford truck and remembered when he and Mary picked it out at the dealership in Johnson City. How long ago was that and how could it still run after all these years? He turned the key and the engine fired up and backfired. He turned his eyes to the daffodils that bloomed on the little hill which was nearly covered by them. Over the years Mary and he had replaced the bulbs as they played out. The rhododendrons were still there, growing spindly with age. The morning sun hit them just right. He would tell Mary about it when he got back, tell her how the sun shone on the daffodils that morning of their fiftieth anniversary.

The ride to Seaton took only a few minutes and Mr. Heaton had agreed to open his shop early so John could get flowers for this special anniversary. It was a Thursday and John walked into the flower shop proudly dressed in his best clothes. "Looking mighty sharp Mr. Ledbetter. Mighty special day too, isn't it?" Mr. Heaton asked.

"Sure is. Today ah been married to Mary for fifty years. Fifty years," John repeated.

"Well, there's not many as can say that Mr. Ledbetter. You're here for the flowers then?" Sure, Mr. Heaton knew he was here for the flowers. They made plans weeks ago, making sure the daffodils would be ready and the shop would be opened early so he could hurry home to Mary.

"Daffodils they were, right?"

Of course they had to be daffodils. Mary's favorite. Daffodils or rhododendron. But the rhododendron wouldn't bloom for another two months so Mary wouldn't expect any of those. Mary was all ways glad to have any present from John that showed he still loved her. But fresh cut flowers were special and he couldn't wait to get home to give them to her. Mr. Heaton took the coffeepot off the burner and offered some to John after John paid for the flowers. The coffee smelled good but he knew Mary would be waiting for him by now. And he wanted to be next to her on this special day. He thanked Mr. Heaton, left the store and drove home as quickly as he could. He parked the tired old truck in front of the house and carried the daffodils to the side of the house. He climbed the few steps to the top of the hill and sat down next to the small headstone with Mary's name on it. He laid the daffodils on the ground just in front of the stone and told Mary that on the morning of their fiftieth anniversary the sun lit up the daffodils like little yellow players on a green stage. From the time they were married they were never apart although her death last year had managed to put some distance between them.

Snows quiet the woods
Anticipating spring's thaw—
a cascade waiting.

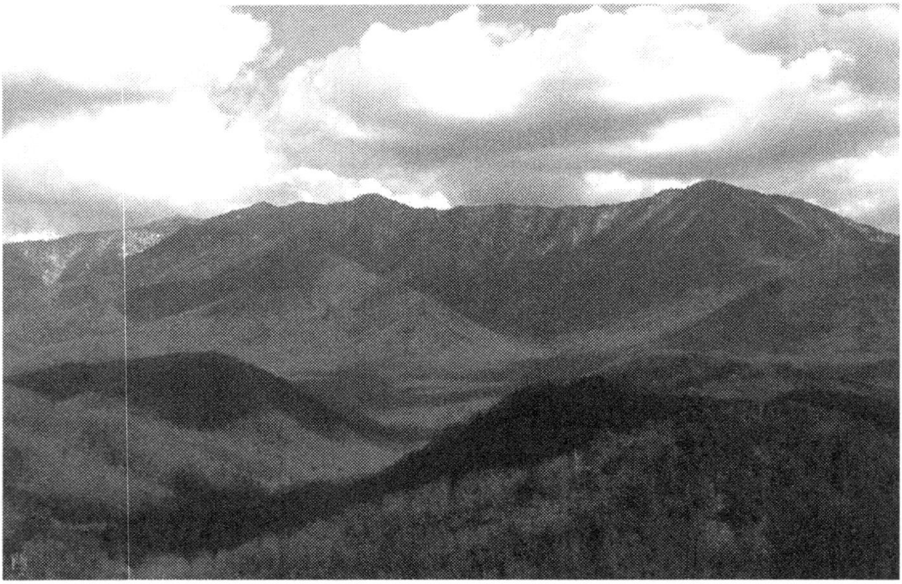

Echoes

I saw Leconte today as it should be seen. I see it most days but usually a haze diffuses the light, muting the mountain and giving it a flat appearance that steals its character. Today the sky was clear and the snow-covered ridges were side lit and defined by the setting sun casting shadows in the ravines. Everything above four thousand feet, the crest of the Smokys, was white against the blue sky. Beyond that line, unseen from my position and a few miles south, lay Mount Kephart, both mountains holding remarkably vivid and timeless memories of my first back packing trip and the path I found.

It was a Friday in late May and Mike, not long out of Vietnam, Thailand and the Special Forces, stopped by my office and asked, "You want to go back packing in the Smokys?"

"Sure. Great. What's back packing?"

"Well, it's sort of like camping only you carry your stuff to a different campsite each day."

He spoke of mountains, crystal streams and bears but I had seen those mountains and streams before, on a camping trip with four friends at the end of our high school years. My memory and fondness for the place remained and was as alive as when I first stood among the stone and tall trees as a teenager. I saw the bears and swam in the creeks but what intrigued me now as he spoke was the thought that trails ran on the crest of those remote peaks. Trails we could walk on and see clouds beneath our feet.

Of course I'd go, but we needed equipment. We spent the better part of the next day rummaging through Army Surplus stores. I bought a cheap sleeping bag, a Boy Scout mess kit, a Sterno stove and powdered eggs. I also borrowed some things from a friend who hunted regularly. Back packing, being a new sport and relatively unknown at the time, equipment, the correct equipment that is, was not to be had. And, more to the point, we had no idea what the correct equipment could possibly be. Tennis shoes wouldn't do; it was too wet. My steel-toed work boots from my rebar days on the Industrial Canal would have to do.

My hunter friend, who also knew little or nothing of back packing, loaned me two heavy canvas rucksacks, a large sheath knife, a hatchet, and a canteen belt with canteen, cup and cover. Mike had his Vietnam issue army pack, jungle boots and fatigue pants. I chose a nice wide-striped, bell-bottomed pair of brown pants from the Vanilla Fudge collection. An army fatigue shirt and the black work boots completed my look, the *tout ensemble* of a complete fool.

We made a run for groceries selecting a variety of can staples: Dinty Moore's Beef Stew (Was there anything else one must bring besides the beef stew?), some canned and very heavy pork and beans, some canned and equally heavy Spam, some candy bars, flashlight, batteries, cigarettes and lighter, knife-fork and spoon set, and, in the Boy Scout tradition, I coated some wooden matches with candle wax. The excessive weight of all this was not considered until well into the hike when the point was made for us with painful and obvious clarity. And, oh yes, beer. Yes sir, lots of beer, which we started drinking early in the day. Two guys can not possibly drive over six hundred miles to walk in the woods without lots of beer.

Having gathered up the food and gear, I was feeling fairly loose and Mike was clearly fried. We ate dinner that evening at my home and as my wife walked us to the door to bid us farewell, she whispered, "You better drive. Mike looks a little funny."

Had she looked a little closer, she would have noticed that I wasn't looking any too serious myself.

During the distant memory of my young adulthood, the interstate was largely incomplete and most of the drive was on U.S. Hwy.11. We hit Meridian, Mississippi about six cans of Dixie later, near 10:00 PM as I recall, where we gassed up and I gave the attendant a dollar to mail my first and last letter home. There were no mailboxes in the woods. Women four decades ago didn't understand things like that about the woods. I didn't try to explain this bit of wilderness esoterica when my wife handed me several envelopes and writing paper, I just took them. Mailboxes? There are no mailboxes in bear country ma'am. Only trees. Trees, and before too long, some empty beer cans and maybe a drunk or two. No mailboxes.

Leaving Meridian to the south, and inside Alabama perhaps an hour, Mike nodded off leaving me to drive and alone with an ice chest of chilled beer. I turned the radio on with the naive hope of locating a jazz station and turned the dial from end to end repeatedly finding nothing other than preachers and country music. I gathered that the late hours of a Saturday night was considered a good time to reach the sinners. To my thinking, word at this hour would arrive a bit too late to prevent the sinning, but it would probably be a damn good time to preach a little repentance. Between the larger cities, there was nothing, just the sound of static and the occasional indecipherable word or two from a station just beyond reception range. Time to reach over the seat and into the ice for another brew.

I remember hitting the outskirts of Birmingham in the dead of night without another car in sight. Highway 11 ran through Bessemer and into the steel capitol of the south and I caught every red light. The green light would blink into being and two blocks away I would see the yellow caution light of the next traffic signal warning me to stop just as I was shifting into second. And then I hit the endless streets with the Lewis Carroll names: Terrace Q, Circle R, Court R, Avenue R, Terrace S, Avenue T, Court U. Time for another cold one. Then with a numbing sameness, the numbered streets started. 17th St. W, 16th St. W, 15th . . . My spirits lifted briefly along this stretch when I caught a glimpse of the familiar. In the cool darkness of the summer night in which we moved, I saw a flame of natural gas on one of the hills on the eastern side of the city. Coming from the uplifted torch held by the cast iron hand of Vulcan, God of Fire, was the symbol and pride of this steel-making town. I had seen it years earlier on that first camping trip and, in the years to come, I would watch that gas flame change to electric lights, then reignited with red and green neon and eventually extinguished.

I was crossing numbered streets again but they were no longer West. North had arrived. 8th St. N, 9th St. N, 10th St. N . . . Like the names, the streets themselves had a sad uniformity. The city was old, dust covered and decaying. Many of the steel plants were abandoned and large equipment lay scattered about lifeless and rusted. I tossed an empty onto the floor of the back seat and reached for another. I continued glancing to the east seeing Vulcan's flame flickering between the trees and passing buildings.

49th St. N. and I was still catching every red light. When Mike fell asleep we had at least a case and a half of Dixie left and I began to worry if the supply would last. Here a scary thought took hold: lost on the never-ending numbered and lettered streets of Birmingham, driving through eternity, with only a sleeping drunken friend and the stoic Vulcan for company with nary a beer to be had. An hour and forty-five minutes after I entered this view from Dante in Bessemer, I finally saw the far side of Birmingham near something named Roebuck Plaza. Plunging my hand into the ice again, I felt around, taking an assessment of the supplies and grabbed another Dixie in celebration of my release.

On the two-lane highway I moved behind a sixteen wheeler barreling through the night, letting him do the navigating. I kept a good distance between his trailer lights but stayed on his tail, both of us speeding, he probably in both senses of the word.

Gadsden was an eternity away and I drove on listening to a fading Birmingham station and Roy Acuff's static filled musical prayer about a great bird, a great speckled bird at that. The silence that followed was welcomed. At Gadsden I pulled into a gas station just before Highway 11 led back again to a completed section of the interstate. Mike woke up and asked where we were and promptly fell asleep before I could tell him. I filled up and pulled into the approach lane of I-59 seized by the wise words of a sincere reverend telling his listeners we were all sinners including himself. Certainly alcoholism falls under the sin of gluttony and seeing as I wasn't capable of other sinning at that moment, and not wishing to disappoint, I reached for another chilled Dixie.

From Gadsden across the northwest corner of Georgia and into Tennessee there was little along the road and only a handful of crossroads. There were no cities, no towns of any size or radio preachers to help the miles go by, nothing except one truck stop. The state highways through Alabama warned night drivers of approaching bridges with silver reflectors embedded in the asphalt. They were arranged in a series of diagonal dashing lines pointing to the bridges. Beginning a quarter of a mile before each bridge, they lit up the complete darkness like hundreds of beacon lights on a runway. They were impossible to ignore but became an hypnotic annoyance well before I left the state behind. For over two hundred miles, Alabama pulled up a chair, suggested a game of solitaire, turned over the Queen of Diamonds and called me Raymond. I fought of the urge to sleep and pushed on.

Many miles later and unsure of the road ahead and the location of another gas station I pulled into the truck stop in Georgia. It was a diner, souvenir shop and home of bizarre animals, named the Georgia State Game Farm. I pumped the gas and went in to pay the cashier in the souvenir shop. Arranged around the shop and diner were stuffed animals; freaks of the genetic code and deceased former residents of the Game Farm. A two headed calf, several two headed snakes, a five legged cow and standing in the middle of this redneck sideshow was the cashier, a girl of my age, with amazing green eyes. And quite unlike the mangled menagerie, she was flawlessly beautiful. She explained, without thought of ridicule or self-consciousness, how there were many more animals in the "farm" out back that were very interesting. I remember asking how the town, Rising Fawn, home of the Georgia State Game Farm, got its name. She did not know but it was her conversation, not necessarily her answers, which held my interest. She spoke with a wonderful southern accent, rich and filled with the scent of magnolias and summer honeysuckle, but there was nothing small town about her except her surroundings. Was she local? Where had she come from? She was from Rising Fawn, she said. How did a girl of such singular beauty wind up lost and unnoticed in a town of six streets and a truck stop and, more importantly, why did she stay? I didn't ask. I paid for the gas and a six pack, just in case, and drove through the embracing darkness and the growing peaks of the Southern Appalachians on to Chattanooga with questions unanswered, seeing her eyes before me as much as the road. I gassed up there on the return trip a week later and she was behind the counter again. Because of its convenient location, I would gas up at the Game Farm at least once a year for the next twenty-nine years. Like a waterfall or any other roadside scenic beauty I would look for her. We hardly spoke that first night and we rarely spoke again but she was there for twelve years after I had first seen her eyes. And their extraordinary quality and her loveliness never faded in all those years.

At Cleveland I quit highway 11 and took U.S. 64 east past the city of Ocoee and the river gorge of the same name. I wheeled the car, feeling the fatigue setting in, passed the dead hills of Ducktown and Copperhill, center of Tennessee's Copper Basin, and the destruction caused by the ore smelting still disfigured the land. For more than a hundred years they mined copper, cut trees for the open-air roasters which released sulfur dioxide killing the remaining vegetation for hundreds of square miles. With the rising sun I drove through an orange clay landscape devoid of all life except the occasional weeds tucked in at the base of unsightly ravines. Deep erosion scars criss-crossed the low hills and the silt-laden streams were umber smears in the early morning sunrise.

Mike was still sleeping in the passenger's seat when we crossed the state line into North Carolina and entered the Nantahala National Forest. Mike, a college fraternity brother, had withdrawn from graduate school lacking six hours for his MBA, joined the Special Forces and volunteered for Vietnam. Instead of the Nam, he was made finance officer for Thailand which was close enough. He did, however, assign himself temporary duty to, "jump on the hostiles" as he said.

During his training and tour of duty we wrote occasionally, and as he made his way through the army and joined the war, I made my way through law school and entered politics. His mother had passed away when Mike was still in his teens.

His father had three sons who he expected to fend for themselves. Their father kept a roof over their heads but food, and the preparation thereof, as well as laundry, was their responsibility. For a period of time, a half-year I believe, Mike was forced to live in his car as he attended college classes. One night, while he was drunk, before he got in shape for the army, I watched him do twenty-six one-armed pushups. He was granted leave before departing for SE Asia and was dutifully drunk every night. But every morning at 6:00 o'clock, he was running at City Park and he ran until he threw up three times, no more and no less. Then he would stop running until he repeated the exercise the next morning. And now, as we approach the thirty-third anniversary of this first back packing trip, he runs daily and still enjoys marathons. As these words find their way to this page, he and his brother are in their third day of hiking in North Carolina. I would be there with them had my lungs not played out. The heart never did.

In college he threw a large paper route from his car. In those collegiate days of late and all night parties, Mike would always pull up when it was time to deliver his papers. I saw him drive in a near coma in the early hours of a New Years Day, still drunk from a fraternity party, to toss his papers. Whether they landed on the correct lawns, I can't say, but I do know he had the character to leave every party to try. I don't think I've ever seen Mike in a fight and I know he is a man of extraordinary honor and bravery. Today it's hard to imagine a young man of his age, left basically on his own, turning out to be the man Mike is. And when his country needed him, he didn't wait to be asked.

We had our own wars, Mike and I, private and internal wars, which started long before Vietnam. Although the cause of the combat that made the world a difficult place for us was certainly different for both of us, the nature of the battle and our bunker was the same: we chose a bottle. In my war, I was angry. Mike, in his, was not. By the time I woke him to say I could drive no more, I had downed over a case of beer. I pointed to our location on the map and jumped into the back seat and was in a dead sleep before we made a few hundred yards.

Just shy of two hours later I heard him calling my name, waking me from a very deep and warm slumber. I sat up and looked around. It was bright outside and through squinted eyes I could see we were in some type of parking area. A very high parking area at that. It didn't look at all like a campground.

"Where are we?"

"Newfound Gap."

"Newfound Gap? What the hell are we doing here?"

"We put in here."

"Put in? We're not going to camp out first? I need some sleep; I've been driving all night while you slept. Hell, I'm still drunk and have a hangover that could kill."

"No sweat. The shelter's only three mile from here."

"Three miles uphill and I haven't had any sleep for God's sake. Let's camp in Cades Cove, rest up and go tomorrow."

"Nothing to it. Jerry and I did this stretch before. We'll be there in no time."

"Not without sleep and me being hungover we won't."

"Once you get started, there's nothing to it."

"You're crazy if you think I'm hiking today."

But we did. He talked me into it. I don't know why or how he did but he did. Probably owing to my fatigue and stupor, he was able to talk me into the worst day I was ever to spend on a trail and that includes one when I was lost and another when I almost died.

We repacked our gear and secured a fifth of Old Whatisits in Mike's pack and began our eastward slow march to Ice Water Spring. The late morning air was clear and crisp and the hike started off easily enough. But before I had gone very far I was doubled over, gasping for breath. Never having hiked in mountains before, I tried to rush the pace, get there quickly to end the ordeal. On that day, drunk and without sleep, there was no pace that could make the hike bearable. I'd trudge on, stop and gasp for air. Mike would wait patiently and tell me to slow down or count steps. I tried both, and neither did much good.

On one of the halts in our upward climb he said, "I think it was here that Jerry tossed a six pack last year."

"A six pack?"

"Yeah. He tried to carry it in his hand and got about this far. Tossed it downhill."

After a night of beer, which now weighed heavily and uncomfortably in my midsection, the thought of carrying six cans of beer up a mountain seemed remarkably stupid. I was half way through this thought when Mike walked off the trail downhill.

"Whatcha doing?"

"Looking for the beer."

While he looked, I sat down and breathed. When he gave up ten minutes later, I was disappointed but not because he didn't find the beer.

With the fair weather of late spring, the trail was crowded with day hikers. Young men, older men, young girls and even old women passed us by. After a half mile of this humiliation I told Mike to go on to the shelter. I was going to sleep right there, right on the side of the trail. When I woke up, I'd find him at the shelter.

"Are you sure?"

"Yeah. Unless I get some sleep, I'm gonna croak. How do I find the shelter?"

"Straight ahead, you can't miss it. You do cross a couple of intersecting trails but stay on the Appalachian Trail until you see a trail sign saying 'Ice Water Spring'. It goes off to the right and the shelter is about a half mile of flat hiking from there."

"Great. See you later."

"Let me carry that front rucksack for you. I can stick it right up here."

I gave him no argument. It would lighten my load considerably but I still had another rucksack, my sleeping bag and several tons of steel hanging from my web belt.

Not quite sure of my decision, reluctantly, Mike went on.

I opened my poncho, unrolled my sleeping bag and crawled in. It was great. I was cocooned in a soft zippered comforter beneath a canopy of spruce, fir and yellow birch and immediately felt the sleep overtaking me. Each time, just a moment before slipping off, chattering teenagers or talkative tourists would stomp by inches from my head. But I was determined to sleep and remained in the slight depression on the uphill side of the trail. I was so fatigued I would soon be able to tune out the noise and the intrusions. During a lull in the passing troops, headed both south and north, I felt the first drop of rain. Then another. And another. I opened my eyes and studied the sheltering leaves of the forest. Could they block most of the raindrops? Sure, I thought and closed my eyes again. It began raining harder. I pulled the poncho from under me and covered the bag with it. Large raindrops on the stiff, thick rubberized poncho sounded like pebbles hitting a snare drum. Then it began raining flat out. I was trying to sleep in a trailside ditch in the middle of a thunderstorm.

I struggled out of my sleeping bag, cursed, packed it into the stuff sack, strapped on my web belt, slipped on the rucksack and covered it all, myself included, with the poncho. I stuck my head through the opening, pulled the drawstring and took off headed east again, this time in the rain.

Rain beat on my head and ran into my eyes. Where had the other hikers gone? I stopped on the trail and lifted the poncho. I unsnapped my canteen cover and took a long and satisfying drink. It hit my stomach with a thirst quenching coolness and I pushed off again. Not far up the trail I felt the first rumblings of my sick, beer filled stomach. In a moment I was leaning against the stone side of the trail with one hand while I held the poncho close to my body with the other and I hurled. I hurled like the universe was inside fighting to get out as quickly as possible. I hurled for what seemed like an hour. When the eruptions subsided I stood, slowly, weakly and waited to be sure. My eyes were filled with a mixture of tears from the straining and the rain that had run off my head. The trail and small plants at my feet looked somewhat less than natural.

I took off lighter but sicker than I had been a few moments before. The rain continued and the heat inside the poncho was building. As sick as I was and as weak as I felt, it was several minutes before I realized I was walking in my very own steam room. That poncho was capturing every bit of body heat and holding it very close to me. In the middle of a downpour at over five thousand feet, I was sweating like a hog. A few more steps and I was once again leaning on the stones, leaving behind more used beer for the tiny woodland creatures.

Weaker and covered now with sweat and rain, I took off the poncho and folded it as best I could over my sleeping bag and rucksack hoping neither would get too wet. A few steps beyond a turn in the trail the geyser was reaching yet another crescendo. By now all pride was gone. I could care less who saw this vile display resulting from a night of over indulgence. In the middle of my next one handed balancing act, bent nearly in half, fertilizing the trailside flora, an entire troop of Boy Scouts walked behind me. I didn't stop or bother to look and they didn't say a word. I only saw them from their olive drab knees down, passing behind me in stunned disbelief as I continued to blow chunks without inhibition. It was a major low point, my trailside nadir, memorable in its lack of worthiness and things civilized, and had I not been so sick, I would have laughed like a madman.

I cleaned myself off as best I could with the rainwater that was running off of me like I was standing under a shower and took another pathetic step in the direction of the spring named Ice Water.

My hair was wet and the rain kept it that way. My clothes were now soaked. My nose was running and no doubt my eyes were red. I was wearing cut and scuffed work boots, striped brown bellbottomed trousers, an army surplus fatigue shirt and carried an old heavy canvas bag of can food. From my canvas belt hanged half of the steel camping implements carried by Sears. And to make this obscene woodsy collage complete, I was still quite drunk. As I trudged onward, stopping to gasp frequently, the rain began to let up. There were moments, all too brief and few, when I would break out onto a flat and move easily, almost enjoyably. As the sun reappeared, so did the hikers who appraised me, judged me and having done so, kept their distance.

To those headed in the opposite direction, I would ask, "Have you seen a guy with an army pack headed this way?"

"Yes."

"How far ahead is he?"

"A mile" or "half an hour" or the informative, "Not far, you can catch him."

"How far is it to Ice Water Spring?"

"A mile to the turn off."

Time to lean on the stone again.

On an uphill of what turned out to be the last pull before the turn off to Ice Water, it began to rain again. Gasping with my hands on my knees, an old lady passed me by. A very old, smiling lady.

"Come on son, you can make it."

At this my embarrassment completed another pitch and the only sound I made was the horrible sucking noises of intaking and exhaling air. Sweet old bird, happy old turkey, I'd like to wring your neck.

I hit the turn off and fairly glided down the trail without stopping. I was no longer drunk, far from it, and I was not nearly as sick as I had been but I was far from having a relaxing great day of it. As I stumbled and lurched the last few downhill yards to the shelter I could hear voices and one of them was Mike's.

"Here he is. He can start a fire. Glad you made it. We can't get this fire going. How about starting it up?"

The shelter was one of the old ones constructed by the CCC. It was a three-sided log structure with a moss covered, wooden roof and chain link fencing across the open front. Two long logs ran from one side to the other and back from those logs, other logs were placed at right angles running to the rear wall. Hardware cloth was tacked across the framework and created space for ten or twelve sleeping bags. It was located in a shady ravine. It was dark and dank with all the coziness of a sewer pipe.

I dropped my pack and hardware store of woodland tools. Introductions were made and I sat on the rack studying the fire ring. The ashes were soaked as was every scrap of wood.

"It's wet. You don't have anything dry?" The rain was beating on the trees and hitting the mossy roof with muffled splats. It was getting cold.

"That's it. That's all we could find. There's more outside but it's wet too."

I made a small tent of twigs and dead moss. I touched a wax covered match to a rock and it burst into flame. The moss and twigs hissed and steamed but did not ignite. There was no glow to blow upon, no flicker of flame to nurse into being. Even when I added a glob of Sterno it failed to start. It would be another year before I would know how to start a fire with water soaked wood, before I would discover the making of fuzz sticks, the wonders of heartwood, the use of resins in the conifers and fuel tablets

Mike, who had camped with me during college and attended many cookout-jungle juice parties when the fire starting duty fell to me, said, without encouragement, "Man, I thought you could light a fire any time."

"Well with dry wood, I can."

"When the sun comes out we can put some kindling on the roof to dry out."

"We need a fire to heat up the food."

"I have the Sterno stove. Be good to me."

We passed the afternoon hanging our finger in the chain link fence like inmates, each two-man team telling tales to the other. One wore an old and much abused hat which he usually carried rolled up in his pack when not on the trail. He had it on now because of the cold. They had started hiking south from Davenport Gap four days before.

"See any bears?"

"Oh yeah, every night."

"What did you do?"

"Nothing you can do really. You just keep the door chained up while you're inside and keep your back pack inside."

His partner added, "There's a pole with a cross piece at Cosby Knob with a pulley on each side. Three guys there had their packs hanging from them so we just put ours inside. During the night a bear came to the shelter, headed straight for the pole and swatted the hook where the cable was tied off until the packs fell. Funny shit watching the bear eating all their food. Ruined a pack too."

"Every night, bears?"

"Yeah and the mice. They're worse than the bears. Get into everything. Eat through your spare clothes and any food not in a can. Climb over you while you're sleeping too."

"Whatcha do for them?'

"Hope they pick someone else's pack."

"Where you headed from here?"

"Up to the shelter on Leconte."

At this I said, "Well, we're headed that way too and I sure hope it's easier than today up Kephart."

"It's longer and harder."

"Swell," I said.

By mid afternoon, the sun was out to stay and we began to move around outside the shelter, looking for firewood and anything else of interest. Someone located the spring, and flowing from deep within the mountain, it was indeed cold to the touch.

One of the other two disappeared over the uphill rise and began yelling. We raced to the top of the knoll and on the other side, awash in brilliant, warm sunshine was a new shelter made of stone and a corrugated tin roof. The inside was warm and more importantly, bone dry with a good supply of firewood.

We moved our gear from the old shelter into the new with spirits rising. I picked a spot away from the stone wall figuring the mice would be more active there. Others began to arrive and soon the shelter, which could hold twelve hikers, was full.

One was an older man hiking by himself. He and another hiker, who was closer to our age, carried small, white gas mountain stoves. Mike and I stood in amazement as the younger one fired up his stove for a cup of afternoon coffee. He was tall and had little to say to anyone. Mike and I quietly nicknamed him only to ourselves as Woodsy Guy. The basic principle of the stove was simple enough, but to us, we could have been ape-men staring at a light switch. After pumping the stove and allowing a bit of gas into the priming ring, he lit it and adjusted the flame.

"White man make fire with fire thing."

"Fire thing strange and evil."

I spoke with the older man. He was an orthopedic surgeon from Florida, he said, and he hiked in the Smokys a few days each year. He was doing the reverse of our route, coming down from Mt. Leconte where we were going the next day. His wife dropped him off at the Alum Cave Bluff trailhead two days before and would meet him at Newfound Gap the next morning. He was a birder and during our conversation, as he heard chirping or caught a form darting across the sky, he would pause and identify it. There was a gentleness about him and an open friendliness as well. It seemed, after a while, that whatever enjoyment he found in these mountains was increased by his bird watching. It was because of that brief encounter with the birdman of Ice Water that I bought my first book on tree identification several days later. It was to be one of many which would lead to my becoming fairly competent at identifying trees, wild flowers, weeds and edible plants. It added another dimension to the deep enjoyment I was to find in wild places.

Deciding wisely to save the Sterno for emergencies, Mike and I and a few others gathered around the fireplace to heat our beans. We were standing inside the shelter as night fell and Woodsy Guy again fired up his magical stove. The rest of us, except the surgeon who had his own, again studied this novel device from an advanced culture. This time he over primed the fire ring, waited too long allowing the fumes to spread, and when he touched a match to the burner, the thing ignited in a ball of flame that sent him falling backwards with a loud whoosh. It was immediately apparent that this tight-lipped, standoffish fellow had harmed nothing more than his pride and I turned to laugh quietly in a satisfying moment of backcountry class envy. That type of stove is still in wide use but because of that early demonstration, it would be several years before I would trust them enough to carry one myself.

Gradually the pain and humiliation of my morning faded as the day moved on to dusk. I became aware of the distinct and pleasant scent of the spruce-fir forest through which we hiked and which surrounded our shelter. I noticed how alive everything seemed. Chipmunks scurried under and over logs and hopped from spruce branches. Small red squirrels tried to steal from our packs. But the life I felt was not just the woods and the animals. The forest floor, the air and even the quality of light itself pulsed with it. Wilderness had a heart and I was standing where I could feel it. The next morning, sunrise woke me, and from my rack I saw the golden ball rise over the ridges to the east. There was something essential in the moment. It was the glimmer of a lifetime of discovery that began with this awareness that there was something simple about being here and within in that simplicity something healing. Perhaps being in wilderness it is some atavistic need we have or a familiarity that's locked in our genes but I felt a deep contentment away from the distractions of the city. Away from law and politics, down to the basics, I began to feel the things I knew as a child.

After a breakfast of sliced Spam and powdered eggs warmed over an open fire in the aluminum frying pan component of my Boy Scout mess kit, we packed up and walked back the half-mile to the junction of the Appalachian and Boulevard trails. I was far from being in shape but compared to the crippled movements of the previous morning, I flew down the trail. At the junction we turned onto the Boulevard towards Mount Leconte. The next mile we descended Mount Kephart and began a long series of undulating rises before we would hit an uphill. From the real back packers around the shelter the afternoon before, we received several comments about the weight we were carrying. While a 15-inch Bowie knife had its place, back packing was not it. Same for steel hatchets and anything that had to be carried on your belt, canteens included. Cans of food were definitely foolish but the bugle Mike carried drew only puzzled looks. It was just too bizarre to recognize and discuss directly. It was along this stretch of rising and falling trail that I noticed, strangely enough for the first time, the noise coming from Mike's pack. From his heavy military pack dangled his red drinking cup and, on the other side, an aluminum frying pan, each tied with lengths of cord so he'd clank like a chuck wagon in an old cowboy movie with each step. His poncho liner, while it made no noise, was stuffed in awkwardly and appeared a moment away from falling out. From another corner poked a good portion of his sleeping bag. Added to this sight was his apparently inexplicable carrying of six-pound bugle. He looked like a physically fit version of Ignatius Reilly on a Boy Scout outing.

Near a hairpin turn in the trail, the halfway point to Leconte, another hiker coming downhill greeted us. He was a tall fellow about our age and of the two neophytes who stood before him he said, "Well, looks like we have a couple of bear killers here." I think we both assumed correctly that this was the local way of saying "idiots".

The next year we both had lighter and better equipment, which improved with each hike, but for years the bugle remained a constant. In this subculture where each ounce is given careful and precise consideration, the presence of the bugle remained an enigma. On back packing trips, hikers headed in opposite directions would stop on the trail and exchange information for a few moments. It was a great way to get not only the latest news but also the lay of the trail ahead. For reasons which I could only guess, they rarely questioned the bugle but their eyes would return to it repeatedly. They were seeing a guy carrying what amounted to a brick under his arm up a mountain. The bugle was like the old family uncle at a wedding reception who speaks too loudly, belches and farts and whom no one really wants to acknowledge. And even the "bear killer" guy felt no compulsion to ask. But once, perhaps in our third year of back packing, we had been talking to a hiker for some time and I guess he assumed we were sane enough for him to risk a question or two.

"Uh," he started as nonchalantly as he could, "is that some sort of bugle ya got there?"

"Un huh," came Mike's reply, which added nothing to the guy's body of knowledge.

"What do you use it for," he pressed.

"I check out echoes with it."

Certain now that his assumption was incorrect, he offered no smile of understanding, no nod of approval and no further questions, just an eagerness for departure.

The final mile before topping out on Leconte was a steep uphill. Again Mike was forced to wait as I gasped for air but our slow progress was not the snail pace I set the previous drunken morning. Puffing and stopping we finally reached the intersection on the center peak of Leconte, High Top. The forest of single canopied spruce and fir had only a handful of species in the understory. The clouds had moved in and we walked through ancient softwoods shrouded in fog. In the gray which mantled the mountain, gossamer wisps of thicker fog moving slowly past our vision on the gentle breeze. It hushed the sound of our boots on the trail and even muted the clanking of Mike's dangling kitchen. The shelter was located in a sway between High Top and Cliff Top. Around it grew a new generation of spruce and fir no taller than six or seven feet. Someone had secured a large section of Visqueen to the chain fencing. It was flapping loudly in the wind. Fog was blowing into the shelter and inside our two friends from the day before were waiting for someone to build another fire.

* * *

Later in the day I stood off to the side of the shelter with Mike watching a mother bear with her cub amble about, eating huckleberries in a thicket. The red squirrels played in the shelter trying to get in our packs. The remaining daylight hours passed as they passed the day before and much like they pass every day at a backcountry shelter. Conversations center on the trail condition, people seen or the lack of them, what each one did back in the world and food. Always there was talk of food. It has been estimated that pack packers burn between 4,000 and 7,000 calories a day. Even with freeze-dried meals and pasta it was impossible to carry enough food to equal the caloric demands. Back packers were always hungry after the first day. It was during one of these conversations when the hat-wearing member of their team noticed his inside hatband was swarming with maggots. He sounded a half disgusted-half angry sort of grunt and slammed it against the fence.

"Maggots! How in hell did they get in there?"

"Damn," someone said as we huddled around the wounded hat lying on the muddy floor of the shelter.

"It's been raining every day since we left. I guess a fly laid eggs in there."

"What have they been eating?"

"They look thin. Maybe nothing."

"Maybe the hat?"

"Maybe your head."

He picked up his hat and swatted it several times against the fence and looked inside. Maggots went flying to the left and right. He swatted it again a few times and looked inside the band.

"That did it," he said and put it back on his head.

"You going to wear that thing," his partner asked.

"Damn straight. It's getting cold."

I looked at Mike and said, "Plenty of protein in those. You want them?"

"Maybe tomorrow. Tonight it's Dinty Moore."

"Is there a difference?'

"Well, those maggots are fresh."

Others began arriving, mostly men. There were three hippie looking young men (as if we all didn't look like hippies by now), and several other guys came in twos and threes. No computer system monitored the number of hikers in the Smokys then and getting a rack in the shelter was on a first come, first served basis. Number thirteen and above had to sleep outside or on the mud floor.

To make the sleeping situation a bit more complicated, they still allowed horse back trips to Leconte, a practice which ended a few years later. The horseback group that stumbled in that evening was eight drunken fraternity guys and the total at the inn was now over twenty. Mike and I kept a watchful eye on our racks and laid claim thereto with our packs. These guys came for a good time and several of us gave them food, for while they had plenty of booze, enough to get everyone in the shelter slightly buzzed, seems food had been overlooked. One fellow was very upset he had forgotten his toothbrush but he had a saddlebag which produced pints like the loaves and fishes. He would need much more than a toothbrush to cure the hangover that awaited him.

The group of three hippies stayed mostly to themselves and spent most of the evening outside, several yards from the shelter, sitting on a ground cloth. I noticed them there when I went outside to look at the night sky. They were off to the side and I sat on a log looking at the stars.

The sky had cleared and remained so for a few hours. I was in a small clearing more than 6,500 feet above sea level. There were no interfering city lights. There was no light at all except the soft glow coming from the fireplace to my rear and the thousands and thousands of overhead stars. The Milky Way lying on its side was running in a distinct line from horizon to horizon. Stars covered the summer sky like pinhole sized jewels stuck in the black ceiling of the world. In their faint light I could see the spruce and fir trees in front of the shelter. Turning around to take it all in I saw people inside standing near the fireplace talking and the starlight reflecting off the tin roof of the shelter. The orange glow from the fire spilled out along with the quiet laughter from within. I turned my back to the cold night breeze and saw a shooting star moving from right to left low on the horizon. It was a remarkable night and the moment brought the nearness of both magic and deity. I was feeling the peace of belonging and the sense of being very near something vital.

We learned the next morning that the hippie group dropped acid that night, one of them for the first time. Why they felt the need to distort a perfectly wonderful night was just another bit of human behavior that made no sense to me. But I didn't understand much of the 60s and 70s and much of myself would remain a mystery until the 70s were just bittersweet memories.

The fraternity group started the night sleeping outside but they came in when the rains returned. It started late and continued throughout the night. Water ran downhill from the front of the shelter and onto the mud floor. The brotherhood of Lambda Delta Drunks walked around trying to find a place to lay their bags and, in the process, churned the floor into slush. It was fortunate that they had a lot to drink because they had to sleep in oozing mud or drown outside. The next morning when we awoke, they were still sleeping, their sleeping bags resting comfortably in three inches of soft mud.

We walked past the trail that led to Cliff Top, where we failed to see a decent sunset the evening before. That short trail, once it reached the top of the rise, meandered through low plants that hugged close to the exposed rock, seeking protection from the cold and often heavy winds. Thick and green mosses, stunted sand myrtle, dwarf fir trees and gnarled and ancient rhododendrons formed a natural bonsai garden. We passed the spring where we filled our canteens the day before and again after breakfast that morning. We passed the rustic lodge which housed the probably more intelligent Leconte visitors. We walked across all of this on relatively flat terrain until we reached the steep downhill of the Alum Bluff Trail.

Being the poorer hiker, I took the lead setting the pace. The trail dropped quickly and skirted the perpendicular wall that was the base of Cliff Top. Every crack and crevice along its rust and pink colored stone face was home to members of the heath family: sand myrtle, mountain laurel, rhododendron, and blueberry. As we moved lower, the spruce and fir trees resumed their grand size leaving their stunted cousins on the windblown slopes of Leconte's peaks. Red spruce with trunks more than three feet in diameter and huge firs kept the forest floor in shadow. We passed a few of these giants uprooted when the weight of their ice covered limbs caused them to tip over in the howling winter winds. Lacking a taproot their roots spread out in a circle around their trunks, and when they went over, they ripped up large irregular clumps of soil and rock fifteen or twenty feet across.

Wood sorrel with small white flowers streaked with minute red lines on hair thin stems were everywhere and most importantly, the downhill trail was far easier than the climbing of the past two days. On the previous two days Mike had blown his bugle several times but the echoes were few and muted. On the higher section of the Bluff trail, he found and tested many promising spots. Yes, to my unending joy, there were many promising spots.

Perhaps three-quarters of a mile from the trailhead, we came to a section of mountain that had been sheared off years before. A narrow exposed ledge, perhaps two feet wide, had been fashioned for the trail which circled the rock face and ended somewhere beyond our line of sight. A steel cable handhold was anchored to the wall with very large eyebolts. I glanced down to the skree pile some forty or fifty feet below. It looked a great deal further and I could picture my broken body lying there, twisted and soft among the angry blocks of jagged stone. I saw that the cable had too much play in it and I suggested to Mike that he wait until I was safely to the other side before he started across. I began inching my way around that memorable stone wall, my knees increasing their shaking with each shuffle step I took. I slid my hands along the cable and froze when I came to an eyebolt and had to release one hand at a time to pass it. I was nearing the half way point, where the wall bowed out, when Mike, unaware of my rising terror, chose that precise moment to hit a shrill, blaring note of exquisite volume that almost blasted me off the face of the rock.

More than a little rattled and clutching the too loose cable in a death grip, I heard the faint sound of a distant echo. After it faded and I could speak again, I turn to Mike and quietly asked, "Mike, if you're going to blow that thing, yell to me before you do, ok?"

"Sure" he said, thinking the first blast was sufficient warning for the present wall. "Did you hear the echo?"

I was moving again and managed to squeeze out only, "Un huh."

Summoning up my now thoroughly destroyed confidence, I continued to inch my way to the other side. After a few very uncertain steps, another high pitched "BLATT" knifed through the silence of the eastern forest and struck terror into my core. I began vibrating at the end of the loose cable back and forth between the wall and over open space feeling like a paddleball in slow motion. When this stopped and I regained my equilibrium I continued my stutter motion to the other side of the slide area.

I waited for Mike to cross and then said, "I thought you were going to warn me if you blew that again."

"I didn't think you meant now," he said, somewhat confused.

"Mike, if we come to any more of these narrow spots, let me know before you blow that thing. You scared the hell out of me."

"Sure, no problem."

We took off again and in only the briefest span of time, we came, as I was sure we would, to an even larger area that had to be traversed. Inching my way across again, face to the wall, hands sliding along the cable, I heard in the highest possible decibels from only a few feet from my ear, Mike yelling, "Hey, Buz!"

The force of his scream almost knocked me off the wall and I went into my back and forth rubber band vibration wondering why the stinking cables had so much slack in them and asked, "What?"

"I'm going to blow the bugle again."

I got to the other side and as he was coming across and I looked around for a good-sized stone to heave at him. He breathes today only because I found none. There were a few more of these slide areas and each was as frightening as the first two but after a serious talk with Mike, he blew the thing only when I was on solid footing.

Three miles down the trail we came to the large stone outcropping which gave the trail its name: Alum Cave Bluff. We stood at the upper corner from where the trail ran down and across the bottom of this concave stone face.

Eons of water percolating though and across the stone had eaten it away, leaving a fine dust of powdered rock. The trail ran along the base of this massive stone wall a hundred feet high and twice that in width. In a wilderness of trees and shrubs exposed rock this size was a thing of rare and enduring beauty. We crossed the face and ate a snack on the other side and drank from our canteens. From where we took our break, we could see a weathered circular hole in the razor-thin ridge running out from the base of the bluff. A peregrine falcon darted from overhead, skated along the face of the ridge and disappeared from sight.

Rested we headed steadily downhill and the trail floor began to sink between its two sides. We entered an area of rich soil built up from years of decaying vegetation. Between the stone path and the growing plants was three feet of soil that looked very much like coffee colored peat moss. The plants again were heaths but unlike on Leconte, here they were their normal size. The trail led to a rock ledge which overlooked the Pigeon River Valley. We stood on the ledge, studying the valley and the ridges beyond it and enjoyed the wind rushing up the slope. At this point and below, the forest changed. The softwoods began to play out as we lost altitude and the beech, birch, maple and basswood were understoried by rosebay rhododendron. We reached Arch Rock where the trail dropped twenty feet rapidly inside that rocky passageway. The stones which served as steps were ice covered and we bounced our packs on the steps as we eased our way down through the stone. Once through, the trail became gentle and garden-like. Rhododendron lined the stream-following trail, which jumped from one side to the other, until we reached the trailhead and the parking lot where Mike hitchhiked to the car at Newfound Gap and the remnants of our beer supply.

* * *

We slammed down a couple of Dixies and picked up a few more six packs and ice in Gatlinburg. We bought some franks to spice up our beans, a pack of hot dog buns, some chips, mustard and canned chili. We headed to Cades Cove, paid for a tent site and drove to a nearby stream to wash off several layers of sweat, dirt and campfire smoke. Standing in waste deep water we soaped ourselves with our clothes still on and gradually peeled off each layer as they became a little cleaner. Even in the heat of mid-day the water was chilled. By the time our clothes and bodies were clean enough, we were shaking, our skin was pale and our lips were blue. We sat on the rocks in the sun warming ourselves until our clothes were dry. The process took several more beers.

At the campground at Cades Cove we tied off a poncho to cover our sleeping bags. I worked on a fire while Mike introduced himself to our camping neighbors, a man and his wife in a small trailer. About the time I had our dogs and beans ready, Mike came back with a plate loaded with real food compliments of his new friends. We piled that along with my campfire fare onto two plates and stuffed ourselves and proceeded to get drunk.

Throughout the day, bears would wander into the campground, inspect the dumpster for human chow, make a racket while nearby campers gushed and giggled. That night, they didn't find it so amusing. Mike and I, safely under our poncho, were set up maybe twenty yards from the nearest dumpster. We were sleeping soundly when the first one came. This bear knew the ropes. Before going to the garbage dumpster, he tried to sample the contents of the ice chest left on the picnic table by a young couple tent camping. I heard the crashing of the plastic chest and then the screams of the female member of that lucky group. A male voice was demanding that she be quiet. A flashlight was turned on which lit up their yellow two-man tent like a bright neon sign, which said "beat me" in bear talk. The bear lumbered over to the tent and gave it a few swats. Mike and I were out of our bags and moved closer to the tent, shouting to distract the angry and confused bear. A fellow in a pop-up camper across the road yelled at us to shut up and go to sleep. The woman continued her near panic screams and her silhouette danced on the wall of the tent which now moved, not from the bear any longer for he was now at the dumpster, but from their frantic efforts to retreat without leaving the imagined safety of the tent.

"Oh my God! Is he gone? Where is he?"

"At the dumpster. Stay where you are and put out the light."

"Shut up and go to bed for Christ's sake."

"There's a bear out here bothering these people."

"Oh God!"

"Well let him alone and go to sleep. People are trying to sleep here."

"He's coming back your way. Be quiet, he probably just wants the ice chest."

"Can you get it away from him?"

I replied, "Er . . . no."

Mike, with characteristic sympathy for fools said, "Hahaha."

"Oh God."

Crash. The bear threw the ice chest to the ground breaking it open. This time from within the tent the male asked, "What does he want with the chest? It doesn't have anything in it."

"He won't know that until he opens it up."

"Hahaha."

"Oh God. Oh God."

When the bear finally lumbered off and we informed them, they exited the tent and inspected their chest, now broken. I suggested they place it in their trunk as it would certainly attract another or the same bear. While they rearranged their site, I asked Mike the maximum range of his camera flash and set the focus for that distance. Fifteen feet.

I asked Mike, "What do you think he'll do when the flash goes off and I'm fifteen feet away from him?"

"Don't know. Might come after you."

"Yeah. Gimme another beer."

We were both sure the bear would return and maybe an hour later he woke us again. He stood on his hind legs with his head and front paws in the dumpster. Again we heard, "Oh God," but it was quieter this time, more like a prayer. I slipped out of my bag and walked slowly over to him. He stood upright, balanced with his paws on the dumpster looking straight at me. I got about fifteen feet away, probably more, and pointed the camera at him. There wasn't enough light to see anything in the viewfinder. I released the shutter and was immediately blinded. I was hoping the bear was as well.

I asked Mike, "Where is he?"

"Still by the dumpster, I think. I can't see a damn thing."

Some of my night vision returned and I told Mike to close his eyes so he could warn me of the bear's movements when I took another picture. The bear, bored by whatever I was going to do to him now, returned to his rooting for tidbits. I braced for whatever the bear would do and steadied myself for the next shot. Brer Bear would not look my way and kept his head in the trash bin.

"Hey," I yelled.

He did nothing so I threw a beer can against the dumpster. He leaned back and I yelled again. He looked at me and I told Mike to close his eyes. I pointed the camera in the direction of the bear, closed my eyes, and pressed the shutter. We continued this game with the bear for several more frames and I retired under the poncho for the rest of the night. He returned a few more times and I took another picture without leaving my bag. The pictures turned out fine but lacked the excitement of standing so close and flashing a thousand candle power in a bear's face. Lacked the warm glow of all the beer too.

The next day we drove the loop road in the Cove stopping at the old homesteads and reading the self guided brochure. We returned to our poncho campsite and ate lunch. Mike's friends in the trailer called for us. They sat at their table and the woman held a horse hoof shaped, white platform fungus upon which she had drawn a Christmas looking tree next to a log cabin, a stream and smoke rising from the chimney. Beneath the mountain scene were the words "Great Smoky Mountains".

"We find them in the woods. They grow on old oak trees and she makes these drawings. After they dry out for a few days, we varnish them and they make wonderful souvenirs." Mike and I, afraid to look at each other and bust out in maniacal laughter, told them it was an extraordinary idea and suggested they sell them to tourists.

"Do you really think so," she asked.

"Absolutely. Tourists would love that sort of thing, right Mike?"

"Sure. They buy all that genuine Indian stuff made in Taiwan don't they?"

The husband gave us a conspiratorial smile and asked us to step to the other side of his trailer. He opened a large wooden panel and beneath it he had constructed six or seven narrow shelves each crammed with scenic fungi.

"Whoa, that's really swell."

"We look for them in all the parks and we bring them home for the family and friends."

"Great."

"Here," he said handing one to his friend Mike, "take this one."

"Oh, I really couldn't do that."

"It's ok, we have plenty and we're going to get more tomorrow."

Before we left them the next morning Mike had parlayed his new friendship with the slightly goofy trailer folk into the artwork fungus and two more meals for us.

* * *

The next morning we drove to Clingman's Dome, the highest point on the Appalachian Trail and the second highest in the park. From the parking area we climbed the graded trail up to the observation tower through a spruce-fir forest which is now gone, destroyed by an insect from China. Tourist at the tower, seeing our packs, asked where we were going and when we answered Silers Bald they looked at us in obvious puzzlement.

"Where's that?'

"Five miles that way."

"You going to stay there over night, in the woods?"

"Un huh?"

"Aren't you afraid of bears?"

"No. On this shelter there's a door which you can shut. On Leconte the whole front is open."

"Were there any on Leconte?"

"Before we got there, two guys saw one milling around, and we saw one later on in the day with a cub but they didn't come around that night."

"Well, that doesn't sound like my idea of fun."

"Mine either. I rather collect horse hoof fungi," I said.

The Appalachian Trail dropped off the top of the Dome and we headed west, downhill but still in the Canadian softwood forest. The distinct smell of the resins and the decaying needles wormed its way into my memory and took up permanent residence. That delicate scent, both unique and familiar, formed one of my core recollections of that trip and all that were to come. From the fog shrouded ancient firs on Leconte, haunting and remote, to the deep canopy they formed along the high peaks, they remain fixed and beautiful for all time. In their deep shade sorrel, ferns and club mosses flourished. Fallen trees were everywhere and in their cycle of becoming soil again, mosses grew along their exposed side. Lichens and algae, insects and weathering were breaking them down, converting them into nutrients for countless plants which covered the decaying giants in a green mantle. Young trees sent their roots deep into their hearts, gathered molecules from the dead so they could grow and the dead could live anew. Death, decay and rebirth. This same cycle was everywhere, in the sunrise and set, in the changing seasons, offering hope to the cynic provided they chose to see. Witch Hobble bloomed and their seeds turned cherry red in winters highlighted against a background of fallen crystal white, pure snow. But this May morning, spring lingered and summer was near. Deep red Rhododendrons bloomed on the grassy balds on the south side of Mount Buckley. There were orange lilies tucked along the trail where it broke into the sun and everywhere the air was sweet, alive and holy.

The ridge connecting Clingman's with Buckley was exposed layers of metamorphic rock, broken and tilted on edge. Slabs of it were thrust upward at a forty-five degree angle and across the top ran the trail. The ancient spruce and fir still found footing in the thin soil and dressed the ridgeline with green sentinels, mute guards that stood at attention for our passage. From this open knife-edge we could see far to the south and west. Ridge upon green ridge, mountain after mountain, we could see past Fontana Dam and its silver-blue lake, past the Snowbirds and as far as Georgia. We could see the crown jewels of the Southern Appalachians, their peaks embraced by the blue sky of late spring. Here was beauty with power to open the eyes.

We crossed Buckley and descended in a series of flats and declines. In two hours we entered Double Spring Gap where water from a spring on the south side of the trail ran into North Carolina and one on the north side spilled into Tennessee. The shelter was located in a stand of birch and in the open field before it grew wild mustard, their yellow cluster flowers dancing in the wind which blew trough the gap. We were less than two miles from Silers Bald.

We moved again on a ridgeline but it was broad and rounded unlike the narrow one we crossed just south of Clingman's Dome. I was in the lead and I saw a young man, his pack on the ground, busily scooping bear scat into a small plastic container. Feeling as I had stepped through the looking glass again, I had to stop.

"Hey. How's it going," I asked.

"Fine and you?"

"Great. Beautiful day isn't it?"

"Sure is." During this exchange he had continued with his strange predilection. I could now see he was using a regular kitchen spoon to scoop it up.

"Er, is that bear crap you're picking up there?"

"Yes."

At this point, Mike amused and overcome with curiosity asked, "Why?"

"I go to UT and a professor in the biology department pays me to walk the trails collecting this stuff."

At least he was now looking up at us and smiling.

Mike laughed and said, "You're kidding aren't you?"

"No. Really. They're trying to check on the health of the bear population and this is only one part of what they do."

Fishing through a pocket of his pack, he pulled out several sheets of paper and handed one to us.

"This is a questionnaire if you see bears tonight. Where are you staying?"

"Silers Bald."

"Well you're going to see one there for sure. He's been bothering people for weeks. When you see him, just fill out this form and mail it back to TU. The questions are fairly general. His aggressiveness, the condition of his coat . . . that sort of stuff."

"Getting paid to walk these trail sounds like a pretty good college job."

"Yeah, but over the weekends I have to keep the stuff in our refrigerator until Monday and my mom isn't too understanding about that. She doesn't like the idea of bear crap being so close to Sunday's dinner. I put some in once without telling her. She opened it and like to went nuts."

"Every job has its downside I guess."

"Do you get to keep what they don't use?"

Down the trail a bit Mike said, "Won't that look super on his resume: 'Picked up bear shit in the woods for UT.'"

"You heard what he said about the bear tonight?"

"Sounds like grins."

The last half-mile to Silers Bald was steep. On that climb I repeated my moving and gasping method of covering the uphills while Mike waited. The bald itself was a large grassy area with shrubs scattered about randomly. The forest was already reclaiming this summer pasture used even before the white man entered the area. Service berry and yellow birch had sprung up. Thornless blackberry formed the southern edge of the bald. From its eastern edge, looking back over the trail we had taken, we could see the ridge running back clearly to the gap where the twin springs were located and the dense forest at the base of Mount Buckley and the long, narrow ridge east of Buckley's crown. And five miles away was the massive form of Clingman's Dome and the tower at the very top. A few degrees to the north and nine miles past Clingman's we could see the three distinct peaks of Leconte. From where I stood on that windblown point of rock, I could see the crest of the Smoky high country, this perfect land, and I felt as though I owned it. I was overcome with the certainty that I was feeling the way I should feel in church but no longer did. Seeing the view of where we walked and the ground we covered, my thoughts were conflicted. I felt some pride in standing there, proud of some accomplishment, but seeing the rugged vastness in which I stood, my pride was mixed with a feeling of my absolute insignificance. I knew clearly that this complex and perfect world of shifting energy did not occur by some cosmic accident but by design and I was part of that design. Walking these days along stream and trail I knew without question I belonged here and in that fleeting moment when my mind and the world embraced, I became convinced of the existence of a Creator and I did not have this epiphany in a traditional church. I had sensed it here in a temple fashioned by the hand of God Himself.

* * *

We spent the afternoon and early evening gathering firewood, refilling our canteens, laying out our sleeping bags and preparations for another tin of Dinty Moore's. As the day moved slowly to its demise, we began wondering if the two of us would face the night bear alone. We were sure the chain fence was a barrier in a psychological sense only. Even a small bear could rip it down should it decide to do so. As we had done each night before, we washed our pans completely not leaving a trace of food odor on them. The shelter was located in hollow down the west side of the bald. The area to the front was open only to the treeline some thirty feet away. A bear could be on us with out much warning and for that reason we kept the door chained each time we entered or exited the shelter. No sense letting one get in with our food while we were outside with the woods. But it was not a bear that would first ease up on us; it was a human. Making no sound as he moved down the trail, he appeared silently and suddenly at the door. Wraithlike he stood there with the expressionless stare that long distance hikers acquire at the end of each long day. He was young, perhaps sixteen or so, and was at least six inches taller than six feet. He sported a crop of red hair common among the Scots-Irish of these mountain folk. He entered with barely a grunt of recognition and immediately fell soundly asleep on one of the racks.

When he awoke an hour later, he was only slightly more animated. He moved like a slug around camp. He would reach for things in a painfully slow motion and spoke in a drawl that matched the speed of his movements. As he made a meal of corn flakes and powdered milk he told us that his brother, a cousin and he had put in at Mount Springer in Georgia with the intention of hiking the entire Appalachian Trail, a distance of over two thousand miles. Somewhere south, probably around Wesser, NC he grew tired of the muse, abandoned the arena and left the trail. After a few days of guilt and missing his friends, he caught a Greyhound and rode north, got back on the trail headed south to catch them. He had eaten only corn flakes for days. Perhaps in part the lack of calories accounted for his lethargy but certainly not all. We told him about the UT kid and his promise of bears that night. Our anticipation was lost on him as he told us he had seen the things almost every night on the trail.

The bear did come that night, slipped quietly out of the woods directly to our front as expected, had his portrait taken and then came again an hour later. And then an hour after that. We banged on our pans when he moved close to the fence and yelled but he remained unflappable. His mind was on food, be it on the ground or in our packs. Then Mike, in a moment of Gestalt insight, blew his bugle so piercingly loud that people in shelters miles away had to whisper, "What was that?"

The bear, in cartoon fashion, lowered his rear end, let lose with a frightened grunting huff and ran back into the woods as fast as his four legs would carry him.

While Mike and I laughed, Corn Flakes said with snail-like speed, "That there trumpet works pretty fair, didn't it? Is that what y'all carry it fer?"

"Well, that and the echoes. Mainly the echoes," Mike replied.

"Echoes? Y'all hered any?"

"Coming down Leconte a few days ago we heard a bunch but Buz here didn't like them too much."

"And why was that," he asked turning to look at me.

"Gave me a feeling I wouldn't live to see my family again."

"Oh," he said, as if I had responded to his question in a way he could understand. Mike laughed.

We would walk back to Clingman's Dome the next day and when we finished our evening meal, our hike nearing its end, we gave him the extra ration of food we each carried. He wolfed it down with his slow motion tempo. For a sleeping bag he used an Army surplus woolen blanket folded in three lengths and fastened with very large safety pins. Because of his height, his shoulders were completely outside the bag. It almost froze that night and I'm sure he had spent several uncomfortable nights below freezing, particularly when they began the trip weeks earlier in Georgia. He carried no change of clothes. He was going super light, super hungry and super cold. The next morning, Corn Flakes ate another bowl of his namesake, threw on his pack, told us good-bye and moved down the trail with speed that surprised us. I watched as he turned on his afterburner and rocketed off. Mike, poking around in his pack, looked up and said, "Where'd Corn Flakes go?"

"South, with the other birds."

I began the day with some dread. Beyond Double Spring Gap lay the steep uphill to Buckley and Clingman's itself. We got a late start and stopped to eat lunch at the gap. We sat on the racks eating and listening to the blowflies buzzing around something left in the fireplace. The day was bright and the wind had a chill which made for an easier hike. We were quiet for the most part, thinking about the last seven days, when the first group of a twenty man Boy Scout troop ran into the clearing, crushing the wild mustards. The stragglers arrived followed by a volunteer dad who brought up the rear. They fixed their lunch with as much noise as they could make. There were three men, two were fathers of scouts and the third was the Scout Master. The dad who came in last sat on the rack to my left.

Our beards hadn't seen a razor for a week and our clothes were filthy. Our hair was uncombed and I was still carried two rucksacks and my woodsy utility belt. Why he asked advice from us is one of those unanswerables that usually has to do with there always being a greater fool somewhere. And I had apparently found one of mine.

"How long you guys been out?" he asked.

"We hiked up and around Leconte for three days, took a couple of days off just camping and this is day two of this leg. Our fifth day of hiking," I said.

"You see any bears?"

"Sure, some at the camp ground, two during the day on Leconte and another one last night at Silers Bald. He came three or four times."

"At night?"

"Yes."

"We're going to stay there tonight."

"Well you'll see him for sure."

"What did you do?" he asked.

"Nothing. We took some pictures and after awhile, he just went away. Bang on something and they usually just move away. Mike here has a bugle which works really well."

Looking furtively around, he reached into his backpack and before removing his hand, he glanced around one more time. Satisfied he was not being watched he said quietly, "Well, I got something right here for them," and pulled out a .22 the size of a cap pistol.

I didn't laugh; I just said, "Well don't shoot them with that. All you're gonna do is really piss him off."

That night in the campground, standing so close to the bear, I understood part of this foolishness I had fallen into. Among my cans and useless pounds of camping tools were three extra pounds which were totally useless: a 9-mm pistol and extra rounds of ammo I carried for the bears. Not only were guns in the park against the law even then, I knew when I saw one up close, that it would take well over a full magazine to bring the thing down. I didn't tell volunteer dad this. I just urged him to use a Boy Scout whistle instead. For the next twenty-three years and countless days on the trail, I never again carried a weapon, a hatchet or any knife weighing more than a few ounces.

My speed increased over the years but looking at the seemingly unending uphill between where I stood that day and our car parked a half-mile below the summit of Clingman's Dome, I already understood something and I would come to know it with a deeper certainty in the years that followed. Back packing isn't about finishing. It's about moving forward. Just keep putting one foot in front of the other, enjoy the view and look for mystery even in the small stuff. Especially in the small stuff. Feel the sheer ecstasy of being completely free; free to have options, free to create, to love, to rage against fools, to enjoy thoroughly our all too brief time. Move through it with purpose, never aimlessly. Hiking is an exercise of the head and heart, not the body. Hiking aimlessly would be passing through these countless gifts and never asking why they're here and who we are. Being aimless is looking at a flower and seeing a flower. Aimless would be never confronting fear or seeking an understanding of its cause and being held captive by it. Aimless is living on one's knees. Aimless is being someone else and never knowing it.

And as often as necessary, breathe.

The Boon

We are outside in the cold. Joe and I. But I can't look at Joe right now. He's changing into a gorilla again. Instead I look at the leaf stuck to my shoe. I move my foot to the side trying to shake it off. It sticks like a magnet. I move it away and something pulls it back and it sticks again. I keep scraping my foot but it still sticks. Maybe it's not a leaf. Maybe it's nothing. Maybe it's part of this movie that's running in my head. But I keep trying to get whatever it is off. Joe's looking at me without saying anything. Maybe there's nothing there and Joe knows I'm crazy. Maybe I should stop. Joe knows I'm not right. I better stop.

It's cold and the wind's blowing. We're outside the glass doors of the hospital. Joe and I. At least I think it's Joe. It was Joe. Christ, since my brother went inside, Joe keeps getting hairy and his nose is flared out. Sometimes he's Joe and sometimes it's part Joe and part gorilla. I keep looking back to him, watching the change. I don't want to watch, but I do. It scares me but it scares me not to.

"George, you ok?"

"Yeah." I look down at my foot and the leaf. It's a large brown leaf. A sycamore. Sure, it's a sycamore leaf. Don't look at it anymore. It might change like Joe or something. Christ, I'm scared. I'm screwed up bad. What's happening? I'm trapped here . . . trapped in this place where everything keeps changing. How do I get back? My brother's back. He's back from inside.

"He ok?"

"Yeah, he's fine," Joe tells him.

"Let's go. He's been admitted."

Christ. This is it. Holy shit. The nut house. I gotta get help but they can't help. They'll lock those doors and I'm never getting back. I'm fucked up for good. Shit, Nat's got paintbrush strokes all over his gray leather coat. How did that happen? Don't say anything. Maybe it's not paint. Maybe it's not there. Jesus Christ, stop this.

"Come on George. You'll be alright." Joe's calling me George. He's always calling me George. He's scared too. He knows I'm really fucked up. Nat opens the door and we go in, inside out of the cold, up the elevators, the elevator with the red doors. We turn down the hall to two more red doors. Large red double doors. The nurse says something to the other side. I don't know what she said. It doesn't make sense. Sometimes I hear people speaking English but they don't make sense. Sometimes I speak but not English. Strange jumbles of words come out and nobody can understand me. I try to tell them shit but junk comes out and they can't understand me. They know I'm screwed. They just look at me. It scares them and that scares me more. It passes and I can speak again. And then it comes back. I keep sliding back and forth from a world of terrifying slipping reality to a surreal world of ever changing images that seem somehow familiar.

The voice on the other side of the double doors turns a key and slides a bolt with a clang. It's loud . . . so loud I flinch.

And then I go in.

* * *

I had been going to the hill for some time. Even before I stopped drinking I had been going there. It was quiet and grass covered and I could see the tall buildings of the business district off in the distance. It wasn't much of a hill, maybe 30 feet or so. Several years before the city piled up chunks of broken concrete and unwanted bits of steel and covered it with clay and river sand making a hill-like mound in the park. Trees, mostly tallow and willow, had sprung up here and there giving it a nice look for a man-made hill. Just before dusk, the sun would set over the sweet gums that lined the lagoon to the west. The lights of the city would dot the night sky and the stars overhead would out shine their glare on the clearer nights. I would sit and watch the sun go down and then lie on my back and wait for the stars to appear. I could close my eyes, feel the wind and hear it gently moving the leaves.

I was coming here almost every day since I quit drinking. I'd go to the hospital, work through the programs and come out here to relax and watch the sun go down in patterns that never seem to repeat. I could feel the panic rising inside. I felt it start when I couldn't remember phone numbers, not the office number or my home phone, for that matter. I told the hospital staff about it, even my therapist, but none of them were concerned. They said I was just juggling too much and to take it easy. Let the office work go and concentrate on the program, they said. Get off that sauce. I had to. My liver was already enlarged. Matter of life and death they said. But I had to calm down, had to shake this terror rising in my gut. Christ, I can feel it like a living thing growing, getting stronger until it takes me over and I'll be out of control, stark raving nuts. No, stay calm, get to the hill. You'll be safe at the hill. Think about the hill. That's it. That's better. It's passing. Easy now. Easy.

I drive out there slowly, not sure of my reactions and whether the panic will return while driving, so I go slowly to the refuge of the hill. I pull off the dirt road and drive across the grassy field to the base of the hill. I can feel the car slipping in the wet grass. Christ, beneath the grass, the ground is a morass. I feel the car sinking. Hit the gas . . . move out of here. Ah, the son of a bitch is spinning. Wheels are digging in! Reverse. Easy, ease out in reverse. That's it . . . it's moving. Easy, easy. Shit, it's spinning. Try forward now. Easy, don't panic. Ok it's going, it's going. Goddamn! Slipping. Spinning again! Shit! Hit it! Floor it! Now reverse! Now forward! Rock it! Reverse! Shit! Ah shit!

I open the car door and the son of a bitch is dug in almost to the frame. My feet sink in the muddy grass. Got damn! Shit! Got to get out of here.

Here's a car coming. Thank God. He offers help and has a rope. Thank Christ. He stays off about 70 feet and we run the rope from his bumper to my frame. We'll get the car out of here and on the road and I'll walk to the hill and relax. Meditate myself back to calm. Will myself to relax. I'll be up there and safe in just a few minutes. Thank God.

Here goes. The rope is lifting off the ground. Easy now. Ok, it's taut. Now pull. Easy. His wheels are spinning. Christ is my car stuck. No! No! Don't accelerate! You'll get stuck! Christ he's spinning like mad. Is he crazy? Stop! Stop!

Ah shit, now he's stuck. How stupid can ya get? He'll walk to the gas station across the park and get a tow truck and be back in a few minutes . . . as fast as he can, he says. Call my wife. Here's the number. Tell her to bring the station wagon but tell her to stay on the road. He leaves and I walk to the hill and climb up. Up to the safety of the hilltop.

I lay down. I don't look at the sky or the trees or nothing. I lay down and close my eyes and start counting backwards. Start the ritual of relaxation. Of self-hypnosis. Of calming down. At forty I'm feeling better. At twenty-five I'm relaxed. Thank God. I'll be ok. I'll be ok

That feeling in my gut. It's coming on again. No, hold on, hold it down. Force it down. Calm. Take a breath. Hold it. Relax. It's going. It's . . . going.

Ok. It's all right. I'm all right. We'll get the car out of here and go home and sleep and I'll be ok. Ok. I'll be ok.

I go deeper into a restful state and wait . . . wait for the tow truck and my wife in the station wagon. On that hill in the center of a quagmire in a grassy field. I could feel the dread of panic waiting out there beyond the boundary of this hilltop. Waiting for me.

The tow truck comes with the other guy and they were pulling out his car when my wife got there. They get the other car free. The driver of the tow tells me his cable isn't long enough to reach my car and he can't get off the road or he'll get stuck too. By this time I don't know what to tell him. I can't think. Maybe I curse him. I don't know what I'm saying. He's looking at me strangely. He knows I'm losing it. I don't know. Maybe my wife tells him we'll get it tomorrow, I don't know. We're in the station wagon leaving the car by the hill stuck in the mud. I've got mud all over me. I'm driving the station wagon. Out of the corner of my eye I see my wife looking at me. She knows I'm fucked up. She can tell. Act normal, damn it. Say something normal. I can't speak. I can't say anything. That feeling's back. Terror. I feel it moving all the way up the back of my neck. I'm losing it! I'm going crazy!

"Buz where are you going?"

"Home."

"You're driving in circles! What are you doing?"

"I'm just driving around. I'll go home now." Where am I? I know this neighborhood. It's near my house. But where's the house? How do I get there? I've been here hundreds of times but where am I? How do I get out? Christ, I'm gonna yell or hit someone. Shit, where am I?

"Buz you're scaring me! Are you all right?"

Christ quit yelling. I can't think. You're fucking me up more. "I'm ok. Nothing's wrong. Here you drive. I'm just confused. I'm all right. I need sleep, that's all."

I'm in my bed. Is it the same day? No. I don't think so. Or is it? Take more Valium. That's it. Take more. Calm down. Christ the guns. If I lose it and grab the guns, the cops will kill me. Get the guns out of the house. Get 'em out now while I can.

"Where are you going with those?"

"Getting 'em out the house."

"Why?"

"Just because. Bringing them to mom's."

Good, that's over. No guns around. Don't want to lose it and hurt someone and don't want some scared shitless cop blowing me away. Calm down. Lay in bed. Meditate. Relax. Seventy . . . sixty-nine . . . sixty-eight . . . take a deep breath . . . . Sixty-seven . . . . Sixty-six . . . sixty-five . . . relax your legs . . . exhale . . . sixty-four . . . before twenty-five, I'm asleep.

* * *

I awake with a vague feeling of the start of an understanding, of understanding something very important, the faint beginning of grasping a truth. And in an instant it comes with a fleeting but certain clarity.

That's it. I've got the key. I understand now. That's how it's done. I see it. I see.

"You awake?"

"Yes."

"Are you all right?"

"Yes, I've got the key."

"Key, what key?"

"The key. I understand now."

Later I hear her on the phone talking to the shrink. They've been talking for awhile.

"Bobby wants to talk to you."

I pick up the phone. "Bobby?"

"Yeah Buz. You ok?"

"Yeah, I'm fine."

"Michele says you've been acting kinda strange and she's a little frightened. What's happening inside?"

"Nothing. I was scared but I'm ok now."

"Scared?"

"Yeah," It's getting harder to keep it together. Harder to talk. Harder to hold on to the clarity of a moment before. How can I explain the key? It's so clear but what words do I use so he'll understand? He'll never understand. Maybe no one will.

"Are you scared now?"

"No."

"How did the fear pass?"

"Don't know. Just woke up and I was ok."

"Michele said something about a 'key'."

"Yeah, I found the key."

"What key?"

"The Key. The key to all of it. I can't explain it. I'll talk to you later." Click. Take some more Valium before it gets bad again. Before that terror that feels like bugs in your gut. Yeah that's it. Like bugs . . . lightning bugs blinking and flying and making my gut jittery. I'm sitting on the bed and my wife comes in. She sits on the bed and takes my two hands in hers. "Buz, what's the matter? Can you tell me?"

"Look, I'm all right. I'm ok." I try to tell her about the key. I try to explain it and I start off slow but before I can finish the first few sentences, my words speed up faster and faster until I'm talking so fast I sound like a tape being played in fast forward and my mouth and thoughts are moving just as fast. Faster. I feel her hands tighten on mine. She doesn't understand what I'm telling her. I'm going so fast, I can't understand it either. Why can't I slow it down? I keep talking faster and faster . . . the tape has no speed control. It's going to break. Stop. Stop! It slows, it's slowing down. Breathe. Slow down. Slow . . . down. There. I'm back to normal speed. Michele is really frightened and I'm scared shitless.

I try to tell her it may come back. and I've got to explain the key to her before it happens again. I try to speak but the tape begins to speed up again.

"Buz you have to get help. I'm calling your brother."

"Ok," I'm terrified and it's getting worse.

I sit there and hear her on the phone in the next room . . . speaking to someone . . . probably Nat . . . very low. After that she comes back.

"Nat and Charlie are coming over. They'll take you to a hospital. Can you rest until they get here?"

"Yeah."

And I take her hands this time and try to talk to her. I try to say . . . say anything . . . to say I'll be ok and it happens again. The tape speeds up and I'm talking high-speed nonsense and my thoughts come so fast I can't keep up with them. Faster. So fast they aren't fully formed. A fragment of a thought, a word, a syllable and then random garbage meaning nothing. And then it passes.

A demon. A devil! That's what it is. I'm possessed. Like that kid in the Exorcist. That's it. A demon. Pazuzu! The same devil. I've got him now. He's inside me. Driving me nuts. I'm in bed scared to death. Praying to myself. Shaking. I lay on the bed and Michele sits next to me. Her hand is resting on mine. A knock at the door.

"That's Nat and Charlie," she says and stands up.

"No. It's not," I say calmly, "It's Nat and Joe. Charlie couldn't come."

Michele just looks at me a moment and then turns to answer the door. I hear the door open and in the corner of the room I see my carbine. How did that get here? I brought it to mom's. The cops, they'll kill me if I'm nuts and have that. I'll give it to Nat. He'll keep it for me. I pick it up and hold it until he walks into the room. He and Joe, not Charlie. Charlie couldn't make it.

"Whatcha doing with that?" He's looking at the carbine and he's scared. He's scared 'cause he doesn't know how screwed up I am. He knows I'm wigging and maybe I'm violent too. I see his face and he's scared.

"Nothing," I say.

He knocks it out of my hands into the corner of the room before I can tell him I just wanted him to keep it.

"What's got you fucked up?"

"Nothing. I don't know."

"Come on. You got to get to a hospital until this shit's over. Come on with Joe and me. We're gonna take you. Ok?" Joe is there in case I say no. But I say ok. I need help or a priest or both. I say ok.

Riding into the center of town I could smell gas and oil. Not just a little odor but like I was surrounded by it. Like I was inside the engine. It was everywhere. Oil burning from friction. It permeated everything. A sickening overwhelming odor of spent oil and brake fluid and gasoline. It was making me ill.

"Slow down! You're going too fast!"

I kept telling them over and over, pleading. We were going to crash into something. Slow down! You'll kill us! Look out the window. Look at something. Focus your thoughts. Ignore the terror. The buildings. Look at the building go by. There's the Tidewater building. And the hospitals. The Tidewater building! It's gone! It disappeared! It's gone! Christ, it's gone! And that one, the one on the corner . . . it's gone too! They're all going! There . . . another one! Stop it! The Oil! Stop it!

"Slow down, you'll kill us!"

"George, it's ok, man. He's not speeding. You're just nervous, that's all. They'll straighten you out at the hospital. A day or so and you'll be straight. Just relax, we're almost there. Ok?"

Shit, that's not Joe! It's a gorilla in Joe's clothes! Christ, they're gonna kill me. Nat and this gorilla. No. No. Not Nat. Nat wouldn't kill me. This is crazy shit. It's Joe. It's really Joe but he looks like a gorilla. No, now it's just Joe again. Joe as Joe, not as gorilla.

"You'll be ok man. Those doctors, they know their shit. They'll have you fixed in no time." He laughs an adds, "They straightened out your brother's ass, remember? You'll be ok. We're almost there."

* * *

"His room is right over here." She opens the door and goes in before us. It looks like a motel room. "Which bed would you like? No one else is in this room so you can have your pick."

I can't speak. I can't decide. Everything is too screwed up to decide anything.

"He'll take the one by the window so he can see the trees. He's crazy about trees, right Buz?"

I look at my brother. He's standing next to a gorilla in Joe's clothes. His hands are jammed into the pockets of his long gray leather over coat. The coat is covered with white and blue paint.

"Ok . . . the window . . . ok."

"The nurse says we can visit tomorrow. Michele and I will be back tomorrow. Ok?"

"Uh huh."

"You ok?'

"Uh huh."

"Take care of him."

"We will. He'll be fine. Won't you George?"

"Buz. His name is Buz. Everyone calls him Buz."

Joe laughs. "Not everybody, huh George? I call him George 'cause it aggravates him," and Joe laughs again.

"Well, ok, great. You'll be fine, won't you Buz?"

"Uh huh."

"We'll give you a shot and some medicine to help you sleep. And then the doctor will be here in the morning to check on you, ok?"

I'm looking out the window into the branches of a green ash some three or four flights up. I feel the wind on the hill in the park. I can smell the stale water in the lagoon beneath me to the west.

"Buz, Joe and I are going to leave. You need anything?"

No. I don't tell anyone about the paint I see on his coat. Is it a test? Is it really there and am I supposed to notice it and tell them about it? No. It can't be there. It's part of what's going on with me. Part of this place or time zone I'm in. Yeah, that's it . . . some sort of a time dimension jump or something. I'm in the wrong dimension. How do I get back? Shit, there's those bugs in my gut again. Stay calm. Get rid of that idea. Get rid of that dimension shit. Scary time shift crazy shit. Don't think like that. Christ that building across the street is gone.

"Buz, you ok?"

"Uh huh."

"Ok Buz, let me help you get your coat off. There ya go. I'll hang it up over here. How about some juice? You want some juice about now?"

"Ok," I tell her. I could still smell the engine, the overpowering odor of smoking, burning oil. Maybe the juice would help. When did I eat last? Three, four days? What's today? Where is this place?

"Joe and I are going to go. I'll be back with Michele to see you tomorrow. Ok?'

"Uh huh, all right."

The paint on the coat. That's not Nat, its Pablo Picasso. Pablo and the gorilla say good-bye and leave the room. I could hear the large red double doors clang behind them down the hall. I had my shot and pills and then I lay in the bed. Next to the window in the upper corner I find a tiny web like fracture and stare at it. It becomes mold growing and mutating as I lay in the bed transfixed. It expands until it covered the wall and then the wall is no longer there. The filaments of mold become a pathway up the phylogenic scale. Branching and dividing. One-cell plants shifting to blue-green algae. Tendrils of mold spreading up the plant kingdom, each segment or branch adding another element of complexity. Budding. Rhizomes. Asexual reproduction. Sexual reproduction. Monocots. Dicots. One celled animals. Pseudopods. Now flagella. Cilia. Cell colonies. Cephalopods. Invertebrates. Like frames in a fast forward slideshow. Frames superimposed over the ones that precede them. Faster and faster . . . now movie-like. Centipedes, millipedes. Black swirling tangles of bugs and beetles. Worms. Eating each other. A beetle eats a worm while a centipede eats the beetle from the rear. I hear the beetle's shell popping and cracking in the centipede's mouth. Its life is oozing out and it's being devoured while it feeds on the worm without stopping. Vertebrates. Amphibians. Reptiles. Faster and faster. And then Mammals. Monkeys. The great apes. The evolution of man. Man's violent evolution. Christ, stop it! Baboons, monkeys, apes running and fighting each other. Faster and faster. Neanderthal. Cro-Magnon. A club in his hand. Christ, he crashes in the skull of another man-ape. Now sapiens! And then . . . and then a fiery mushroom cloud and then another and then all over the world. Another one outside of my window off in the distance. I see the thermal blast rushing towards me. I feel its heat burning the flesh from my body. It melts and sloughs off my limbs. I writhe in unimaginable pain and scream in unending agony.

"God! God! Stop it! Stop it!"

Nurses and aides and all the free staff pour into my room. I am up on my feet and hysterical. Two attendants in white uniforms grab me and I fight them. I am yelling in terror. The nurse barks instructions. They throw me to the bed. Another nurse comes in just out of the cold still with her cape on. A black cape with a red liner. A vampire! A Goddamn Vampire! Shit, I see her fangs. She snarls and sick saliva drips from her huge fangs. The big black attendant snarls and bears his fangs. Jesus they've all got fangs! I fight like mad. I am mad.

"Restraints! Get the restraints."

They strap my feet and hands and abdomen. I am yelling in sheer terror. They're gonna tie me down, drink my blood and change me into a vampire! I'll be a ghoul forever and ever! Pray stupid, Pray!

"Jesus! Mary, Mother of God, help me! Please help me! God help me! Help meeee!

I feel the shot go in my arm as I yell in terror and keep yelling my prayers until I fall asleep.

I'm insane and I'll have this insanity forever. My life will be one of constant agony . . . one imagined violent death after the next . . . suffering torture after torture without end for all eternity. I am being dealt with for my violence, for my selfishness, for the life I lead. I am everything I despise. I am vile and loathsome. In Hell. I'm in hell. For years I lay in endless hopelessness. There has to be ways out of hell. There's always something . . . some thing.

"There's no way out! Haha. No one ever leaves. Never . . ."

"There is, there has to be. God teaches hope."

"He teaches that in that book . . . you should have read it. Haha. Too bad."

"I read it! I read parts of it!"

"Then say it backwards. Backwards, word for word and I'll let you out of hell!"

And the vision fades like all the rest.

In hell forever. The horrible visions continued for days, for eons and in-between overwhelming hopelessness. In hell forever. The bible backward. "In the beginning God created the heavens . . ." What next? I couldn't say the first sentence forward. How in God's name could I ever say it backwards?

I wake up strapped to a gurney across from the nurses' station on my left. Two sets of double doors are on my right. Red elevator doors to hell.

"Are you all right?" The nurse comes from behind the counter over to me. "Are you feeling ok?"

"Where am I?"

"By the nurses' station so we can watch you. So we can help you if you need it."

"Why am I strapped down?"

"Because you became very agitated. But we gave you something to relax you. You should start feeling better but you really need sleep. Your wife said you've been up for days except for cat naps."

"What's behind these doors?"

"Elevators."

"I'm in the way."

"They don't run up here now that the ward's closed."

"I hear them."

"Yes, but they don't stop on this floor. They can't anymore. Get some rest and I'll be right over here if you need me. Ok?"

"Uh huh."

Bullshit. They're gonna wait until I'm asleep. When they think I'm asleep, they gonna throw me down the shaft. Throw me back to hell. I'll lay here and pretend to sleep. When they untie me and open the doors, I'll jump up and kick their ass and run outta here. Yeah, that's it. I'll wait for them to try. What if they don't untie me? What if they open the doors and just shove the gurney down the elevator. Get up. Get out of here! Kill yourself before you let them throw you in hell! Fight! Kick off the restraints! Pull!

"Calm down. Calm down! Miss James! Miss James!

In no time the floor was alive with people again. This is it! They're gonna shove me! "Fuck you! Fuck you, you vampire cocksuckers! Untie me! I'll kill you, you rotten blood-sucking bastards! You ain't killing no one! Fuck you!"

"Quiet room! Put him in the quiet room. He's waking up the other patients."

I'm pushed down the hall yelling as loud as I can on the gurney. A door opens and we turn to the right into a smaller hallway and up to one of several small doors. It opens and I'm pushed in.

"You can get out of here when you calm down. We'll be checking on you."

The door slams and a key loudly drives a bolt in place. It thunders in the small room.

Overhead an incandescent bulb burns dimly in a round reflective fixture. I'm strapped to the gurney under a light cotton sheet. I am clothed in nothing more than a flimsy hospital gown. A leather strap is pulled across my ankles holding them tightly in place. Another strap is pulled painfully across my stomach. My wrists are in leather cuffs attached to the side of the gurney. Except for my head and chest, I am immobilized. The room is small, not much larger than the gurney. The light casts a bizarre orange luminescence in the room. It turns the sheet and gurney a pale golden hue.

There is a small window in the door and the light from the hallway beyond shines a bright white in contrast to my golden room. My golden coffin. I am buried here for eternity. Left here to die and then rot, far away from anyone who knew me or loved me.

From time to time a face appears at the glass. Sometime the face asks if I am ok and sometimes not. I scream to be let out, to be let out of my coffin and the face disappears.

Occasionally the door opens and a nurse gives me a pill or a shot. Sometimes water. I yell to get out, yell for them to take the restraints off of me.

"Not yet. When you are stabilized, we'll let you out of here."

Christ the strap across my stomach hurts. How long have I been here? How long do I have to stay? I stare at the orange light overhead. It grows larger and larger and draws closer to my face until I can feel its heat. I can now read its wattage and the circle of information in its center. It's growing hotter. It begins to burn my face! I can feel my skin form blisters and feel them burst. My face is on fire!

"Help me! Help me! For God's sake! I'm on fire! HELP!"

And the episode fades like the others. A male face appears in the window and smiles and turns away. I'm on a spaceship travelling to a distant star system. The voyage is so long most of the crew is in suspended animation. We take turns awaking from our down periods to run the ship and then return to our cubicle for years of sleep. Eons of sleep. I am part of the crew now running the ship. I'm the entertainment for my crew on this shift. The window is some sort of TV screen and the crewmembers stop by when they're bored. I make faces at them to make them laugh. They keep coming by to see me between their duties. They enjoy me. But it's been too long. I've been in this TV for too long. They screwed up the shift schedule. I should have had down time years ago. They forgot about me. It's a new crew . . . many new crews have come and gone. My crew has been asleep for years and I'm still up performing. I'll die if I don't get sleep. They forgot! The schedule is screwed up. I'll die!

And then I scream again.

* * *

Monkeys running, chasing each other, some squealing, fleeing their pursuers. No, now it's baboons. The monkeys run from the baboons in panic and the baboons fight among themselves . . . snarling . . . screaming. But I am above them. I'm on a hill in a green meadow looking down at the baboons killing and beating each other. I am looking down at them from the hill in the park. They run in circles beneath me . . . fighting and clawing each other to a bloody death. Some are torn apart and devoured by the rest. I am sitting on my haunches and . . . and I am a baboon also. I am the alpha male and my mate sits next to me on the hill. The hill in the park. I stand and the rest fall silent and move to the base of the hill and look up . . . up to the top of the hill . . .

I am filthy. My pants are filthy, urine stained khakis that are falling from my hips. I am on the street, stumbling down Camp with a sick taste in my mouth. I can smell the foulness of my body. I feel a sickening sweet nausea filling my gut. I want to puke. I have no socks. My shoes are too large and the strings are broken and untied. I hold my pants up with my left hand and I brace myself against the window of a car dealership. I feel the urine running warm and wet down my leg. My stomach turns in disgust. It's not my face in the window. I am Andrew. Andrew the street drunk who was in the program with me. I'm Andrew but it's me inside Andrew. Me living Andrew's life. I see all of his life with his eyes but my understanding. I live it in fast forward. I am forced to live it all. I see me as Andrew beg the bartender down the street for a pint of Mad Dog. I hear him say he'll sell me a half-pint for one of my shoes but only if I come back two hours later and sell him the other one. Then he'll give me a full pint. I hear the men at the bar laugh. The men in the vomit, cigarette smoke, piss smelling bar. Andrew hands him a shoe and the men laugh louder. I hear the sick, sadistic louts laugh at Andrew and I want to kill them. I have to live Andrew's life . . . and then . . . and then I have to live the life of everyone who was in the program with me.

I'm Bob, the architect who became a street drunk. Bob who hit bottom when his brother slammed a 45 caliber through his skull and blasted blood and chunks of brain all over his office. His brother, the doctor, the family patriarch, who's sound judgement directed the family's affairs . . . who always knew best. I'm Bob weeping like a child plucking the embedded pieces of his brother's skull out of the wall before his mother comes in and sees Cain's blood and brains splattered all over Able. And then . . .

And then I have to live everyone's life. Everyone alive and everyone who ever lived. And then, before the end of the circle of time, I'll get back to me. I'll get back to my life and the people who know me. An eternity. They are out there . . . the people I love . . . millions upon millions of life times away. I learn to be patient. To anticipate is to suffer more. I live inside everyone. I live as they live but I'm fully aware of my presence with them . . . not in control but as them . . . inside. A dual identity . . . I am them . . . I suffer with them . . . I can feel and understand but not direct. They are not aware of me. I observe and feel; they decide and act. One story after another stretching endlessly across history, across reason, across time . . . until I get back to me . . . until I understand . . .

I am in the grassy field near at the base of the hill, fighting with the others. Fighting and snarling and my mate is fighting too. Another alpha pair now sits on the hill and we run and smash into other baboons until the alpha call us all and we gather at the base. I must live the lives of all of the baboons . . . my mate and I . . . and then . . . and then it will be our turn to sit on the hill again.

* * *

How in God's name can I say the Bible backwards? Why . . . in God's name stupid. Believe. He'll show you the way. Faith, that's how. Calmly accept that he'll show you. Don't force it . . . accept it. Relax. Meditate and accept. Seventy . . . sixty-nine . . .

The first word, what is it? No, no, the last word. What is it? This is impossible. Relax. "Amen." No . . . no . . . that's not it. Wait. That is it. "Amen" is the last word of the Bible! What's the next? Could be anything. How long will it take to run through every word combination of the English language? "Charity." No . . . that's not it. Have faith . . . it'll come. Accept that He'll show you. "Love" No . . . that's not close. I run through thousands of word . . . lifetimes of words . . . I must not quit . . . I must return home. Don't think . . . just let the words come . . . don't direct the search . . . just accept . . . "All." That's the second word! It fell into place like a tumbler in a lock. The hair on my neck raised up in cold fear. The next word formed on my lips and then they poured out in a flood. And then I slept.

* * *

"How ya feeling?"

"Better, much better but I'm thirsty."

"Here, take this pill with this orange juice."

I take it and tell him I'm still thirsty. He returns with a glass of cold water. I drain the glass in one pull. "I need more," I say.

I drink the second glass down without a pause.

"You want anything else?" he asks.

"Yeah, this strap across my stomach. Can you take it off? I'm not going anywhere and it hurts like hell."

"I can't take it off yet but I can make it loose for you. Ok?"

"Yeah, sure," I reply.

He adjusts the strap and turns to leave. Stopping at the door he turns to add, "If you keep improving, I'll take the strap off soon and after that, maybe you can get out of here before long. Ok?"

"Uh huh."

The stomach strap still hurt like hell. It was looser for sure but it still hurt. Maybe because it had been on for so long and so tight, it hurt now with just a little pressure. I've got to get out of this damn thing. It's hurting badly. I close my eyes and focus my attention on my legs. Relax your legs. First the right one, the toes first and then the foot. Seventy . . . sixty-nine . . . inhale and hold it . . .

I reached zero and started slowly pulling my right foot from beneath the leg strap. It held fast. I gradually increased my pull. Not suddenly but slowly and gradually. I use more strength while I focus on the strap. I felt the skin on my ankle scrape off as the strap releases its hold. My foot is free. After the first, the left one released easily. Both feet are now free but the belt across my lower stomach is still there. I push to the head of the gurney as far as I can, my progress halted by the wrist restraints. The abdominal strap is now across my hips. The squirming and pushing against its hold tore skin off the points of my hips. I rest for a long while and refocus on my relaxation. I visualize the wrist restraints and the strap that now hold my hips. I pull slowly with both wrists. I felt the thick leather straps dig into the flesh of the base of my thumbs. I feel no pain. I relax my shoulders, let them drop further and continue the pull. The cuffs inch down the back of my hands. I dig into the gurney with my heels and push as hard as I can until the pressure on my hips eases and the waist strap lays loose over my thighs. I relax, breathing heavily from the effort. I am exhausted and it takes a few minutes to catch my breath. It is now easier to pull up to the top of the gurney. I relax as deeply as I can and slowly I begin to pull my right knee up to my chest with my leg out to the side. I had lost so much weight that the move is even easier than the strength moves that preceded it. My right leg lays stretched out on the gurney but now on top of the restraint. The left leg is easier still as I could roll onto my left hip and just bend at the knee naturally. I grab the sheet and arrange it as best I can with my hands still in the leather cuffs. And then I sleep. A very peaceful sleep without dreams.

Sometimes later the door being opened awakens me. The male attendant has a candy bar in his hand. As he holds it up, he asked, "Would you like this?"

"Yes," I reply, "it's from my wife, isn't it?"

"Yeah, how did you know?"

"Because that's my favorite candy. It's her way of telling me she's outside and she waiting for me."

"That's right. That's what she said to tell you." After a pause he adds, "If you keep improving, the next time I come, I'll take off the abdominal restraint."

"It's already off."

"No, it's still on. But the next time . . ."

"No, it's off. Check if you'd like."

He pulls back the sheet to see me lying across the loose restraint. I had slid my feet back under the strap that had held them. "How did you do that?"

"It was still hurting, so I got out of it."

"But how?"

"Don't know, I just did."

He was feeding me bits of candy as we spoke. "I have to put it back on," he said.

"No you don't. I'm not leaving and if you put it back, I'll just take it off again."

"I have to. Doctor's orders. But I'll take it off on my next round if you're still ok."

"What the hell happened to me?" I asked.

"DT's. Doctor said it was DT's but you're all right now. Or soon will be." He begins to replace the strap across my stomach. and adds, "I'm going to tighten it up some more so you can't take it off again. But don't worry, it will be off for good the next time."

It was tighter than before but not much of a problem. Once I knew the technique, and had faith, it only took a few minutes.

Monticello, Dove and The Cove

I
I remember the light
of your eyes
dancing with your smile
as my words
found a place
where your thoughts were quiet.

II
I remember the light
on your shoulder
that spring day
of our love making
filtered through a dark curtain
soft as your touch.

III
I remember the light
caressing your hair
framed by a pillow;
Zeus thrilling to Io everyday.

IV
I remember the light
from the campfire
throwing patterns
on your skin
while I lay protecting
your form
from Orion's autumn gaze.

V
I remember the light
of April's sun
hitting our tent at dawn
and the frost covered ground
held us . . . .
and your lips
warm
on my stomach . . . .
both of us dying into the other.

VI
I remember your light
finally touching
what I had hidden
from harm, saving . . . .
Before the words became our child.

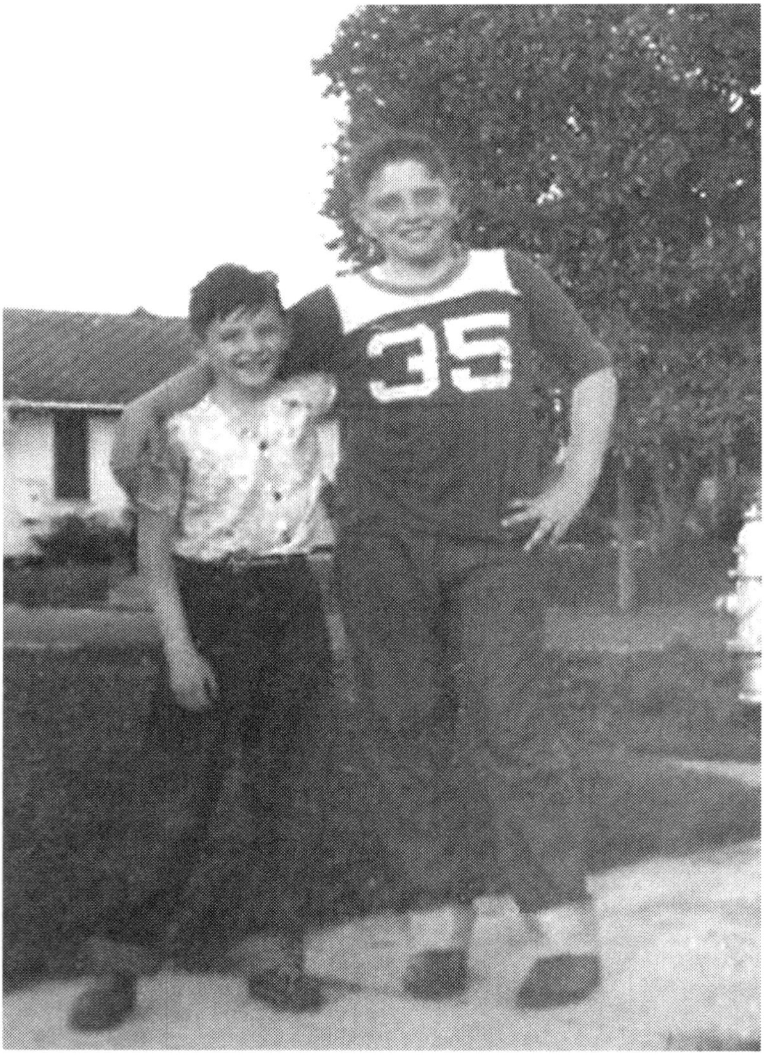

All That Live

Years before my brother's life became public property, when his magic was known to a much smaller circle, we would gambol like wild dogs in backways of Gentilly, each running with his own pack but sharing tales in the cave that was our bedroom. It was in this same room that we, in the winter of '58, responding to an atavistic urge, pieced together a loosely conceived plan for our first duck hunt.

He could borrow decoys, one pirogue, and a shotgun from his friend, Steve. I had a single-shot twelve gauge and enough shells for the both of us. We needed another pirogue.

"I'll get one, just be ready at two," he said.

"It's already seven-thirty. Where are you gonna get another pirogue?" I asked.

"Don't worry. Just be ready at two." It was part of his magic that you didn't worry. He'd have the pirogue.

Stumbling out of the kitchen door at 2:00 a.m., one hand holding my shell bucket and the other balancing the shotgun on my shoulder, I walked to his dented chocolate-brown Belair in the cold and shadowed street. He had the pirogue all right, but how does one carry two of them in a '53 Chevy convertible? Easy. The larger one was on the roof, tied precariously fore and aft to each bumper. The smaller one was placed through the unzipped rear window, across the seats, with its bow resting on the dashboard above the radio. My brother, wearing a "so-watcha-expect" look, sat bundled in a long, woolen overcoat behind the wheel, hands jammed deep in his pockets. Sliding into the passenger seat and looking over the bow of the boat into his face, I asked, "Is this gonna ride like this?"

"I got it this far," he replied.

"How far we going?" I asked.

"The other side of the lake." While the frigid implications of this sank into my sleep-deprived numbness, he added, "I had to hold the one on the roof with my left hand. It's only tied with one rope in front, and the wind is pushing it pretty good. Couldn't find anymore cord. You hold it from your side while I drive. I'll need both hands on the wheel when we hit the highway."

We were off before I could mutter a word of protest, but that too, was part of his magic. Sliding down a Chef Highway now lost to time, and turning at Powers Junction onto Highway 11, my already numb right hand was now fully exposed to the unobstructed north wind blowing across open lake and low marsh. I had him slow down while I squeezed out of the window and sat on the door, feet still in the car. Now able to hold the boat with my left hand, I plunged my wind-frozen right hand into the warmth of my carcoat's woolen pocket. This worked fine until my face, now blasted by moist, near-freezing wind, began to burn painfully. Wind-formed tears took shape and inched down my cheek. Needing warmth after several minutes, I slid down and into the car, and trusting the rope to hold awhile unaided, I spoke in shivers, "Damn, it's cold out there."

"I'll hold it a while," he said, slipping his arm out the window onto the roof. "Try to warm up before we get to the bridge," he added.

"I smell whiskey," I said with hope rising in my voice.

"Yeah. I have half a fifth of bourbon on the seat somewhere."

"Man, let me have it. I'm about to die," I said.

"Can't reach it while I'm driving. Wait 'til we get there. It'll warm us both up."

After a brief rest, I twisted back onto the window ledge and somehow managed to hold the pirogue in place until we arrived at our put-in, somewhere southeast of Slidell. This once rich marshland, nursery and breeding ground for uncountable fish and shellfish, is now filled in and reclaimed, ruining the landscape, but not my memory of it.

We pulled past parked cars. Their occupants, hunters all, were milling about, speaking the language of small boys in hushed tones in the pre-light hours of that long-ago winter. Our rig, looking as though borrowed from the Joad family, caused heads and voices to raise as it lumbered out of the early fog into full view. My brother, ignoring the bewildered looks from the real hunters, began to feel for the bottle of wintertime, anytime elixir. He found it all right. The cork had come out—he having sat on it—and the bourbon that was not sponged up by the seat was soaked into his thick overcoat.

"Great," he said.

"There's nothing left?" I asked.

"Half a shot. Take it, I had some before I picked you up," he replied, handing me the bottle. His side of the car smelled like a still. I didn't argue. I threw back the shot and flipped the empty bottle into the back seat.

In the silent darkness, other hunters who had thought to bring lights, or who knew their way without them, pushed off. We watched as they slipped from sight and sound, disappearing into fog and marsh. With anticipation we unloaded out boats and gear and waited for the first rays of soft light before dawn.

Since I had never been in a pirogue before, my brother volunteered to take the smaller, almost childlike boat while I would take the gear in the larger one. He weighed, at the time, some 90 pounds more than I. Both boats were placed in the water, their sterns resting on the soft mud of the marsh, just inches from the shoreline. He waded through the water to the mid-line of the boat and climbed in. Tipping the boat slightly side to side, he adjusted his coat beneath him and held his paddle chest high, at the ready.

"Push off," he instructed.

I did and hitting the deeper water he sank like a stone. Sitting in water up to his waist, his boat and coat secure beneath him, his elbows out to the side, protecting the still ready paddle from the water, he said without turning, "I'm too heavy."

"No shit?" I asked, as we both began to laugh. We traded boats, and as light as I was, I still only had an inch or so of freeboard.

"Where'd you get this from?"

"From a friend of Steve's," he replied.

"Who?"

"I don't know. Just a friend."

The answer sounded purposefully vague, seeing whoever upped with the boat did so only a few hours before, but I let it slide. Maybe he was still cold from his recent plunge.

The east rising sun over our left shoulder, we paddled down a tranarse to the south. Getting a late start, each blind we passed and each promising spit of land was already occupied. Onward we pressed, Quixote followed by his younger Sancho Panza, until at last we found an unwanted blind, in disrepair, and as foul in appearance as we. It was nothing more than a knot of mud, eight by four feet, covered by roseaus. The center had been beaten down, and a port for the pirogues had been fashioned by the removed plants now stuck in the mud behind the island. Although muddy and damp, it was at least partially out of the wind and provided some cover from the birds. We emptied the decoys from the oyster sack which held them, freed their anchor lines, and threw them down wind from the blind. We did some things right.

"Only eight? Steve only has eight decoys?" I asked.

"That's all he had. I guess Big Steve is using the rest," he answered.

There was that vagueness again; the feeling of being conned once again. But that too was part of the magic. Any number of men are runaway optimists, but unlike him, few had the genius to match. And if his genius reached its limit, his will propelled him far beyond that limit. The idea that anything was beyond him simply was not considered. Self doubt, suffered by all to some extent, was never allowed to surface. High spirited and jovial, this ringmaster of political campaigns would, in later years, enter the battle with his cadre of troops like a M.A.S.H. unit. His enthusiasm and confidence spilling over and infecting all he touched, he engineered victory where many candidates surely would have failed without his help. When caught in an exaggeration, I mean caught, with no room to wiggle, he'd just laugh and give you a "Yeah, ya right." Like a kid, his hand in the cookie jar, he'd merely laugh and hand you a cookie. From accuser he'd shift you to co-conspirator, and you'd love him for sharing the joke with you.

His magic was not merely believing in himself, but instilling in others an almost absolute belief in themselves. If he said you could do something, you learned, by God, you could. And laughter. It seems all men of extraordinary will, warriors, regardless of their paths, are gifted with laughter. It's the perfect mask and refuge for the conflict and pain swirling inside. So they laugh loudly, drowning out the voices of doubt and fear. Bravery is not the lack of fear, it is succeeding in spite of it. And bravery was part of his magic, too.

Only a select few achieve Order of the Coif at Tulane, fewer still become Editor of the Law Review. He did, despite having three children and holding, for a time, four jobs to keep school and family going. He graduated third in his class but, cliché or not, he was in a class all his own.

The eighteen year-old boy driving that rag-tag Chevy down that ice-age Chef Highway would, in nine years, become the Senator for that district, the largest in the state. When he entered politics, I entered law school, my path made easier following his blazes. Years later, I would, without success, try to show him a few things I had discovered on my trek, but it was too late. Eyes set on different horizons, our struggles, while having common elements, were largely ignored, each by the other. His challenges were external; and if his road led to terrain unfamiliar to me, I am sure my inward journey made little sense to him as well.

* * *

Jesus, Nat, are you really dead? Why do I still hear your laughter and hear you speak to me in a language I do not understand in late-night dreams? Why do I, my mind preoccupied, still see you walking on Baronne or Common, just ahead of me, just out of reach? And why, after years, is there still a hole in my gut, and why have I not cried my last tear? And why . . .

* * *

I remember when he was sixteen he opened his wallet, unfolded a small bit of newspaper and I read those sacred words that would or had become his anthem:

"The credit belongs to the man in the arena; whose face is marred by dust and sweat and blood; who strives valiantly, who errs and comes short again and again, who knows the great enthusiasms, the great devotions, and spends himself in a worthy cause; who at best, if he succeeds, knows the triumph of high achievement and who at the worst, if he fails, at least fails while daring, so his place will never be with those cold and timid souls who know neither victory nor defeat."

His life, burning meteor-bright, ended far too quickly. At age 46, pursued by demons of his own creation, finding each goal he reached less fulfilling, he met his enemy and understood its nature too late to avoid the inevitable self-destruction. Men like him don't die—they're not supposed to—and when they do, our own mortality is made more real and our security becomes the illusion that it is. When he died, that bit of time-stained newspaper was found still in his wallet. Those words, carried so long in his heart are now on his tombstone, a fitting epitaph for an impeccable warrior.

* * *

We shot a few birds, spoke of football and my high school and his college, not watching the sky as intently as before.

"How many decoys did we put out?" he asked during a pause in our rambling.

"Eight."

"Count them now," he said quietly.

"Nine."

"That one, over there to the right, is that a duck?" he asked.

"Yeah. Let me get it!" I said.

"No. We'll both shoot at the same time so we won't miss." Sportsmanship went only so far when you were cold and hungry teenagers. Cold anyway. That was one duck who had greeted better mornings. Two twelve gauges at thirty yards brought him a quick, if not quiet, peace.

Sometime later, when the ducks were not moving as much, we noticed a large raft of them sitting in the open water to the east. I got into the toy-like pirogue, shotgun between my legs, and tried to close for a shot. Halfway they spooked and I let fly with a shot straight over the bow. Not a bird fell, but fog-muffled words of anger, vile no doubt, were heard from a pair of hunters, their blind obviously in my line of fire beyond the birds and fog. Undaunted and unflappable, I was merely amazed at the range of birdshot.

Returning to our blind, a few of the now scattered ducks circled from the north, coming in perpendicular to the boat. A moment later, with sudden insight, I learned it was unwise to shoot to the side in a pirogue. The pellets go one way, and you, like a top, spin overboard on the other. I walked the rest of the way back to the blind, towing the boat behind, staying in the water which was warmer than the wintry air. I can still hear his laughter, muffled in the gray morning marsh, mine as well. Wet from head to tennis shoes, carcoat included, I hunkered down behind the patchy vegetation of our blind, partially out of the wind. Hypothermia was no problem; it would be years before it was invented. It took a lot back then to pierce our shield of youth, laughter, and the warmth of brotherhood.

"What's that?" he asked, pointing to a large brown and white bird drifting among the decoys.

"I don't know. A goose?" I offered.

"It's big; maybe so," he said as we both raised our guns for another dose of double-barreled sureness. The deed done, he paddled over, gathered the broken bird into his boat and returned for closer examination.

"That beak doesn't look like a duck or a goose," he said, getting out of the boat and throwing the bird on the mud floor of our reed fortress.

"The feet are webbed like a duck," I said holding up a leg.

"Dad will know. Just put it in the sack with the rest." We busted a few more birds that day, poule d'eau for Dad mostly, but a few ducks as well. We picked up our scant decoys and paddled back the lonely route to shore and car. The other hunters, knowing their business, were long gone. Our Grapes of Wrath special still reeked of whiskey, and we were both a little damp, but the drive back home was much warmer, sun and spirits both rising.

Carrying our sack of birds and decoys, we opened the gate to the backyard. Dad, hearing our arrival, came off the porch asking how we had done. His two teenage sons, proud and smiling manfully, dumped the contents of the game bag on the grass for their mentor's inspection.

"Aah!" he commented with obvious pleasure. "Dos gris, but a couple of pintail, too. Poule d'eau . . . great! But why did you kill that sea gull?"

Sometimes the magic failed, but not often.

The Summer of the Best Purple Seedless Grapes Ever

One summer years ago, the purple seedless grapes were remarkable. The skins were uniformly crisp and their sweetness was never equaled before or since. Or so they tell of.

We got the word early from Aunt Granny who called to say the purple seedless grapes at Dixon's were the best she had ever tasted. We all discussed this as soon as Elie got off the phone with her. Uncle Vud said Aunt Granny always had been given to exaggeration. He concluded the grapes might be really good but not the best ever. Elie said she liked grapes regardless.

All the kids got so excited about the grapes that they wanted to buy some that very day. Uncle Vud said we couldn't just spend hard-earned money on grapes like that unless they really were the best ever. He said he'd drive over to Aunt Granny's, taste the grapes, and if they were the very best ever, well, by God, he'd just buy some. He rounded up the money from those that had some: Elli and me, the older kids, and ever Earl, the hired hand pitched in a few coins. We sat out on the stoop and waited for him to return from Dixon's with the grapes. We sat there until near dark.

Well, the grapes were the best ever and for years after that summer, one of us would ask the other, "Y'all remember the summer of the best purple seedless grapes ever?"

Uncle Vud never got home with those grapes though. Three hours later, Earl found him out under the cottonwood tree off the road to Dixon's. He was laying with his back propped up against the tree, his belly swollen, and the sweet juice from the purple seedless grapes running down his chin. He had a smile wide enough that his missing teeth made him look like a Halloween pumpkin. The empty brown bag from Dixon's was crumpled up next to his leg.

Earl asked him, "Uncle Vud, was they the best purple seedless grapes ever?"

Vud rolled his eyes, lifted his chin and let out a small burp. "Yep," he said.

Years later, I was out back, putting a new clutch in the pickup. My hands were greasy and sweat was running into my eyes.

Earl and Uncle Vud ambled up to the truck and I asked Earl to hand me the three-quarter open-end wrench. He bent over and slid it under the frame where I could reach it.

I took a few turns with it on the bolt, and like so many times before Earl asked, "Do you remember the summer of the best purple seedless grapes ever?"

I stopped turning with the wrench and pulled my way out from under the truck until my head and shoulders were clear. I looked at him straight in the eye and said, "Well, yeah, I do."

He said, "Vud does too."

I looked at Vud and said, "That so?"

He said yeah and they walked off.

Things have been like that around here for as long as anyone cares to remember. Except for the year the pole beans were really, really good.

Rain, soft on the trees,
carried gently on the wind
moving to the sea.

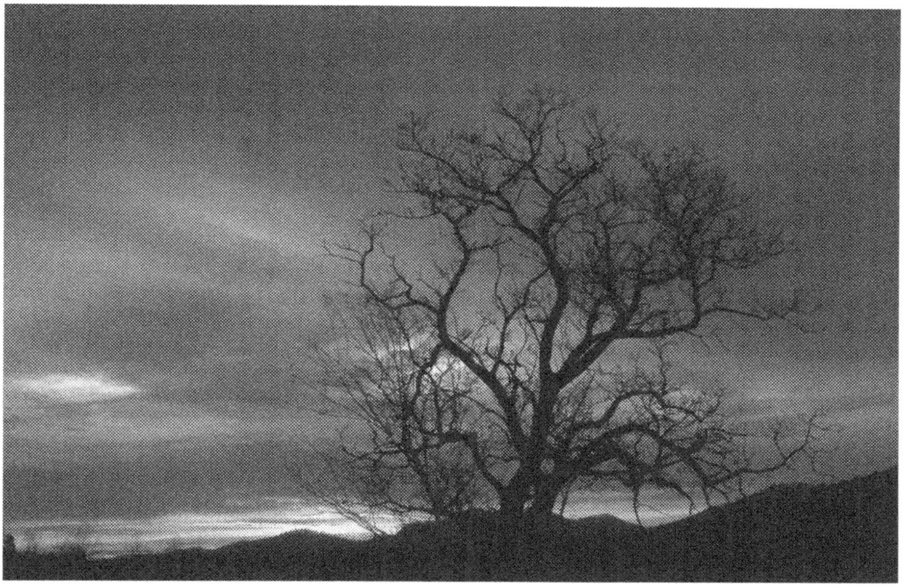

Nightfall

The afternoon sunlight eased between the blinds and cast parallel stripes on the floor near where he sat. A heavy photo album, its cover cracked and flaking, laid open on the desk against the wall. The man, thin and frail, sat in a wooden chair and soundlessly turned the pages. The chair was thick and solid; the armrests were worn and dark with age. He studied a picture, and after he succeeded in putting the puzzle of time together, he looked at another. He lifted his head when he heard them at the rear door. He heard his daughter-in-law enter followed by his granddaughter. She called to him, announced their arrival, and by a simple reply, he let them know he was in his room. He heard the little girl's voice and it stirred a moment of expectation that faded when he heard her turn on the TV. In the winter, when he came to live with them, she would run to his room with excited squeals but in a child's world his newness withered quickly. An old man with stories of another time and a few card tricks couldn't long compete with today's distractions. In spring he heard the mother hushing the girl when she said his room smelled and he felt another small fire flicker and die out. But he understood. He was grateful for the time they did share.

His eyes fell to the photos again, his hands resting alongside the album. He turned a page and found a familiar black and white, now browning with age, of a young man and woman. She wore a white dress, her arm looped through his, bent at the elbow. He displayed a ring on his lightly closed hand for the camera. It was formal photo with neither of them smiling. His eyes went from the photo to the ring on his hand. He raised both hands, looked at them as he turned them over and held them to the light. His hands seemed strange and alien. The wrists were too thin. How could these hands have worked a lifetime on the big engines, fought in war and caressed the girl in the photo? He turned his head to the side and looked at his bent legs. Beneath his tan trousers were thighs that belonged to another man, a weaker and older man.

He heard his son in the driveway and listened to the footsteps carry him to the kitchen door. He heard their greetings. The old man heard the wife say something which sounded purposefully muted. The son then yelled to him but did not come to his room. He returned to the album and smiled at his wife. He turned the page to another sheet of photos, the pressed flowers of his spring, and an image of him in his uniform appeared. There was one of his son by a decorated tree opening presents on a tinseled Christmas morning and another, out of place, of his wife in high school. He held the page slightly above the next. Having lost pigment, the photos were faded and the paper was cracked. They were as frail and delicate as the fingers which held them.

He narrowed his eyes to see photos of vacations beneath the sun, on boats and on sandy beaches. There were frozen moments of parties, graduations and another life. The album was put together by his wife who labeled each photo. He lingered over the final page, the carefully trimmed and taped, single entry made by him: a notice of death.

He closed the book and sat in the darkening room. Dinner would soon be ready and the old man considered his movements, weighing the necessity of each against the probability of being heard, discovered and remembered.

The call of a loon
a reminder of freedom.
How I miss the peace.

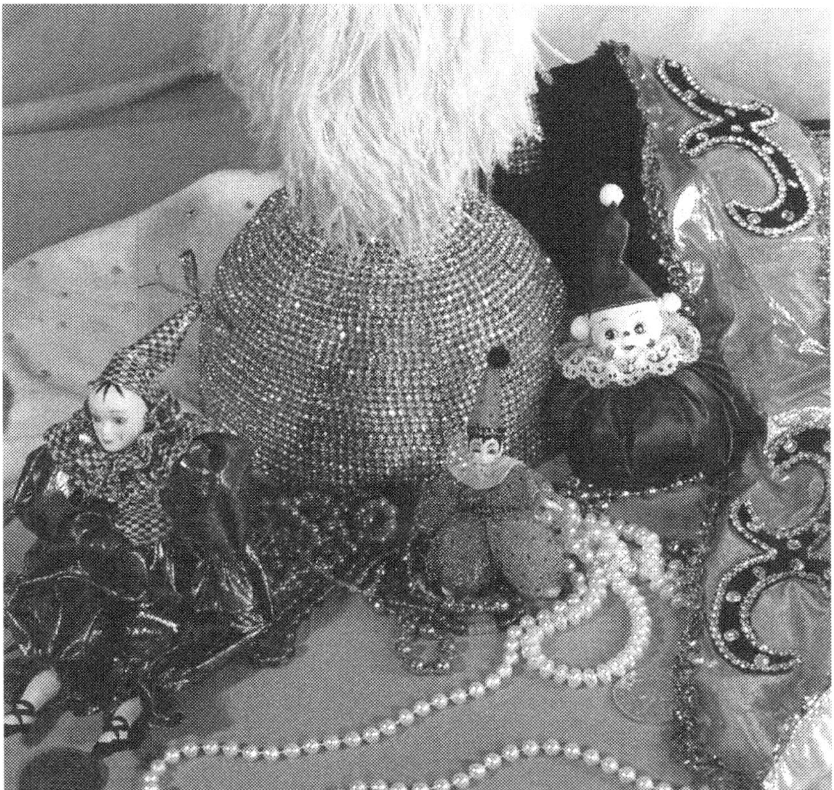

Don't Rain On My Charade

(or Why Fat Tuesday is Wearing Thin)

Life sometimes forces you into unavoidable activities which cause enough discomfort that you become convinced you are being dealt with for some wrong you've committed; a penance, perhaps, for some venial transgression. I look upon Mardi Gras in that light.

Marrying into a Mardi Gras family is a bit like marrying into a cult. The machinations of merriment would begin several weeks before the fattest Tuesday of the year. In almost imperceptible fashion the tempo of the household would quicken while I quietly braced once again for this silly ritual. The queen's flag would be removed from its sacred location, unfurled and displayed on a length of pole for the hoi polloi to envy. Purple, green and gold would appear about the house along with unattractive displays and centerpieces of doubloons and multicolored beads. King cakes would become a daily affair, achieving the significance of the Mardi Gras eucharist. For my part, I would slip further into my foxhole of despair, awaiting fruition of the three or four commitments I had made and resign myself to another season amongst the krewe-krewe birds. My only defense was to stand detached and watch with embarrassed amazement as the possessed carried out their ceremony. I watched, with apparently the only eyes that could see, that this year's king was not only unbelievably tacky, but clearly he would much prefer to be the queen.

Mardi Gras krewes remain in existence from year to year, and it is in their ranks that the pecking order of nobility is most firmly fixed. Officers, Riding Lieutenants, Dukes, Float Lieutenants, all pyramiding up to the head honcho—the guy who really runs this bogus bonanza—the Captain. It's his show, his party, but the trick is to get the King—a new one being selected each year—

to pay for the bulk of it. This poor ego-involved boob is treated royally—and make no mistake, those involved in the upper echelon of Mardi Gras clearly think of themselves as royalty. They bow and scrape to one another in what outsiders would assume, at first, was jesting. Then, like the fog lifting at the lakefront to reveal the Mardi Gras fountain, one sees that these schmucks actually have a hierarchy that each member fosters. They grant unearned respect to those above their own position in order to secure standing from those below. Those higher in ranking or on equal ranking are spoken of in reverent terms to members and outsiders alike, even if they belong to another krewe. The idea is to create not the illusion but the "reality" of royalty. The folks on the street could care less about this phony pecking order but, at its core, this is what Mardi Gras *is* to those who put it on.

One remains Captain for years until either the krewe folds or the reins are voluntarily turned over to a younger cretin on an ego binge, usually the son or daughter of the predecessor. At these changings of the guard, other Captains, their officers and their wives (the literati of bogus heraldry) tense while the neophyte shows his stuff for the first time at the ball. He or she is graded, criticized, weighed, and measured by the "strut". This opening prance across the ballroom floor is the papier mache' equivalent of the State of the Union address. "Doesn't have the command of his father." "Amusing, but a bit pretentious." "Stiff, and yet not quite formal enough." These are killer comments for the emerging larval-Captain. "My God," I'm thinking: "Didn't they see this boob getting dressed, with his pot belly, his support hose under his leotards, and his sequins falling on the floor? Wake up. It's an illusion! The guy sells insurance, for Christ's sake!"

I had escaped the balls early in my Mardi Gras career, and, with similar skill, I declined several invitations for a "ranked" position with a club. I remember telling my then father-in-law, a captain of some note, "You don't ask me to ride in a parade and I won't ask you to backpack." I am sure from his exalted position he looked upon my refusal as more than just a minor depravity, but it worked. We now have far better reasons to dislike one another, but my trails, as well as his streets, remain unsullied by the other's footsteps.

Early in the afternoon of parade day, the officers and near royalty would gather in the Captain's suite. Everyone was dressed in tuxedos or sequined gowns, and each was straining at the seams. The plastic smile each of us would adopt for the next ten or twelve hours was firmly in place. Not that there weren't some genuine people there, for there were. I met and enjoyed two Captains, each self-made men who appeared to have had their egos in check at one time. Some kink in their self-image had brought them low, I surmised. Why else would such men need others to grovel about in this surreal pretense?

As the tedium of the afternoon wore on, occasional titillating moments of excitement would spread through the gathering. The first was usually when the Captain's wife would make her entrance. Then a silence from a far corner of the room was followed by the "oohs" and "aahs" of nearly orgasmic older females as, yes, the Captain himself would appear. The high point of this charade was played out with the arrival of the King. He was greeted with feigned deference and then ignored for the most part. This unfortunate mark was footing the bill and, like all drones, was superfluous after his function had been performed. But, unlike other drones, he was the recipient and not the giver of the screwing. Oh sure, he would be propped up for his ride before the masses and toasted at Gallier Hall, but his reign was merely titular. This, after all, is the krewe's party and the King is here simply by virtue of capital and is not actually one of the anointed. So much for relying on the kindness of strangers, Blanche.

Grey-haired, tuxedoed gentlemen, dignitaries from another time and a more gentile Mardi Gras, would mill about, stroll through the crowd, and assign seating on the waiting limousines for the ride to the viewing stands at Gallier Hall. As the recalcitrant in-residence, I would be placed in charge of a group of officer's wives, my own among them, and would see them to the proper car and happily situated in the ballroom to await the parade. On those magical years when weather and time permitted, the caravan of over-packed limos would, after much pleading and whining by the wives, engage in a perplexing migration as bizarre as that of the lemmings. It was called "buzzing the parade route." Six or seven limos, with police-sirened escorts, would tear down St. Charles Avenue without apparent purpose. Spectators already lining the streets would strain to see who or what was seated in these rented carriages. I remember on one occasion, as the car slowed and stopped before making a U-turn, I turned my head and peered bewilderedly into the bleary eyes of a street drunk who stared back into my eyes with equal bewilderment. He obviously wondered who in hell I was and I . . . well, I just wondered if I could join his krewe.

Arriving at Gallier Hall we would mill about for hours awaiting the parade, acting civil in our phony finery. We would get periodic updates on the location of the parade and its progress along the route. I would pretend it mattered.

Even as a child, I never understood this rite, this eagerness of people to degrade themselves at the mere passing of a parade.

Years ago a local economics professor outlined several ways in which the uptown clique retarded city development. The clannish nature of their social order, all but closed to new entrepreneurs both from within and without the city, was held to be the iceberg's tip. This characteristic is admittedly more obvious and more stifling among the old-line organizations. Those who spend the year dumping on the common folk gather them together in this springtime ritual for one final humiliation. The masses, although willing, are herded into the streets to behave like mindless beggars, groveling and shoving each other in order to catch the worthless baubles thrown to them by their economic and social masters. Their lordships stand poised and aloof and occasionally let fly with a doubloon to a worthy subject, not because they have to, but, by God, because they can. They wallow in their warmth and savor the unbridled largess. Here, the inner voice whispers, "Let them eat king cake!"

In no parade was this more obvious than in the now safely departed Comus. Those pompous gasbags would ride unflinchingly for blocks clutching a single strand of beads, basking in the pleading voices of the damned at their feet with nary a show of emotion. Stone-faced and bespectacled, they would stare from behind plastic masks as cold and as bland as their lives. These people have to inbreed; no one else would screw them.

In time the parade would arrive at the Hall, the relatives of royalty would squeal as the space between them and the riders filled with throws. Beads were tossed by the bundle and bunch and caught and kept for purposes I never fully understood. Often I would stand to the rear of the crowd studying the glitter of the sequined dresses and the confining lines of the stiff tuxedos. I stood alone and on the periphery of the action—a lone wolf apart from mankind, ranging just beyond the lights of the city. An unsociable misfit— the voluntary outcast. Looking down on them from the porch of the Hall, I was acutely aware I did not fit in, and, thinking to myself, I would say, "Thank God."

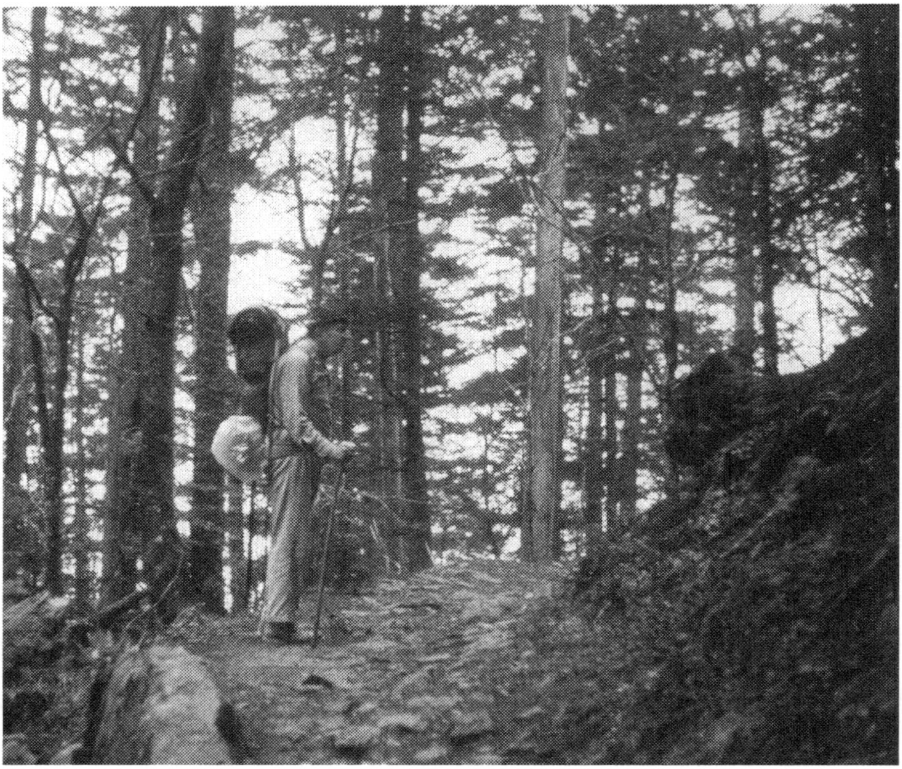

Edouard

Near the middle of the second week of August when I was a young man, I could both feel and smell the promise of autumn. From the northeast a clean air would whisper and carry with it a reminder of Halloween moons, football nights and winter's geese moving south. It was on one of those evenings of summer's demise that I met Eddie.

He was the uncle of a lovely young woman who, within a few months, would be my wife. He sat across from me with the rest of her family seated around her grandmother's massive dinning table. He moved from serving plate to serving plate, spooning mounds of food onto his own. Resting from time to time, elbows on the table, hands perched before him chipmunk-like, he broke small bits of bread and ate them. Peering over his hands, his eyes danced around the table with the devilment of a 10 year old plotting his next move. The corners of his mouth were turned up in a perpetual near smile. He would stand and scoop potatoes and other vegetables onto his plate and wolf them down talking constantly between mouthfuls. I sat there next to my bride-to-be with all the sophistication a 20 year old could muster.

He was half a foot taller than six feet, slightly balding and in spite of his appetite, he was lean and fit. He was 59 and for years he walked every day to his office and back home, a distance of over 16 miles. Years earlier, when my wife's family moved back to the states from France, Eddie announced to the kids, my wife and her brothers who had never met him, that he was, in fact, a rabbit. For months he walked about the house with a white fluffy tail fixed to the rear of his pants. No smile, no further mentioning . . . Uncle Eddie was a rabbit: no big deal. In the morning he would leave for work through the basement door, hiding the tail on a small hook before he left. Upon his return in the evening, he'd enter the basement, put on the tail and climb the stairs to be greeted by the family. Eddie the rabbit was home from work. America was just different from France and so were the people. Here, some people were rabbits, and Uncle Eddie was one of them.

Nineteen or not, Michele, my future wife, was always the proper lady. Eddie, the rabbit, had other plans, however. During a lull in the dinner chatter, he began. "You know, I find over the years if I don't use my French, I forget it. Ordinary conversation is fine, but words I haven't used in years, I'm starting to forget." His sister, Michele's mother, agreed and said she had noticed the same thing.

"Like animals. I don't talk much about animals so I'm forgetting the French name for a lot of them", he added.

"Michele, what's French for hippopotamus?"

"Un hyp-po-pa-tom", she answered.

"And lion?" he continued, "I'm even forgetting the easy ones."

"Un lee-aun" she quickly answered.

"And seal?" he asked.

"Un phuck", she responded without thinking. Her brothers almost fell out of their chairs, her mother gasped and I shuffled my feet turning red, fighting back my laughter. The rabbit just smiled broadly and reached for more potatoes.

Some years later when Eddie was 67, I asked if he would like to disappear with me for a few days on a backpacking trip. He smiled and studied my eyes, first one and the other, deciding whether I was serious or not.

"Mr. Buzzy, you really think I could make it?" he asked. From the time we met, for some reason that appealed to Eddie, he always called me Mr. Buzzy.

"Sure, all the walking you've done? And those long legs of yours, you'll have no trouble. We'll only be out for a couple of days. Want to try it?"

I didn't have to push too hard. Eddie's take on life was to find adventure, large or small, in everything. Like two kids waiting for Christmas we planned and selected supplies and counted the days until the end of April. We drove overnight and set up our tent in a campground on the Tennessee side of the Smokys. We hung out a day or two, biking around a loop road past farmhouses of early settlers. Eddie struck up a conversation with a photographer from Germany and before we began our trek, he invited him and his family to stop in New Orleans and join us for dinner. Two months later, they did.

We struck out early the morning of the third day with me in the lead. I would turn from time to time to see how he was doing and he would look uphill at me with a wide grin. The cool April morning was perfect for hiking.

At each spring and trickle we passed, Eddie would slip off his pack and drink a cup or two of water. He would let it run over his balding head and would rub his face and head vigorously with the cold mountain water.

"Man, Mr. Buzzy. There's nothing like this back home. This is great! Woo, feel that!" For years after that day I would perform the same ritual and think of Eddie with his natural, easy exuberance. He was right. The rush of cold clean water on your skin while high up a mountain is one of the finest simple pleasures around.

We stopped for lunch and I took a few pictures of him on a turn in the trail. With his back to a drop-off and spruce trees rising behind him, he stood leaning on his walking stick standing with the same natural strength as the trees that framed him. I enlarged a print of that shot which he kept on his desk for years. It amused him when one of his amazed patients would ask if it were indeed their doctor in the picture.

We spent that first night at a shelter three miles up the trail with several other hikers. Eddie listened to their stories, watched their camping routines and pitched in where he could. We left the next morning for an eight-mile climb to the summit of Mt. Leconte. The shelter was empty and wrapped in clouds when we arrived. The stone lean-to was built in a grove of low spruce and fir trees. The clearing just to the front of the opening was piled with broken limbs and partially cut trees. Spring clean up from the nearby lodge was placed here for firewood. We slipped off our packs and Eddie, all 67 years of him, after an eight-mile uphill with a pack, tore into that wood. With a small camp saw he reduced it to manageable lengths of firewood. It took him hours and he smiled and joked the whole time. As other hikers arrived, they'd offer help, which he declined. He was having too much fun he said. He cut more wood than we used that night. I'm sure hikers were able to use his wood for three or four days after we left. Eddie had paid back someone for the joy he felt.

We descended the next day and passed through a heath bald of low shrubs overlooking a fine valley. We both stood looking for a long while scanning the view back and forth, each pointing out to the other features we had seen from some other point on the trail. The Chimneys beneath us, the ridgeline we walked the day before, a hawk gliding on a thermal. I asked him to stand on the stone that laid exposed on the trail. I took another picture of him, this time with the valley to his rear, as he stood surrounded by rhododendron and mountain laurel. Eddie was huge for his generation. He stood six-six with short cropped hair, a balding top, and very large ears. His nose was hawk-like and his features when taken individually were not becoming. But the whole of it—the total composition—worked. Whether it was the joy in his bright eyes or the laughter in his voice, everyone was attracted to Eddie.

Reaching the roadway, Eddie was able to hitch a ride back to our car and returned to pick up our gear and me. Driving to a lower level, we bathed in a stream, our first bath in three sweaty days.

I've always seen Eddie smiling. I did not know him any other way. I did not know him when his son died. He died in a mountain stream like the one in which we were bathing. A cold, clear stream with rounded, smooth rocks along its bed and border. His sixteen-year-old son stood on one of those smooth stones, slipped backward and struck the base of his skull on another. They carried him from that stream in the Ozarks to a hospital in Mobile but he died before Eddie reached him. My wife told me a big part of Eddie died too. But you'd never know it. He never spoke about it. Not then, not in that stream and not for the more than the 20 years I knew him. Never.

Long past the time most people hang it up, Eddie finally retired. He took to riding a bike from one side of the city to the other. He'd ride all day, thirty miles or more. He'd stop by our house from time to time to say hello and grab a glass of water. He said he was visiting his little worlds. Eddie collected interesting people like some people collect books, and like a good book collector, he treasured his finds. He'd visit these little worlds where one might be a sculptor and another might be a teacher. His worlds were worlds of his eclectic interests, worlds of exciting, unusual characters, who tended to create rather than critique and laugh rather than complain. Eddie's worlds were peopled with characters like him: interesting, joyful, civilized folks with an appreciation for life's small and obvious gifts.

Eddie began to paint in his seventies. He dabbled at first and then took classes. Within months he was competing and winning regularly. I liked his style and obviously others did too. To me it resembled a merging of Utrillo and Braque. He did a street scene of my first office and I still feel proud that he made a gift of it to me. It still hangs in my home more than twenty years later.

Before his eyes failed, at the young age of eighty, Eddie was teaching painting. His studio became a fine little world for others to visit.

I did not see Eddie for over ten years after his niece and I were divorced. I missed him but felt a contact would be awkward for both of us and embarrassing for me. I learned his eighty-fifth birthday was at hand and I searched through my slides from that long ago backpacking trip. I found the original of those two slides and had a print of him on the heath bald enlarged. I wrote a few words on the back, slipped it into an envelope, sealed it and drove to his home. Driving past slowly I could see part of his yard and it appeared that no one was home. I parked a short way down the street, walked to his mailbox mounted on his rear fence and placed it inside. Turning to walk away, I heard his familiar call, "Mr. Buzzy! Is that you, Mr. Buzzy?"

"Hey, Eddie. Yeah, it's me all right. I just dropped a little something in your mailbox for your birthday. Nothing much, just a thought to wish you a happy birthday. I don't want to disturb you. Take a look at it and I'll see you later."

After all those years, I still couldn't face a man of his character after I had shown so little. I was gone before he could reply.

Eddie died last year. I should have spoken to him that last time. It's not that this story would not have been written, it's just that we could have remembered it one more time together.

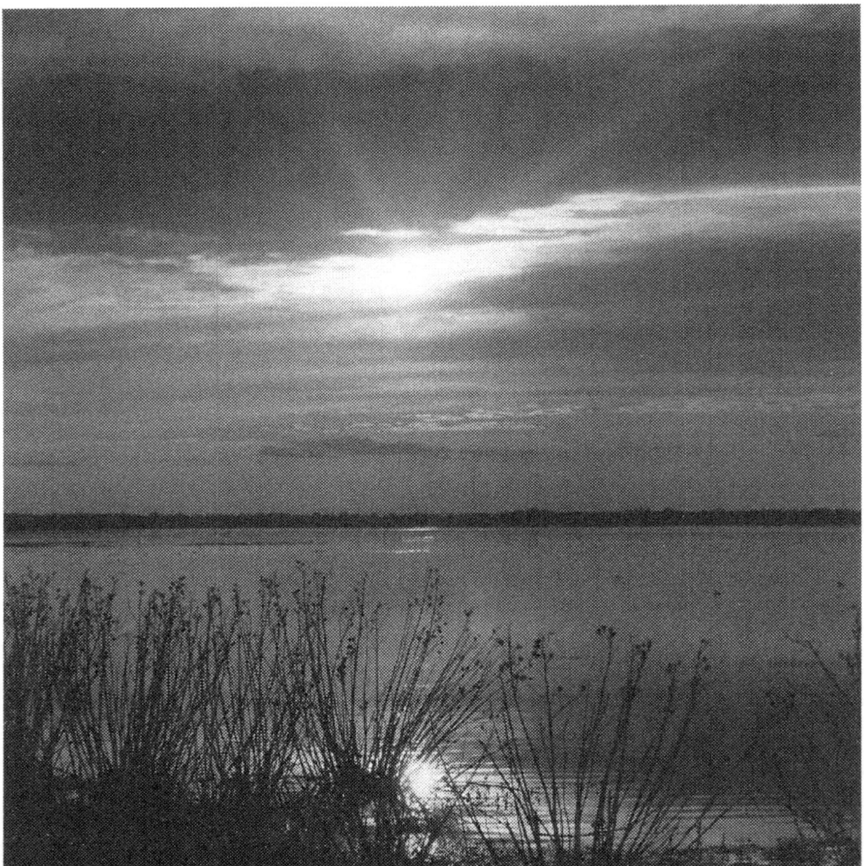

Softshells and a Hard Row

I met Vernon almost 30 years ago, and you don't find many of his kind anymore—not living this close to a city anyway. He came from a time when trust was given freely, a time when you went about your life with dignity and a stoic appreciation for courage and humility. A time when nobility had little to do with wealth and more to do with chivalry.

I had met his wife long before I knew him, and before I knew what made him tick. We hardly spoke the first few times we met, usually because there was a large crowd or a party of some sort going on. I suppose he was 25 years older than his wife, but his years in the sun and in the open marsh made him appear much older. His face was deeply furrowed and pulled from years of smoking and leathery from the time spent in an open boat. The back of his hands were as weather-beaten as his face, and his palms were thick with calluses. They were rough hands that had seen coarse ropes and wooden oars, hands that had repaired boat motors and fired more than a few shots. He stood about 5'8" and weighed at most 150 pounds. On his left hand, parts of three fingers were missing, and in spite of this, he had the grip of a man twice his size.

After several months, perhaps a year, of seeing he and his wife at meetings and parties, Vernon began talking. He was a shy old fellow, but he took pride in his ability to support his family off the land. He and Beth had four or five children and he kept a roof over their heads and food on the table by catching soft crabs. Some of the largest and better-known restaurants paid him well for his crabs.

He and his wife and house full of kids lived on Slip Bayou east of the city where she and he were born and raised. The house was a simple shotgun with green asbestos shingle siding. Simple as it was, it was warm in the winter and home year 'round.

We spoke of hunting and fishing and my love for the mountains. He spoke of his time on the bayou, where life in the outdoors was a necessity, and not merely a hobby.

Before alligators were put on the list of endangered species and hunting and trapping them was still legal, he had done that for extra cash. He and a companion would take off in a flat boat and he would plum the bottom of a likely spot with a long pole. Finding a hole several feet deeper than the nearby water, he would slowly move the pole around and locate the gator. He would then slip over the side and slide his legs into the hole, keeping them close to the side. This, he said, decreased the likelihood of the alligators biting his legs. Once his feet were firmly on the bottom, he would slip them under the gator's head. Having determined where the head was located, he would slip both arms into the water and suddenly clamp down with both hands on the gator's jaws. He would pull the gator up, a task made easier because the gator's claws would be climbing up his torso. The head under control, he and his partner would tie off the jaws and the legs. He used this method for years and swore it was safe, although the missing finger parts were proof that the method had its drawbacks. Speed and agility were necessary and no small amount of courage. Vernon was not given to exaggeration and told me he had once taken a ten-footer this way, although he did not know its size when he grabbed it. He said he couldn't just let go of it as both of them were tossing and rolling and splashing like mad. His helper had to jump in and grab it before they finally tied him up.

When he told me this story, I had just enough beer in me to say, "Man, I'd like to give that a try sometime."

"Anytime," he said, his eyes fixed on a short piece of rope he was fooling with, "but it's illegal to kill 'em now."

"Hell, I don't want to kill 'em; just wanna grab the sucker and tie it up."

"Oh," he agreed softly. "Just don't go sticking ya fingers in his mouth like I did." After a pause he added slowly, "Seems to me a lawyer might need all his fingers."

After a longer pause, while twirling his rope, he asked, "When you wanna go?"

"I'll let you know."

Still twirling the rope, he added, "Know where a hole is right now. Big hole. Should be a big gator."

"How big?"

"Seven, eight feet."

"Great, maybe next week."

Several weeks later, while camping by myself, I happened upon a five-foot gator and got close enough to grab his jaw with one hand. He pulled his head away with such speed and strength that I felt like a child. I never brought the subject up again with Vernon and he didn't ask.

I met him several mornings before sun-up to run his crab traps with him. Blue crabs would leave the deeper waters of the lake and enter the shallow backwaters to shed. They would hide in the grasses of the marsh, away from the deep-water predators. When the old shell is sloughed off, the crab is helpless until the new shell hardens. If discovered in this state, even smaller fish and other crabs could eat the defenseless softshell. Vernon's traps were not for catching the softshells; softshells can't move. But, placed as they were in the saltwater marshes bordering the lake, he would catch a large number of crabs just a day or two before they actually shed.

He had better than a hundred traps set out, and he would run them every morning. Each trap was located by a nylon cord tied to a float. He'd cut his motor and drift to the float and pull in the cord. The trap would be pulled on board, the crabs dumped out and the bait, chunks of trash fish, replaced. Ever so often, he'd grab a crab and show it to me.

"See the yellow near the long points on his shell?"

"Yeah," I replied.

"This crab will change tomorrow." Picking up another he asked, "See the difference?"

"No."

"This one, the one that's gonna shed, its yellow is different. See it?"

"No. They look the same to me."

"Here, look on the other side. See the corners? And look at the base of its big leg, see the yellow there? It's from the fat. They store fat to live off of while they molt."

"Yeah, but they both look the same."

"Here, look at this one, it's a buster, real close, see how yellow it is?"

"Yeah, I see it."

"See the difference from this hard crab?"

"Yeah."

"Now look at this one again. Can you see?"

"Nah."

It went like that all morning. I could see the difference in yellow coloration in the busters, the ones that were just hours away from shedding, but the others, forget it. But Vernon kept trying, and so did I, without luck. I'll be damned if I could ever consistently tell the crabs apart.

"Damned sure better stay a lawyer," he said.

After taking a pull on my beer, I said, "You're bullshitting. There's no difference in those crabs. You're having a little sport at this boy's expense. Now, ain't that it?"

He laughed and added, "How in hell you read all them law books and you can't even see a little yellow on a crab?"

I was usually freezing by the time we finished the run. We'd dock the boat in the bayou across the highway from his house. His crab house, with its large stainless steel tanks, was here and we'd bring the crabs in from the boat. The hard crabs, he'd sell by the hamper. The other crabs in various stages of molting were placed in tanks according to the degree of their hardness. Every two hours he would check the tanks, throughout the night as well, moving the crabs from tank to tank and before the harder ones would destroy the softer. Once they were soft, he would stack them upright in refrigeration boxes and place them in a large unit to keep them cold. They would be sold the next day. It was long, hard work, and the hours over open water had to become more difficult with the years. But, hell, the man never complained. Not about the work, anyway. He did complain that the alligators had recovered and that they should allow a season every once in a while. He complained that the marshes were over-trapped and there wasn't enough muskrat to fool with anymore. He complained that there were too many crab traps in the lake and too few deer along the cuts. But about his lot in life, hell, he never complained.

He had been living off the bounty of the lake and marshes since he was a young boy. I remember his crystal blue eyes gleaming like a young buck's behind that leathery and deeply furrowed skin when he told me of his shooting skills.

Before the Second World War, different gun manufacturers would stage shooting competitions to promote their company's lines of firearms.

"I did pretty well at those things and I guess word got around. Some fella from Winchester came and talked to me and my paw. Said they would give me one of them Winchesters proofed "One of a Thousand" and pay me to travel with the show doing fancy shooting. Hell, I weren't but a teenage boy and hadn't been off these marshes except to go to Canal Street a few times. Didn't have much education. And, man, the money was good but me off with all these city fellas, what did I know? Had to turn 'em down. It was my big chance, but with no education, hell, I had to say no."

From time to time, he'd grab his .22 and we'd plink at a few targets. Back then he was in his late fifties, I guess, wore no glasses and could shoot like a pro. He never bragged when he out-shot me, he just did it, easily, and at that time, I was better than most.

"Not bad for a lawyer fella," he said.

He and Beth had four children and I asked her one time, before I knew Vernon, how she came to marry a man so much older than she. She was a blonde with a nice figure, blue eyes and a fine face. Pretty when she smiled and she smiled often. She read a lot to pass the boredom of life on the bayou and began working with community problems and politics to fill the hours. She needed the excitement, I guess.

"I was about 16 and got pregnant from my boyfriend. But he was just a boy and you couldn't get abortions back then, not legally, anyway. Not that my Catholic family would have allowed it. No way."

I was sorry I started this conversation. She rolled over on her back and continued.

"Vernon was all alone and my daddy went to see him. He told him I was pregnant and needed a husband and told Vernon he needed a wife and I'd make him a good one. So, he married me and I had that child and three more for Vernon."

I wanted to ask if she had ever loved him, but I didn't.

"Sounds like one hell of a decent guy," I said.

"Yeah, he is. He's very kind and he's good to me and the kids."

I'd still see them from time to time but spent most of my visits with Vernon. The more I saw of the man, the more I thought of him. I was never alone with Beth after that conversation.

Coming back from camping or hunting, I'd take the turn off to Slip Bayou and look for Vernon. Usually he was in his shed tending to the crabs in the large tanks. By this time his wife was working in town and I rarely saw her. Occasionally I would hear word of her getting wilder and that she was now taking pills. Sounded like bayou life had lost its charm and she was using chemistry to cope. Some of the stories reaching me were fairly outrageous but our friendship by now had been over for years.

"Hear you a judge and all now," he said.

"Yeah. How about that?" I replied.

"Bet ya still can't pick out a crab that's gonna shed, now can ya?"

"No, but I still got all my fingers."

I wondered about Beth, his wife, from time to time. I'm sure, from her point of view, life was far from satisfying. She was near thirty now, and in, on her part at least, a loveless marriage to a man much older than she in surroundings far less than palatial. She should have left sooner, I suppose, while she still had some dignity. It would have been kinder to him as well.

I suppose it is widely accepted that men are reluctant to commit to a relationship. Perhaps this is because men do not fall in love as quickly as women but, when they do, they fall deeper. I don't think Vernon ever recovered from losing his wife and children. He did not, to my knowledge, break down or beg. He took his loss with expected stoicism, but I don't think he will heal. A wound that deep takes time and Vernon's too old.

He still gets up before dawn in a silent house to begin his day. His scarred and cracked leather fingers make coffee and pull in the cords tied to his traps. He still awakes every two hours throughout the night to move the crabs. His life is tied to his routine and to the marshes. He goes about his chores in silence, alone with his thoughts.

Sometime after hearing she left him, I stopped in one day in the afternoon. We sat at his table and, over coffee, I asked about the break-up.

It's hard to explain how clear and blue his eyes were. They did not go with his aged and weathered face. With a look I had only seen on broken and beaten dogs, he gazed into my eyes and said, "She shouldn't have ought to done what she did."

He began to tell me about how she started taking pain pills and she had reached a point where he no longer knew her. He told how she became very friendly with a lot of different policemen and how he suspected they were giving her the pills.

"One day two of 'em came over, and the four of us were sitting around this table drinking coffee, and they're laughing and cutting up. She writes something on a piece of paper and hands it to him. He reads it and laughs. He crumples it up and flips it into the ashtray."

"They stayed a while longer and left. Well, I can't read, but I took that piece of paper to a friend who can and he told me it said, 'I love you.' She shouldn't have done that. Not in front of me like that and the both of them laughing."

I would still see him every now and then and we would talk about crabbing or hunting but clearly the light was out. Perhaps it was the loss of love or the loneliness or the depth of the betrayal, but Vernon was no longer a complete person. There was a large hole in his gut where a family and trust once lived.

Vernon could tell crabs and weather and tides by just looking, but on his map there was no area marked "deception" so he didn't recognize it when it stared him in the face.

I knew Beth long before I met Vernon, but once I had, I mean once I got to really know him, my friendship with Beth changed. I don't guess you can really betray a man you've not yet met, but I think I did.

And I still see those sad blue eyes looking at me across that table years ago.

Jerry, Johnny and My Season at Zatarain's

Boiled New Orleans seafood. Crabs, crawfish and shrimp tumble and roll in waves of warm memories lying just beyond the present. Cayenne pepper, mustard seeds and bay leaves bubble up bringing tears to the eyes and anticipation to the initiated. Louisiana Crab Boil. This magical blend of spices was a mere sampling of the rich and unique flavors of New Orleans. And in New Orleans, these pungent ingredients were prepackaged, usually at Zatarain's, where I worked the summer of 1960. The plant's ever present, stinging odor of vinegar and crab boil forms the matrix from which my memories of that summer before college rise.

The original plant was located uptown in a residential neighborhood of old and elegant Victorian homes whose moment had slipped. It looked small tucked in by homes and trees on both sides and in front by the sidewalk and granite curb of Valmont Street. Nevertheless, the red brick building was three stories high and extended fully to the rear property line. It was as out of place in that neighborhood then as I am now.

Jerry, who ran the mustard mill, was the first co-worker I met there. He was a few years older than me and on my first day he walked me around the warehouse explaining how the plant operated.

"In the warehouse we keep the boxes of empty jars, all the barrels of produce from overseas—the pickles, olives, capers, onions—all that stuff and the boxed up extracts. All the spices are kept over by the pepper mill or on the third floor. That's where we mix the crab boil, on the third floor. When the upstairs ladies on the second floor need stuff to put up, they call down to us for different size jars and whatever food they're putting up. These are olives in this cask. See the marking on this thing here. That tells you the size of the olive and what kind it is. We stack all of it on these pallets until we have to bring it upstairs."

"You can get the fork truck in here to move the stuff?" I asked.

"Yeah. It's close but there's nothing to it. I'll teach you how to run it. The main thing you have to remember is to tilt the forks back a little bit towards the machine after you lift the load a few inches. And take your time. Things are pretty tight in here. Ya see those groves in the asphalt here."

"Yeah."

"See that wooden tank over there?"

"Yeah."

"That's the vinegar tank. They just fixed the thing. Last week I ran the forks into it making the turn into the shipping department. Busted out a few slats and a few hundred gallons of vinegar ran all over the place."

"Ya kiddin?"

He laughed and said, "Bigger than hell I did. We washed the warehouse down with the fire hose and the stuff still ate these trenches in the floor."

"I thought you said there wasn't anything to running the truck."

"Well maybe a little but you'll do ok. Don't sweat it."

"Man, vinegar can eat through asphalt like this?"

"Yeah but that's pure vinegar, not what you get in a bottle at the store. We dilute it with four parts of water to every part of vinegar before we bottle it. That stuff in there is like acid as it is."

After a week at the plant, the vinegar residue in the asphalt ate the soles off of my shoes, chewed right through the stitching holding the soles in place.

The warehouse crew did a little of everything at the plant but I worked primarily in the shipping department with Johnny. In a matter of days he and Jerry taught me to run the forklift and I taught myself to turn the corner near the vinegar tank very slowly. Pallets of goods were lifted off the rear of delivery trucks and stacked in the warehouse along both walls until needed. Jerry was at most three or four years older than I was, maybe 20 or 21, but he was already married and had a child. I never understood how he managed to make it on the dollar and a quarter an hour he was paid. I started at a dollar an hour and could hardly cover my bar tab. In my mind, he was trapped at an early age in my brine and pickle Zatarain summer where he would always remain. He had black hair and, like most of us, worked in blue jeans and a white T-shirt. I never came close to being acclimated to the mustard when

Jerry ran a batch of seeds in the grinder. On those days I would try to spend time on the second floor, hiding from the burning, throat-searing miasma that was Jerry's present and future.

Every few weeks, in government stamped, black metal barrels, pure grain alcohol would arrive for the extracts. Two hundred proof alcohol. Among several things I could not sort out at the plant was how vanilla extract could smell so wonderful and taste so much like brake fluid. Lemon, almond, coconut; they all smelled delicious and tasted horrible. But Sid liked them well enough. Sid looked to be in his eighties but he had to be younger. He was a helper assigned to one of the local delivery trucks and wore a khaki shirt and khaki pants every day. They were clean and ironed with starch so the creases stood sharp and straight. His heavy black shoes were shinned neatly. In contrast to his clothes, he was wrinkled, hunched over and walked like a man drained of energy and purpose. He had gray hair and mumbled softly to himself. The company had Sid work with a dark skinned, large Italian driver. Ray was his name and he was strong and apparently kind enough to do much of Sid's work along the route. The drivers and their helpers arrived for work earlier than the rest of the plant employees. They loaded up their quaint open sided trucks and made deliveries to grocery stores in and around New Orleans. Ray took care of the old man: he enjoyed his company, he said. The two of them, along with the other five or six team of drivers and helpers, usually finished their routes half an hour before quitting time. In the late afternoon, while Ray made his returns in the office, Sid walked, ghost-like, past the shipping department and into the warehouse, mumbling quietly. He'd reappear minutes before the bell sounded the end of the workday. I noticed on his return trip that the mumbling was gone, the voices he heard apparently were stilled and no longer needed a response. After several days watching Sid's ritual, I asked Johnny about it.

In a whispered voice, heavy with his Cajun accent, Johnny said, "He's in there drinking the extracts."

"Extracts? That stuff tastes like turpentine. Why?"

"Sid's an alcoholic. A bad alcoholic. They don't even give him his paycheck. They used to but he got so bad, he'd drink all weekend and not show up for work on Monday."

"Man, a guy his age a drunk?"

"Yes. His wife comes to the front office on Fridays and picks it up now. He never even sees it. No one can trust him with his money."

"So he can get loaded on those extracts?"

"Oh, yeah man. Read the labels. Those little bottles are mostly alcohol. They taste like hell but you can get loaded on them if you can stand the taste. I can't."

"How many does he drink?"

"Enough to get a buzz on. Four or five maybe. Jerry and I always find an empty box or two back there. It takes him awhile to empty one and he hides the one he's working on until it's empty."

"There's twenty-four bottles in those boxes."

"Yeah. It takes him a few days."

"They know about it in the front?"

"I think so. The foreman does. I guess they don't care as long as he gets his work done and Ray won't let him drink on the delivery route. The bottles are cheap enough and he's worked here forever. He'll retire soon so I guess they just let it slide."

"I think I'll stick to Dixie."

"Yeah, me too."

The alcohol barrels were brought by hand truck up to the lab where, under lock and key, one of the owners mixed the formulas for the many extracts Zatarain's bottled. In that locked lab they also blended the sacred Zatarain's Shrimp Roumalade and the secret Seafood Cocktail Sauce. But it was the black barrels that held our interest, not the formulas, and they always returned to us with three or four ounces still in the bottom. Jerry and I, along with Johnny, would turn the things completely upside down and salvage enough for a few drinks. We cut it with V-8 Juice, a half an ounce to an eight ounce glass. It wasn't enough for the three of us to get loaded but it was more than enough to make us feel humanly devious and get a bit of a buzz.

The company allowed the employees to eat any of the foods they processed provided they weren't already packaged for sale. I had no taste for pickles, olives or pimentos but I had my share of V-8. Zatarain's was a distributor for canned V-8 juice and I rationalized this breach of company rules by taking into account I never touched an anchovy stuffed olive. Never.

On the second floor, ladies in two lines facing each other along two long tables packaged and bottled the line of Zatarain's products. Colossal Olives, Jumbo Olives, Giant Olives (all the same size but marked with different labels) cherries, pickles, Chow-Chow (both fine cut and regular), onions and yellow and brown mustard moved down the line and were placed in bottles and jars. The second floor, hair-netted ladies looked so much older but I'm sure they were, for the most part, only in their late twenties or middle thirties. They wore white dresses with their hair curled up and tucked under nets in a style reminiscent of the 40s. They were allowed to speak quietly but never stop working while the line was in production. They were under the direction and stern eye of the forewoman, the master sergeant of the second floor. The only respite from work was their lunch break or when the line stopped to change to another product to be bottled. When a run was close to being completed the sergeant would call down to the warehouse and we'd bring up another 500 pound barrel. One man with a large steel hand truck was able to move the wooden barrels heavy with produce from the Mediterranean up to the second floor. The freight elevator was an open cage with sides as high as a man's hips. Instead of doors, flimsy wooden gates located on each floor closed off the shaft. The control to start and stop the old dinosaur was two ropes that had to be push-pulled with both hands at the proper time to align the bottom of the elevator with each floor. If the floors were misaligned, it was impossible to pull the heavy barrel truck off the elevator. It took practice to do it smoothly and even the long-term employees would miss occasionally. If we were delayed or if the forewoman mistimed the line, the ladies could stand and chat, leaning on the tables. None were attractive but they were friendly and smiled often. I often wondered what caused or allowed them to stay day after day, doing the same repetitive work in this fixed Orwellian scheme. But I came to learn that they were happy, and except for Betty, happier than most.

 The shipping department was located just inside the wall of the main warehouse. The vinegar tank was just over my right shoulder, eyeing me, waiting for me to make the turn a bit too quickly, biding its time. The different Zatarain products, once bottled and boxed, were located randomly on two of the three floors of the plant without apparent order or reason. The boxes were stacked in piles and the drivers and the shipping department would take them when needed. Johnny and I would work quickly through the day's work, actually running at times to get an order out in time for the shipping trucks' arrival. Several times we even bypassed the packing ladies to fill our orders, bottling whatever we needed for ourselves. When our work was done for the day, Johnny, Jerry and I would shoot the bull leaning on the shelf desk in the shipping department. Taking a lesson from Sid, I kept an open box of V-8 juice beneath my feet under the desk. Our foreman, an ex-navy man, knew our work was finished and never jumped us for hanging around still on the clock. On Fridays he'd bring in a six pack for the three of us. He told us that during prohibition he had waited for that black government barrel to come downstairs himself.

As the Shipping orders were being filled, we placed them on a row of pallets behind us. On the wall behind them, from floor to ceiling, perhaps twenty feet high or more, Johnny pasted Playboy centerfolds. Each month he'd bring in the new one and he already covered most of the wall. On the surface, looking at the plant itself, those pasted and creased magazine photos were the only hint of color and beauty in the whole building.

I liked Johnny. He was Cajun and spoke with the strong accent of those strong and self-reliant people. Johnny was older than Jerry and me, perhaps in his early thirties. He and I both drove 1950 two-door Ford coupes. I bought mine the year before, quite used and now quite abused. They were the same dark blue color.

"I ordered mine from Delta Ford," he said. "I picked out the model and the extras I wanted from a book in the showroom. You know, the radio and color and seat covers. It took a few weeks for them to get it ready and ship it into the city." He was smiling broadly and his eyes danced as he relived that high water mark of his life. "My father wanted to go with me and we watched as they drove my car off a boxcar at the dealer's warehouse. He really liked that car. Still does."

"What did you pay for it."

"That car, brand new with all the extras, cost me six hundred dollars."

As we came to know each other, he told me as a young man he wanted to be a priest. But his tattoo and the care his father needed sealed that door. On the underside of his forearm, there was a large tattoo of a bare-breasted woman in a grass skirt. One drunken night while in the service, she was inked into his skin, ending forever a future hope. Most religions, Catholicism included, tend to focus on the surface or the ceremony, never seeing the man or the deeper meaning within. He laughed about it and although he was at peace with himself, there was a sadness there, a morose sort of drifting. Johnny, it seemed to me, was living half a life. Near the middle of that spice filled summer his father became very ill and needed Johnny to care for him. He was granted a leave until his father passed away less than a month later. I had been there for maybe three weeks when he left. One of the Zatarains stopped by that day and asked if I thought I could run the department myself until Johnny's return. It was then that I learned only the Zatarains, one secretary, Johnny and I had a high school education. Sure, I said to myself, after all, I was making a dollar and a quarter by then. In truth, I was glad to have the job. The one I had the previous summer paid sixty-five cents. But gas for my Ford was only twenty-eight cents a gallon and the car itself, nine years old when I bought it, was only a hundred and fifty. The cost of my living was twenty-five cents a longneck and fifty cents a shot. I lived at home and except for replacing transmissions blown while drag racing, times were good financially.

It was during this time of Johnny's absence that Gus was hired to help in the warehouse. Gus, like myself, had just finished high school and he planned on joining the police force. He was thin, a bit taller than I and had a quick, twisted sense of humor so he fit in well with Jerry and me. Unfortunately for him and hilarious for us, he would trip, stumble and fall over the boxes and pallets scattered on the three floors of the plant. Leaning on the shipping department desk one afternoon, checking a partially filled order, I heard a crash and Gus yelled, "Holy shit". I walked the few steps around the wall of stacked boxes and he was standing in a red-orange, gallon-size puddle of Louisiana Hot Sauce. His face was a mixture of helplessness and confusion. Broken glass was around his feet and the sauce had splashed on the walls, the boxes and covered him like a Jackson Pollock canvas. By way of sympathy, I roared with laughter. When my laughter subsided, along with that of the other workers who gathered to see Gus' latest pratfall, we pitched in and helped him clean up. Vud told him to take his shirt and pants off and wash himself immediately. The cayenne pepper in the sauce would burn him painfully unless he washed with soap. Vud was right about that. When the cayenne sacks were moved by hand, as they had to be, we had to do the same thing. The burlap sacks had an inner liner that looked like thick linen but the powered pepper came through easily. Carrying a sack over a shoulder or close to your chest, it penetrated clothing just as easily. Sweat caused it to cling. In a hurry one hot summer day, I decided it had to be mostly shop myth and passed on washing off. Within the hour my skin was on fire. Washing off then helped little as it was too late. The stuff had worked into my pores and inflamed them so the water and soap could not reach its hiding places. I never made that mistake again.

Vud too was a Cajun but unlike Johnny, was a little light on gray matter. He wore blue jeans rolled up on the bottoms and the sleeves of his signature plaid short-sleeved shirt had a similar roll. His hair was slick with Vaseline and appeared to be cut daily by someone at home. Never a hair out of place, he looked like a young Moe Howard with a bowl cut. Always wearing the same emotionless face, he had the unmistakable textbook look of a man sporting a new lobotomy. Rarely did he speak and when he did he was impossible to understand. When he was forced to speak to me, bearing some urgent message, his Cajun accent was so thick I could never understand him. He'd say something unintelligible and I'd ask him to repeat himself. He'd mumble something again, I'd say "huh" or "what" and he'd try again. He would then begin charade-like arm movements trying an improvised form of sign language with little success. Frustrated, he'd drag one of the other employees over to translate. On those occasions when even the translator failed, he'd walk off in a huff to reappear with someone who would speak for him. Most of the time he'd just walk past the shipping department and offer a shy nod without comment. Vud was the only man I ever met who signed his name with an X.

Moving along the line of ladies, selecting bottles and jars to fill a box for a rush order, I'd exchange a quick word or two. Betty was in her thirties, tall, very thin and gawky. Her face was thin and arrow shaped, made even more memorable by her buckteeth. The combined effect gave her a horse-like appearance. She was a blond; a horse-faced, blond, hair-netted vision of Rosy the Riveter decked out in white. She and a few of the other ladies would help me box things that were needed quickly for a truck. She was kind and funny and her laughter was uninhibited, still filled with hope for another day, for some other place perhaps.

I guess if you open enough oysters, a pearl will eventually show up. In all the years along the packaging lines, enough oysters had passed through for the pearl to appear. Her name was Gwendolyn. She was my age having just graduated from high school that year. She had dark hair, an attractive face and a good figure. We nodded and the ladies looked at each other. We spoke and they began whispering. After a few years, what can you say about pickles that hasn't been said before?

After that first week I drove her home. She had an easy smile and said the line work had bored her already. I spoke about college in the fall. I did not mention I was still spitting out the ashes of a busted relationship. I asked her out for the following Friday and she accepted. Most of the line ladies and the other workers lived in the neighborhood near the plant but on the other side of Magazine Street, closer to the riverfront. She lived there with her family in a modest shotgun double and planned to leave Zatarain's as soon as she found another, better paying job. But her optimism for her future did not include education. Her horizons, while higher than the packing line, were still without dreams.

Perhaps it was the whispering, the smiles from the ladies with the knowing looks or maybe I just didn't want to be involved again or just climb into the sack with a decent girl. Or, if I did, I didn't want it to be the subject of gossip with the line ladies. Perhaps it was snobbery but I don't like to think that of myself. More likely it was the subtle realization that we had nothing in common. On Wednesday, I broke the date. I wasn't sure of the reason then but it probably was a combination of all of them. I just did and it made me feel terribly guilty.

The large Italian, Ray, who worked with Sid, would stop by my department to pass the time or ask if I knew where a case of one product or other might be located. Like everyone there he had an easy laugh but his anger was easier to see, beneath the laughter and very near the surface. The drivers only made a few cents more than the plant workers and he felt none of us were paid enough. Seeing the orders first hand, the salaries paid and the drayage slips on the incoming produce, I had to agree. I just listened at first but in time our conversations included Jerry and became conspiratorial. Ray began to speak with the other drivers and raised the possibility of a strike.

After he left one afternoon, I asked Jerry, "Whatcha think?"

"Man, I don't know. I need this job but they sure don't pay us enough. How do you feel about it."

"Me? Hell Jerry, I'm going to college in a few weeks so it doesn't matter too much one way or the other. But you're right. From what I've seen on the paperwork around here, they could be paying you guys more."

The plant worked half a day on Saturdays. We were paid time and a half and when the bell sounded, several of us walked a short block down Magazine to the corner bar. They also served lunch and po-boys sandwiches. Often four or five of us would make an afternoon of it, drinking beer around a wooden table and wolfing down shrimp po-boys. A group of the second floor ladies sometimes showed up for a beer and spoke shyly to us. As the beer and the hour put on larger numbers, they would laugh and join us. In a few hours we'd go our ways, they to their neighborhood homes and I to mine across town. Those were Saturdays of lazy, laid back, easy laughter. Nothing was serious and no one had reason for the mask of social pretense. We were just plant workers, male and female, having a few beers after work; the work which was the thread which held us together however weakly.

Gus was usually there with Jerry and me. Our foreman would stay for a while but leave before breaching that line that separated management from labor. Johnny was always there before he took the leave of absence during his father's illness and he rejoined us after his death. A driver or two completed the usual male portion of the circle. Betty and a few of the older women from the line joined in. On one of those po-boy half Saturdays, I had a few free minutes so I gave Gus a hand with the Spanish olives. These broken bits of olives were mixed in Spain with pimentos and brine and shipped to us in huge vats four feet high and perhaps five feet across the middle. They were far too large to fit on the elevator and I doubt if that old horse could lift them anyway. Instead, we'd take the vat down from where they were stacked on pallets in the warehouse, open the wooden lid, and using simple household metal frying baskets, we'd hand dip the stuff into a barrel placed next to the vat. Once filled, it would be moved to the second floor ladies with the barrel truck by hand. Those vats held five or six full size barrels of Spanish olives. As the runs of Spanish olives were finished, the level in the vat dropped below the level a man could reach with his basket. We placed a box next to the vat so the worker could stand and lean into the vat to reach the bottom. We—Gus and I—were filling a second barrel that morning when I was called to the office to pick up another handful of orders. I was at my desk laying the orders out according to their level of importance when I heard a piercing yell for help coming from the warehouse. I ran down the short hallway, turned the corner by the evil vinegar tank and saw Gus standing with his hands held at an awkward angle away from his body. One hand still held his dip basket. He, having fallen into the vat, was covered from head to toe with red and green bits of Spanish olives. From where I stood, it looked like thousands of Christmas colored slugs were having their way with him. Once again, overcome by sympathy, I roared.

Gus didn't join us that Saturday. He punched out early to go home for a bath.

I hated the third floor; everyone did. The windows were closed unless we were working up there, which we did rarely. The ceiling wasn't insulated and the summer sun of the 30th degree north latitude beat down on that roof turning that top floor into an oven. In seconds, sweat poured out and soaked our shirts and the top of our jeans. Only boxes were stored there. Boxes and the crab boil hopper. Several of the larger boxes near the hopper contained the ingredients for making the crab boil. We'd remove the metal cover of the hopper and fill the bin with measured amounts of pepper, mustard seeds and the rest. Two of us usually did the job so it could be done quicker. Cayenne and other sharp spices rose in the air and were drawn into our lungs and stuck to our skin. Within minutes we started to cough and our skin would burn. Sweat made the cayenne sting more painfully. Once the bin was filled, we stirred the concoction with an ancient wooden canoe paddle, its blade worn smooth from years of moving through the spices. The blade of the paddle had a reddish tint from the cayenne that had worked its way into the wood fiber. It had insinuated itself into the wood, squeezing between the tissue like the hopelessness of the place which was slowly eating into me. The handle end was smooth as well, worn smooth by hands of sweaty men working quickly to escape the heat and the fiery spices.

The bottom of the hopper ended just above the far end of one of the production tables on the second floor where the forewoman worked the control. Thin cotton bags, each with drawstrings, were in boxes at her side. In a mechanical manner she'd open a bag, slide it over the large nozzle end of the hopper and fill it with spices. Pulling the strings tight, she'd toss the filled bag onto the table where others put them into individual boxes with the familiar Zatarain's logo. Another lady placed them into larger one dozen boxes for shipment.

Johnny returned after his father passed away. He was still carrying the usual heavy burden of loss and unnecessary guilt. He told me of his near lifetime of caring for his invalid father and the pain they both felt as the end drew them both into the cruel dance of endless and eternal parting.

"The house is so lonely now. He stayed with me for so long. I still see him everywhere. He was my best friend."

"Johnny have you thought about becoming a priest now?" I asked him. "Maybe if you cover that tattoo with something else."

"Yes, I have but I'm too old now. They'd never take me."

Self-sacrifice should never work from the bottom up. In Johnny's case, I believe, the son died with the father in small doses of an unfulfilled dream.

Jerry and I felt a few beers would pick him up and that Saturday, after the full plant worked on running the crab boil, we managed to see that the turn out at the corner bar was larger than usual. I wore a beard then with short hair. I was reading a paperback written by Lawrence and placed it on the bar as we ordered our beer. I paid for the first round and the barmaid, putting my change on the bar, looked down at Lawrence's picture on the back cover. It was a photo of him as a young man with a beard and short hair. "You wrote dat book, hawt?"

I picked up the book, looked at old DH and saw for the first time the resemblance.

"No", I answered, "but I wish I had."

I didn't wish for much then. I had most of what I needed but the idea of writing was conceived at that bar however vague in conception and distant in time it was.

As the afternoon wore on few of the crew left. Everyone was ordering beer and for a period of time, I had three full ones in front of me. Johnny was slowly showing early signs of life without dad. Betty's husband Ted phoned and then came over. She introduced him to everyone and he ordered the next round. By now we had ten or twelve of us at the party and it was turning out to be Johnny's debutante ball. He was dancing with the older women, smiling and laughing as he tried out steps which needed more practice or less beer. Jerry and I watched him with unstated satisfaction and damn if everyone wasn't having a great, if slightly drunken, time of it.

Ted was civil enough for an hour or so but as the party continued to grow away from him, he began to shrink back, withdrawing. I could see it in his face and tried to bring him closer to the circle. He spoke a bit but clearly he was feeling the distance between the workers, including his wife, and himself. Abruptly he left with normal good byes to the group. Betty remained with us and was fairly gone on the Dixie. Someone started telling jokes and fueled by the beer the laughter was loud. Others at the bar joined in. The whole place was now one big celebration. An hour later Betty got a call from Ted. I could hear her over the din telling him she was having fun and she was staying. Remembering what I saw in his face, I felt uneasiness. Spend enough time on the street or in the French Quarter and you can smell trouble long before it goes down. She rejoined the group and one of the ladies asked if everything was all right. She told us Ted was angry and wanted her home but added he could just kiss her ass and then she let out an awkward laughing sound an embarrassed mule might make. I realized she was not used to ignoring or joking about him.

In another hour, as the sun neared the end of its western descent, the more sober among us began to leave. Betty asked if I could ride her home but with an angry husband waiting, I didn't want to be drawn into any hassle. Being her co-worker and not wanting to be seen as anything other than that by her husband, I said sure but asked Jerry to ride with me. I'd return him to his car by the plant.

The three of us continued to laugh and Jerry and I both left the bar with open bottles of beer. She rode in the back seat and when we let her out she climbed the short steps to her door. It was locked from the inside. She ran the bell, knocked on the door and finally beat her fists on their bedroom wall. The door flew open inward and the fiery-eyed Ted from behind the screen door looked at Betty off to the side and then he looked at us. More to the point, he stared angrily directly at me. Great, I was thinking. Without comment or curse, he walked away from the door and Betty stepped up to and opened the screen. "Are you going to be ok?" I asked.

"Yeah, sure. He's all right."

"Ok, see ya Monday," I said and I took off headed for Jerry's car. Half way back to the plant, that nagging street sense made me speak out, "Jerry's, he's going to hurt her. I saw it building all day. They're going to get into it and he's going to beat the hell out of her."

"Yeah, he was pissed at something. You think he might?"

"Yes. You wanna go back with me to check on her?"

"Yeah, sure", he said.

"Damn, how in hell can a guy be jealous of a woman that ugly?"

Before we pulled up to the curb by her door, we could see that the screen door was knocked off the top hinge. I parked and we knocked on the doorframe of the open kitchen door. I yelled her name. I knocked again and yelled louder. We heard a moan and I walked in with Jerry close behind. She was hidden from view by the kitchen table but once in the room I could see her feet. One of her shoes was off and she was lying on the floor face down. I rolled her over carefully and her mouth was a mess. She was split from her lip up to the base of her nose. The bottom of the cut was wide, wider than the two or three teeth I could see even with her mouth still closed. Blood had spilled down her white work dress and had pooled on the linoleum floor. I turned and headed into the house looking for Ted. He was drunk, lying on one of two twin beds, the one furthest from the kitchen door. He stood when I entered the room and started in my direction. I hit him with every bit of contempt I could muster. The punch caught him in mid-stride and carried him over the bed and into the corner. He was unconscious and I let him remain there in a heap.

Johnny had stopped the bleeding with a towel and Betty was sitting on the floor. It was a ghastly cut and on a woman, even more so. Working herself senseless at a maddeningly repetitious job and now, as if life hadn't crippled her enough, she had to face this further disfigurement. Ted deserved more of a beating. What level of self-contempt and cowardice would allow a man to do such a thing? I wanted to kill him.

"Is it bad?" she asked.

"Well, it doesn't look so great now but after a few stitches, you'll be fine" I said.

"Are you sure?"

"Positive", I lied.

She gave me a number to call so her mother could meet us at Baptist Hospital and she did.

Monday morning our foreman found Jerry and me talking near the shipping department. "I heard what you two guys did. Don't you know you both could have gotten killed pulling that stunt?" he asked. But he was wrong. I was seventeen and I was going to live forever. I had the suspicion he would have done exactly the same thing were he in our place. There were no more comments about it, even when Betty returned to work a few days later. And when the bandages came off, the cut had healed better than I had expected.

Time had rushed past the solstice and the siren song of autumn college grew louder in my ear. Drunken weekends spent at a piano bar on the lakefront took most of my earnings from Zatarain's. Gus managed to misalign the elevator on the second floor and tried to force the barrel truck over the rise. A moment later, 500 pounds of Fine Cut Chow-Chow splashed, splattered and oozed its yellow and green way down the walls of the elevator shaft. When I saw him a few minutes later I told him it was different, at least, seeing him after an accident not covered in some condiment.

Near the demise of summer and the end of my season among the spices, Johnny, Jerry, Ray and I now huddled in the warehouse. The drivers would go out but the packing line would have no part in it. The warehouse crew and the drivers could stop the plant themselves. The line wasn't essential.

College started before the strike did, but over Christmas I returned to see Jerry and Johnny and the rest of them once again. They filled me in on the strike. The rest of warehouse crew crossed the line after two hours, gutting it before it really got started. Johnny and Jerry stayed out until the drivers folded. With guys like Vud and Sid, it was Zatarain's or a cardboard box on Camp Street. In the afternoon they called in the drivers one at a time. Two of them were cut three cents an hour. The rest were allowed to stay at their present salary except for Ray, the large Italian. He got a nickel raise. So the long awaited autumn strike at Zatarain's ended with the company saving a penny an hour, forty cents a week or roughly twenty dollars and eighty cents a year.

The plant moved across the river years ago and I never returned to see them after that Christmas visit. In the years that rushed me forward from those days to these, I often wondered what became of these people who earned both my respect and sympathy. They may have wished for a better hand but they never tossed theirs in or complained. I don't think young people would work that hard for next to nothing today but maybe they do, somewhere. Gus I know became a police office and I hope Jerry moved on to something better. Did Johnny end his days of longing still inhaling mustard seed and brine? And the crab boil. Do men still endure the spices that burn their skin, their throats and eyes in that quick trip to hell? And what became of the canoe paddle, its edge s smooth and orange from endless years of passing through the spices?

Merchant of the Eight Part Street

The hour of the slouching draws nigh
And I, with flaccid tool in hand,
inch towards home
on the eight part street
to prepare for my accounting.

The night chill lies gray on my coat.
Tedious footfalls
ease me through
the damp
of evening's demise.
We are bathed in dew,
my words and I,
clothed in crystal beaded pretense.
A moment, Lord, hear my words.

Form without substance . . . .
shadow of a shadow.
Let me pretend
someone mattered.
Let me pretend

I had a cause
instead of a diversion.
Death is difficult
for those
who have not lived.

I shall say
(with determined eye)
that I have traded well
and greeted each in turn with outstretched hand
and superficial smile.

I have risen through
the ranks of givers,
pandering for their respect,
performing mitzvahs,
leading parades,
easing pain
(provided it gives me none).

Did I take my measure in other eyes?
Surely
I fashioned my front to curry favor
and held conformity's coat.
I did not even dare
to eat Prufrock's peach . . . .
except when no one looked.

I puff my breast
and strut my well-earned position.
I rarely feel the hollow . . . .

Seek my friends and inquire.
Surely they speak well,
for if I have not cultivated deep,
a large number I acquired.

From my storehouse of wares
I have granted
largesse of keystone plus ten.
illusion,
but a gift nevertheless,
like a smile,
like flattery,
it cost me not.

I am well-regarded.
I have sacrificed
for my esteem.
I shall say I have traded well;
I have turned a profit
(and my back to principle).

With measured words
whispered
over time,
a bit of fact, a bit of spin
(all right reasoned)
I have turned mother against brother
and usurped
his birthright.

I disclaim any blame
from the years of formation.
I have my pride intact.
True, I caved to demanding shrill voices
finding it easier
to abdicate
without a shrug.
Can one impart what one does not possess?
can one?

I sat with idle hands
when my issue,
with talons of abuse,
tore the heart
from the deaf.

I shall say
I have traded well
and refused to rein in
the harpies
and witnessed their evil unfold.
instead,
I traded my grandchildren
for a little peace.

an impotent intruder.
a pebble striking
the water's edge,
causing not a ripple.
Even the hyla fails to note
my passing.

I have traded well
and my name causes no echo

Beddy

"I believe there is only one story in the world, and only one, that has frightened us and inspired us... Humans are caught—in their lives, in their thoughts, in their hungers and ambitions, in their avarice and cruelty, and in their kindness and generosity too—in a net of good and evil. I think this is the only story we have... the never ending contest in ourselves of good and evil."

John Steinbeck, "East of Eden"

Beddy Forrest wasn't right. On the day of his birth Doc McGill said as much to his father but Beddy was his only child and he loved him dearly. Maybe he loved him more than a he would a normal boy because was a sweet child never leaving his father's side for very long. But problems or no, James Forrest didn't dote on his son and allowed him to do everything normal boys did. Physically he was fine. He could climb trees better than most and could run faster and longer than the other boys in their small farming town. Beddy liked to walk and he ran with a peculiar stride, picking his knees up higher than normal. The boys teased him about the way he ran but his pa told him that that was ok. He said it would make his legs strong and soon he could move up hill as fast as a deer and just as quietly. His mother Elizabeth loved him because he was always smiling and he'd come up behind her and hug her for no reason and sometimes it seemed he could tell when she needed more than one.

Much of the work on a farm is repetitive and Beddy was good at those things. His father had a fine farm located at the base of Feather Mountain and it prospered. He had to show Beddy how to do things more than a few times but, once the movements were locked into his slow firing capabilities, he rarely forgot. As a child he had to collect the morning eggs and feed and milk the cows. On many of those early farming mornings he forgot the basket of eggs by the cow pen or next to the barn door.

"Beddy, where's tha eggs?"

"Ah don't know ma."

"Did ya leave them in tha barn again?"

"Ah don't know."

He seldom looked at his mother's eyes or anyone's for that matter. Beddy was more comfortable looking at the floor or the walls instead.

"Well Beddy, go take ah look. I'll bet that's where they are."

He returned a few minutes later with a short stick. "Look ma, this stick looks like ah bird's head."

"Let me see. Why sure fire Beddy, it does. It does indeed look like ah bird's head. What kind of bird does it look like to you?"

"It looks like one of them candied gooses ma."

"That's what I was thinking too Beddy, a Canada Goose, sure enough."

"Beddy, you didn't forget tha eggs in tha barn did ya?"

"No mamma, they're out in tha barn."

"I see. But ifin ya get them, weuns could have our breakfast. Aren't you hungry yet?"

James Forrest grew good, sweet corn, broad fields of it, and had some fine pigs and mike cows but the money he made from that barely kept the family together. His home was at the base of Feather Mountain and when his pa died, he left James the house and over a hundred acres of bottomland around it. James' father had done well and James eventually did better than his father but not from the farm. James, like his father before him, ran a still and did very well with that. His father started as a sharecropper and eventually bought the land with money he made from the still. It was found by most to be the smoothest shine in the county. His father taught James his recipe and a few suggestions on how to keep the law at bay. Just as his father did, James shared a reasonable bit of his profit with the sheriff and it was in their nature to tithe a bit to the church. But profit had nothing to do with caring nature of James and his father. Having gone hungry enough times themselves, they never let another valley family go without help if they needed it.

One autumn, when James was a young man, Ezekiel Lawson took ill with pneumonia and his son Oliver, just few years younger than James, had to turn the fields for winter and run things by himself. Try as he may, the Lawson family was still having a bad time of it. As Ezekiel slowly recovered, still unable to work, his family was running out of money with little for food and none for seed in spring. The loan on the place hadn't been paid in months. His father took James when he went to see Mr. Lawson. It was a lesson his father taught in a time when the doing was more of a lesson than the telling. His Father loaned Mr. Lawson enough to get the family through winter and guaranteed credit for seed and farm tools if necessary.

"I won't be forgetting your kindness Forrest."

"I know that."

"Would you be wanting my note?"

"Ifin ah did, ah wouldn't be here."

"Than you have ma word."

"That's more than enough Lawson."

"But ah would be liking to do more than just repaying you for this."

"Your boy here, Oliver, he wants ta go ta school. You and the boy work tha farm hard and when ya can, send him."

Neither James nor his father could explain why their shine was as good as it was but they felt sure it had something to do with the spring. It flowed over a slab of limestone a half mile from the farmhouse, a half-mile up the east holler on Feather Mountain, and became the stream that ran by the house and through the field. It flowed deep from within the heart of the mountain and never failed in the dry season. It smelled sweet and was clear. They watered the stock and the fields from it. They washed their clothes and bodies in it and, as James told Beddy, it was the spring that feed the body and soul of their family. From it's pure water James made more shine than his father ever had. It was his idea to pay a man in Seaton to run the liquor for him to the three counties bordering his. He'd load his false bottom wagon with shine and cover it with corn or hay and make his rounds, returning to James for his pay.

Greed was a terrible thing in a man, and like lust, it could turn a man into a thing of awful corruption. It could blind the smartest of men to the most obvious risks, even those a fool would avoid. Doing business with a greedy man could not only bring ruin to him but your business as well and James didn't want to ruin this Seaton man or his business by letting him fall to greed. James, on horseback, would collect the money himself a few days before delivery.

You could do good with money but James knew from The Book that if a man took to loving it for itself, that was the way to a man's undoing.

James Forrest wasn't turned by the power of money although he made more than his father could have hope. And with it, he bought more land in

Horton County and added to his holdings near the Feather. He even bought a large share of the county bank. He bought all of Feather Mountain and large tracts near the county seat. James was quietly becoming the wealthiest man in Horton County but an outsider would never know it. His family still lived in his daddy's house and they still worked the farm every day. "The land," he told Elizabeth, "is the only wealth a body can keep regardless. Work the land like the Lord meant us to do and tha land ain't never gonna fail yer." Among the few luxuries he allowed was a phone and electricity. The phone was for his business and a few friends and the electricity was for Elizabeth. She loved the radio and would turn it on when she cooked or did laundry on the porch. At night, she and James and Beddy would listen to news before turning in. The radio brought word of how the world was changing, and James worried about Beddy and how those changes could hurt him. And James hoped, with a little money, he could keep the changing world away from Beddy a little longer.

When Beddy was very young, his father walked with him to where the spring broke above ground. "We have to do this Beddy; we have to come here and keep the spring and its stream clean cause we drink of it. The winter sometimes causes trees and branches to fall across the stream and we have to clear it. In autumn too. Sometimes the leaves are so heavy they block the stream near the spring and foul it. We have to make sure no deer or some other animal doesn't die and lay in it. That would make us all powerful sick. Come up here now and again to see if them wild pigs don't get to wallowing in it. That could make us sick too. This spring is special Beddy. Take care of it son, keep it clean, and it will always take care of us. It's strong like medicine Beddy and it feeds us. It feeds our soul and the soul of the farm and it keeps them strong."

"How does it do that pa?"

"It keeps us alive son, it's the strength of this place and the valley around it. A spring like this can only come from God Himself and He done give it to us. Up here where it starts, it's clean and fresh and it stays that way, running over these stones and in the shade of these rhododendrons. That water brings up tha very nature of Feather Mountain to us. We have the sweetest water in the valley and it makes us healthy and strong and lets us grow fine crops and keeps our animals healthy."

"Moms says the birds and other animals drink from it too."

"That's right Beddy. That's why there so many deer on the mountain and other animals down in the fields where the stream runs."

"What if they drink all of it pa?"

"They won't do that Beddy. There's more than enough for them. That's one fine spring son. Maybe the finest and it will always be here if we take care of it."

Beddy grew strong and raw boned working hard in the fields and felling trees. While he was still a teenager, Beddy could till a field as good as his father. When work was to be done in the valley they'd help others bring in crops, cut tobacco and sort it or raise a new barn. Beddy didn't speak much but the valley folk were kind to him. He could bring a tree down quicker than most men and climb a frame and move a log into place in no time. Beddy, they knew, wasn't right but he wasn't what they'd call wrong either.

The valley folk knew full well what James, and his father before him, made and sold and thought little of it. Most of the valley men would stop by James' house and knock quietly on his back door during the night. James had customers from all over and many had been his father's customers or their sons.

Beddy asked about these men and his father told him they were friends just stopping by to politely say hello. As a youngster, because it had gone on for so long, Beddy saw nothing peculiar in this practice. And being polite, he'd often knock on a neighbor's back door himself.

"Hi Beddy. What can ah do for you honey?"

"Jess saying 'hi' Mr. Clayton."

"Well ain't that nice Beddy. Would you stop for a glass of buttermilk or cider."

Not having much to add beside his greeting, Beddy would just say, "No sir, jess wantta say 'hi' so 'hi'."

"You stop by anytime Beddy and tell your folks hi for us."

And knowing Beddy, the neighbors didn't find it very strange either.

When he was older and began doing this in the middle of the night, James knew he'd have to have a talk with his son. One afternoon after the three of them had finished hoeing their corn, James said to his wife, "Elizabeth, Beddy and I are going for a walk up tha holler a bit to get out of this heat. Beddy, you feel like heading out for some shade?"

"Yes sir, ah do."

Walking across the field they hit the stream running through the middle and turned to follow it upstream. A few feet past the edge of the cornfield the stream entered the woods under a canopy of oak and maple. Beddy could feel the coolness rising up from the stream, lingering in the shade of the trees. A few feet into the shade James knelt on one knee and cupped his hands to drink from the cool water. Beddy could smell the forest now. The wild mints that grew along the stream, bruised by their passing, sent their aroma into the air. The resins from the hemlocks mingled with it and perfumed the mountain. "Grab yerself some water Beddy," said James.

Beddy knelt on the ground with both knees, put his arms on the ground and leaned his face forward and into the stream gulping down the water. Then he plunged his head full into the pool and held his breath. The water was so cold it made his head sting on the inside and when he could stand it no longer he pulled out, shaking his head, yelling, "Ya-hooo, a-hooo, that's colder than cold daddy!"

His father smiled and said, "Ain't no colder than it was Tuesday Beddy and you said tha same thing then. But yer right. It's always cold. It stays cold underground and stays that way until long after it leaves our farm."

James picked up a handful of pebbles from the creek bed and looked at them lying in his open palm, figuring out the right words. Like those pebbles, the truth of it and all truth, just was. "Beddy, ah want ta tell ya about this here stream and those men that come late at night to our door. Beddy, have you ever heard of moonshine? Not the kind that tha moon makes but tha kind that men drink?"

"I heard the word before Pa. I heard a boy talking about it before. And I heard Mr. Alton saying it were the devil's doing but ah don't know nothing of it myself."

"Beddy they's some that take to it and some that don't. Even tha law takes to it but they say they don't because folks like Mr. Alton have too much ta say about it. Come on Beddy, ah want ta show ya something."

When Pa walked to the spring, he never walked over the same ground. He told Beddy many times, so Beddy would understand, that he didn't want to make a trail others could follow. He told Beddy it was best to stay in earshot of the stream so he could follow it himself one day. Away from the stream the uphill was a hard climb. Over moss covered rocks, around boulders and beneath the thick, lush laurel patches and on slippery ground they moved up the mountain. Very near the slab of stone and the spring, a small sway in the ridge opened to a low flat area on the other side. Once through it, his pa stopped and pushing aside leaves and small branches, he picked up a black hose which ran in both directions, back through the sway towards the stream and onto the flat.

"This brings in the water Beddy."

"For tha deers daddy?"

"No Beddy. For the moonshine."

It didn't come easy to Beddy, not the making of it, not the selling of it nor the reason for it being at all. But James patiently showed him and explained it enough times that Beddy remembered and was making good shine before the year was out. He had tried the taste of it but he didn't like it. "Daddy, that shine burns ma mouth all tha way ta ma innards."

When James died, Beddy was in his forties and had been making the shine the family sold. Beddy never cried when Pa died. He had seen farm animals die and had hunted the hills with his father enough to have some understanding of death. Everything died sooner or later. His Pa was with God and that was all right with him although he would miss him. "He's in a better place," Ma said.

"Is they a spring and good land there Ma?"

"Yes Beddy, I suppose there is."

"And plenty ah deer and shine, like here?"

"Yes."

"Then why didn't he jess stay here with us Ma?"

"God wanted him Beddy and he was a-hurting something bad."

He heard the words that Minister McComster said about his Pa. They didn't sound like his daddy but the minister did say he was a good man loved by his family and that did sound like Pa. Two days later Beddy took a bottle from under the floor in the barn and walked into the woods, up Feather Mountain. He came home the next evening.

"Where have ya been Beddy?"

"Up on the Feather."

"What were ya doing by yourself out there, over night?"

"Talkin'."

"To who Beddy?"

"The Feather's soul mama. Ah figure daddy's there too."

She looked at him and he looked at the floor.

"Well ya should have told me Beddy. I was worried half to death."

That was that for Beddy and the matter of Pa's death. The talking of it ended there but he thought of him often.

When James passed on Elizabeth built a new home with plumbing and running water. Beddy and she, when the farm work was done, would still sit quietly for hours by the radio. On one of those evenings Elizabeth turned the radio down and looked at Beddy.

"Beddy, me and your pa done talked about you some. James didn't want you ta be making shine after he passed. I told the Seaton man that we weren't a-doing it no more and he understood. But your pa knowed it's in your blood so you can still sell it out that back door if you want but you still have to work tha farm. Beddy, we done got us all the money we can use and then some, so you don't have ta sell shine a'tall. You understand Beddy?"

Yes ma'am ah do. Ah do."

"Good Beddy. Tomorrow a man, a man and his son, friends of your father's, will be a-coming ta tha house. I want ya ta meet them. They's my friends too. They's both lawyer fellas and yer pa trusted this man and he says his son's a good man too. Ah want you ta meet them Beddy. In case anything happens ta me, this man's a-gonna watch out for you. His name is Oliver Lawson and his son is Boyd. You understand Beddy?"

"Yes mama ah do. But ah believe I'll go ahead and still be a-makin shine ifin you don't mind."

"No Beddy, that'll be jess fine with me."

Nelson Bridges

Nelson Bridges sat in his office looking at the skyline with what for him would have been boredom but others would have recognized as longing. Nearing fifty, with some wealth, he was feeling the tedium of the days beginning to wear on him. He wore a dark pin striped suit with a signature rosebud in his lapel. A bright red tie matched the shade of the rose. Renting rundown property to the have-nots ran a man down and played him out too soon, he was thinking. The tenants, for the most part, all carried the same anger and the lack of hope that gave it birth. He was weary of the endless grumbling about the plumbing, the roof, the lights and the way they destroyed the places themselves. Government subsidies made their rent payments dependable and profitable and, with the right connections, very profitable for him. But he needed something, some excitement or maybe another challenge.

At a cocktail party fundraiser for a commissioner he knew, Nelson ran into a fellow, an acquaintance from his days in college. There was a time, when they were both younger, that they were friends but Nelson could not remember ever seeing him in all the time stretching back those thirty odd years. And he was no one Nelson hoped or planned to see that evening. Vance Coleman was a slight man and one who would go unnoticed in a full room. Like another piece of furniture, he was just there. It was he who walked to where Nelson stood with his date for the evening. Nelson had been busy, surveying the room expectantly, with drink in hand and an insincere smile, ready to make eye contact with anyone he figured had pull. Networking he called it. Groveling is what it was. Vance Coleman had long fingers and narrow shoulders. He spoke in a whisper, making even the innocent mentioning of collegiate memories sound conspiratorial. He had become a chiropractor.

Having failed to connect with someone of substance, Nelson Bridges was stuck with this wisp of a man from his past.

"I do well Nelson. The government . . ." He had gotten no further than this when Nelson, eyes still shifting, gave him his full attention. "The government keep a loose rein on Medicare payments to doctors and I do quite well."

"Oh?"

"Yes. In the early days of my practice I started getting referrals from an attorney I knew who did personal injury work, you know whiplash . . . that sort of thing. Soft tissue stuff. That was soon going so well that I told him I couldn't take on any more clients. He told me to hire someone else to help out. Well, I had a good thing going and I didn't want to give part of it up and told him so. He said he owned a building and had a lot of space available. He told me he had someone in his office, and ex-government employee, who was expert in getting people cleared for Medicare. I could move into his building and she could work in my office. He would send me his business and the business of other attorneys and I could hire another guy or keep it all myself if I were smart enough."

Before Vance Coleman neared the middle of his story, Nelson had told his date to sit out on the balcony and watch the sunset. As Vance Coleman spoke, Nelson could see her sitting at the bar, eating finger sandwiches and doing some of her own networking. Nelson's eyes continued to dart around the room and he was now speaking in hushed tones himself.

"How could you keep it all for yourself?"

"Well these people aren't really hurt, see. I manipulate them three times a week, treating nothing and it gets to be a pain in the ass for them to come. Some stop coming and the attorney has to chase them back to me. Instead, I began to see them maybe once every two weeks and when they come in they sign the book for the visits we skipped."

"Doesn't sound too kosher, Vance."

"Hey, I don't know about it. The Medicare gal and the office personnel set the system up. I just move from room to room treating these people who tell me they hurt. I'm doing some good for somebody. That's all. I'm easing everybody's pain, even a little of my own."

"Well you just make the money from your treatment, right? You don't get part of the case do you?"

"Sure. If I got part of the attorney's fee, that would be unethical."

"Well, if it's just the fee for your treatment, you don't have to work for just attorneys, do you?"

"What do you mean?"

"Look I have this rental property see. A lot of rental property, maybe a hundred families, three hundred people, counting their wives, live-ins and kids, right?"

"Yeah, I guess so."

"Look, these folks are down and out. They need a break. What if we treat them, you give me . . . oh say a third of what you make, I throw them a bone and we all make a few bucks. Whatcha say?"

"I say twenty-five percent. I'm taking some risk here."

"If I hear this right, you don't need nothing more than their name, their signature and their sosh, right? I mean you don't have to even treat them, right? Maybe once, twice tops, right?"

"Ok, thirty percent."

"Done. Watch them attorneys Vance, they'll screw you one day. I never use the bastards."

The moving of so much cash from Vance to Nelson did pose a problem but Vance's attorney set it up so Nelson was paid as the office manager. He had to recognize the income for the Feds but, as the attorney pointed out, even after paying tax, he had a sweet deal and a lot of cash for doing nothing. "Pay the gotdam taxes Nelson, for Christ's sake. You don't want the Feds cracking you for evasion and looking into Vance's books do you?"

Nelson agreed and when he left, Vance's attorney said, "Don't trust them slum landlords, Vance. They'd cut their mother off in a bicycle race if there was a buck in it. And what's with that rose anyway? Is the guy a fag or what?"

From this slow start, Nelson soon realized the potential market was wider than his tenants. Much wider. He hired one of them, one of his tenants, a street-smart woman. She was soon driving a van, collecting up neighborhood folks to be brought to "Dr. V's" clinic. On Christmas Nelson threw parties for the children with Santa being played by a large black man from his growing staff. Vance Coleman now had three clinics and Nelson was living large on his thirty percent. And if folks got a little too nosey, for a few hundred, the neighborhood crack gang would do a little chilling out for them.

Life was sweet but after several years, Nelson was ready to pull up, go elsewhere, Colorado maybe. Go anywhere but where he had been. The aftertaste of his hustles was becoming repugnant even to him. It wasn't his conscience that was bothering him. He was starting to sense that people didn't treat him with the respect he felt he had earned. Nelson was now widely known in Miami as a large and regular contributor to political campaigns. Knowing powerful people was good for his business and by association, it allowed Nelson to feel his own importance, even if he had to pay for it. But Nelson had come to believe that people could see him for what he was and not the successful businessman he pretended to be. Lately even the commissioner seemed to avoid him except when he needed a check. At one of the many parties held for shaking down contributions, a lowly county clerk snubbed him. Or maybe it was just the paranoia that came from breaking the law too often and too long. To his date that night he said, "That two-bit thieving pawn. Who does he think he is? I made the little shit what he is." The truth was, the man held the office long before Nelson became a political player. But even a county flunky could detect the fog of sleaze about Nelson and not even the rose could dress it up or make it smell any better.

Maybe it was just the routing grind getting to him, he thought; the same thing day after boring day. He needed a jolt to make him right again and maybe a vacation could do that. And, who knew, maybe the road held an opportunity. But what Nelson was really feeling was a gnawing understanding of what he was and he feared that others were coming to that same understanding. Nelson needed someone to forgive him but being incapable of feeling even guilt on a conscious level, escape would have to do.

Horton County

Nelson Bridges had driven into Seaton almost two weeks before, put his luggage down at the reservation desk of the Seaton Resort and checked in. In his room he drank the larger part of a fifth of gin and fell soundly asleep. The next day he awoke, bathed, dressed and walked down the carpet covered wooden stairs to the dining room. Seated near the window, dressed as he was, he looked out of place. Unlike the casual vacationing guest, he wore an expensive suit and tie with the same withered rose he had worn yesterday. He studied the mountains and the menu, each in turn. He ordered country ham and eggs and a pot of coffee.

Perhaps it was the fresh air or the long ride and sound sleep but after breakfast he felt rested and unaccustomedly pleased with himself. He called for the check and to the waitress asked, "What's the name of that mountain over there, the big one."

"We get the name of the town from that one. That one there's Seaton Mountain. Them three peaks are sure pretty ain't it?"

"Yeah. And that one, just to the left, lower down?"

"Oh that's a beautiful mountain. That one's the Feather. Feather Mountain."

"Really? What do people do around here? I mean besides tourism?"

"Well some do arts and crafts, you know, quilts, rocking chair and that sort of stuff. There's a Wal-Mart, the quick food places but mostly it's just tourists."

"Just here in town? The resort and the motels?"

"There's that and the cabins. Most city folks come for the cabins. They's always rented. And they's always building more."

"People do well at that, do they?"

"Lordy yes. Ifin you have the money to buy two or three, a body wouldn't never have to work a lick again."

"You don't say? By the way, my name is Nelson Bridges. I guess you're Mae, judging from the name tag."

"Yes I'm Mae. Very nice to make your acquaintance Mr. Bridges."

He spent the day driving around the small Victorian town, past the square with the obligatory large oak in front of the court building. The streets were without curbing and most of the houses had gardens. The landscaping of the homes in the town had a similar appearance although no two were exactly alike. Flowers were usually planted near the front of the lots and in beds around the porches and shade trees surrounded the houses. Groomed maples were everywhere and the dogwoods were blooming. Small, quiet and the word "quaint" came to him although he couldn't remember ever using the word. It felt like a good place; a clean town with people who cared for its upkeep. He drove into the countryside, along tree covered lanes, past grass covered farmland with white wooden house and further on, log cabins on the side of hills. It was different but he saw potential here as he drove back into the town. And perhaps more importantly, the people he spoke with that day were accepting of him. The cynical eyes he had grown accustomed to in Miami had not followed him here.

The next morning, after breakfast he asked for a phone book at the desk and looked up real estate offices. There was one on Magnolia Avenue, the same street as the resort.

"Where is 476 Magnolia Ave.?"

"It has to be right near by. This is 220 Magnolia. What are you looking for?"

"Craig Morton's Real Estate."

"Oh goodness me. Craig's office is the little blue house down two blocks on the right. It has the cutest white trim and shutters. You can't hardly miss it."

He walked the few blocks feeling better than he had in months. Yes, he said to himself, this air has to be good for people. Morton wasn't in but when he told his secretary he was interested in buying some rental property she said, "Craig's just over at Alf's eating a little lunch. I'll give him a call and he'll be right over. Have yourself a seat and I'll get him for you."

Morton was dressed in khaki slacks, penny loafers and a blue oxford shirt and Nelson was relieved when he saw Morton without a coat and tie. Nelson Bridges weighed a man's worth and ability by the things he could see and understand. Being what he was, he saw very little except the superficial and that he understood. He could spot a hustler in the beat of a heart and a man's weakness in two. He explained he was interested in buying a few pieces of rental property and asked if the agency could manage the property locally for him. He pegged Craig Morton as a fool.

Morton opened the latest edition of the local listings and showed Nelson several, trying to get an understanding of what Nelson had in mind.

"I could drive you to a few places that I know are on the market but have a look at these and let me know what price range you're looking for. I'll tell you this: if you're looking for a couple of pieces, you get a bigger bang for your buck with the two bedroom units. We're basically a family destination here in Seaton. You know, kids and fishing, canoes in the lake, horse back riding and of course, the big amusement park just outside town. That thing draws them like flies and it keeps getting bigger each year."

"That so?"

"Yes and there's a parcel, a very large parcel, that recently sold to a national concern and they've already started to build an outlet mall."

"But won't that change the place into something that it isn't now. The way this place looks, the town, it's like stepping back in time. Won't that all change? Won't people stop coming when that happens?"

"No. We won't let that happen. The whole town is zoned residential all the way to the lake and the lake is owned by the state and is part of Horton

State Park. This place is pristine and except for the corridor leading to the Interstate, it's going to stay that way."

"Sounds like the town folks thought about this."

"They did and they're good, God fearing people."

"Are you from here?"

"No. I moved down from Ohio a few years ago. Didn't like city life anymore."

"Yes, I can understand that. Too much crime back there."

Nelson Bridges spent the next two weeks driving with Craig Morton looking at property, until it all merged into a blur of log cabins, deck railings and mountain views. They ranged in price from a hundred and fifty up to four hundred and fifty thousand. He saw promise in at least twenty of them and figured on buying three. With the size of his down payment, financing locally would be no problem and he had plenty of idle cash. His take from the Medicare game alone was more than enough. Morton's office managed a large amount of property held by non-resident owners. He ran all the ads, handled the rental agreements, collect the fees, hired maids to clean and wash the linen, and generally did everything for the owners, even the cutting of grass. For this he received forty percent of the gross which was the going price for this service in Horton County. It cut heavily into his profit but from the P & L sheets Nelson had seen it was a sure moneymaker with very few headaches for him. He also liked the idea of writing off a few items he'd buy for his home: a riding lawn mower, power tools and a speed boat which would appear on the expense sheet as being at one of the mountain houses. He knew over time, he would think of others.

Toward the end of this searching, Craig presented another idea to him. "Nelson, maybe I should have mentioned this deal to you before. There's a fellow, a local man, who has eight cabins up on the Feather. I know that's more units than you have in mind but they're really nice places. None older than six years, well cared for and he's asking two and a half million for the bunch. They sit on twenty-five acres on the very top of Feather Mountain and the views are some of the best we have around here. There's plenty of room up there if you'd want to build a few more cabins later on. It maybe more than you wanted to spend but maybe you should take a look before you decide. It could be a fine opportunity Nelson."

"How far is it?"

Craig pointed to a mountain just to the left of the highway maybe three miles away. "Right there. That's the Feather."

"Sure. As long as we're this close."

The road was blacktopped and wound up the side of the mountain following the ridges and sways on a relatively easy gradient. The cabins were fine, better than fine, they were beautiful and well made. The chimneys were made of fieldstone, not the cheap cement kind, shaped and dyed to look like fieldstone. The finished carpentry work was well crafted and mitered in the joints. In some of the other cabins, the cheaper ones, unsightly trim work met at right angles. Some of the joints weren't even chalked.

The furnishings were better quality and the final house, the one at the very top of the Feather, looked more like a luxury home and the windows in the large den looked out over Horton County in three directions. Recessed, built-in bookcases lined the walls. Should he ever live here, this was a house befitting him. A huge stone fireplace dominated the room. This, he was sure, was a house that people would notice.

"The fellow that owns this, why is he selling?"

"His name is Reilley. Owen Reilley. He figures the market is right. He had it built before prices exploded here. He's a country guy. He figures he's got enough now to sell these and move to Florida, take in the sun with his wife."

"Florida? Go figure. That's where I'm from. Two and a half mill is more than I planned to tie up. Let's get the P & Ls and I'll look over them tonight. We'll talk again tomorrow if it looks good."

That night Nelson ate at the hotel as he had most nights. He had the chicken fried steak with mashed potatoes again and when the waitress brought him his food, he spoke to her.

"Mae, you know much about Feather Mountain?"

"I guess everyone around here knows something about the Feather, Mr. Bridges."

"Do you know about those rental cabins on top?'

"Lordy, Lordy, do I? Why them's some of the nicest cabins around and the view! Why it's enough to die for, is what it is. Why, I've even been there myself. Christmas Eve it was. My husband is the day manager over at Billy's Big Barn and two years ago his boss, Mr. Billy Gidley, had the employee Christmas party in one of them houses. Houses, that's what they is. Them's not cabins. No sir, them's fit for homes for somebody.

Mr. Billy had us a big Christmas tree with all the trimmings and had food brought over from the Big Barn. Mr. Billy had presents for all us and all the kids. Mah old man got hisself a five hundred dollar bonus. We had hams, turkeys, pumpkin pies, ice cream and we had us a time, yes sir, we did. And then, as we were leaving and on the way home, it snowed."

Nelson watched her as she remembered the night and the snow of Christmas Eve on Feather Mountain. That, he figured, that was the kind of place that could bring in the people. The P & L statements had looked strong, strong enough for him to start a negotiation.

The next morning he waited for Morton to phone him. He let the phone ring without answering. He looked at his watch. Exactly fifteen minutes later the phone rang again.

"Hi Nelson, Craig here."

"Craig, I was just going to give you a ring. Just stepped from the shower. I looked over those statements last night and the thing is . . . well it's awfully iffy."

"You mean Feather Mountain?"

"Yes, and the whole idea of it Craig. Buying property here. Here I am, eight hundred miles from my home, and I'm thinking about dropping my life savings on something that looks too iffy."

He let this idea sink into Craig, let him realize he had a fish on the line that was just about to shake the hook. Let him realize he probably had lost two weeks of his time, several tanks of gas and a hell of a commission. A commission his wife probably already had made plans for.

After a perfectly timed pause, when he was sure all of this had flashed on the movie screen in Craig's head, he said "The only way I see this deal coming together is if the price comes down and your commission is cut a little."

"Well Nelson we can always talk to the owner about the price but my commission is fixed."

"Cut the bullshit Craig. You have to get the price down a quarter a mill and drop two percent from your side of the deal. Sure you lose a small piece but you're still at a hundred large and that ain't bad for two weeks of work, now is it Craig? And you can manage the rents for thirty percent."

"I'll have to think about it Nelson."

"Sure Craig think about it. Think about losing a hundred grand. I'll hold the phone while you think about that."

There was silence on the phone. Nelson could hear the wheels turning. Craig owned his agency. The property was his listing. He didn't have to split the fee with an owner's agent.

"Ok, Nelson. I'll cut my commission but the rentals have to be at forty percent."

"After you pick up nearly a hundred Gs for driving me around a few days? It's thirty or nothing Craig and we'll put it all in writing so there's no misunderstandings down the line."

Another pause and Craig agreed.

"Fine Craig, fine. And look buddy, anything you can get the owner to knock off more than the two fifty, I'll split seventy-five-twenty-five with you."

"No . . . I can't do that. I'll give it my best try but whatever I save you on the price will be yours. We don't do things like that here Mr. Bridges."

"Have it your way sport. Call me here when you know something."

Nelson then phoned his office in Miami making sure his twice-monthly check for managing Dr. Vance's office had arrived. It had and, as usual, the check was slightly more than the last one.

Before he went down for dinner that evening, the call from Craig came.

"I spoke with Mr. Reilley and he says he'll sleep on it. I'll phone him tomorrow near twelve and get back to you, ok?"

"Fine Craig. I know you can land this one for us. I have faith in you big guy."

He hung up the phone and snickered before lying back on the bed. Nelson was in the zone, high on the adrenaline of a deal. He was playing Craig like a drum and this Reilley, this Hee-Haw, he could be dealt with just as easily.

Craig called back the next day at noon to say Mr. Reilley had gone into town and would return shortly. His wife said she'd have him call the office. Nelson hung up the phone and threw his pen against the wall. He drove around to kill time and he planned not to be in his room when Craig phoned back. He drove over to Feather Mountain and up to the big house at the top. Damn, it was a fine looking place. Thick wood, heavy stone, lots of glass, low stone planters enclosed a large stone patio, manicured flowerbeds. Impressive. Nelson had violated the first rule of the deal. He let himself like the thing more than the investment.

Craig called again at six, after Nelson had returned. This time he didn't let the phone ring. He answered it. Craig told Nelson that Mr. Reilley wanted to meet with him; wanted to see the purchaser personally. He said for Craig to bring him over the next morning.

"What time?"

"He didn't say Nelson, anytime in the morning."

"OK, pick me up at ten."

"Morning starts early for these folks Nelson. Seven-thirty would be better. That would put us at his place for eight or so."

"Fine," he said and placed the handset in its cradle.

The drive out to Reilley's place was somber, neither man now liking the other very much but they were held together by the hope for a concluded deal and a profit. The Reilley home was set back from the road and was framed by two heavily pruned maple trees on the front lawn. It was a white-board house resting on white painted cinder blocks. A porch swing was off to one side. The front door was centered and had a screened outer door. Craig Morton knocked on the wooden frame of the door.

Owen Reilley had gray hair and wore glasses with wire frames. He wore brown slacks and a maroon plaid shirt. Nelson guessed his shoes to be well-worn Rockport walking shoes. Nelson had a difficult time locating the proper pigeonhole. He greeted Craig and took Nelson's extended hand when Craig introduced them.

"I was just going to have some iced tea. Can I get you boys some with a little lemon?"

"Well thank you Owen, I think I'll have a bit if is isn't too much trouble."

Nelson accepted the offer as well. It had been a long drive out to Reilley's home, long and uneasy.

Owen brought them a glass of tea, a saucier with wedges of lemon and each a paper napkin. He spoke of the fall in tobacco prices, the rise of tourism and the weather. It was Nelson, his patience played out, who brought up the cabins on Feather Mountain.

"Owen, I know that Craig has conveyed my offer to you for those cabins up on the mountain. I've seen your P& L statements for each unit and I feel it's a fair offer."

"Well, now, it might be."

"And you might be getting the better side of it too Mr. Reilley," said Nelson with a smile.

"Owen. Call me Owen. My father was Mr. Reilley." He and Craig Morton smiled at each other and Craig nodded his head.

"Fine. Owen it is. Owen, prices here have sky rocketed in the last few years. You and I both know this can't go on forever. I may damn well be paying top dollar. The very top of the market."

"That's true. That sure could be true enough."

"I know about what you paid for the places and I know if you get the two and a quarter mill you'll be set for life. You and Mrs. Reilley will have enough to move to Florida and have a time of it down there for the rest of your lives."

Owen Reilley turned and looked at Craig Morton for half a beat and then studied Nelson's hands. They were soft and fleshy. The nails were clipped and manicured. "Is that a rose you have in your lapel Mr. Bridges?"

"Yes Owen, it is. I love flowers and things like that. 'God's little gifts' my mother called them."

Nice touch thought Nelson. Owen Reilley thought something else.

"Well Mr. Bridges, the land values may have peaked and maybe not but I'm sure you've noticed that much of that acreage is undeveloped. You could subdivide what's left and build a few more cabins up there."

"I had a soil engineer take a look at the place Owen," he lied, "and he said there's plenty of shale up there. Much of that ground is loose and unstable. Maybe I could build a few more places but not on the whole thing."

Owen Reilley raised his tea glass and took a slow sip. He was looking over the glass, out the window.

"Mr. Bridges, that place has a limited water supply. I have the rights to the water it uses from a fellow who lives at the base of the mountain. I pay him about two hundred dollars a month. He's a good old boy, a little slow, and he sold me the water rights at that price but it doesn't transfer to any successor in title. I've already spoken with him and I don't expect any problem or I wouldn't have put the places up for sale. Tell you what. We'll go see him and if he takes to you, you have a deal at two million, four hundred."

"My offer was for two and a quarter."

"Yes, I know and I was asking two and a half."

"Two mill and three hundred."

"Mr. Bridges . . . I gave you my last price."

Nelson looked at Craig who was staring at the tabletop, saying nothing. He looked back at Owen Reilley who looked as though he could have been at a church social or sorting tobacco somewhere. He was drinking his tea, knowing Nelson Bridges was the kind of man he wanted to sell this land to.

"Done and done Owen. Let's go meet this fellow. What's his name?"

"Beddy. Beddy Forrest."

"Beddy Forrest. What kind of name is that?"

"Oh it's a good name Mr. Bridges. And Beddy's a good man; he's just a little slow. His folks passed away some time back and Beddy's all alone now. Folks kind of watch out for him and a lawyer in town handles all his business, what there is these days anyway. He's Beddy's guardian, Beddy not being able to handle his own affairs.

"I think people don't understand about Beddy. He never could learn from books but he's got a knack for things. He makes a little corn liquor up in the holler behind his house, mostly for himself. When his mom passed, Beddy turned to the bottle I guess. She used to take that boy everywhere with her. He was well over forty years old and he would follow her into town like her shadow, not saying very much to anyone. Some folks figured the state would take him once she died but his pa left him with a little something. And his guardian, first it was Oliver and then his son Boyd, well, they try to watch out for him. Lawson's their name. Oliver and Boyd Lawson.

"Beddy has an old pack of dogs up at his place. Some old Blue Ticks and a few Walkers. Good dogs but mostly too old for anything but pets. A little like Beddy in some regard I guess. Beddy doesn't cause anyone any problems and he likes people but he's short on talk. Doesn't much care to, it seems. I suspect he stays drunk most of the time now and he still runs everywhere. Says his daddy told him it would keep him strong as a deer, so he never stopped running places. He runs into town to buy his food and runs home. Must be ten miles round trip and he's getting up there now. Maybe sixty-five or so. The store delivers his groceries and keeps his bill. They send it over to Boyd's law office and they write the check.

"And he still works every day. Grows corn for his shine and a garden for his house. Things for the table that he eats you know. And he's given to howl in the middle of the night every now and again, when he's had too much to drink I suppose. One night he ran down to the Henry place and beat on their door. Lord, lord, ha-ha, he was a fright. His eyes were bugged out; he was panting and speaking in short jumbled up, bursts of words. Claimed to have seen what he called a Goller Roosie up on the Feather. Said it looked like a deer with a goat's head and could run like the wind. It scared him something awful. It chased him and he ran all the way from his place down to Henrys. I don't know what he thinks he saw but it was enough for him to want to sell the top of the mountain. He's a character, nothing more. Harmless really."

"He owned the top of the mountain?"

"He owned the whole thing, all of the Feather. His pa and ma left it to him. And he owns the farmland near his house. His father did well here and I think there's more property he owns. But after that night, he was hell bent on getting rid of that mountaintop. Said the Goller Roosie lived up there."

"Sort of the village idiot?"

"No Mr. Bridges. He just had too much to drink and scared himself. That's all. He's more of a reminder of the good things about this town and its people, its kindness. Seeing Beddy is sort of like looking at the soul of this place."

And after a short pause Mr. Reilley added, "And I understand he's makes a fine jug too."

Craig spoke up at this, "I'm sure he does Owen, I'm sure he does."

And the two of them laughed for reasons Nelson, being an outsider, could only assume.

Beddy and Nelson

Beddy lived in the same house his mother built the year after his father died. It was back against the base of the Feather protected from the north winds in winter. In the summer large oaks and hickories shaded it. There were apple tress and plums beyond his vegetable garden. The rows were neat and well hoed. Corn was just getting tassels and the beans were ripe and full, climbing on poles. Tomatoes were red-orange and weighing down the vines supported by stakes. The roof of Beddy's house was sound and the place was freshly painted. Even to Nelson's eye Beddy worked hard at keeping the place up.

The barking dogs brought Beddy to the screen door before Craig's car pulled to a stop. The three men walked through them and up to the step.

"They's won't hurt ya now. They's jess letting me knowed somebody's here. Bo Thomas, hush up dog. Hush ah say."

The dogs lowered their heads and fell silent. They walked over to the men, sniffing the air. "You all go on now. Go on, git. Ain't nobody wants you bothering no one."

"Thank ya Beddy. Beddy, I brought you a man I want you to meet. Do you think we can go inside and out of this heat?"

Beddy's eyes shifted nervously. He looked at the floor, at their feet and turned to face the door. He turned back around facing Mr. Reilley looking at his shoulder.

"Yes sir, you can."

The house was dark on the inside. A radio was playing softly in another room. Beddy was in overalls and wore a long sleeved shirt even in the heat. He walked over to the table in what Nelson assumed was the dining room. He stood by the rear of the table looking at the floor as the men pulled out their chairs and sat down. Beddy remained standing.

Beddy," said Mr. Reilley, "I know you know old Craig Morton here. He helped us when I bought your land up on the Feather. But I want you to meet this gentleman."

Beddy interrupted Owen to say, "Hi Mr. Morton, sir." He was looking at the window shade.

"Beddy, this here is Mr. Nelson Bridges and I'm thinking of selling him that same property.

"Hello." Beddy was now looking at Nelson's shoes.

Beddy," said Nelson, "I don't believe I've ever heard that name before. Are you named after your father Beddy?"

"No sir. My Pa was James Forrest. James Donald Forrest. Ah was named after my great, great, great uncle, Nathan Bedford Forrest."

"Nathan Bedford Forrest was your great uncle Beddy?"

"Great, great, great uncle. Yes sir, he was that. Yes sir."

"Beddy, your namesake was one of the best generals the South had."

"Yes sir, mah Pa told me that. Did you fight in his army?"

"No, no Beddy. That was a lot before my time but your being related to him, well that's something to be very proud of Beddy. The South had some fine generals and Nathan Forrest was one of the very best."

"Nathan Bedford Forrest and mah name is Beddy, Bedford James Forrest. I'm named after him and my Pa. Beddy. Short for Bedford," and looking at his shoes he added, "yes sir."

"Yes, I see that now Beddy. Very good."

"Beddy, Mr. Bridges is wanting to buy the land from me up on Feather Mountain."

"Yes sir."

"And he needs the water to run the place Beddy, the water rights you sold to me."

"Yes sir." Beddy was looking over their heads at the front door.

"But I can't sell those right to him unless you say I can. Do you understand Beddy?"

"Yes sir, ah do."

"Do you want more money Beddy or is the two hundred dollars still ok with you?"

"Ah don't spent any money Mr. Reilley. Mr. Boyd does that for me."

"We're going to talk with Boyd, Beddy. I just wanted you to meet your new neighbor and see if you were willing to let him buy the water from you."

"That water's special Mr. Reilley. My Pa told me it was."

"Yes Beddy it's very sweet water and it's always cold. A body doesn't need any ice for that water. But will you sell what you sold to me to Mr. Bridges? Would you want him to be your neighbor up on the Feather?"

"Are you from the north Mr. Bridges?"

"No Beddy, I'm from Florida. Miami, Florida. A good southerner . . . like you."

Looking at the floor again but speaking to Mr. Reilley, Beddy said, "Well, he knowed my great, great, great uncle so I guess so."

"Will you tell that to Mr. Lawson, Beddy?"

"Yes sir, ah will."

"That's fine Beddy, that's just fine."

Owen caught Craig's eye for a moment as the men walked to the screen door and the car. Neither man could see anything good or southern about Nelson Bridges.

Boyd Lawson

Craig spoke to Boyd and it took a few days for Boyd to get back to Craig at his office. He had spoken to Beddy and drew up the lease of water rights to Nelson Bridges for the same terms and conditions. At Boyd's office, Nelson read over the document which seemed clear enough.

"No, Mr. Bridges, Beddy just likes to have neighbors he can get along with that's all. Apparently he took to you and he's leasing you the same amount of water for the same price that he had with to Mr. Reilley. Is that right?"

"Un huh."

Well, here's basically the same agreement with your name inserted for Owen's. You see the rights to the water are personal to you just as it was to Owen and the lease is for a hundred years. That's sort of standard for these things. The lease can be broken for cause by either party."

"Cause? Like what?"

"If the well goes dry or becomes too silty to be filtered or if you change the amount of water you use. But that would be pretty hard for you to do. There's a meter at the well head on the Feather and the water Owen uses now is just a little over half of what's allowed. You could build six or seven more units up there and still have water to spare. Here's the clause that covers it. There's no chance of that well playing out. Even in the worse drought it runs full out."

"What if the pipe breaks and water runs all over the place or if the pump goes down?"

"You have to maintain the pump Mr. Bridges and Craig tells me he's going to manage the property for you. If it breaks in any manner, he'll call you, have it fixed and any water wasted by the failure of the well or it's casings are covered here. You can see that wouldn't be "just cause" provided you use due care and it's fixed in a reasonable amount of time. Worse that can happen is you have to drill a new well. The going rate for that is ten dollars a foot. And that well is down over four hundred feet. The casings will cost you a few hundred more. But I'll tell you this, that's the sweetest tasting water you're going to find around here."

"Ok then, this will do."

"I'll sign for Beddy as his guardian Mr. Bridges but don't you want to have your lawyers look this over before you sign?"

"No, I know when I can trust a man."

"That's fine then Mr. Bridges. Lots of us folks here find a man's word better than a written contract. Of course that does hurt my business a little."

"How did you come to be Beddy's caretaker Boyd?"

"Our families go back a long way Mr. Bridges. My family and Beddy's family have been here since the early eighteen hundreds. We watch out for those who need watching, that's all. Beddy's a fine, hard working man. I think he took a liking to you because you knew about Nathan Forrest."

Nelson laughed. "You mean Nathan *Bedford* Forrest. Yes, a fine, fine General." And to himself he added, " . . . and the dumb bastard started the Ku Klux Klan. What rube would want that on his résumé?"

"Yes, Bedford. And Beddy is very proud of his name and his family. To his way of thinking, it connects him with something. Gives him a sense of belonging, I think. We all need that, don't we Mr. Bridges, and Beddy's no different from all of us in that regard."

"It's good that he's here Boyd. I don't think he'd do well in a city. They'd take advantage of him or worse down there. I hate to be returning, to tell you the truth."

"Oh? When are you leaving?"

"Now that the water rights are straightened out, we'll be passing the act of sale tomorrow or the next day. Craig's already cleared Reilley's title and my financing has been lined up for days. It's more than I planned to put out but I think I'll make a few dollars up there."

"I'm sure you will Mr. Bridges."

Sheriff John H. Meyers

Three years later Nelson Bridges was in his Miami office for the last time. He had sold his interest in his run down properties to an acquaintance of the commissioner in Boca. He worked out a time buy-out for his management arrangement with Dr. Coleman to the Medicare coordinator in his office. It was a sweet deal for both of them. He'd continue to pick up fifty or sixty grand for a few years and she would be doing a hell of a lot better than the salary he paid her. The property on Feather Mountain was doing better than he expected. The new outlet mall was bringing them in just as Morton has predicted. Nelson had built ten more cabins using the same contractor that built the original cabins for Reilley. He wanted the same look for the new places, the same upscale feel. From the beginning he had placed guest books in all the cabins. They had space for his visitors to leave a comment or two and their names and home addresses. He had his office send each family a Christmas card from "The Happy Folks on Feather Mountain". He sent them another greeting in early spring, just about the time they'd be making their plans for summer vacation and had built a good bit of repeat business this way. In a few years, with the repeat business, an Internet site and some direct mailings, he would be in a position to eliminate Morton's thirty percent if he chose.

The big place on the top he now kept for himself and had moved most of his furnishings there already. He had bought some massive pieces, which improved the look of the long windowed and bookcased den with the huge stone fireplace. His home in Miami was on the market and he was looking forward to a new life, a life without the same glitz perhaps, but one in which a community would look up to the man who lived atop Feather Mountain in such a grand house.

He knew how things worked in small towns. It was no different than a big city; you just had to get connected. The main difference, he figured, was that the price tag wasn't nearly as high. After he bought Reilley out, he stopped off at the sheriff's office and asked if he could have a moment with Sheriff Meyers. John H. Meyers, Sheriff of Horton County.

"Mr. Bridges, the sheriff will see you now sir."

He walked past the woman, slightly bumping her without acknowledgement, and into the office. Perhaps had he known she was related to the sheriff, he might have excused himself. Things like politeness were noticed in Horton County. Unlike the cities, politeness and civility to those on a lower rung was expected.

"Yes sir, Mr. Bridges, what can I do for you?"

"Sheriff, I'm Nelson Bridges and I guess I'm Seaton's newest resident. I just bought Owen Reilley's cabins up on Feather Mountain and I though I'd come by and introduce myself."

"Well, you're a welcome addition to the community Mr. Bridges. You planning to live here are you?"

"No, not yet anyway. My business in Miami will keep me there a few more years but I hope to be spending my free time up here."

"You'll like it here. Plenty of fresh air, good fishing and real nice folks. And you bought yourself some mighty fine cabins Mr. Bridges, mighty fine."

"I've been here a few weeks sheriff and I have to agree with you. The air is as good as it gets and the people couldn't be friendlier. But sheriff there is a small matter on my mind. Craig Morton here in town will be managing the renting of the units but I'm a little worried about vandalism and, well, you know . . . burglaries, that sort of thing."

"None of the local do much of that Mr. Bridges. And living around here doesn't give a man many places to hide himself. We know who the bad apples are and the little thievery we do have comes mainly from some of the tourists who come up here with the wrong idea. We tend to come down on those boys pretty hard so word gets around. Tourism is the lifeblood of the county now and our judges here aren't about to let outside riff-raff ruin it for everybody."

"Glad to hear it sheriff, glad indeed. Look," he said, reaching inside his suit jacket and removing a folded check, "I know you fellows have a lot of responsibility and on top of all that you have to run for re-election every few years. Here's a small donation for your past campaigns and please put me on your list of contributors for your next one. I understand these things are expensive."

The sheriff unfolded the check and seeing it was for a thousand dollars said, "Mr. Bridges, I've never had a hard race in my life. My father was the sheriff before me and his uncle was before him. In Horton County, people just know who's who and re-election comes sorta easy for us."

"Well sheriff the check is made out to you personally, so use it how you see fit. I'm sure you have some good community purpose you can use it for."

"Well, on behalf of the community, I thank you Mr. Bridges."

"My pleasure sheriff," said Nelson Bridges as he rose and turned to leave. The sheriff stood and when Nelson opened the door, he turned to Sheriff Meyers and said, "Sheriff, if it wouldn't be too much trouble, could you have one of your units drive to the cabins every now and then, just to keep check on the place?"

"A marked car is usually up there twice a day Mr. Bridges. Been that way since Owen built the first one. Every county road is cruised twice a day, every day here. Your cabins are safe."

"Well, I couldn't ask for more than that. Thank you sheriff and I'll be seeing you."

"Have a safe trip home Mr. Bridges."

When he left, the receptionist walked into the office. "Uncle John, who was that awful man?"

"Just a fellow from Miami who brought some cabins here. A man with his eye on something bigger I think."

"Well that foolish rose and his rudeness ain't going to help him none around here, that's for sure."

A few weeks later, balancing his bank statement, Nelson noticed the check had been endorsed over to the Seaton Baptist Church Auxiliary. He held the check in his right hand while he studied it a few moments. His left hand was bent up towards his lapel fingering his rose. Then, with a flick of his wrist, he let the check sail into an open file marked "Feather Mountain Properties".

Feather Mountain

With the satellite dish, the football package and his cell phone, Nelson Bridges was ready for the start of the football season. He enjoyed the quiet of the place but he couldn't watch the Dolphins or the Canes without at least a dime on the games. He even had rose bushes planted in the sunny parts of the garden around his home. When dressed for town, his last steps were to the garden, to select a bud for his lapel. The folks who stayed at his cabins were gone for most of the day, off boat riding or at the amusement park or spending money for things they didn't need at the outlet shops. Occasionally Nelson would drive into town for a meal or into to Knoxville for the day. The mortgage on the place was sizable since he added the new cabins but the guests were booked for months in advance and he had no cash flow problems. By all measures and accounts, he was set and never felt healthier in his life. He had briefly met the Mayor of Seaton, a judge or two and the county commissioners for Horton County. Things, he hoped, would take a definite turn for the better after he hosted a party for the mayor at his home. Nelson had gone to the county clerk's office and paid for a printout of the new voters who had registered in the county over the past five years. With that list in hand he made an appointment with the mayor.

The name on the glass door read Mayor Orin Tunney, III and his receptionist rose to hold it open for Nelson's entry.

"Afternoon Mayor Tunney. Perhaps you heard of me. I'm Nelson Bridges and I own the cabins up on the Feather."

"Mr. Bridges," he said as he stood to shake his hand, "yes I have and good morning sir."

For a few minutes they made the small talk of a small town before getting to the reason for Nelson's call.

"Mayor, you run a nice town here and I know that's not an easy thing to do. Lots of things are changing. The amusement park and mall are bringing in a lot of new folks and a lot are moving here because of it. I see all the new homes going up and I don't think it going to stop anytime soon either. And all those new folks moving here may not see things the same way we do. A few days ago," at this point Nelson began opening a folded spreadsheet, "I had the clerk's office run a listing of the voters registration of people who were newly registered just over the past five years. It's over fifteen hundred new votes around the county and almost five hundred of those are right here in Seaton."

He rolled out the sheet on the mayor's desk allowing it to fall on the floor and run a few more feet. He had the mayor's attention.

"It's something I was aware of Mr. Bridges but didn't realize the full extent."

"I was thinking the best way for these new folks to feel welcome and to get to know you would be to have a get together for them where they could meet their new neighbors and the mayor.

"Mr. Bridges, that's a fairly large crowd and I . . ."

"You wouldn't have to do a thing Orin. I figure out of five hundred maybe half will show up. Three fifty tops with their kids. Why we could easily handle that at my place on the Feather. I'll put on an old fashioned bar-b-que with all the trimmings. You know, hot dogs, hamburgers, chicken, potato salad, some sodas for everybody . . . that sort of thing. Families with kids. Balloons. Be a good chance for them to meet their mayor and to remember you come election time.

The mayor held up the spread sheet, looking at the names, addresses and party affiliations of the newly registered. "How much will this be costing me Mr. Bridges?"

"Nothing Orin. Nothing at all. I'm only too happy to sponsor this party. My chance to pay back my new community for all the good things going on here. I like living here. I like the way you do things and I want to do my part to see that the town continues to prosper. As long as it continues to do well, so will my business."

Nelson Bridges was smiling broadly and nodding his head at this last.

Mayor Tunney moved his eyes back to the sheet in his hand. "When would you wanting to have this party?"

"Three or four weeks depending on when we can get the invitations printed. A few days to have them addressed, dropped in the mail . . . not long."

"You may have a fine idea here Mr. Bridges and I appreciate your doing this. For the town."

"I do need just one thing Mayor. Parking is going to be a problem. There's no way all those cars can fit on top at one time. Now I can arrange to have a crew of drivers running folks up and down the mountain if you can talk to Beddy Forrest about letting the folks park somewhere on his land."

"I believe that can be done. Beddy's a good old fellow and I'll run out to his place tomorrow and clear it with him. I'll give Boyd a call about it today."

"Great mayor. Do you know Beddy very well do you?"

"Most of us old timers know Beddy, Mr. Bridges. A little eccentric maybe but a good man."

"And Boyd Lawson. Does he sort of steer Beddy around, does he?"

"No, not in that sense," the mayor was smiling. "Beddy has a knack for things. He may not understand things the way you or I do but he understands in a good enough way and things are usually right for him. Makes most of his own decisions himself. Boyd just makes sure he's protected, you know, contracts and legal matters. Watches his money because Beddy would most likely give it all away. Mostly Beddy just makes a little shine and minds his own business."

"Well, if you can handle the parking mayor," said Nelson rising to leave, "I'll take care of the rest. I'll give your secretary a call on the date just as soon as I work out the invitations and the rest. One other thing. The party is going to be in your honor but maybe you'd like to invite your staff here and Sheriff Meyers and a few commissioners . . . and any members of the community you feel should be there. It would be good to have a mix of the old and new people. Get to know one another, don't you think? I can just get the list from your people and just add them to the invitations."

"Fine idea, Mr. Bridges, mighty fine."

"Call me Nelson, Orin. Nelson will do just fine."

Hunter Henley

The bar-b-que at Nelson's place was better than Mayor Tunney had hoped. A crowd of newcomers, larger than he expected, and a good mix of county and town folks turned out. It seems there was a lot of curiosity about the cabins on the Feather, the view from the top most had heard of but few had seen, and about the new owner himself. Nelson made a short, very short, welcoming speech and introduced the mayor, Sheriff Meyers and the handful of commissioners who though it in their interests to make an appearance. They smiled at Nelson Bridges and shook his hand and the community folks, it seemed, were taken with this man of apparent substance who came from Miami to live here. Nelson mingled through the crowd, shaking hands, laughing at bad jokes and was pleased with himself. He judged that these people, including the sheriff, were seeing him in a different light. He could feel their eye upon him and Nelson Bridges felt strange receiving their approval and admiration and he smiled in return.

As the day was drawing to and end, just as the sun was starting to touch the top of Seaton Mountain, Nelson moved a bit close to the edge of the garden wall and watched it set. He could see lighter rays being sent skyward, framing the crest of the mountaintop. He was thinking a shot of that would look great on a printed ad for the place. He was still thinking of that when a well-dressed man and his wife approached him.

"Mr. Bridges, allow me to introduce myself. I'm Hunter Henley. This is my wife Eleanor." Nelson had noticed the couple earlier. Even at a distance there was a noticeable ease about them, an air of polite confidence. Now seeing them nearer and hearing the man's voice, Nelson understood that ease to mean they were neither envious of the surroundings nor overly impressed. They were comfortable in a home like this.

"Very pleased to meet you. May I get either of you something? A glass of Chardonnay perhaps?"

"No, no thank you Mr. Bridges. Very kind but we have to be on our way. Eleanor and I wanted to thank you for the day and tell you that you have a lovely home."

"Thank you and I am very pleased that you could come."

"What a lovely sunset. I'm afraid I find myself quite jealous Mr. Bridges," said Eleanor.

"It does seem extra nice today. I was just noticing it."

"Mr. Bridges, I see that you have a considerable amount of land here that remains undeveloped."

"Please Hunter, call me Nelson."

"Fine, Nelson it is."

"Yes, there's several acres that could be developed but, for the moment at least, I like the appearance of the trees and having the cabins scattered about. Adds a feeling of nature and privacy to the place I think."

Hunter Henley made a slow turn and he, his wife and Nelson began walking across the stone of the garden walkway towards the house. "I have an idea I'd like to put to you. Would you mind if I phone sometime? Are you in the book?"

"Yes I am. Call any time. Perhaps we could have dinner sometime."

Again Eleanor spoke. "Yes, that would be wonderful. There's an adorable little restaurant on Cove Road. La Cuisine. Do you know it? I don't know if I prefer the food or the ambiance more. And for a small place, it has a remarkable selection of very good wines."

"No, I haven't heard of it. Perhaps we can do that soon. In fact, I insist we do it this week but the night shall be on me. Would Thursday do Hunter?"

"Yes Nelson, we'd love that. Thursday then. I'll make the reservations for six o'clock, call you to confirm and give you the directions."

They had crossed on the walkway to the front of the house and Nelson waived to one of the men driving the vans shuttling the guest to their cars. As the van drove up, Hunter turned to face Nelson and shaking his hand said, "This was a fine day Nelson. Thank you again and we'll see you for dinner."

"My pleasure" and turning slightly and nodding to her, Nelson said, "Eleanor."

The van turned in the drive and Nelson walked in through the front door. Most of the guests had departed but Mayor Tunney and Sheriff Meyers were still there with their wives. The mayor turned to Nelson and said, "Nelson this was a fine idea. I believe I can't remember a finer party. And these newcomers seem to be fine, fine citizens."

"I believe it went well mayor. We'll match all the names in the guest book with the voters' registration for their addresses and follow up with a personal letter from you saying how nice it was to meet them. I'll have it all at your office by Friday ready for your signature.'

"Well I'll be. Is that how you fellows do it in Miami?"

"That's part of it mayor, just part of it."

The mayor and Nelson laughed. The wives looked at each other and Sheriff Meyers just smiled politely and watched Nelson's eyes.

In the van driving down Feather Mountain, Sheriff Meyers looked at the mayor. "Mr. Mayor . . ." and switching to the mayor's first name, he continued, "Orin, I just . . ."

"John, do you really think it's necessary?" And the mayor grinned. His wife smiled and the three of them looked at the sheriff.

He laughed and said, "No. Orin. It ain't. Just making sure I knew which way the wind was blowing that's all."

* * *

The call from Hunter Henley came the following afternoon and dinner plans for Thursday were finalized. That morning Nelson had driven to Craig's office and the two of them reviewed the monthly receipt and expense statement for the cabins. When they were finished, Nelson asked Craig if he knew Hunter Henley.

"They moved here about three years ago I think. Quiet; go to the United Methodist. Wife's name is Eleanor. Children are grown and live elsewhere. He was in the hotel business as I recall. Picked a wonderful old Victorian near the lake. A fine home with a wonderful view of the lake and well away from the noise of the town. I believe he's looking for a site to build a lodge or a small resort."

"You don't say?"

"He was shortly after moving here. Maybe he's changed his mind since then. I showed him a few places I thought had promise but nothing came of it. I know he also had Dub James show him some properties after that."

"Interesting. You know where they're from?"

"Michigan, up state New York maybe. Not really sure. Why?"

"They were at the bar-b-que and we spoke briefly. Curious is all. Look, instead of my waiting, just mail the check out with a copy of the summary sheet. I've got to do some work around the house today and I best be getting to it."

Craig rose when Nelson stood up to leave and as he turned Craig said, "That was some party you threw Nelson. Lots of folks are talking about it."

"Glad to hear it Craig. Maybe we'll make it an annual thing."

"If you do, me and the Missus will be back for sure."

Nelson turned to leave thinking Craig was starting to sound a little too much like the locals. Before he left, he said, "Take care Craig, keep up the good work and keep making money for both of us."

"You know I will Nelson, that's for sure."

Idiot thought Nelson.

Nelson pulled his car to the side of the last cabin. He opened the door and stepped out onto the broken granite chips of the parking area. The stones crunched beneath his shoes as he walked to the edge of the drive. He continued to walk on grass to the rear of the house. A broad, gently sloping field, seven acres more or less, was covered with shrubs and a few small trees. It had been lumbered over certainly. He planned to use part of this site for his next expansion. He turned to the west and looked at the massive form of Seaton Mountain. From where he stood, he was certain that from the center of the field and perhaps at an elevation of, say thirty feet or so, the view would be spectacular. And in the opposite direction, the view of sunrise would be unobstructed. A lodge? Hotel?

He drove past the lower cabins up the gentle grade to his home at the top of Feather Mountain. He sat at his desk, turning things over. Why would he need Henley? He knew immediately that he lacked the organization skill and know-how to run such a place himself. And all of his money, or most of it anyway, was tied up in the cabins. The mortgage on those had him stretched as far as his credit would take him. So doing it on his own was clearly out.

What did Henley have in mind? A partnership? A buy out? Selling the cabins and his house was definitely out. Things were just falling together for him here in Horton County and he liked being on the mountain. That left selling him the seven acres or a partnership. If a partnership were on Henley's mind, the only thing he could put up would be the land, no cash. And for the land, he'd have to get a big piece of the pie. It was then that Hunter Henley phoned to confirm for Thursday.

La Cuisine

The directions to the restaurant were easy enough. A right along Cove Road about three-quarters of a mile on the left. A small hand painted sign over the door read "La Cuisine". There were two bay windows in the front and the lawn was covered with climbing ivy. Small trees hid most of the building from Cove Road. The golden-yellow light shown through the windows and on to the ivy. Nelson parked in the side lot and walked up the stone walkway. He could see through the two windows that the walls were thick and sealed with a coat of heavy mortar. They appeared old. The rear wall housed several large recessed wine racks. A single small candle was on each table. Several simple brass chandeliers with no more that six or seven small, dim lights illuminated the dining area. He saw Hunter and Eleanor immediately and Hunter stood as Nelson crossed the floor between the tables of other diners. They shook hands and he greeted Eleanor. She mentioned his rose as he pulled his chair beneath him.

"Yes, it's become something of a habit I'm afraid."

"Well it's one I find charming Mr. Bridges."

"Nelson, please call me Nelson, Eleanor. And you certainly were right about the ambiance. Understated and lovely. Excellent and if the food is as good as the surrounding . . . and the company, this will be a wonderful evening."

"The company will do its best Nelson but I assure you, the food will surprise you."

Nelson could care less about the food. He was consumed with the hunt and high on the adrenaline of the deal. But he maintained his most polite face and spoke words of appreciation for the food. For dessert Nelson had the almond tart and it was over coffee before Hunter brought up the purpose for the evening.

"Nelson, you might remember my discussing the mountain when we were there the other day."

"The mountain?"

"Yes. I had mentioned I had an idea I wished to discuss with you."

"Yes, of course, I do remember now. Forgive me."

"Nelson, I was in the resort and hotel business most of my life. I've had a few places of my own and I worked for several of the larger chains as well."

"I see," said Nelson in a manner to convey that he did not see.

"I retired several years ago but the business . . . I'm afraid it stays in the blood and I found I don't retire very well."

"Oh, he does well enough but I think he just needs a small place to run for a hobby," said Eleanor with a smile.

"I have more than a hobby in mind Nelson. I have a number of financial backers and I've been looking for a suitable place and I think I found it."

"Oh?"

"Yes. I believe that large field just beyond the cabins you have would be just right for what I have in mind."

"Really? I was planning my expansion in that direction Hunter."

"It would be a natural for your expansion, I have to agree with that, but we are prepared to offer you a considerable sum for that location and the use of the existing road. You also have the right in your act of sale to widen that road by three feet on either side. We, as a part of the agreement would want to do that widening. At our expense naturally. And we'll have to secure water from your well head or be permitted to dig our own well. Actually, we prefer the latter and you would have to obtain that right for us from the present owner."

"It would have to be a serious amount Hunter. That parcel has a fine view of sunrise and sunset. I've already had my contractor have the health department run soil tests for the field lines and I'm planning the location of the new buildings. What figure did you have in mind."

Hunter slipped his hand into his jacket pocket, retrieved his pen and wrote a figure on his napkin. Nelson, reading the numbers upside down, struggled to keep his disbelief and his emotions on a tight rein. Hunter slid the napkin over to his side of the table and turned it around so Nelson could see it. Three million, two hundred thousand.

Nelson picked it up and looked at it without emotion.

"You're right Hunter, it is a fair offer I suppose." He placed the napkin back on the table and paused before he spoke again. "I hope you understand. I never expected to sell any of the place. I have plans to expand as I said. Mind I'm not saying no; I'm saying I'd like to sleep on it awhile and see how this would affect my business. The extra traffic, the noise . . . Construction on that scale will certainly have a bad effect on my revenue. I just want to weigh these things. But in all fairness Hunter, I must tell you that I'm at a point where things were just starting to jell up there. This would take things into an entirely different direction for me."

He could feel the tension rise in Hunter; he caught the slight twitch in the corner of his eye. He knew there was more to be had if he let Hunter run a bit.

"We believe we took into account your possible loss during construction but I certainly understand Nelson. I know this has to come as a surprise. Take some time thinking about my offer but I will have to know something by Friday after next. In the meanwhile, I have a few places I'm still looking at. Give me a call when you've decided."

"I will Hunter. I certainly will. Would either of you care for a brandy," Nelson asked, but his mind was now on water.

The Deal and Beddy

Nelson phoned Boyd Lawson's office and made an appointment to see him the next afternoon. A simple matter, he was sure. Just a matter of how much the simpleton would want for the water. The following day he had lunch at the Seaton Resort before walking to the law office.

"I'll have just the soup today Mae."

"Fine Mr. Bridges. Forget your rose today?"

Nelson raised his lapel and saw he had forgotten his rose.

"I guess my mind was on the weather today Mae. I guess I did forget."

"You don't kook like you without that rose Mr. Bridges. Better get you one."

"It's quite a ride back to my garden Mae."

"Well, you jess be careful now. Without your rose, you might have bad luck today."

"Not likely but I'll be careful. I always am."

"Oh I'm jess teasing you Mr. Bridges. Let me get that soup."

Boyd opened his office door when his secretary let him know that Nelson had arrived.

"What can I do for you Mr. Bridges?"

"Boyd I plan to see Beddy about this but I wanted to touch base with you first. It's about the water on Feather Mountain Boyd. You know I've built a few more cabins up there and I'm thinking about adding a few more."

"How many more?"

"I don't know for sure. Things are going well and adding a few cabins would sure bring in some more tourists into town and help me with the mortgage on the place. Maybe five or six."

"I'll have the figures run on the meter we have at the wellhead. Those monthly figures are sent directly to Beddy so I don't know how much you're using now. But you've added quit a few cabins already and you might be close to your limit as it is."

"I'll probably go over the limit for sure and I wanted to see Beddy about, oh, maybe doubling or more it just to be on the safe side."

"If it's ok with Beddy, Nelson, I have no objection. Of course we'll have to increase the fee accordingly but . . . Look, I have to tell you, Beddy's funny about that water. It's part of the same flow that forms that stream by his house. He's always making sure it flows free. He uses it to water his corn and garden. It's his drinking water too. I guess he sold those rights to Owen because he wanted to sell the top of the mountain and he liked Owen. A big reason was it didn't cut noticeably into the flow rate of his creek there. I figure he was sorta used to the idea when he sold them to you. Don't be surprised if he says no. To you and me, and to most people I suppose, it's just a creek. But to Beddy it's something sacred; something that keeps him going. Maybe it gives him a purpose. It's like he's caring for something that needs him as much as he needs it. Beddy's got his ways and some are strange alright."

"Beddy's a fine man Boyd. We always wave and he comes up to look at my flowers every now and then. We get along fine. Why, he even gave me some vegetables from his garden. I'm sure he won't object."

"Well good then. Have him give me a call and I'll take care of everything."

Nelson drove home and changed into a pair of blue jeans and a plaid shirt. The blue tassel loafers he wore removed any doubt about his ease in such an outfit. He drove downhill and turned into Beddy's drive. The home was back against the base of the mountain and nearly hidden by the trees. The corn was high and the breeze was tossing the yellow tassels. He blew the horn about half way down the drive to alert Beddy of his coming. When he pulled even with the house, Beddy was standing at the door.

"Hi ya Beddy."

"Mr. Bridges. Yes sir. What can ah do fur ya?" Beddy was looking at a post on his porch.

"Beddy I have a couple of things to ask you."

"Yes sir."

"Beddy my roses are looking bad. Not dying, just looking weak sorta."

"Yes sir." Beddy was looking at Nelson's car.

"Do you have any idea of something I can put on them to pick them up?"

"You still using 10-10-10?"

"Yes, sure am."

"Sulfur, Epsom salts and cottonseed meal, um huh, yes sir. Mix it up together. Cup of sulfur and a tiny cup each of salts and cottonseed meal. Yes sir."

"Think that will do it?"

"Yes sir it will."

"Fine Beddy. That brings me to something else I have to ask you."

Beddy was now watching the corn move in the breeze.

"I'm thinking about putting a few more cabins up on the Feather Beddy."

"Yes sir."

"And I might be needing some more water."

"Yes sir."

"Would you be willing to sell me some more Beddy?"

"I don't know Mr. Bridges."

"Why Beddy? Is there a problem?"

"How much would you be needing then?"

"About the same amount as I'm getting now."

"You already have that much, yes sir."

"No, no. That's not what I meant Beddy. I wasn't very clear was I? I meant I need that amount plus what I'm getting now. Maybe a little more."

"That might would dry up mah creek. And mah daddy told me to take care of the creek."

"Beddy we could get one of them scientists from the Agriculture Department to come and run tests on it. They have ways of telling how much water can come from that flow. They call that flow an aquifer and they have ways of knowing how much water can come from it."

"Depends on the rain," said Beddy watching the funny looking strips of leather on top of Nelson's blue shoes.

"What?"

"Water depends on tha rain. When it don't rain, the water don't flow as much. Them fellas with their books and papers. I don't trust them, no sir. Mah daddy told me, 'Beddy', he said,' Any man come to your door with a bible or a bunch of papers in his hand, run him off. He's meaning to sell yer something or steal something.'" These were more words than Beddy had spoken all week and Nelson could see his deal with Hunter going quickly south.

"Beddy, it's important to me. It's important to the roses. We need some more water for the roses and some more cabins."

"Roses have enough water. They need sulfur, Epsom salts . . ."

"Beddy," Nelson's voice was rising. "Beddy, do you want more money because I'll triple what I'm paying you now."

"Mr. Boyd's got mah money. Don't need no more."

"Beddy perhaps I wasn't clear enough. I need that water and I'm willing to pay a lot for it. Will you please help me."

Beddy was looking at Nelson's hands.

"Ah'll help you Mr. Bridges but ah can't be selling you that much water. Mah pa always told me to take care of the spring. Yes sir." Beddy was looking at Bo Thomas lying in the sun.

"We'll take care of the spring Beddy. I promise. You and I. We won't let anything happen to it."

"You don't know about this spring, no sir. And you don't know about tha land or any other land either. Yer hands, they's too smooth and yer got no dirt under yer nails. No calluses either. You don't work for your money. You live offen those who do."

Nelson grabbed Beddy's shirt beneath his collar and twisted it. "You ignorant son . . ." He got no further than those words when Beddy placed his right hand on his chest over Nelson's and hit Nelson's elbow locking it straight. The jolt gave Nelson a sharp pain and it increased as Beddy held the pressure on the joint.

"Don't do that Mr. Bridges." Beddy was now looking directly into Nelson's eyes.

"I'm sorry Beddy but . . ." Beddy released him. "I'm sorry. I was carried away Beddy. I have a bad temper but I meant no harm."

"I want you to leave Mr. Bridges." He was still looking at Nelson's eyes and Nelson knew enough to know he better leave.

"Leave now."

The next morning Nelson showed up at Boyd Lawson's office without an appointment. He was told Boyd would be out but could see Nelson the following Monday at three in the afternoon. Nelson used the pay phone in the lobby of the Seaton resort to phone Hunter Henley.

"Hunter? Yes, Nelson here. Hunter I've given your proposition some thought and it may be doable. I'm leery, as you know, about my loss of income. If your team is willing to assure my same gross income as last year plus an expected growth of, say ten percent, we may have something."

Nelson switched his weight to his other foot while listening to Hunter's reply.

"Yes, that's what I mean. If there is a short fall from last year plus ten percent, than you fellows have to make up the difference."

Another pause.

"Yes I know that your offer was to include any potential business loss but . . . what if construction runs over schedule and what of any future construction? These things have to be considered. You've got me interested in a general way, I like the concept, but these things have to be worked out."

He shifted his weight again and held out his lapel. Today's rose was bright red but one petal already had a dark edge.

"Hunter perhaps if that's not possible, than a percentage of the net profit would work. A small percentage."

Pause. Shift.

"Yes, yes, I understand. Can you get back to me, oh say, next Wednesday then?"

Short pause.

"That's fine Hunter. Yes, yes, of course. Until then and please say hello to Eleanor."

Leaving his car parked in the Lawson parking lot, Nelson walked to city hall and into the mayor's outer office.

"Is Mayor Tunney in? Tell him it's very important."

"Yes sir, Mr. Bridges, I'll see." She entered the mayor's office closing the door briefly behind her but opened it again almost immediately.

"Mayor Tunney can see you Mr. Bridges."

Nelson walked to where the mayor was standing and extended his hand.

"Nelson, good to see you. But you look upset my boy. What can I do for you?"

"Orin, I need your help and the influence of your good offices."

"Meaning?"

"I need you to talk to Beddy for me. I'd like to buy a little more water from him and, well, he says he can't do it. I know he respects you. Look how easy it was for you to get us that parking space for the party."

It would have been wiser for Nelson not to have been so transparent but either way, the mayor would not be able to help him with Beddy.

"Nelson, have you've already spoken to Beddy?"

"Yes. But I got no where. Maybe I lost my temper a bit."

"Oh?"

"Yes. Probably said the wrong thing."

"Nelson, as much as I'd like to, I can't help you with Beddy. Particularly when it comes to that water and his spring. Beddy's, well you know Beddy's not as right as he should be, and he's set in his ways. He figures that spring is what keeps his crops and that valley alive. I know it's sounds strange to you but we grew up with Beddy and we're used to the way he thinks about these things. I could ask but it won't do any good. Once Beddy's made his mind up, he sticks to it. Them Forrests are a strong willed people."

"Yeah, I know about them Forrests all right. I know who started the Klan around here too."

"Yes," Orin Tunney stiffened but not enough for Nelson to notice, "there's that too and none of us around here are proud of that and I doubt if Beddy ever heard of the Klan. That's part of history Mr. Bridges, nothing we can do except see that it doesn't happen again. But that was over a hundred years ago and I was talking about the will of those people. Beddy's grandfather and father made it here when many couldn't and they both helped other folks when they could. Yes, Nathan started the Klan and you're free to think of him as you want but let me tell you about Nathan's mother, Marian. She was married to William, Nathan's father, who died and left her with eleven kids, Nathan among them. Nathan was sixteen years old when his father died. Marian and her son, Nathan, raised those kids. Mirian and his aunt were returning home from a neighbor's one night with a basket of chickens. They were on horseback and they noticed a mountain lion was following them. They figured the cat wanted those chickens but Mirian was of no mind to lose them. As she crossed a stream, the lion leaped on both her and her horse. She reached home, her clothes badly torn and her back and shoulders bleeding. The horse died but she still had the basket of chickens. And it didn't stop there. Nathan took off with his dogs and shot the thing after they treed it. He came home with the ears and scalp of that beast.

That's an historical fact Mr. Bridges and that's the bloodline and the will you're up against. And all the Forrests from here have it, even Beddy. If his mind is made up, that's all she wrote son."

The days remaining until the following Monday and his appointment with Boyd Lawson passed with agonizing slowness for Nelson. Boyd would talk to Beddy, he told himself. Boyd Lawson was a reasonable man. He was an attorney wasn't he? They spoke the same language. He could be reasoned with. Sure, he knew he was more than set for life even if this deal fell through but with a windfall of this size, he could go places. Maybe buy a winter place. Or maybe a small apartment in Europe. Yes, he could see that. He laughed to himself: Nelson Bridges, slum landlord and Medicare hustler in a room overlooking . . . overlooking what? Some place in Paris maybe. Some place with a name people would recognize. And thinking these thoughts, he was able to sleep nights peacefully until Monday finally arrived.

At one o'clock, Nelson bathed and laid out his clothes. He selected a black double-breasted suit and a white shirt with French cuffs so he could wear his onyx links with the single centered diamond. He gave more thought to the watch should he wear. A dress watch for sure. The Cartier or the Rolex? He quickly decided that Boyd would see through his reason for wearing the ostentatious Rolex so he decided instead on the understated Jump Hour Cartier. Having selected the Cartier, he replaced the cuff links he had chosen with a simple gold pair. His tie was black. He stood before the full-length mirror studying himself, making sure his appearance conveyed exactly the right message.

He stepped out the rear door and walking to his car he stopped to select the proper rose. A deep red for sure.

He timed his arrival at Boyd's office to be fifteen minutes late. Once there, he had to wait an additional fifteen minutes before he could enter and that unexpected delay disrupted his rhythm a bit. Boyd sat on the sofa against the wall at a right angle to his desk. Behind the desk sat his father, Oliver Lawson.

Pointing to the chair at the front of the desk, Oliver Lawson said, "Have a seat Mr. Bridges. I'm Oliver Lawson and Boyd tells me you have some business you wish to conduct today." Neither man stood as Nelson entered the room.

"This is an honor Mr. Lawson. I've heard quite a bit about you since moving here."

"Really? What have you heard Mr. Bridges?"

"That you're one of the first attorneys in Horton County and the very first in Seaton. I know that you are Boyd's father and I also hear that you are a fine gentleman and a damn good lawyer." Nelson emitted a small nervous laugh. The men sat silently until the older Lawson spoke again.

"Those are kind words Mr. Bridges. What can I do for you?"

Nodding to the side to where Boyd was sitting Nelson said, "I was hoping Boyd, or perhaps you, if you would, could intercede on my behalf with a client of yours."

"And which client would that be Mr. Bridges?"

"Beddy. Beddy Forrest."

"Beddy's more than a client Mr. Bridges. The court says he's under our care but he's more. He's a friend of our family. In fact, he *is* our family Mr. Bridges."

Sensing the shifting wind, Nelson said, "Yes, I certainly understand the closeness of the relationship Mr. Lawson and that is why I'm here today."

"Please, go on."

"I went out to see Beddy the other day and things didn't go very well."

"We heard."

"I assumed you did," Nelson lied, "and that's why I came here, to make things right with Beddy."

"Oh?"

"Yes. You see, I've got some expansion I want to do up on the Feather but to do it, to build more cabins and bring in more guests and visitors to Seaton, I have to buy more water from Beddy. As you know, Beddy limits the amount I can use up there. I went to see him about it and things sort of got out of hand. You gentlemen know how things can get heated in even the smallest of business dealings. It was clearly my fault and I'd like to tell Beddy how sorry I am and . . . at the same time I'd like to retain your firm to negotiate the sale of the new water rights for Beddy and I."

"That would create a conflict of interest for us wouldn't it Mr. Bridges?"

"I don't think so Oliver. It's just a small agreement between two friends put together by two other friends."

"How much are you willing to pay Beddy for his water?"

Nelson felt relief for the first time since he entered the office. He could begin to feel the familiar tapping coming from the end of his line. In a moment he'd pull back.

"I pay two hundred a month now and that takes care of the cabins and then some. I don't plan to use much more than that but I'd like to change it to, oh say, that plus a similar amount. Even more if it would help Beddy. Like I said, I probably won't ever use close to that amount but rather than fine tuning it every time I add a cabin, I'd just pay for that amount even if I never use it."

"So you'd like to double the water amount, is that correct?"

"Yes, I'll never use near that much, as I said. And it should work out fine for Beddy. I'll even pay more than twice what I'm paying now."

"How much more?"

"Five hundred a month. Five hundred seems fair."

"And how much will you pay us for negotiating this for you?'

"Whatever you fellows think is fair Oliver."

"I guess you'll want us to draw up the agreement too, right?"

"Yes, of course."

"And file it in the county office?"

"Yes certainly, the whole enchilada. What will it run me?"

"Nothing Mr. Bridges, not a thing. Beddy's not interested."

Nelson felt Paris slip away and his stomach filled with a familiar emptiness.

"But . . . I'm sure . . ."

"That's the end of it; the answer is no. Beddy told us what happened out there Mr. Bridges. He didn't mention your grabbing him at first but it came out. Beddy's a simple man and he simply doesn't understand why you or anyone would want to hurt him. He's an innocent Mr. Bridges, much like a child. And like a child, he's trusting and kind. He doesn't recognize greed because there's none of it in him. We'd all be better off being more like Beddy instead of the other way around. He's a strong man Mr. Bridges. I'm sure you noticed that the other day. To Beddy you're not a threat, you're nothing more than an unanswered question. To me, I know what you are, and if you lay another hand on Beddy Forrest I promise you I'll pursue it to an end you won't find very pleasant."

"I . . . Mr. Lawson surely . . ."

"Good day Mr. Bridges. Our business is over."

Nelson stood and turned without saying more. As he grasped the doorknob, Oliver Lawson spoke again.

"Mr. Bridges."

Nelson turned to face Oliver Lawson.

"Folks in Miami, are they impressed by Cartier watches, are they?"

The Still on the Feather

Nelson put off calling Hunter Henley until the next morning. When they did speak Nelson told him that the offer, while good, had too many unknowns.

"I was primed for it Hunter, I was, but there's too many variables that I'd have no control over. It could turn out that a resort would steal my guests away. In the long run, I could be destroying my own business."

"I certainly understand Nelson and, to tell you the truth, I hadn't thought about that possibility and I can well see that happening alright. Better luck next time as they say."

"Hunter, should I change my mind, say in a few months, should I phone?"

"Yes of course Nelson but as I said the other day, I'm still looking at places and until I find something that works, we can always talk again."

"Right Hunter, that's fine then. Perhaps we'll dine again soon at La Cuisine. Please remember me to Eleanor."

Nelson didn't like losing money. It affected him deeply on a level he and most people couldn't understand. To Nelson Bridges losing money, a lot of money on a deal or gambling or anything, confirmed for him that he was a pretense. Regardless of how well he hid it, behind the clothes, the jewelry the roses, behind all of it, he felt he was nothing more than a street hustler, and large setbacks in money matters destroyed the psychological veneer that concealed the lie. And he couldn't let a thing like Beddy Forrest do this to him and there was always the long shot.

He though about little else since leaving the Lawson Law Office. First he'd put a little pressure on Beddy by contacting the ATF folks and informing them about the still Mr. Forrest ran at the foot of Feather Mountain. A rather large still at that, he'd tell them. He was sure that would be enough of a distraction to occupy the Lawsons while he dealt directly with Beddy. Or more correctly, while some of his more physical associates from Miami dealt with Mr. Forrest. He was sure they would deal with Beddy in a manner even his simple mind could get around. Perhaps Mr. Beddy Forrest would see the light after all. It was a long shot but either way, Nelson would have his measure of satisfaction.

That afternoon, after contacting the authorities, Nelson called Vance Coleman and discussed the problem with him in purposefully vague terms. Coleman understood only that Nelson needed two street toughs and he, Coleman, was to call Nelson back when he found the right men.

"This isn't my thing Nelson."

"Mine either Vance. I just need someone spoken to in strong and certain language. Like we had to do a few times a few years ago. Nothing physical but be sure they're capable of that should the need arise."

He would explain to the men themselves precisely what he wanted said and done.

At the end of the third day after speaking with Coleman he didn't hear from him but he heard a knock at his front door. He opened it and standing with Sheriff Meyers were both of the Lawsons.

"Mr. Bridges, you mind if we come in?"

"Certainly Sheriff, certainly, come in," and turning to lead the way Nelson said, "The den will be more comfortable. What can I do for you gentlemen."

The den was the center of activity the day of the bar-b-que but then it was crowded and much of the furniture had been moved to make room for the guests. Today the large room was far more impressive. Several large leather wing chairs were placed near the stone fireplace. A large and heavy wooden table took up much of the far side away from the fireplace. The walls where filled with books, perhaps a thousand of them. And the view from the room was extraordinary. Walking to one of the chairs, and seeing the house again, Sheriff Meyers wondered at the level of discontentment that ate at this man.

When the four of them were seated, the sheriff spoke.

"Mr. Bridges, I received an interesting call yesterday."

"Oh? Nothing bad I hope Sheriff," Nelson said as he shifted his weight in the chair.

"It could be Mr. Bridges, it could be. It seems someone who wouldn't leave his name, phoned the ATF office complaining about a large still here in Horton County."

Nelson said nothing but stared without blinking at the Sheriff waiting to hear more.

"Well they ID every call coming into those offices Mr. Bridges, even if the caller has an I D blocker. Did you know that Mr. Bridges?"

"No I didn't but wha . . ."

"I didn't think you did. The person who called their office said Beddy Forrest was running a large still. A very large still. The ATF office, like most law enforcement offices, gets plenty of crank calls, you know, just people getting mad at someone and send out the law on wild goose chases. Happens all the time. Anyway they contacted the state attorney's office about it and passed the complaint and your name on to the state office for preliminary investigation. That was the call I got this morning. The state attorney's office, a Mr. Bollinger to be exact, wanted to know if I knew about any of this."

"My name? Surely you . . ."

"Hold on Nelson, there's a little more and then you can say your piece. I told Mr. Bollinger I knew old Beddy all my life and I didn't believe he could be involved in anything illegal, particularly at his age. I told him Beddy hasn't been a lawbreaker for over sixty years and I couldn't imagine him starting now. I told him I'd get a man right on it and get back to him. And I did. I put two men on it to be exact. I phoned Boyd here and told them what happened. I suggested that Beddy shut down his still until this blew over and I sent two deputies over to help him sort of clean up the place. They should be finished with that directly. I gave Mr. Bollinger a call before we came up today. I told him I checked up on you. I told him how you threatened and manhandled Beddy over the water you needed and then you called his office hoping to make trouble for the simple old timer because he refused you. I told him you're just a no-account, son-of-a-bitch from Miami cause that's what you are."

"Don't you for . . ."

"Now wait just a little longer Nelson; you'll get your chance. Right now Mr. Lawson, Oliver here, has something on his mind. Then I promise, you can have your say and we'll listen."

Nelson, thoroughly shaken but trying desperately to maintain his control and piece together a story, looked at Oliver Lawson. The man's eyes were cold as the bottom of a mineshaft and his voice was low and menacing.

"Mr. Bridges, when you came to our office about the water rights on Feather Mountain, Beddy had already brought over the monthly figures on the water consumption. We didn't have a chance to look them over until a few days ago. Seems you're over on the water limit. Quite a bit over, as a matter of fact. It would appear you built a few too many cabins up there."

Oliver Lawson turned to his son and Boyd handed his father a sealed envelope. Oliver took it and handed it to Nelson.

"This is a formal notice of your breach, Mr. Bridges. Your rights to any and all water from the well on Feather Mountain are terminated for cause effective immediately. There's a copy of the written contract enclosed along with your notice in case you've misplaced yours."

"You red-necked sons . . ."

"And Mr. Bridges," the sheriff interrupted, "should you decide to build a tank and truck water up there, you'll find there's a little problem with that. On roads of that grade we have a weight limit in this county. And by tomorrow, you won't be able to find anyone in the county who will sell you water anyway."

"Nelson looked at Oliver Lawson, "What in hell am I going to do without water up there?"

"I don't know Mr. Bridges. I suspect you'll loose your ass and go bankrupt. Can't imagine anyone buying those cabins. Not even in a foreclosure. No water up there will be a problem for anybody. Then there would be a deficiency judgment against you, probably taking whatever you have left and can't hide. I wouldn't be surprised if Beddy wound up with them, seeing no one else will buy them. He'll probably get them for next to nothing I feel. And that would be fitting too. Around here, we sort of owe Beddy a lot. In a manner of speaking, he let us know where the road is. And Beddy, he says he doesn't like you very much Mr. Bridges and that's good enough for most of us."

Nelson had turned to the side as Oliver Lawson spoke. Now it was time for him to speak but he was silent. The few thoughts he did have were of Paris and the long road back to Miami. He was still silent when the three men stood and left. He was watching the sun as it began to slip behind Seaton Mountain. Finally, in the last bit of light before nightfall, he lowered his eyes to a point just outside the window. A rose bush and on it a single bright red rose was being gently moved by the invisible hand of the wind. With his left hand Nelson Bridges fingered a similar rose in his lapel. And seeing them for the first time, he was struck at how really lovely they were.

LaClede

"Tho' much is taken, much abides; and tho'
We are not now that strength which in old days
Moved earth and heaven, that which we are, we are;
One equal temper of heroic hearts,
Made weak by time and fate, but strong in will
To strive, to seek, to find, and not to yield."

"Ulysses," Alfred, Lord Tennyson

The sun had set already and a light breeze was moving down the canal from the river. It carried with it the muffled voices of workmen and the occasional clang of steel from the plants just upstream. The leadman and I had crossed the water of the slip to the barge on a wooden plank and were unloading rebar with the overhead crane and another two-man crew inside the plant. It was cooler over the open water than under the steel roof of the shop but the mosquitoes were thicker. Throughout the summer night workers at LaClede sprayed ourselves with a mixture of DDT and diesel fuel. The spray mixed quickly with sweat and wore off in less than an hour and the mosquitoes would find us again. With a bit of luck, by that time the horn would sound for lunch. After eating we sprayed again before returning to work and we would spray ourselves several more times before the shift ended.

The leadman and I would slide three cables under each five-ton bundle and attach them to the equalizer that seesawed from the hook of the overhead crane. We gave each bundle a slight push so it would be parallel to the storage racks by the time the crane reached the two other men who guided the bundle into place. They'd unhooked the bundle and give the equalizer a similar push returning it to us. New men on the job would occasionally push too hard and brace for the string of obscenities that would come from the other men in the crew. Some of it was in play; some of it was not if it happened too often.

The steel rods that became the support skeleton for bridges and office buildings were extruded in the company mill in St. Louis and floated down river to the plant on the Industrial Canal for fabrication. The bars from the barges were placed in long dusty racks that held hundreds of the sixty-foot bundles until needed. When the crane lifted the load out of the barge, the leadman and I had a few moments to speak before it returned. Small talk among the men was limited not only by the company but by the constant crash of the shears and the roar of the huge fans by each workstation. For much of each eight-hour shift the workmen lived within their heads, alone with whatever thoughts pleased or haunted them.

The leadman, Mickey, finished high school a year before I did. Our teams played each other my junior year and I remembered his name. At the end of that season he made All-State running back. He had college offers he turned down, he said, because he wanted to marry his high school girl and start a family. College, he decided, was not what he wanted. Four years later he was in a barge, unloading steel, married with two kids. I was a college student working summers on the canal between semesters. The second shift, our shift, ended at midnight and in spring and early summer Mickey drove the marsh-lined highway east of the city and ran his crawfish traps. He'd sell his catch before dawn, grab a few hours sleep and work with his uncle building homes for a few hours in the afternoon. He was back at the plant at three-thirty when his day would repeat itself in what I saw as a numbing sameness. Mickey's way was hard work and, for him, just as natural as breathing.

"How long ya married Peter?"

"A year."

"Whatcha do on ya anniversaries?"

"The only one we had so far?"

"Yeah."

"Ah, we went to out to eat, then to a movie and ended the night at a lounge out near the lake. Why?"

"My fifth anniversary is next week and I'm thinking about taking my wife to the A & G."

"The cafeteria?"

"Yeah, ya ever been there?"

"No but I've heard it's pretty good."

He smiled. His blue eyes appeared deeper next to his sun-darkened skin.

"Yeah, she's always wanted to go there, ya know, so I've been saving up. Money she don't know nutting about."

"Yeah."

"I'm gonna surprise her."

"Taking the kids?"

"No, just her. Kids are staying with my momma for the night."

The crane and the equalizer appeared over the edge of the barge and we each grabbed an end to hook up another load. I finished with my cable and Mickey, having finished with the far end, walked to hook the middle. I pulled off a glove, lit a cigarette and squinted against the stinging smoke rising up to my eyes. He slid the middle cable under the bundle and slipped the end loop onto the hook of the equalizer. With his mind on something other than his work, he was smiling. I looked up past the overhead lights into the dark of the night trying to see stars but the floodlights over the slip were too bright.

The plant ran two shifts and occasionally a third as work would rise and fall with the seasons. As construction work picked up in summer the company hired extra men, usually college students. I worked there the summers of my college years and in my senior year, I worked the winter and spring as well. After graduating from college I hid out from the world for three years in an office before returning to law school. Because it paid more than other summer work, I returned to the plant four years later, the summer after the first year of law school. In those years from 1960 to 1968 I went to college, married, became a father, and like the country, I grappled not only with tomorrow but yesterday and the uncertainty of both.

New men were watched, prodded and measured until accepted or, like a few, driven out. One of the older men, over weight and lighthearted Stanley, would christen a newly accepted man with a nickname. Dudley Do Right was so named because he had the quick mental skills of a ball peen hammer and the template he used to establish order in his chaos defied both logic and common sense. He earned his name from Stanley because he had all the wrong answers and shared them eagerly.

Dudley worked briefly with Siam Sammy on a bender as his helper. Sammy was a short but powerfully built oriental fellow with thick glasses. One evening Dudley told Sammy he bought his wife a piece of furniture that morning. At lunch Sammy said, "Dudley, tell the guys whatcha bought today."

"Got tha wife a piece of Eye-talian furniture."

Mickey caught Sammy's eye and asked, "What piece did ya get Dages?"

"A chest."

"I guess an Italian chest like dat runs pretty high, huh?"

"Yeah, the thing is hand polished," Dudley said.

"Really, "said Mickey, "how they do that?"

"Hand rubbing man. With their hands. They use their hands."

"No sand paper, no polish?"

"Nope."

"No electric buffer, nothing?"

Big Nose started to snicker. Sammy turned his back to the group and shoved his hands in his pocket. He exhaled a cloud of smoke over his head. I could see his body shudder from stifled laughter.

"That's got to be rough on their hands, huh Dages?"

"Nah, they used to it. Built up calluses with all dat rubbing."

We finally lost it when Stanley, who had been leaning over the table with one leg propped up on the bench said, "That's amazing. That the most amazing fucking thing I ever heard. Son, who handles the money in your house; you or your wife?"

"My wife."

"Thank Christ."

My hair was cut short in the style worn by a TV detective who frequented a jazz club. That and because I hung in jazz joints, I became Peter Gunn and then Peter and eventually just Gunn. To Johnny the night foreman I was, along with everyone else in the world, Dages. It wasn't meant as a slight nor was it taken as one. Johnny was a raw-boned Frenchman who looked like an angry jockey in need of a serious mount. There were Germans, Irish, French and Italians working at LaClede but to Johnny we were all Italians, Dages— his way of saying Dago. Even Antonio Ragusa. Antonio was very large, very dark and very obviously Italian. He spoke broken English in a heavy Sicilian accent. So with this array of obvious ethnic characteristics, the choice was clear to Stanley. Antonio became Frenchy. The rest of us, even Antonio, to Johnny, were all simply Dages. Johnny was one of the very few men at the plant who didn't smile or laugh easily. Perhaps he was angry at the hand he was dealt in the unknown part of his life but more likely he was just caught up in his idea of how a foreman should conduct himself. I believe he decided that a scowl kept production up and was a necessary part of his mystique. While waiting for a bundle of steel to be brought to your station, you could occasionally get water but sitting or too much conversation was not tolerated. And too much was often defined by how much tonnage you put out. No one even leaned on a machine. Except for break time we stood all night. Johnny usually sat on the lunch table and glared over the plant. With his bony face, protruding Adams apple and darting eyes he sat motionless, resembling a vulture waiting for a hitch in the flow so he could swoop down on the unwary.

I got along well enough with him, as well as anyone, simply because I worked hard to make the night pass quicker. Each time I returned to college in the fall, I'd lose the seniority that I accumulated over the summer. After the first summer, I knew the plant and several of the machines better than the men who were hired the next spring and who were up for operator when I returned. Johnny would put me with these new operators until they learned the job.

"Dages, work with Rodent for a while. He's starting on the big shear tonight. He don't know from his ass but he's senior and he's up for it. Give him a hand, show him tha ropes and help him get his steel out."

I am sure it occurred to Johnny, as it did to me, that had I slow walked it or didn't do much teaching, these new operators would lose the position. And if three or four of them lost the position, I would have enough seniority to be the operator myself. But in the meantime, the tonnage for Johnny's shift would decline. The union rules required each man, when his name came up, to have a two weeks trial period to learn the job before he could be passed over. Operators were paid more than their helpers but not enough for me to lie down on the job. These men were married and I was single, lived at home and worked primarily for spending money. They had families and needed all the money they could earn. So of course I helped them. I looked upon it differently after I married.

After I broke in a new operator, Johnny would put me with the leadman. It was an easy job as the work changed throughout the night. It also allowed for a few stolen minutes to walk out to the slip, feel the breeze and watch the tugs move along the canal. A few minutes to leave the steel behind and feel human again even if only briefly. The leadman and I directed the crane, picked up the fabricated steel and replaced it with more steel for the next job. We loaded flat bed trucks with the completed orders. Boredom seldom found you while working the chains and the pace of the night became tolerable. It was Johnny's way of playing out his role in our symbiotic relationship. I taught the new operators, Johnny got his tonnage out and the front office stayed off his case. When Mickey and I caught up with our work and after we had thrown enough scrap bars at the needlefish, I'd go to the shears and whip the long bars onto the rollers for cutting. One shear cut the smaller bars, the size of the bar being numbered and determined by its diameter in eighths of an inch. A single number 11, an inch and three eighths through the center, weighed more than 300 pounds. We wore heavy stiff gloves and at the end of a week of whipping bars holes appeared in them. At the end of three weeks our hands were heavily callused where the holes exposed our hands to the bars.

Each shear had a long steel rack which held the different size bars. Steps led up to three levels where a man stood to whip the bars down to the rollers. As unlikely as it seems, a long bar of steel could be whipped like a rope, even the larger bars. A slow upward lift followed by sharp downward motion sent a wave down the length of the bar that made the other end snap up wildly three or four feet once it was freed. A badly twisted bundle often required a man at each end to free the tangled bars. Occasionally, due usually to inattention, a man would whip a bar while his coworker was trying to free the other end of the bundle. If he whipped the bar free at that moment, there was a fair chance that the scalpel-edged, opposite end would slice an arm cleanly and deeply. Given time a man's senses became attuned to the sounds and pulse of the plant. The movement of the overhead crane noted unconsciously; Johnny seen moving silently among the racks and sensing whether a man's next move brought you danger. Above the roar of the shop, eyes fixed on your hands digging into a bundle to free a bar, one could hear the low whispering whine of a bar moving swiftly along the bundle and you pulled your arms back a moment before the dancing razor ripped at your arms. A glare at the other man was usually message enough. But if he were known to be careless too often, a loud string of obscenities would alert the plant that he messed up again. There would be a price for him to pay at the next break.

"Dages," Mickey started on the new man, "ya like to got the Truck Driver tonight and we just started working." The crew, partly in imitation of Johnny and because names were always changing, took to calling newer guys Dages.

"Man, I told the man I was sorry. Shit."

Brooklyn spoke next saying, "Last week ya like to knocked the Preacher on his ass at the spiral machine and tonight you whipped a bar while Driver had his hands in the bundle. You trying to kill all the operators or what?"

"You drinking Dages?" asked Rodent.

"Aw, get off my ass. Ain't like none of you sons-a-bitches never done the same thing a hundred times. The man ain't saying shit. Let it go. Damn."

Truck Driver, the frail country boy who dreamed of running his own Peterbilt rig, sat nibbling on the sandwich he held tightly between his two mousy hands.

"Truck Driver, you ain't saying shit. You don't mine if Dages over here puts a few more stitches on your arms?"

Behind his weasel eyes the Driver was mad but he weighed the situation. He wanted his tonnage made for the night, so he couldn't anger his helper or he'd dog it, lay on his leg. Finally the Driver swallowed and said, "He's right, we all done it. Just don't going do it again."

Big Nose, Mickey's younger brother, started laughing and said, "Mickey, who you to be knocking this man? You forgetting what you did Dages on the German bender? You got four of that poor bastards fingers."

The crew broke out in laughter and Mickey smiled sheepishly before he said, "Dumb son-of-a-bitch oughta watch where he's putting his hand."

There was more laughter.

John, the particular Dages that Big Nose was talking about, was Stanley's brother. He was the operator of the German bender on the day shift. He was bending simple hooks by himself and had placed four small bars between the steel wheels of the bender. He began talking to Mickey as he walked by looking for part of an order. John placed his hand on the outer wheel, his fingers dangling in the space between the bars and the stationary wheel. Mickey, lost in the conversation, put his foot on the lower ledge of the machine and his hand on the upright control lever accidentally engaging the bender's gears. John's fingers were immediately pinned and they remained pinned until the machine took several seconds of indescribable pain to complete its cycle. When the machine tripped itself out of gear, the first joint of four of his finger had been crushed off and laid on the bender. They were still there when I punched in an hour later. During lunch they were still there, a dozen feet from where we were eating.

That human fingers stayed there for hours I found bizarre if not disturbing. I assumed that no one had the stomach to move them, so I spoke up. "Johnny, ya want me to do something with those fingers?"

"Nah Dages, leave them there." He turned to spit out the door and turning back to me he said, "Let dem guys on tha day shift see 'em again so they remember to be careful around here."

These men had more than stomach enough and I should have known that. Most of the older, full time men had seen combat in Korea or in World War II. Those fingers belonged to Stanley's brother and his indifference to that fact could not have run deeper. I recalled when he told us of collecting gold teeth from dead Germans by smashing their mouths with his rifle butt. He started laughing one night when some spoken word or gesture reminded him of the winter he fought in Europe. During a lull in the fighting, he said he was sitting with a few men in their foxhole, relaxing with the remains of a cigar. In the snow within arms reach was a dead German, frozen. Down to the last half-inch of cigar he nonchalantly placed it in the German's mouth. "Fucking guy looked like he could use a smoke."

These men and the younger ones who held these jobs permanently had seen how hard life near the bottom could be. The fingers were just another curious event and the ripple they caused had faded already. What did I know?

From the big shear I saw Dudley punch out and leave with Johnny. At lunch Sleepy told us what happened.

"We was running spirals back ina shed and I just got the pitch right and ran about six or seven of dem. I cut the first one off wit tha torch and that dumb sum bitch grabbed the hot ends. Grabbed both of them wit both his hands. Burned right through tha gloves."

"No shit?"

"Burned the hell out of dem. Looked like barbecued shit to me."

"What he do that for?"

"Said because they were bouncing loose, springing back and forth. Hell they always do that, dumb shit."

"That boy's gonna kill himself one day or one of you guys," said Stanley.

"Yeah," said Sleepy, "that's it for me. I ain't working wit his ass no more. Johnny came back there and told him to piss on his hands to take the sting out."

"And he did it?"

"Yeah, ain't dat a bitch? Jumped around like he grabbed the ends all over again. That shit had to hurt."

* * *

The helpers on the shears rolled a heavy gauge tray to the proper length and pegged the tray in place with heavy steel pins. Once the tray was pinned the operator would turn on the rollers, grab the steel bars as they ran to the shear, lift them above the blades and let them run out along the table. The roar of the fans and the rollers against the steel bars was deafening. When the two men were ready, the operator stepped on a foot pedal that caused compressed air to drive a large flywheel and brought the top blade down with a terrific force. The big shear had enough power to cut five number 11s at a time. It could go through flesh and bone quickly and cleanly and it did more than once.

Big Nose broke me in on the big shear that first year after I worked on a bender for almost a month. After several trips with him to the racks for more steel I noticed the pigeons roosting high in the beams of the metal shed. The beams, the corrugated tin of the shed, the bars of steel, the heavy steel frame for the overhead crane, the shears, the tables, all of it, the entire plant was a monotonous, spirit stealing gray. Except for a splash of white, even the pigeons were gray. If boredom could choose a color, it would have to be gray. Among the dust and bits of wire and other debris, hundreds of feathers were scattered about the floor. Big Nose was reading the tags on the bundles, looking for the grade and length he wanted.

"Dages," I asked, "what's with all the feathers back here?"

"From the pigeons. The cats that live around the shed nail one every now and then and they molt a lot too. You work around here long enough, you get enough feathers, you can fly the fuck away."

"You planning to fly the coop anytime soon?"

"Me and Mickey wanna do more house building with our uncle. Soon as his business picks up enough for us to be with him full time, we're both gonna leave."

"Better money?"

"Nah it's about the same but it's easier work. We're too soft to work around steel Peter. All of us. Look at the ends of these bars. Each one of them is sharp as a damn razor. We're all too soft, our bodies are too soft for steel. Someone's always getting hurt here and tha longer ya work here, the quicker ya luck's gonna run out on you. We weren't built to work around steel for too long."

I worked with Phil's nephew for a few weeks on the little shear. Phil was a Cajun in his thirties, stood a few inches over six feet and said little. Word was he had spent time at the state penitentiary and no one made him the butt of a joke, not even Stanley. He alternated between being the overhead crane operator and running a bender. His laughter was infrequent and around the lunch table his eyes moved to each man as they spoke but he rarely turned his head. His nephew came from Tennessee and was soon christened Red Neck and eventually Red by Stanley. I don't believe his real name was ever used. I know I never heard it. Shear operators would match the orders to the different lengths of steel in such a way as to limit the waste as much as possible. During those few minutes of calculations, a few words shared between the operator and helper were enough to sustain the need for contact. With only a sentence or two exchanged before you'd have to return to your workstations, the conversations could take hours. Other times, alone with my thoughts and the repetitive motions, I'd memorized passages of prose or poetry to pass the time. In one of those hurried snippets of conversation that took place over several hours, Red told me he'd been reading the insurance and workman's compensation benefits. He found it interesting that a severed finger joint, a single finger joint was worth five hundred dollars. Apparently to him this was more than a fair sum for the fractional loss of a digit. His eyes told me more.

A month or so later Red punched out for good. While I was working elsewhere in the plant, he lost the first joint of his index finger in the little shear. Later around the lunch table, among the young men, there was talk of a strange aspect of his glove. The thick material was barely cut but the severed finger and the blood was inside. They had to be shaken out by Johnny, the foreman. The older men told us the material is squeezed and somehow actually bends around the blade while the finger and bone inside just shears off. They'd seen it before they said.

Later, walking past the shear table I asked Red's helper how it happened. "Gunn, the son-of-a-bitch just hung his finger over the bottom blade and cut the son-of-a-bitch off. Crazy bastard asked me to trip the pedal. I told him he was fucking out his mind."

Five hundred dollars. Maybe five weeks work before deductions. The helper spread the story to most of the plant but word never reached Johnny or the front office. The line between management and labor wasn't voluntarily crossed but Johnny probably figured it out. For us, it was enough that we knew Red was nuts and for Johnny it was enough that he was gone.

Cutting his finger off was perhaps Red's personal symptom of the insanity that was taking place in the world outside the plant. The Cuban Missile Crisis came and went without too many realizing how close to the end we were but the tension at school was palpable nonetheless. Nine hundred and thirty civil rights demonstrations were held in the southern states in 1963 where over twenty thousand people were arrested. The Black Panthers were gaining airtime by breaking from King's nonviolence and advocating robberies and shoot-outs with the police. On a highway, civil rights marcher and SNCC organizer Willie Ricks hit media pay dirt and made more than a few whites pale when he coined the phrase "Black Power". The racial ranks formed a little tighter when SNCC later tossed out their white members. Soon the Panthers demanded black exemption from the military, for blacks to be tried by all black juries and the freeing of all blacks presently in jail. To the little known and backward nation of South Vietnam President Kennedy sent several hundred "advisors" to train an army to stem the tide of Communism and the military situation soon began deteriorating. The world couldn't help but take notice when Buddhist monks publicly burned themselves in protest over the repressive Diem government. The immolations captured on film showed the monks in their brightly colored robes sit calmly in the lotus position, douse themselves with gasoline and light off without further sound or movement until very slowly they'd keel over to the side. You tend to remember that sort of thing. And each of the many times I saw it, I tried to see the why and how of it. Diem was overthrown, probably with CIA assistance, and a string of coups followed. In November of '63 President Kennedy was assassinated in Dallas and most who followed the story closely were convinced the assassin had not acted alone. America was in the throws of witnessing its adolescence fade but still it clung to its naiveté. A U.S. destroyer, probably assisting South Vietnamese commandos in the waters of the Gulf of Tonkin, was fired upon. Twice it was claimed. In short order, and after much embellishment by the media and the Johnson administration, Congress passed the resolution allowing the President "to take all necessary steps, including the use of force" to prevent further attacks against U. S. forces. At that same time in 1964 when Red traded his finger joint for five hundred U.S. dollars, Vietnam was costing the country over two million a day or roughly four thousand finger joints. In human lives, the cost was higher and going much higher. In December of that year Nguyen Cao Ky seized control of South Vietnam and the U.S. was just eight months from the start of the seemingly unending race riots which began in the Watts area of Los Angles. The country did not just come of age in the 60s. During that decade and for a while thereafter it grew old and feeble, bypassing maturity in the process. It seemed the whole world was going insane and I saw no compelling reason to be among the few left standing. I hoisted a few more eighty-proof glasses on my way to oblivion.

The foot pedal that Red had stepped on engaged the shear blades. Not that it mattered for Red's purposes but after the pedal was pushed, a puff of compressed air signaled that the flywheel was beginning its rotation. Like the near silent whisper of those whipping bars, that puff gave the wary a one-second warning before the blades would meet. On the big shear the covering over the foot pedal was defective. Anything accidentally hitting just the covering with enough force would trigger the blade. That foot pedal remained a danger throughout my working years at the plant. It was never replaced, never fixed and experienced operators stayed well away from the pedal until they were ready for the cut. It took new comers a while to distinguish that warning puff from the incessant roar of the plant.

It was hot, noisy and dirty work. Each time the shear slammed into the bars, coating and rust flew into the air and covered everything with a fine layer of dust. It was in the fibers of our clothes, in our hair, our nostrils and ears. The diesel fuel and DDT mixture glued it in place and at the end of a shift, we were filthy.

My third year at LaClede I began working in December. In those cold winter nights work inside the shed was much better than in the summer's heat and we worked so hard we rarely felt the cold until break time. And better still, there were no mosquitoes. By late spring I had enough seniority that only one man was ahead of me to make operator. I was married, in school, with a child on the way. Johnny asked me to work with that man on the big shear. I did but I didn't teach him nor did Johnny ask me to do so. I slow walked it and I damn sure didn't show him how to hold a job that he wasn't ready for. Two weeks later, I was running the big shear. Fuck him.

Like men anywhere, a pecking order had to be established and maintained for the place to run smoothly. And so there were competitions in the plant. The most tonnage cut, the best put down at the lunch table, bending the biggest bars by hand, any contest to occupy your thoughts and make the hours pass was welcomed. Perhaps the most peculiar involved hitting needlefish with scrap bars as they swam in the slip. Most of the men could bend a number 4, a bar of steel four-eighths of an inch in diameter, with their arms straight out to the sides and drawn together in front of the chest. Only three ever bent a number 5, a bar one-eighth of an inch larger than a 4, in that manner and Mickey set the tonnage record when he was the operator on the big shear.

Mickey was as large as Phil and both towered over me. Phil rarely spoke and he seemed to barely tolerate me when I worked with him. Both could bend a number 5 and when Little Brother announced to the lunch table that I bent a number 5 before break the reaction was as expected.

"No fucking way".

"Bullshit."

"Your ass."

There is something unique, almost mystifying, about men thrown together in dirt and grime for some purpose that involves hard work, sweat and the nearness of physical danger. They are compelled to speak the tongue of the street and in places like LaClede it was common, no necessary, to use as many coarse words as possible when speaking to one another. Nothing, not the weather, one's car or family escaped this obligatory show of mindless testosterone grunting. And it's a hard habit to break.

"I'm telling you the fucking man did it asshole. Gunn, tell 'em. Tell 'em you fucking did it."

Roland smiling from the far end of the table said, "Mah man Peter. Go on."

Truck Driver, looking like a beady-eyed chipmunk nibbling on his snack and knowing better than say anything directly, looked at Do Right and said, "You're fifty pounds heavier than Gunn and you can't do it. You believe this shit?"

Do Right looked at Truck Driver, then at me and then at his sandwich and said in a low voice, "Horse shit."

Mickey was smiling from ear to ear. "Gunn you bent a 5?"

"Yeah."

Phil looked up, "You did?"

Johnny, sitting on the pipe railing around the lunch area said, "Dages, show us. Sleepy go get a 5 bar. I wanna see this shit."

Phil began speaking to me after that night. Not too often in front of the other men as he rarely spoke in the group at all but just when he could, in snatches of conversations around the plant. He'd talk about fishing, the front office, his paycheck, anything the rest of us spoke about. Whatever club he and Mickey were in, I was now apparently a member and the seventy or so other men at the plant couldn't join.

At lunch one evening it began to rain. I jumped up and ran to my car. The window cranking mechanism had broken inside the door and I had to pull the glass up by hand.

"Dages, what's the matter with your window," Sleepy asked when I sat down again at the table.

"Damn window crank's busted."

Mickey caught my eye, smiled and said, "Do Right, tell Peter what's wrong with his window."

"The glass won't go up?" he asked.

"Right."

"Here's what ya do. Open the door and look for the screws holding the door panel onto the car door, ya know. Unscrew those and take the panel off. Once you're inside, that's where the problem is."

"That's where the problem is?"

I heard suppressed laughter escaping from the guys around the table. I looked at him and asked, "So if the window doesn't work, I should take the door panel off and look for the problem?"

"Yeah."

"How do you know? You ever have something like this yourself?"

"No but it just figures."

"Thanks ya fucking moron, I'll give it a try." Even Johnny the foreman broke into laughter.

After I made operator on the big shear and broke in a new helper I began to think of Mickey's tonnage record. I lost twenty pounds running around in a nightly contest with Mickey's record and with myself. One night I cut over 48 tons of rebar, a record that was still in place when the company closed its door fifteen years later. Now, from my perspective of some thirty-five years after the fact, I blame that sort of foolishness on the pervasive boredom of the plant and the same hormone that puts hair on your ass.

Drinking a few beers with the guys after work was routine and often we'd have more than a few. I started drinking heavily before my days at the shop and I knew it was getting out of hand. I did well enough with my studies but too much of my free time was spent in barrooms escaping a dissatisfaction I sensed but didn't understand. It is from ourselves that we hide most effectively. There were several places around the canal that didn't mind serving grubby workmen in filthy jeans and T-shirts. They were restaurants, lounges and pool halls that began their slow demise when the interstate choked the economic life from Highway 90. They welcomed the workers and their paychecks. Brooklyn and his brother Johnny, both from New York, were two of the regulars and their accent was close to the New Orleans Yat dialect that most of us commanded. Identical, in fact, except to all but a practitioner or the trained ear.

After a few beers Brooklyn brought up Truck Driver. "What's wit dat guy? Christ, wit da truck t-shirts all tha time and that Peterbilt belt buckle. Damn thing's as big as his ass. That's all the guy talks about."

"Yeah," I said, "that's his dream; to hit the road, driving for days by himself. How's that for a surefire way to go bugfuck?"

"Damn right. What's up with him," Johnny asked.

"You see the way he looks at those rigs when they pull in the shed to load up? He's like a dog in heat. Ever see his wife?" I asked.

"Yeah, at the company picnic and a few times when she dropped him off."

"Have you looked at her?" I asked.

"Yeah, she makes three of him for gawd's sake."

"And ugly as hell too," Johnny said.

"I heard she beats his ass," I said.

"Ya kiddin."

"No, that's been the word around the plant for years. He can't weigh more than 140 pounds."

"Yeah and she probably goes two and a quarter at least."

"Right."

"Why she beats him?" Johnny asked.

"Don't know but with her looks and her kicking his ass, it sure explains why he wants to hit the road."

"They got two kids too."

"Yeah, I seen 'em," said Johnny. "Nice kids, quiet."

"Yeah, just like the Truck Driver," Brooklyn said.

"Bitch must run them all ragged," said Johnny

"Gotta feel like shit with that kinda life," I said.

Sometimes even the insignificant can have unexpected consequences. A pebble strikes the water, ripples move out touching things that weren't seen. It was Johnny's suggestion and innocent enough. "Next time we go out, let's axe him to come wit us. Maybe a few beers and some laughs will loosen him up, you know, give him some backbone maybe."

It wasn't the next time or the next but after a few weeks, after he cleared it with his wife we figured, he joined us. Six or seven of us, grimy and needing shaves, went to a 24-hour dive enticingly named The Dollhouse. The place smelled of stale beer and disinfectant. It was dimly lit which served the dual purpose of cutting expenses and concealing the neglect of the place and patrons. There was a payoff pinball machine in a front corner, a jukebox, the bar, several booths along the wall and tables in the center. It had two winning features: cheap booze and we met the dress code. The booths were upholstered in ratty red plastic with contrasting black swirls but they were softer than the chairs at the bar. Two guys from the day shift were there and were already drunk. A few women, whores probably and drunks certainly, were also there. One, an extremely overweight woman wearing an eye patch, was noticed by Truck Driver. Soon they were alone in a booth. If I were forced to choose which of the three to touch, the booth, Truck Driver or the woman, it would have been an unpleasant tossup.

Nodding in their direction, I asked, "Brooklyn, how ya figure that shit?"

Jerry, the crane operator said, "Bastard just likes fat ugly women."

"Gotta be," I said. "Barkeep, give us another round. Shot of Old Crow with a Dixie backer here and two more Dixies for these guys."

"Peter, you really like that shit?"

"No, but the effect is nice."

The bartender placed the drinks in front of us and Brooklyn took a long swallow from his bottle before saying, "I'm gonna go over there and make Truck Drive sound like a prince to that bitch. Maybe if he gets pumped up about himself and she's thinks he's ok, he might get lucky." He was smiling as he said this.

"Lucky wit that? How lucky is that?" Jerry snickered.

"Fucking right," Brooklyn said. "Anything besides jerking off is lucky for him." The three of us laughed as he turned to the booth.

Jerry and I sat at the bar and talked to the other guys from the plant. I put a quarter in the jukebox and returned to the bar without making a selection when I found only country music, no jazz. Brooklyn came up behind us and placed his hand on my shoulder. He leaned in and started to laugh quietly. "Youse guys ain't gonna believe dis shit. He's pissed. He thinks I'm trying to take a shot at the broad."

"No. You're shitting."

"Really, the fucking guy thinks I'm trying to cut him off. Took me aside and told me to get the hell away from his broad."

"No wonder his wife beats him; he's a fucking moron."

At the shop the next day it was apparent that Truck Driver did get lucky. He walked in holding his brown lunch bag and with a changed light in his eyes. Throughout the early evening there was teasing from the crew. He didn't answer or even acknowledge the questions but he was smiling and that was good. A few months later he quit LaClede and was driving a rig. I laughed when I heard of it. The oddest thing can put wind in a man's sail. A roll in the sack with a fat whore wearing a black eye patch gave Truck Driver enough madness to follow his dream. And that was good too.

It was a cool night on the barge, and before Mickey and I climbed down to the steel, we watched a school of shiners feeding on insects attracted by the lights over the slip. Hundreds of the small fish were there and as they cut and turned erratically their silver sides and bellies flickered beneath the green water. From the darkness surrounding the circle of light a foot-long needlefish darted in and took one of the shiners in its mouth. The shiner's belly showed brightly as both fish disappeared. In a moment the impassive school regrouped and returned to feeding. As Mickey and I moved to the steps we heard the crane horn sound loudly. It was not the short note to get someone's attention but a long, uninterrupted blast. In the crane Jerry was waving his arm and pointing to the other side of the plant. Then the alarm bell by the office went off. We ran across the plank and sprinted to the front of the shop. Men were crowded around the lunch area. A new man lay on the ground. A blood trail led to him. Johnny the foreman was using his belt as a tourniquet around the guy's bicep. The boy, in agony, moaned and twisted in pain. His right hand, still in his glove, had been cut by the big shear. I remembered Red, Phil's nephew, and his glove bending around that blade with his finger sheared off inside.

Johnny speaking to all of us said, "We've got to get him to Mercy but I can't hold this tourniquet and drive."

"Here, give it to me. You drive," I said.

The boy was pasty and weak. Some men half carried him to Johnny's car while I held the belt. Along the route, I loosened the belt from time to time. When the dull pain rose to an unbearable crescendo he moaned and rolled his head. I tried to keep him talking.

"Let me take the glove off so I can see how bad it is," he said.

If he took the glove off, I thought, and half of his hand stayed in the glove, it was going to get very messy in the car for the both of us. With a forced calmness I said, "Nah, don't do that. If you start to pull on that glove you could make it worse. Let the doctor cut it off. You don't want to damage it any more than it is."

He repeated his request several times before we arrived at the hospital and each time I told him the same thing. I assumed wrongly that once at the hospital, the nurse would take the belt from my hand. Instead the doctor asked me to hold it as he and the staff removed the glove and worked on the hand. From the look of the wound he had placed his hand on the edge of the blade as the cut was across the hand from the outside edge almost to the base of his index finger. The stubs of bone were white against the bloody flesh and sinew. It was a smooth cut but the wide blades forced the hand open in a wedge shaped gash. I tried to keep looking at his eyes so he would focus on what I was saying. I kept him talking; telling him it wasn't as bad as we thought. After seeing it, I was convinced he'd lose his fingers and the distal part of his hand. I was hoping they would be able to save his thumb.

After they cleaned the wound he was taken to X-ray. My hands were cramped from holding the belt. Looking at the X-rays the emergency room doctor told Johnny and me they could save his index finger and thumb which was one finger better than I figured. The first orthopedic surgeon said he could also save the middle finger. His partner came shortly after, looked at the images and said without hesitation that he could save the entire hand. And he did.

Roland was the second black man hired at the plant. Integration was still making its tentative way through the south and the angry crowds that rose up in protest in New Orleans gathered less than a decade before. He had a semester of college before dropping out and was hired in 1967. By early '68 he made operator on the little shear. I was his helper that spring and again in summer. In those conversations shared a few seconds at a time during a night's work we spoke to escape the boredom, each uncertain of the other. I was in law school and my brother had been elected to the state house the previous summer. He represented the district where Roland and I both lived. Roland's brother was living in Detroit and had taken part in the riots of that same summer of 1967. Roland had visited him over that winter.

"No shit Gunn, he's got rings and watches and all kinda shit last July. Damn, you should see what he got hisself. Fine shit."

"Really? He wasn't protesting then. I'm mean he was more interested in the looting than the protest, right?"

"Well shit Gunn, he was protesting. When the police raided that club, they started the shit. Damn right he was protesting."

"Did he get arrested."

"No."

The overhead crane stopped above us and we chained up a rack of cut steel, tied it with bundle wire and stood back as it took it to the leadman before returning for another load. Signs were placed throughout the plant where they could be read easily. Bold black letters on a yellow background told us not to stand under loads but it was understood the warnings had to be ignored. The crane was constantly moving overhead and to move each time meant the work, your work, would not be done. Occasionally, very rarely, a load would come down. So we stayed by our station but watched the crane out of the corner of our eye. If a very heavy or a very large load were overhead, we'd stop and look at it until it passed. The company gave us yellow plastic hats to wear for protection in case one of the 5-ton bundles came down on our heads. And that was good for a few laughs.

"I heard on the news that they arrested over 7,000 people."

"Yeah man but not him. He runs with a bunch of brothers that have their heads on right. Everybody was snatching up cars and using them with chains to pull down the bars covering the doors. He said everybody was doing that shit. But the other people, they were going in furniture stores, grocery stores. They were carrying all that heavy shit like TVs, radios, fucking recliners. They were the ones that got caught. My brother and the dudes he ran with went after the jewelry stores. One guy in the car, the others on foot. They pulled the bars down, broke the glass and just left the car there. They'd take all the good stuff and run like hell before them other fools would jump through the window. They'd be long gone before them other fools got caught. Man they done good."

"You think we'll have riots down here?"

"I don't know Gunn. There's a lot of us that live, you know, all jumbled up, mixed together. Y'all don't like us worth a shit, no more than we like you, until we know each other and then it's cool. With all these mixed neighborhoods, lots of people knowing each other, I don't know. Maybe. Maybe not. What you say?"

The crane returned and we sent out another bundle. "I don't know either Roland. Shit, things are so messed up right now, nobody knows from their ass. Like Nam. Good? Bad? Nobody really knows but they all act like they do. Like this Tet shit. Cronkite's saying how we got our asses handed to us. Westmoreland and the rest are saying we beat all hell out of them. Who knows? Who the fuck knows? Look, I know blacks have taken shit for so long you got a right to be pissed. But damn, like your brother's riot, how's that make sense? People get pissed at the way the cops treat some brothers at a nightclub. They roughed them up. Yeah get pissed, protest, sue them but burn down stores in your own fucking neighborhood? Loot them? How's that make sense Roland? How's that help? Yeah things were shitty and still are. But give it a chance. Change is coming, it has to. Take you. You work here now and this shop was segregated."

"Yeah, I do. One fucking black guy, two of us in the whole plant, and more than seventy of you white guys."

"Yeah and they probably hired you because you're so white looking. They thought you were a white man."

"That's it. That's right you crazy fucker, they thought Roland Rudy Brown was a fucking white man."

We laughed and I said, "Roland a lot of us don't like the way it is."

"Yeah, I know, but shit Peter, you don't have to fucking live it."

"No? Come to my law school and see how happy them uptown fuckers are to see a Yat in their school. It's not only about race, my man; it's about economic and social class. And me and you, my nerve, are from the wrong part of the sit-tee."

"Yeah but they let you eat with them don't they?"

"What the fuck makes you think I want to eat with them?"

"Crazy bastard. If we do have a riot, I'll call you."

"To represent you? Think I'll be practicing by then?"

"Hell no. I'll call so your ass can come wit us."

* * *

That spring in '68 the world didn't awaken with freshness and renewal: it exploded into unparalleled confusion that reached chaos by summer. The previous winter Eugene McCarthy announced he would take the extraordinary step of running run against Johnson, the sitting President from his own party because of Vietnam. By December U.S. troop strength in Vietnam reached over 450,000. Ten days before launching the February Tet Offensive General Giap attacked Khe Sanh. The Marine garrison encircled at that isolated base would draw the attention of the world as they held out for 77 days before the siege was broken. Nightly news brought us graphic color footage of the battle there and at Saigon and Hue. Americans watched in stunned disbelief as their fathers, sons and brothers contested streets, city blocks and jungle in a land 10,000 miles away and died. More than 500 U.S. soldiers were dying each week but the Tet Offensive ended in a military disaster for the VC and the NVA. The expected general uprising never occurred and their troops were decimated. But the word we received from the media and the dissidents was that a rag-tag guerrilla army had bested America's fighting men. And that word, repeated until believed in the States, brought Giap the victory his troops could not bring about on the field of battle. Walter Cronkite after returning from Saigon announced that he was certain that " . . . Vietnam is to end in stalemate." In the fallout of Tet, we lost the political war. Student anti-war protests were common place and in that spring some thirty schools a month erupted. At Columbia University they held five buildings for several days before the students were violently removed by the police. In March a high school student, this time in Syracuse, New York not in Saigon, soaked himself with gasoline and ignited himself in protest.

In the New Hampshire primary Johnson defeated McCarthy by a mere 300 votes. Four days later on March 16, 1968, Senator Robert Kennedy announced his candidacy for the presidency. Johnson's vulnerability was carried by the waves of nightly news and the swelling tide from Vietnam. On the same day that Kennedy announced, in the small hamlet of My Lai, over 300 civilians were slaughtered by members of the U.S. Army. Two weeks later President Johnson stunned the world when he announced that he would not seek re-election. General Westmoreland's request for an additional 206,000 soldiers and the call up of reserves was denied in early April. And on the 4th of the month the man who shared his dream with us, the man who offered hope for a better tomorrow when many felt their tomorrows were slipping away, was shot to death in Memphis. The assassination of Martin Luther King ignited race riots across the country. The death of this man of peace brought mayhem to Baltimore, Boston, Detroit, Kansas City, Newark, Washington D.C., and many other cities. Forty-six died.

The misguided nightmare of the 60s played on and needing a suitable soundtrack it contorted rock & roll, morphing it into acid rock. Sex became a toy without commitment and good girls did, easily. Drugs, marihuana and speed in particular, were ubiquitous and eventually ushered in the age of lysergic acid, not Aquarius, and like a bad trip, Nam kept flashing back on the nightly news. Long hair and paisley dreams. Body count and bodybags. The doors were cleansed and the perception for many was one of infinite cruelty. Tell me more lies about Vietnam.

Within days students in Paris protested in support of unions and the ensuing riot turned the streets into a battle zone complete with barricades and tear gas. The French student protest that started with twenty-five grew in weeks to fifty thousand and by May swelled to ten million, paralyzing the entire nation. Increasingly students around the world, in Poland, France, Japan, Germany and Czechoslovakia, were protesting the war and the status quo. The Southern Christian Leadership Corps lead by Rev. Abernathy camped on the Mall in Washington. They were forcibly removed a month later. 124 were arrested. And then, when the world was turning on itself, came the news hitting like a thunderbolt straight in the heart that Robert Kennedy, after winning the South Dakota and California primaries, was assassinated.

I went into work the next day and Roland was already by his shear before the bell rang. I walked over to the gauge where he was standing with his head down, staring at the tickets. The bravado was gone and in its place was despair; a despair and a hurt I saw in the eyes of a man who admitted of no hurt. In a voice I could barely hear over the roar of the fan motors he said, "They're gonna kill us Gunn. They gonna kill all of us ain't they?"

After Jack and Birmingham and Malcolm and Watts and Nam and King and now this, I had nothing to say. Nothing that would make sense for either of us. Hope lay dying on the ground, its stomach split open, its guts spilling out and there weren't enough hands to put them back or hold the rest in. We just went through the repetitious motions that night and cut our steel. Where did it go after it left on those trucks? Did they really build bridges with it or office buildings as the tickets read? Or did they just dump it in a landfill somewhere? Where we stood that night, dumping it made as much sense as anything else. Pointless, repetitious work that served no purpose other than to keep us busy and silent.

The days drifted, merged into each other in a numbing confusion. It wasn't too long after that that Roland said, "Gunn you know all those pigeon feathers lying around in the racks back there?"

"Yeah."

"Well I've been picking them up for some time, ya know. I got me a whole bunch by now and I figure I've got enough so I can fly the fuck outta here."

"You're quitting?"

"No Gunn, hell no. That ain't how it is. I'm gonna get myself hurt, collect a little comp and hit the road. My brother phoned and wants me to come up. The riots are still going on and I can pick up some change man, some real change."

"Bullshit."

"You watch Roland, Gunn. I'm telling ya what tha Lord loves."

Abbie Hoffman took his Yippie sideshow on the road. They disrupted the New York Stock Exchange, destroyed the clocks at Grand Central Station and made plans for the Democratic Convention in August.

Several days later I was pushing the gauge down the rollers to the proper pin and kicked a wooden 4-by out of my way. We piled the cut steel in racks and separated each order with the 4 X 4 wooden logs so we could slip the chains under the steel. They were scattered all over the shop and those by the shear that weren't being used were kept beneath the roller table. I had just kicked another one when Roland came over to me. "Damn Gunn, quit moving my fucking 4-bys."

"Your 4-bys? Whatcha talking about?"

"Man that's how I'm taking the fall tonight. Just leave the mother fuckers alone."

"You out ya mind?"

He laughed and walked back to the shear. I left the 4-by where he had placed it. It was there for less than an hour.

You know how a slight-of-hand artist loves to impress his crowd? He pulls a move two feet away from you and you wonder how in hell he did it. So he shows you. He shows you very slowly so you can follow his hands. You see it done, you know how he does it and then he does it again so fast you see nothing at all. Later that night Roland walked over to my gauge stepping over the 4-by. The overhead crane began to move from the rear of the shop. Roland looked at me and said, "Here goes Gunn. I'll see you around. Watch this shit."

He started to walk back to the shear, looked up and began talking to Jerry in the moving crane, yelling back and forth about a bundle we needed. As he neared the 4-by I knew it was coming but damn if I know how he did it. It looked for all the world that he actually broke his ankle. And for the briefest moment, I thought he had.

Roland grabbed his feathers that night and flew north.

* * *

I was working with Mickey again and the trucks were loaded for the night. We had just removed the cut steel from both shears and I was talking to Big Nose who was running the big shear. His helper, a new man, a boy really, was whipping bars for the next run. I was standing near the shear blade. The fellow finished and was stepping down to the floor. He tripped and one of his boots kicked the cover of the defective foot pedal. He fell forward with his arm going through the shear blades a heartbeat after I heard the distinctive puff just before the blades met. I grabbed him with both hands and spun around throwing him against the wall of the shed. He fell to the floor after bouncing off the wall and rose to one knee looking at me with puzzled anger.

"What tha fuck you do that for?'

Before I could speak Big Nose answered him. "The fucking man just saved your fucking arm asshole."

Nothing more was said and I walked away wondering what would have happened had he been 60 or 70 pounds heavier.

Towards the end of August 4,600 tanks and 165,000 soldiers of the Warsaw Pact invaded Czechoslovakia ending the brief show of liberty and defiance known as the "Prague Spring". As young, longhaired Americans converged on Chicago, unarmed young people filled the streets of Prague trying to stop Soviet tanks with their bodies. In the end, 72 Czechoslovakians were killed. The Democratic Convention, in the face of nightly demonstrations and protest, nominated Hubert Humphrey for president. I would leave work and get cleaned up in time to catch the final few minutes each night. The Wisconsin delegates wanted to debate the anti-war plank for the platform and Mayor Daley who ran the convention with a steel fist wanted the debate to take place that night, right then, after 12:00 AM when America was asleep. The delegates from Wisconsin refused and began giving their reason for wanting it heard during the day. The camera shifted to Daley, his face red and contorted in anger, as he drew his finger repeatedly across his throat signaling the control booth to cut the sound off from Wisconsin. And they did. During the course of 1968 14,589 American soldiers died in Vietnam.

In the street the protesters and police were locked in the performance that symbolized the country for me for more than a decade, the we against them dance of self-destruction. On Saturday and Sunday I saw the events of that weekend. I watched in a slow motion disbelief as the Chicago police played into the protestors' hands. Their prodding and name calling led to a police riot. On Sunday, August twenty-fifth, after driving the protesters from Lincoln Park they continued to beat them in the street, they beat innocent bystanders who were watching from their front steps, they beat journalists, smashed cameras and clubbed anyone they could find as they fanned out for several blocks. And the nightly beatings continued for four more days. Film and tape on TV showed police and national Guardsmen beating people with clubs and rifle butts leaving many unconscious and bloody. They beat the fallen and even the elderly. Protesters, male and female, were dragged through the street by their hair and tossed into paddy wagons while others chanted, "The whole world's watching. The whole world's watching." And they were right. The world and I were watching and I along with the world shifted uneasily in our chairs. This was the pivotal event. This night the seeds of change, for better or worse, were cast far and America was never quite the same.

As August drew to a close I was spending my last days at LaClede. I would come to miss the place and the sweaty hard working men there. Except for Roland none of them paid much attention to the world or when they saw it, it was to them, much like watching a movie. A few beers, a couple of hours of overtime and their families was world enough for them and their concerns took in little more than this. The war in Vietnam had touched none of them that I knew of nor did they seem to care much about the riots and the assassinations. These events were not part of their lives nor did they become involved in them and if their world appeared grotesquely limited to some, it was nevertheless, happier than the one I was watching.

On November 5th, Richard Milhouse Nixon was elected the 37th President of the Unites States of America. Four years later, after many years of pain and confusion, when I saw clearly the face of my enemy and knew he had to be stopped, I quit drinking.

I never saw Roland again.

Above Timberline

I belong in tundraland
above treeline
where life is
tenuous.

Where stunted life
hides
from wind howling at all hours
and freezes teach the meaning
of A bit of heat.

Where the grip on
life
    slips
        a
            little
every now and then.

How precious it all is
when it
hangs forever
in
the
balance.

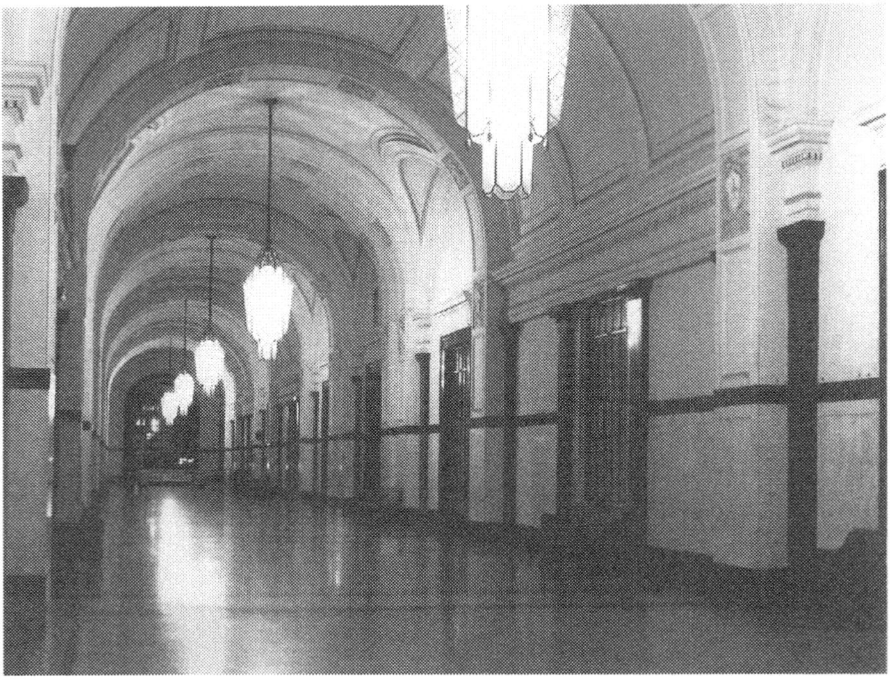

When Words Fail

I don't know what they'll do with the body. I mean after the cremation. His wife's family won't care, not after he killed their daughter. His mother may take him back to California where she lives, or maybe to El Salvador where his father still lives. His sons may want to keep him here. Don't know how his ex-wife feels. Probably go along with whatever the rest want. Christ, if they take him home to El Salvador, he'll be like some phantom that blew into town 30 years ago, lived quietly and one day shattered the lives of so many people, and disappeared to be spoken and felt but never seen again.

His bullet tore through the front of his face blowing out his teeth and nose. Hope he didn't feel much. I hope the terror of his wife's final moments were dreamlike in stead of painfully vivid reality. Christ, what terror of loneliness had gripped him so strongly for the weeks before last Friday? This guy was no killer. He adored his wife and kids. Always laughing, always had a joke, always the friend with a hand to offer. Where did this good man go and from what depths of hopelessness did his crazed replacement spring?

* * *

We finished the early session and my deputy came in without knocking, "Judge, Cisco wants to see you."
"Who?"
"The night security guard, you know, Cisco." he said with a smile.
"His name isn't Cisco. You want me to call you Dee-wayne?"
"No, he's cool your honor. Just messing with you."
"Yeah, let him in. What's he want?"
"Don't know. Didn't say." He was still smiling.
"Sure, show him in."

I had a few conversations with Nelson the first months after I was appointed magistrate in the criminal system. He was from Central America and was with the building security that gave support to the sheriff's court security. He seemed to have a better understanding of things than most of the court deputies and appeared better educated. I knew he was studying mechanics and working as a guard until he was ready to start his own place. He said he wanted a fine shop where he would be seen as a reliable alternative to the jacklegs who rip people off doing shabby repair work.

"Señor, que passa?" I asked.

"Que paso?" he said with his come back to our routine greeting.

"What's up? How've you been?"

"Fine. I just came back from my home. I spoke with Judge Jerome the other day and told him how quiet things are in San Salvador now."

"Really?" I said, not knowing where this was going.

"While I was there, I told my father's friends where I was working and they would like for some of the judges to come down for a visit. The country's beautiful and they'd put everyone up and really entertain everyone. They'd feel honored to have a few of you come down for a visit and see our country."

"Well, that's really nice, Nelson but with the rebels shooting all hell out of the place, I don't think I'll be making that trip." I laughed with him as I said this.

"Naw, that's just out in the country side. The cities are safe," he said while smiling broadly, his clear eyes gleaming. "We went all over. No problem. Here's some pictures of the country." He handed me a stack of photos and added, "We drove through the hills for hours. Never had any trouble. Nothing."

"And the people with you were armed, right?"

"Of course but really, it's very safe now."

Nelson's family was from the upper class of El Salvador and he had lived in the US while in high school. He loved it here and decided to stay. Other members of his family were spread through out the world as well. A brother, a physicist, was living in Brazil; another lived further north in the US. But New Orleans was just fine with him. He'd return home every few months to visit his parents and his friends, primarily Oscar. Oscar was the son of the ex-president and Nelson's best friend. Although I never met him, Nelson spoke of him often. He was a pilot for Taca Airlines and had his own private two engine aircraft. I met Oscar's mother though. Years later, when I knew Nelson better and after I had incorporated his heavy equipment company, he formed a silent partnership with her to build a house in the suburbs on speculation. She had a warm but formal bearing, what one would expect from the wife of a former head of state.

Unfortunately the down turn of the city's economy doomed that transaction. After the oil collapse of the mid-eighties, real estate in the area collapsed. After Nelson and his first wife divorced, he and his new wife, Jennifer, moved into that home and planned to sell it when the market improved.

Some years after meeting him, Nelson left his job at the court, not to start his own place but to work for another heavy equipment repair company. When the transmission went out in my Fiat he offered to fix it if I would buy the blow-up book and the parts. He said he could fix it for a few hundred dollars cost to him.

"The dealership wants two thousand to fix it. You ever tear down one of these and repair it?" I asked.

"No, that's why I need the blow-up diagrams in the Fiat book."

We bought the book and to me it looked like the schematics for the space shuttle. I though there was little chance of his repairing it.

"Can you do it?" I asked.

"Ah-huh, I think so," he said.

A few days later he returned and the car worked fine. After a test drive, I told him, "It's running as good as ever. Can't thank you enough, Nelson."

"Well, you can do me a favor, señor."

"What's that?"

"Sell it while it's running so I don't have to work on that damn thing again," he said while smiling. His tan skin and bright eyes shown. Within the week I traded the car for a new one. Nelson had proven to me that he knew his business.

During those years when he worked for another repair company, they sent him out of state to attend various technical schools and classes. He was rapidly becoming a highly trained heavy equipment mechanic. He worked long and hard hours building on his skills. He was given several raises when he mentioned he wanted to try his hand at his own business, but in time the offer of a raise was not enough. He had to try it on his own. He started his shop just before the oil industry collapse. Other major companies were closing and moving just as he was getting started. Nelson never seemed to have luck in business. The course he chose wasn't a bad decision, but the timing couldn't have been worse. No businessmen anticipated the collapse and many large concerns applied for bankruptcy.

But he stuck it out. I remember more than a few conversations with him during those dark days of the mid-eighties. He would complain that he was working harder as an owner than he did as an employee and making less for it.

"Nelson, you've stuck it out this long, stay with it a little longer. Your job is always waiting for you if you throw it in. Most of your competitors have closed down and are gone. At least you're paying your bills. When the economy turns around you'll be still up and running. Stick with it for awhile. Damn, you're still young. Give it your shot while you can."

I didn't talk him into it. He just wanted to hear it from someone who agreed with the decision he had already reached.

When he eventually did turn the corner and started to make things a bit easier, he came to me with another stack of pictures.

"Where is it this time, señor? Cuba?"

"No, señor, never to see Fidel. Brazil! For the Carnival. Great time. Those people know how to party, señor."

We looked at his photos for more than a few minutes and then, playing his best Peter Pan on me he started, "Next year, we take the wives. They'll love it. Rio, the samba, the tongas. You'll love seeing all those lovely ladies dressed at night in their tongas. And here, the mountains," shoving a photo in my hand. "See the hang gliders. That's me and my friend, Jerry. Man, he sailed one of those things over the city down to the beach. It was fun but, señor, I was scared enough not to want to try it. But you, you'll really love it, the way you like mountains. Come on, what you say? Next year?"

"Ah, señor, I have a new child. We couldn't take her and we sure can't leave her that long. But, we'll go. Someday, señor, I promise we'll see the Carnival in Brazil."

It was not the last time we spoke of Carnival in Brazil. We spoke of it often. We spoke of it again just last year. "Ah, señor, now we both have two-year olds. How can we go?"

"Take them with us, señor. My brother lives a few hours outside of Rio. We can enjoy the Carnival and fly to his house for a few days. He has a Ph D in physics and his wife is an MD. They'll love having us. They have a beautiful hacienda in the hills. Pool, patio. Nice breezes. The wives will love it. What are we waiting for?"

"What does the flight cost, señor?"

But we never went. Life moves too quickly sometimes. Too often it moves quickly to no where, and unless we watch it, it just leads to the end.

After my second marriage ended and I was living alone in a small apartment I stopped one day to buy some fruit from a truck on an uptown street. I bought some bananas and grapes and returned to my car. Stepping inside, I heard his familiar call, "Señor!"

Pulling up behind my car was Nelson, whom I hadn't seen in months. It was spring and I hadn't seen him since our families spent two days on the beaches of Gulfport the summer before. He had arranged rooms for everyone who came. He had his jet skies, umbrellas and beach gear set up for the party. Along with his family and friends was his secretary, Jennifer. She was a lovely young girl of twenty-three or four. She was even more than lovely in her swimsuit. She and I spoke only briefly and I left that weekend not knowing her any better than I had before. On those occasions when I would call on Nelson at his office, she was too busy to be very social. She was quiet but had a warm, sincere smile.

"Señor, que passa?" I responded.

"Que paso?" he replied, with his big, wonderfully sincere smile. I was glad to see him.

"Where have you been, your honor, sir?"

"I broke up with my wife. Moved out."

"I know, señor. I phoned your home and got an ear full," he said, dragging out the last syllable for effect.

"I'll bet you did, señor."

"Well, she did not get much sympathy from me. I was there, señor. I remember. So, what are you doing now? Where are you living?"

"Have a little apartment over near the parish line. I've reconnected with someone I dated years ago and I'm happy again. Happier than I've been in a very long time."

"Oh?" His eyes were dancing above his familiar broad smile. "I understand now, señor." dragging the syllables again.

"No, it wasn't like that and you know it."

"Si, señor, I know, but I like to pull your chain, señor."

The often-repeated "señor" over many years had become a thing between us. He and I called each other señor constantly. We would throw "señor", "my friend" and "Ah" around like dialogue from poorly scripted episodes of Zorro in the 50's. I don't remember how or when it started, maybe from the beginning. My children, when they heard Nelson's name, always asked if señor was coming over. He was wonderful with children. When I was busy buying a TV for a new den, he sneaked off with my daughter to another part of the store and bought a keyboard she wanted. He just laughed when I told him it was too much. "Come on, señor, it's just a cheap little keyboard."

His own children were with him always. At the shop, I often found Josh, his middle son, with him while Nelson worked on some large motor. The child had attention deficit disorder and demanded near constant attention. Josh's parents were extremely patient with him; Jennifer, his stepmother, as well. Everyone seemed to understand that stern reprimands would be counterproductive with this child, causing pain to him and everyone else. When the boy was with Nelson, which was often, he received the kind hand he needed. He would get into everything, touching this, moving that, and all the while speaking without stop. Nelson never raised his voice, never got excited with him. He spoke to him with warm, comforting tones which were intended to sooth rather than scold. Clearly he loved the child deeply and on a special level.

His oldest son, Jacob, worked at the shop with Nelson after he married and became a father himself. Watch them work was a scene from a simpler time: the patient father teaching his son his trade. As expected, they would disagree from time to time and Nelson would explain with smiles and laughter a better way to do something. They would end the exchange with a smile on both of their faces.

This was no one-time act for my benefit. I had seen this played out too many times. This was a kind, caring, loving father and friend. This was the core of Nelson. This was Señor; this is not what he became in a few desperate hours in the spring of '98. This was my friend. This was the man whom Jennifer married.

Nelson, on that uptown street, told me he had also left his wife and was dating his secretary.

"The one who was with us last summer," I asked, somewhat amazed.

"Si, señor, that is her."

"Ah, my friend, you sly old dog," I kidded him. "She's beautiful. How's your ex taking it? She's has to be all over you. Is she all right?" I liked his unflappable first wife. Seemed she always rolled with the ups and downs of the bad economic times. She had such a laid back nature that most people were at ease with her immediately.

"No, she's still working at the company. She's accepted it all right. Says we all have to get along for the kids."

"Well, señor, you are a very lucky man, with both women. But my friend, she's young. You hearing those wedding bells, señor?"

His eyes started their happy dance and he, with a smile, answered, "Naw, señor, I don't think so." And after a pause and with a broader smile he added, "but you never know," and we both laugh at our luck for having met someone to love so late in life. In a short time we were both married and happily so.

My new wife, Elaine, and I met Nelson and Jennifer by accident while we shopped and we learned that they had married and were expecting a child.

"Well, señor, now we really can't go to Carnival." I kidded. He laughed and smiled, proudly standing next to his lovely wife and son to be. I remember his smile vividly as I now relive that day of his announcement. Nelson was thrilled. At age forty, he was starting over with a new family. I was happy for him. It was time for something good and fresh in Nelson's life.

Several months after that day, six of us, Nelson, our wives, his new son, Nicholas, Josh and I had a Sunday brunch at Algiers Landing. It was the first time I had the chance to really speak with Jennifer. I had expected a shy girl who would say little during the meal. I was wrong. She was a self assured, confident and well-spoken young woman. What surprised me most was the level of love and respect she had for Nelson. She was not his middle age trophy wife. She was genuinely in love with Nelson, and from what I knew of him, she had good reason. My wife, a woman of uncanny intuition, agreed.

He's not what the news is making of him now. He was not the violent gun nut run amuck. He was a collector of fine, expensive weapons who never before this episode ever acted in a violent manner. But his story is too complex, too hard to tell in sound bites, so they create the cliché that becomes the lie of who and what he was. But beyond this, there is a larger and, most certainly, an unconscious reason to demonize him. If the loving father, the doting husband next door can do this, then how safe are any of us from each other? What is our security if any one of us can snap, given the right pressures? And that is the story of Nelson. A good, hard working father of three who bent and finally broke from multiple wounds. Nothing can explain nor can reason defend his final despicable act and that's the problem for us now: answering the how and why of this depth of illness in a good man.

Several years ago, Nelson expanded his business. Not satisfied with only repairing large equipment, he began to bid on used heavy machines, repair them, lease them out and eventually sell them for substantial profit. At the auctions where he found suitable machines, he often discovered cars selling far below their value. He would bid on a few and occasionally turn a quick profit if the car was in good shape. Last summer, I bought an aging four-wheel drive jeep from him, which I planned to leave at my home in Tennessee. The vehicle needed repairs and a price was agreed upon. Over the Thanksgiving holidays, I planned to drive the Jeep to the mountains while my wife followed in our other car with all but one of the children. Jonathan, the oldest boy, would ride with me. As luck would have it and after many days of test driving, the water pump went out after driving 100 miles north.

I called Nelson and explained I was at a gas station in the middle of nowhere without a mechanic. "No problem, señor. Just leave the key with the people at the counter and I'll get it in about three hours. Go on with your trip my friend and I'll give you a call after I look at it."

Nelson called me three days later in Tennessee to say the car was ready and with unbelievable sincerity, offered to drive it to Tennessee. Not only did he refuse to be paid for the repair, he was genuinely upset that the car he repaired and sold to me broke down and delayed my arrival in Tennessee. "Señor, I can drive it up on a flat trailer and have you cruising the mountains in no time. I can bring it up with Jacob this weekend, Señor."

I assured him that that was not necessary and I could move it up there on another trip. But this offer was so typical of Nelson. Always there, always the friend with a hand to offer. And always, always with a smile.

Jennifer was usually at home when I looked for Nelson during the day. She took care of their infant, Nicholas, and on most days, Nelson's hyperactive son, Josh as well. For a young woman, the stress had to be extreme. It had to be extreme for anyone. Last summer while she and the children were swimming at our house, she mentioned to my wife that the grind was slowly becoming too much for her. She hoped to return to work for a break from the stress. I was not surprised when Nelson mentioned last fall that Jennifer had returned to work for the jewelry store where she was employed before she worked for Nelson's company.

In the summer, his landlord told Nelson that the lease on his shop was coming up and that he, the landlord, would need Nelson's space. Nelson told me he looked at a piece of commercial property on Airline Highway just a few hundred feet from his home. He hoped to buy it and move his operation just down the street from his home. The price seemed right and he was excited over the move. Some time later he called to say he had paid $70,000 for the parcel and he wanted me to see how he had set up his yard for the move.

The yard was large and much of his heavy machinery had already been moved onto the site. He explained with great pride where he planned to place his rail container boxes, his office and work sheds. "And look, I'm right across the street from the house. I can just walk home for a siesta, señor."

He called a few weeks later that saying that the yard was not zoned for his type of shop. I heard the pain in his voice; he was crestfallen. We discussed the act of sale and the attorney who handled the transaction. After hearing his recollections of the sale, I felt he had a cause of action for the return of the purchase price but he was more interested in obtaining a zoning change. He planned to secure written permission from all the nearby landowners and appeal to his councilman for help. We spoke again several days later and he had gathered the signatures. His attorney arranged an appointment with the councilman and was told the gentleman would vote for the variance at the next council meeting. Nelson called the day after the meeting to say the councilman had voted against the ordinance. He said he wanted to protect the adjacent landowners, Nelson's neighbors who had signed the petition for him. Nelson was upset, having been misled, and felt the reason for the no vote was disingenuous, given the fact he had the written support from all his neighbors.

Word reached Nelson that the councilman wanted the area to look more appealing for the residents near the yard. Nelson had a large wooden fence erected and shrubs planted along the perimeter of the lot hoping that that would satisfy the councilman's concerns. He was then told the man could still not support the zone change. Nelson was at a loss to understand what forces were working against him. Without sharing my suspicions with him, I suggested he contact an attorney whom we both knew and who had strong political contacts in his parish. As a last resort, Nelson called and met with him.

Weeks later, Nelson told me that Jennifer was working late hours at her store. "I just don't understand. She now wants to work on weekends. I tell her, 'It makes no sense for you to work weekends, too. If I have to watch the kids, I can't work and I make more in an hour on Saturday than you make all week.' If we use a baby sitter, it costs more than she makes at work on a Saturday. Man, I'm telling you, it makes no sense."

"Ah, señor, who can explain the females. If I could do that, I'd be a millionaire instead of a judge. She probably just needs a break from the house, señor. Too many kids and you, my friend." We both laughed but I could hear the faint echo of concern in his voice.

Near the holidays, Nelson told me Jennifer had moved in with her mother. "What happened, señor?"

"She's not satisfied with a lot of things. She wants to work, she says the back yard is a mess, with all the jet skis and boat back there. She hates the neighborhood and wants to move."

"So, are you two still talking it out?" I asked.

"Oh, yeah. No one's angry. We're trying to work it out."

"Keep talking to her and you will. What do you think you're going to do?"

"Well, I told her we could put this place up for sale, look for a new place and if she wanted to go to work, that would be okay. But I told her if she wants a real job, then go back to school. Go to college, so when she got a job, it would be worth her while."

"Is she going for it, señor?" I asked.

"She says she is. We're still talking. It's going to work out, señor."

Within a few days Nelson called to say he had a wreck with my car. He changed the master cylinder and drove Jennifer to work. On Airline Highway, he bumped fenders with another car. He had not been able to find my insurance papers in the car and received a ticket for not having proof of insurance. I assured him the papers were there or we could furnish the court with sufficient proof in time. It was not a large thing but his bad luck was inflicting a few too many wounds, both small and large.

When I gave Nelson a copy of my insurance he told me that Jennifer had returned home and they had found a house that they both liked.

"I made an offer on the house, señor, predicated on the sale of the house we're in." He described the new place to me. It was a large two-story home in a better neighborhood and it sounded like things improved for him. He even had a purchaser for the yard on Airline lined up and his monetary loss was within reason. "But señor," he added, "I don't know if I should sell. Maybe in a few years I could have the right zoning and it would be a perfect set up for me or at least I could make a good profit, the way the economy is going now."

"True, señor, and you could also drown. With everything else going on—the new house and you're running out of time on your lease on the shop—cut your losses while you can, my friend." I felt Nelson had to resolve some of the confusion in his life. He had too much to juggle.

I heard from Nelson last Thursday. He had a copy of my insurance and was going to court Monday to handle the ticket he had received. I asked how the sale of his house was going and if he got the new place yet. "Ah, shit. No. The sale was ready and it turns out there's a $25,000 lien on my property for unpaid taxes from my business. Can you believe that? Sale fell through so I couldn't get the new place."

"How's Jennifer reacting to that?" I asked.

"Ah, señor, she's back with her mother. She says it's over. I don't know what that woman wants me to do. I don't think she does either." He was confused and clearly frustrated but certainly not enraged. Not then, at least. Less than 24 hours before he would kill the woman he adored and the boy he believed was her lover he had no rage. That was not what I heard in his voice. His concern then and his reason for the call was the traffic ticket. We ended the conversation with my advising him to ask to meet with the city attorney and give him the documents so the matter could be dealt with more efficiently. He said he had an attorney on stand by if one would be needed. We both felt that that would not be necessary. That's how the conversation ended. It did not end with obsession or anger with his wife. Something within the next few hours triggered something dark and frightening in Nelson. Something that clearly was not there for forty-four years of his life. Something that I had never seen or suspected in the more than twenty years I knew him.

* * *

The next day, Friday, I had finished my docket and was dictating at my desk. The phone rang and my court reporter handed me the phone saying it was Elaine, my wife. She told me the TV news just reported a shooting death at Lakeside Mall and they had also found the body of an eleven-year-old girl abducted from Slidell days before.

"Are you ready to leave?" I asked. It had become our often-repeated question when we heard the never-ending crime news of the city.

"God, Buz, the mall is where we send our kids, thinking they're safe. Yes, I'm ready. I've been ready for years. Any time you want to go, I'm ready."

I laughed a bit to play off her fears and she asked, "Doesn't Jennifer work at one of those jewelry stores at Lakeside?"

"I don't think so. I think she's in one of the strip shopping centers out there, not the mall."

We hung up after a few more words and I continued with my dictation. Within minutes the phone rang again and my reporter, said it was Nelson, and gave me the handset.

"Señor, how did it go?" I asked, referring to the traffic court.

He was on his mobile phone. I could hear static and wind rush.

"No, this is serious." I could hear a calm dread in his voice. I could hear a torn soul reaching for someone from the depths of controlled terror. "I'm not calling about that." He continued slowly. "This is important. I just killed Jennifer. She was cheating on me."

"God, no, Nelson! Not Jennifer, you didn't kill Jennifer. Oh, God. Christ are you sure? Are you sure she's dead?"

"Yes, her boy friend too. Four shots with a 10 mm." His voice was low and pathetic. He was bereft of emotion.

"Where are you?"

"No, I can't tell you that. I can't involve you in this."

I began to say something and he interrupted and said, "I'm just calling you to ask you to take care of my boys. Please help them when you can."

"Nelson, what in hell are you talking about. You can't do that! God damn, your boys need you, Nelson. Nicholas needs his father. He needs someone. If his mother is gone, he needs his father. Please don't do this. Don't do this, Nelson." I was on my feet, my arms braced on the bookcase holding my head. The words, Christ, the words. What are the words? I had to give him a reason to live, had to give him something to hold on to. "Don't do this. You're not thinking like Nelson Arrazate. This doesn't make sense. You have to live for those kids."

"Live the rest of my life in jail. I can't do that."

"Nelson, if she was cheating, it's a crime of passion. There was no premeditation. You're going to do time but, my God, you'll be alive, and your kids will still have a father. You'll get out. They'll still love you."

"Nicholas will never love me after this."

"He will, Nelson. He needs his father. In time he'll love you. He'll always love you. He's only three, Nelson. He needs his father. You can't do this." I was almost shouting. I tried to stay calm. I tried to match the measured flat tone of voice. Keep him talking. Keep him on the phone. God, you make a living with words. Find the right ones. For God's sake, what are the words?

"Nelson, good Lord, Nelson, you're at the bottom of a well and everywhere you look is black. You're not looking up to the light but it's there, Nelson. Look up. Deal with this. Live for your kids, please."

"I've had a good life. I really have. I have to go now." Christ no, keep him talking, keep him thinking, keep him . . . "I was just calling to ask you to take care of my boys and to tell you I enjoyed knowing you . . . and you were a good person. Please, help my boys."

"Nelson, don't. Keep talking to me. Keep talking Nelson! Nelson!"

He had hung up.

I called my wife to tell her that Nelson had killed Jennifer at Lakeside. Filled with disbelief and anguish she asked where he was. I answered he was on his mobile phone but wouldn't give me his location. We broke off so I could give his name to the police.

I phoned the Jefferson Parish Sheriff's Office and told them who the wanted person was and who I was. In a few moments my wife called back shattered and in tears, "Buz, I called him and he spoke with me. I asked him to pray with me and he did. I begged him not to do anything until he talked with you again." She was crying from such a depth that my heart was breaking. She had felt the helplessness of begging a friend to live, a friend who did not want to live, and who would not listen. "He said he would talk to you. Buz, he'll talk. I told him we'd both be there for him throughout the trial. That we'd both stand by him. That we both loved him. Please call him before he changes his mind."

I hung up and dialed his phone. He answered.

"Nelson, its Buz."

We spoke. I continued to give him hope for another day, another reason to live.

"If I turn myself in, all those years in jail . . . you know I'll hate you."

"I don't care if you'll hate me. Your kids will have a father and you'll be out in time and they'll still love you and you'll still be alive."

His voice grew calmer and lower. "I'll come in. Call the DA and make the arrangements."

I told him I would set it up and call him back when they were ready. He told me his phone was losing power and to beep him and he would then return the call.

I tried calling the DA of Orleans Parish and during that process Sheriff Lee from Jefferson called in response to my earlier call to his office.

"Buz, Harry. You know this guy?"

"Yes, Harry. I spoke with him. He prayed with my wife and he wants to surrender."

We discussed my office but decided it was better to meet in the open. I suggested the boat launch ramp where Bonnabel meets the lake. We discussed safety for Nelson and the surrendering officers. We pieced together a plan whereby Nelson would meet me, leave his car and traveling in mine and we would meet the sheriff at the launch. He offered to have the media present for the surrender if Nelson wanted that assurance.

I passed the plan on to Nelson and we discussed where I would meet him. I suggested an intersection near the boat launch, "No, that's no good. How about one of the parking lots on Vets? Look," he added, "I'm trusting you on this one."

"OK, you name the place. You pick one."

"Dorignac's", he said.

"Jesus, Nelson. Dorignac's lot is huge. Where? What part? Where do I find you?"

"OK, let's pick another."

"No, Dorignac's fine. You meet me there. Park your truck, lock it up, leave all your weapons behind. I'm trusting you on this one too. Don't come out of that car with anything on you and get us both shot up."

"No, I'll leave everything behind."

"You stand in front and in the middle of Dorignac's. I'll swing by and pick you up. We'll drive down Bonnabel to where the sheriff is. He'll be there himself with just one detective. The detective will be armed with just his side arm. He says he'll have the media there if you would feel safer."

"No, that's alright. I trust him."

"Good, I'll call back and tell him it's ok."

"Ask him to give me safe passage on the way in."

"OK, I'll call you back with that. How long will it take you to get to Dorinac's from where you are?"

"An hour."

"It's twenty of two. I'll meet you at Dorignac's at twenty of three. OK?"

"Yes." He said in a calm monotone.

"OK, wait for my call."

The sheriff agreed to the location and safe passage adding his units would not stop the vehicle if it were headed to the Dorignac location. I beeped Nelson again and waited for his call.

In a few minutes, Nelson returned the page.

"OK, the sheriff agrees to the safe passage."

"Look," he said next, "I've been heading your way since we started talking. I won't take an hour to get there. Leave your office now and I'll meet you there."

"You're twenty minutes ahead of time? OK. I'm leaving after I tell the sheriff about the time change."

My reporter, who also knew Nelson, walked with me to my car. "Dude, be careful. How's he sound?"

"He sounds too calm Vinny. I don't understand why he's so calm."

"Can I do something to help. Anything. Do you want me to follow you and park across the street from Dorignac's?"

"No, Vin. There's nothing you can do."

"Are you sure. Want me to come with you?" he was worried.

"Vinny, just pray. Pray this goes down right. Pray he doesn't freak and come out of that car with a gun and get everybody shot up." We both knew Nelson was not himself, not after he just destroyed the thing he treasured most in life.

I noticed the time as I eased off the Pontchatrain Expressway and on to Vet's. It was 2:05 and I was a few minutes early. I parked near the front of the store and walked to the center of the building where it was easier for him to see me. I walked to the soft drink machine for a coke. My mouth was dry and the taste was not pleasant.

I returned to the middle of the storefront and saw undercover police everywhere. Everyone looked unusual, out of place. I was jumpy and imagining every possible scenario. I had seen a marked unit pulling out as I pulled in the parking lot. I finally concluded it was just a deputy on routine patrol. I fully expected the sheriff to have plainclothes personnel in the lot, but I hoped Nelson had not seen the marked unit and fled thinking the worst. I planned when he approached me to wrap my arm around his shoulders, protecting us both, and walk him to my car staying as close as possible to him.

I stood there watching the minutes dragging slowly by. I scanned the lot without stop, praying silently to myself. I prayed for Nelson, for me, for the police, for our children and for our wives. Please let this work. Please God.

Some say large events are shaped by small events. A quirk changes everything. The horse throws a shoe and the battle lost. At 2:35, just as I was to meet Nelson, an emergency unit from East Jefferson General Hospital pulled directly where I was standing. From within the store, store personnel escorted a customer who apparently had become delusional and combative. Long blonde hair, shirt pulled open; he was rambling to everyone near by. The deputy on paid detail was there, as was the two private security officers and all hell was breaking loose. I walked opposite the ambulance and studied in disbelief the ruckus being created where I was to meet my friend.

I glanced over my shoulder; glanced in the direction I imagined he would be coming from. No chance, I thought. He'll never come in with this going on.

The time came and went. There was no sign of him. I tried beeping him again. Nothing. After another forty minutes, I called the sheriff to tell him what had happened at Dorignac's. He asked that I stay longer, which I did, but I stayed without much hope. I phoned him again before I left and said that if Nelson would contact me again, it would be at home.

I fully expected to see his face on the front page the next morning after his body was found. I was wrong. They found him four days later in his car, parked along the side of Dorignac's, one hundred feet from where he was to meet me. He had been dead since Friday while I stood in the lot so near him, waiting, trying to find the words.

Upon Mine Altar

The coyotes came into the valley years before but as far as he knew they hadn't come to his side. They didn't concern him until the night he was awakened by the barking of his neighbor's dogs. He lay in his bed without moving, listening to the dogs howl. They were downhill from his home and a quarter mile distant. Their pen was located across a broad field that lay on the other side of a tree line thick with oak and maple. Beneath their calls he could hear the low sounds of the coyotes, wild and confident. He estimated there were two or three, perhaps more. Long minutes passed and the barking continued. His own dog began barking, moving from the front porch to the rear of the house. He stayed awake until he felt certain the dog would not leave the house and move into the darkness. Only then did he close his eyes and fall asleep.

He heard them again the next night, their howling mingling with the barking of the neighbor's Retrievers. Again his dog, a mixed hound, joined in with his baritone voice. The dog remained on the front porch and did not move to the rear this night. The man folded back his woolen blanket and moved silently to the front of the house. The floor was cold on his feet. He walked to the window and eased the curtain a slight bit away from the frame. The dog, he saw, was at the side of the door, facing west, barking in the direction of the fields below. He let the curtain slip back into place and returned to his room taking note of the time.

To the east and beyond a tree-covered ridge lay another large field. The approach road to his home cut around the edge of this field and ran along the bottom of a perpendicular ridge. The next afternoon, coming home on this road and just before turning up the last ridge, he saw a coyote break from the woods running at full sprint. Behind it came his dog, chasing the animal across the field. He stopped his truck and watched as the coyote slowly put distance between himself and the dog. Soon, he figured, they would lead him into a trap or come as a pack onto the porch.

That night he heard no sound, but the next, they came again. Once more he went to the window to see the direction the dog was facing. Again he was facing west. He reasoned that the coyotes were feeding on mice and rabbits in the mowed field beyond the tree line. He checked the time again before returning to bed.

It would be cloudy the next night but there was to be a break in the weather the day after that. A cold front, an arctic high, was to cross the plains, pass through quickly and pull wet air in from the Gulf early the following morning. Snow was expected, but for several hours, the night sky would be clear and the moon was just a few days past full. The next day he walked downhill to the western tree line and passed through it to edge of the field. He stood above it studying. The field was "V" shaped, bounded by two branches of a small stream and stretched several hundred yards in either direction. Both branches were tree lined and probably provided cover and escape for the coyotes as they hunted. The branches met almost due west at a point across the field furthest from where he stood. In the middle of the field, two hundred yards away, a small rise ran down the center of the field for a hundred yards. Along the southern branch and near the middle of the field, was a large sycamore, white and brown against the winter sky. To the front of it grew small, thinly spaced shrubs. The creek to the north ran along the base of a low ridge covered with pine and small oaks. In the northeastern corner was a shed. The roof would provide a good view of the field. On the east, the ridge on which he stood was fair but at least five hundred yards from the western edge of the field where the branches met. Depending on the direction of the wind, he would choose one of these four locations.

He set the alarm to allow him enough time to dress and be in one of the hides at least an hour before the time dogs had started barking. It was near freezing when he awoke and he dressed warmly. He slipped on his heavy woolen pants, his woolen socks and thick boots. Over his long john top and flannel shirt, he put on his camouflaged field jacket. The chest and shoulders were now too large for him. He lighted a cigarette, took out a plastic bottle of soda from the refrigerator and turned off the light. He sat in the darkness while he drank his soda and smoked waiting for his eyes to grow accustomed to the night.

After a quarter of an hour, he stood, walked to the faucet and filled the empty plastic bottle with water. He placed it in one of his jacket pockets. He took a piece of white bread off the table and placed it in the other side pocket. He walked to his gun case, opened it and removed a rifle. It was well cared for, scoped and had a leather sling. From a lower drawer he removed a handful of brass cartridges. He held three and placed the remainder in his shirt pocket. He put his mittens under his arm, walked to the door and opened it quietly. The dog raised his head to look at him, wagged his tail, but did not move any further. "Stay you stupid sum bitch," he said.

He stepped off the porch onto the ground. He stopped a moment, drew a deep breath and held it, savoring the clean northern air. He opened the weapon's action, thumbed in the three rounds and chambered one when he closed the bolt. After pushing the safety into place, he put his hands into the mittens and turned to walk in the direction of the field. Twigs and frozen grass crunched beneath his boots. He reached the trees to the west and moved through them, carrying his rifle by its sling over his shoulder. He needed a cigarette. Within minutes he was standing at the edge of the field. The sky had a faint whisper of clouds but in the moonlight he could see anything that moved on the field. The wind was cold on his right cheek and blew in from the north. He had to use the downwind hide, the sycamore, which stood on the edge of the field just above the southern branch. Stepping back into the tree line he moved south, hugging the ridge until it ran close to the branch. Before he crossed the corner of the field he stopped and played his eyes over every foot of it before he moved again. From the sycamore the rise would conceal part of the field from his view. If the coyotes entered the field from the southern branch they would catch his scent but if they came from the north or west this spot would do. He slipped over to the branch and made his way slowly to the sycamore. He stepped when the wind rose and stood still when it died. The shrubs in front of the tree were enough to break the line of his body but would not obscure his view. He unslung his rifle and sat with his back against the tree. He could feel the smooth, convex curve of the tree's trunk, and through his heavy clothing, the tree and ground were cold on his body. He sat with his right knee out to the side, his foot bent back to his centerline. His left foot was on the ground; his knee was up, bent and pointing to the field. He slipped his left arm between the rifle and the slack in the sling. He twisted his wrist back under the front of the sling and then over it to grasp the stock. He brought the shoulder piece up and felt the sling grow taut, pulling his arm, the weapon and his shoulder together. Leaning forward a bit, he looked into the eyepiece of the scope. Slowly he moved his weapon across the field estimating distances. The gun was sighted to be an inch high at one hundred yards and dead on at two hundred. The rise provided cover for the animals as he assumed, but only if they moved west to east and very close to the base of the far side. If they were thirty yards further to the north, he would see them clearly.

He let the weapon slide down the outside of his leg, releasing the tension on the sling, and waited for the dogs to bark. His eyes played the field along its western most point. From the fork of the creek he worked across the field moving to the east. He watched the northern branch and the tree-covered ridge that rose above it closely. It was from there he felt they would come, opposite the Retrievers' pen, and on to the field in search of small game. Repeatedly he worked his eyes over the field in the same pattern.

The wind was blowing directly into his face out of the north. He should have brought a mask he thought. He put his hand in his jacket, felt its warmth a moment, and took out the water bottle. He took a long pull, screwed the top back on, and placed it on the ground near his side. His well was deep, and the water was clean and sweet on his tongue. There was something familiar and knowable about the field, about this waiting, about the silver and shadows he studied. He saw his place among wordless young men sliding through fog to duck blinds and climbing in silence to deer stands before the first light of day. He recalled spotting and stalking elk, each time striking near the heart of some essential importance. Each time taming just a bit more places on the map that once were green.

More than an hour passed and the wind continued to play through the trees and low shrubs. He recalled also his time spent among the green with seven shades where other game lay among the shadows preparing for him.

Stupid dog. The smell and sound of killing lingered unpleasantly in his memory and he no longer found pleasure in the doing of it. And now it was brought again to him because the dog was too reckless to sense the danger. The thing was so wild it couldn't be penned up. The dog had broken a leg and the vet said to keep him from running until it mended. The dog almost killed himself trying to get free. He could hear him from his bed, thrashing about and crashing against the sides of the pen. The next night he tried chaining him and it howled all night. Sometimes the dog wouldn't eat the food he put out for him. On a schedule that only the dog perceived, he preferred to hunt rabbits, field rats and kill small game and eat it instead. Nor could he get the dog to come in on the coldest of nights. He couldn't stand to be confined, had to run or at least have the option. Stupid dog, he thought, almost as wild as the coyotes. They were going to kill you for sure. Nothing's that free, dog.

The clouds were moving in and he worried they would build too fast, turn the night too dark or bring the snow too quickly. His hip began to ache and he shifted his weight to the left slightly. Where were they? The wind was picking up and he lifted his jacket collar higher on his neck to cover his lower face. It had also shifted a bit, now coming from just west of north. He felt it fresh and clean on his face. It raised again and one of the Retrievers barked once, a single sharp bark. He slipped his hands out of the mittens and felt the cold, damp air on his skin. He raised the stock of his weapon to his knee, resting it there. Both dogs began barking wildly. His felt his pulse rise slightly. He raised the weapon and looked through the scope. The coyotes had to be upwind from the dogs just to the northwest of the pen. He strained to see into each shadow along the northern branch. He began scanning the field between that point and the pen. Nothing. He could hear the dogs throwing themselves against the chain link, barking frantically. Still he could see nothing.

He lowered the gun and watched without the scope. He focused on nothing, letting his eyes blur the field, trying to see it all at once, to find the movement. Nothing. He put his scope on the barking dogs. They were not facing north as he thought but east. Somehow the coyotes were past them and had to be behind the rise in the field. He traversed the weapon, following the rise from west to east. He saw nothing. How could they have moved this far into the field without being seen? He stopped the scope at the eastern end of the rise. From his right, he could now hear his own dog barking. Either he was joining in with the Retrievers or he had picked up the coyotes' scent. The wind moved farther to the west. He stayed with the weapon pointed at the eastern edge of the rise. He looked through the scope with one eye and took in the field with the other.

Near the center of the field, wraithlike, they appeared at the same time. They were at the near edge of the rise and moving parallel to it. The animal in front was to the left of the trailing animal and about ten feet ahead. They walked slowly, with controlled, powerful strides. They were alert and aware but unafraid. The familiar returned to him, a vague reminder of something substantial and deeply felt. He estimated the range at a hundred and thirty yards. Perhaps a few more. From where the pair hunted to the nearest cover of the ridge was an open, flat field for well over a hundred yards. He placed the crosshairs on the lead animal, just behind his front shoulder and six inches up from the bottom of his rib cage. The slug would hit at seven inches, near the heart. He took a deep breath, held it for two counts, exhaled slowly and squeezed off the shot. The animal dropped suddenly and without a sound. The other let out a small yelp, dropped its back end and took off for the northern branch and the ridge beyond. He worked the bolt, lowered his eye to the scope and fired at the running animal. It knocked him down, rolling him over. It tried to get up and fell. It was yelping that sick high piercing yelp canines make when they hurt beyond pain. It was lying on its side. "Damn gut shot," he said. He ejected the empty and locked another round into the chamber. He could see the animal's shoulder just above the grass. It continued to yelp and it raised its head once but could not move. It lay there, unable to get up, howling and waiting for death to stop the fiery pain. The next shot was sent through the low grass to where the animal's head had to be lying. He saw the shoulder jerk violently away from him, pulled by the neck and head moving rapidly with the bullet. The echo of sound stopped, and only the wind was heard. The dogs knew that barking was now pointless.

 He undid his arm from the sling and laid the weapon across his leg. He fished out a cigarette, lighted it and inhaled deeply. He took another, deeper drink from the water bottle. It was colder. He put his mitten on his left hand and continued to use his unmittened right to hold his cigarette. The clouds were turning a darker gray in the sky, and he could see the coming of dawn to his right. He sat there letting the tenseness subside, stretching out his legs until he felt the need of sleep. He took another drink from the bottle and put it into his jacket. He lighted another cigarette and inhaled. He blew a cloud of smoke toward his feet and thought again of the dog. More would come. They would be back. They would avoid the field for a few days but they would be back. Maybe the next time, depending on the wind, he would wait just beneath the top of the small ridge to the north.

 He held the cigarette loosely in his lips and smoke slid up his face, burning his eye. He tilted his head away and placed both knees on the ground. They were stiff. He remained there a few moments waiting for the pain to pass and then stood up holding the rifle by its sling. He slung it over his shoulder and stepped out of the tree line and turned east, uphill toward his home. It began snowing lightly and the first few flakes melted on the still-warm animals back in the field. The bread in his pocket was broken and too damp to eat.

The soft April rains
watch the new spring grass playing
beneath Aimée's feet.

KIEFER

Election Day

The years play cruel tricks, erasing bits of the mind's tapes, but the parts we do hold on to longest are the most important. It is usually the spare change of life we forget; the priceless golden moments remain. If there is contained within this recollection errors of fact or omission, it is but a failing of the memory. The feel of it, I know is correct in all respects. I have made no errors of the heart.

* * *

My earliest memory, from the years before I even knew the numbering of years, was of Woody and when he moved into the house across the street. I was four and my mother told me a new boy had moved in the neighborhood and I should meet him. He greeted me on his porch with windmills of fists and sent me running back to our kitchen and my mother. I was perplexed more than hurt. I expected this sort of treatment from my older brother but not from a complete stranger. Mother was washing the dishes and stopped to wipe my face when I explained just how poorly my introduction had gone.

She then continued with her drying of the breakfast dishes as she explained to me, without emotion, that if I didn't go back there and beat him, he would continue to beat me every day. And, she added, he would probably live here for a very long time. The correctness of her observation was apparent and made perfect sense. I returned to Woody's porch and bloodied his nose. The pecking order being established, we became friends. In later years she told me because my father's job had him away from the house so often, she felt she had to be both mother and father to her boys. She was determined, she said, not to raise sissies. We would not be pampered.

"I'll only punish you for fighting for two reasons: if you start one or if you run from one." This was page number one from Thelma's Hornbook on Life.

I never ran from one, although thinking some were not worth it I did decline a few, but I started too many to remember. For the longest time, well into our twenties, our conflict resolution skills, my brother's and mine, were limited to a series of jabs and right crosses.

Mother's father, my maternal grandfather, died of a lung ailment when she was twelve leaving my grandmother to care for five children. He was thirty-six when he passed away and all I know of him was contained in a fading photo she had of him walking a slack wire. He did this for show at street fairs. As for his real employment, that is lost to time. Her Irish family was poor and lived in a poor part of town, the Irish Channel of New Orleans. Mother's father was named William F. Davis and her mother's maiden name was Mary Ellen Gallagher. After his death my grandmother, Momma Mamie as her grandchildren knew her, worked days as a supervisor at a small neighborhood playground. At nights she collected tickets at the neighborhood movie theater. She was a small woman, no more that two or three inches over five feet. She was thin and wiry with penetrating dark eyes. My mother was not her oldest child but the most assertive. She ran the house during her mother's absence, assigning chores to get the wash done and dinner ready for the five of them, three girls and two boys.

Across the street from Momma Mamie's playground a large Italian man ran a small grocery with fruits and vegetables displayed outside on boxed tables. Over time she noticed some of the older boys going to a brick wall near the playground, removing a loose brick and retrieving small objects. On several occasions she noticed the grocer placing similar objects behind the brick. Biding her time until the opportunity allowed she went to the brick, removed it and saw several hand rolled cigarettes. Her sons and daughters played at that playground and being quick to rise, she walked to the Italian's store. Her words came fast and few.

"I know what you're up to and that's your business but if you ever involve any of my children in this, I'll kill you with my bare hands."

Family legend has it that his reply was, "Yesa mame, Mrs. Davis. Ita never happen. You hava my word."

Mamie Gallagher came from a family who used their backs for a living and were not known to shy away from fistfights. Her uncle, Bunch because he was as large as a bunch of men, took on three men in front of their house because they had beaten his brother with a pipe. Bunch beat them with a baseball bat and the neighbors helped wash the blood off the street with a hose before the police arrived. No one had witnessed anything and Bunch was not to be found. When the police left, pales of beer from the corner bar appeared, as did Bunch, and they held a street party. The green grocer had reason to believe Mamie Gallagher would keep her word.

By faith, perseverance and grit the six of them hung on and remained together. If Mamie's kids couldn't have new clothes what they did have was clean and warm and there was nothing poor or lacking in their character. Quitting was not an option when there were no safety nets and with her father's death, mom had to leave school before the eighth grade to tend to her brothers and sisters. I believe it started her on a lifetime of poor self-image masked by bravado, compensation and stoicism to a fault. It was also, I believe, among the reasons that caused her to live vicariously through her oldest son, my brother. He would achieve what circumstance had denied her.

Her two brothers were exceptional athletes and played basketball and baseball before and after they returned from the war. I saw their scrapbooks when I was a teenager and both were filled with their pictures and write-ups from the newspaper in both sports. Beneath photos of their much younger faces several captions mentioned the Davis brothers. My two aunts were champion swimmers and excelled at baseball as well. The Davis family children were known in the Channel for their athletic skills and expectations for my mother were high. Unfortunately, the pressure coming from such a family, she said, was her undoing. She was fearful of drowning and never learned to swim. In baseball she struck out with every at bat. But when it came to running the house, her siblings named her The General and in their declining years they still called her that giving each other a confirming look and a smile. If she wasn't an athlete, she had been gifted with a very large amount of the Davis/Gallagher toughness.

"Fight for the little guy; the big guy can take care of himself."

"Never lower your eyes to another man. You're as good as anyone you meet."

"To hell with what people say, be yourself. Do things that make you proud, that make you happy. Other people will come and go. You have to live with yourself for the rest of your life so you better make damn sure you like yourself."

"You stand with your brother right or wrong but in private, you let him know when he's wrong and get him to see it. And watch out for each other. You're blood."

"If you're going to quit, don't start. Don't even waste your time. Quitters never win."

She would make sure her boys were not haunted by the same voices of failure that she heard. We were taught to swim at an early age and she and my father were determined to see us educated. Sports were not just encouraged, they were expected.

I really didn't know my paternal grandmother as I saw her only rarely and although my memory contains no lasting image of her face, I remember the smell of aging and the shadowed rooms in which she lived. In her front room, next to a white curtained window, was a player piano and a large ornate cabinet containing a number of paper rolls. The cloth covered sofa and winged chairs, having come from a finer home, were too large for the room and were covered with crocheted dollies. Her gait, while not quite a shuffle, was guarded and uncertain. She was bent over slightly and with her arthritic hands she would put one of the rolls in the piano for my enjoyment, something dated and dreary, while she sat at the large dining room table and spoke with my father. There are no warm memories of holidays spent with her or of her visits to our home. I believe, without certainty, that this was due in part because she and my mother were not on good terms. Mother never went with my father to visit her and no reason for this was given. I remember my brother coming with us only once or twice. Reflecting upon my mother's condemnation of my aunt's antiques, and assuming she judged them harshly as we had none, I conclude that perhaps my mother was threatened by my grandmother's bearing and former wealth.

I am told that before and for a while after the Great Depression my father's family was well off. That the family holdings were lost was due to my grandfather having passed on and my grandmother's blind faith that business had to improve. They lived uptown on a fine oak-lined avenue in a home that eventually became the residence of the German Ambassador. My father when he was younger, again I am told, was somewhat of a rake, a devil-may-care handsome man with an eye for the ponies as well as women and a good hand at cards. Occasionally, it was said, he was good with his fists although not quick to anger. When Bayou St. John was still a navigable body of water he won a small cabin cruiser at a poker table. That weekend he hosted a celebration party aboard the boat as it lay at anchor near the foot of Esplanade. As the night lengthened and after the hoisting of many glasses of bootleg gin, someone noticed that the boat was leaking and, indeed, seemed to be going under. Because it held no more importance to him than the turn of a card, at my father's direction, they removed the liquor, stood along the shore, sang and toasted the boat until it sank.

Before he married my mother, according to an uncle, he matured, gave up that life and took a job. He would gamble only occasionally until my mother almost died trying to deliver the first of her sons. Forming a deal my father traded this passion for my mother's life on a promise. The son died but dad never gambled again after his wife survived. My mother told me this story one night when I was still young but old enough to ask about my first dead brother. My father, Ignatz or Big Nat as he was called, apparently never lost the excitement of seeing the horses run and he'd take me to the track when I could not have been much older than six. We'd watch from a spot on the rail just opposite where they broke from the final turn. I could hear and feel in the vibrating ground the deep thudding of flying hooves breaking towards the finish line, throwing mud into the air, and the jockeys going to the whip for the final sprint. Between races I hunted for four-leaf clovers. He would help me look and toss bits of grass into my hair and we'd laugh.

I was the second son born alive to my mother and her final child. The very first son being DOA dragged my mother into a years-long depression, thinking she could no longer have children. When my older brother was born four years later I am given to believe that my mother had a rebirth of her own. A switch was thrown and the light was back in her life and it lit up her eyes. There was no finer son, no better looking, brighter child anywhere. He was told constantly that he could achieve anything, even beyond greatness, if he wanted it badly enough and worked hard for it. The role of willpower and determination in success is without question true to an extent, but coming as it did from his mother, it was accepted by him as bedrock truth upon which all doors opened and where impossibility did not exist. Years later, in 1977 to be precise, after overcoming multiple obstacles and becoming more than successful, he learned that there were limits after all. Meeting with his first real defeat he began his slow decline that culminated in his death some eight years further on.

Mother was a heavyset woman with a remarkably beautiful face. She had blue eyes and smooth white skin that was framed by black hair. Upon his birth my mother bloomed from depression into a glowing motherhood. She now had a lovable companion child to keep her company while my father traveled the state four days a week providing for his family. Her son had clear blue eyes and from my father's Germany side he was given white blond hair. From him also came his broad shoulders. While she was shopping people, strangers, would stop her to look at her beautiful baby. Because of the near matriarchal arrangement our family socialized with my mother's brothers and sisters and their children although my father's brother, for whom I was named, lived only a few blocks away. Perhaps it was because he and his wife had no children. Or perhaps because he was his mother's son.

When I was born, I was given a nickname immediately. On the birth certificate I was given a name that still rings foreign. From the day I came into being, I was called Buz. When old enough to inquire about my two-name situation, my mother told me that my father's mother had asked, or insisted rather, that I be named after one of my father's brothers, George. So certain was she that after conceiving two males, the third child had to be a girl, she agreed to placate the woman she considered domineering. "No one, not even your father, liked the name George so we gave you a nickname. I wanted to call you William." Bill was a powerful name, worthy of boyhood respect; a name that not only fit in but made a statement about its owner. George was weak and foolish sounding. I went through life despising my own name. My brother was named after my father, and became Little Nat. Nat was a great name; everyone knew it.

At the lakefront, walking on the green space separating Camp Leroy Johnson from the seawall, or while we were in the back yard, my father would throw pebbles or small berries at me while I was looking elsewhere. He'd tell me the Japanese were shooting at me. Knowing the familiar game I'd run to him and he'd grab me under my arms and raise me high into the air. I would yell my excitement and he would laugh. There was power in his arms and chest. Dad had dark brown hair that was thinning and brown eyes that could convey deep affection or fix you like a pinned butterfly.

Mother, constantly goading my brother to do better in school and in sports while overseeing his life, became active in the PTA and became his den mother when he joined the Cub Scouts. His neighborhood friends joined the den and they gathered once a week in the back room of our home. I would watch from the edge of their fun and play with my dog. In three years, when I was to join the Cubs, Nat joined the Boy Scouts and my mother became the troop mother. I remember a photograph of the three or four troop masters and my mother proudly standing on the school stage, surrounded by flags, bedecked in ribboned chested uniforms and military caps, smiling.

Mother arranged for me to join Mrs. Braden's den. I went to the same school as the boys in that group but they were a year or two older than me and were from another neighborhood. Dad drove me to the Friday meetings and picked me up when they were over. It was not an easy fit in the beginning. I was the outsider and my friends were back near my home but my years in Mrs. Braden's den were enjoyable enough and I earned my arrows.

It was during this time of my brother's scouting and of my finding my way in Mrs. Braden's den that the annual jamboree was held at a campground across the lake. The scouts had camped for two days and we drove over for a Sunday picnic and to pick up my brother. There was a swimming pool and boys of all ages were jammed in splashing and yelling. We parked in a lot some distance from the pool. The air was filled with the smell of pine and the needles formed a cushioning mat along the clay road. Chairs for parents were spread around the pool but set back far from the edge in multiple rows. I saw Nat immediately. He and his friends were tossing a ball trying to hit each other. I ran to the dressing room and changed into my suit. I ran to my mother who was seated in a chair next to a gray haired, heavyset Italian woman. I handed my mother my rolled up clothes and she told me I had to find a swimming partner before I could go in. I only vaguely knew the purpose of the partner and I searched for a kid to be mine. I asked my brother and his friends if anyone needed a partner. No one did. The pool was filled from an artesian well and the water was dark with tannin. Through the water I could only see the top six or seven inches of their chests before their bodies were lost in the deep amber of the pool. I asked kid after kid if they needed a partner until I saw a boy walking to the pool with a dry suit. Yes, he said, he needed a partner. I told him my name and he told me his. We ran for the pool, I jumped in beside him and swam to my brother and his friends. Finally liberated I joined in their game of tossing and hitting. Loud yells and kids were everywhere and after ten minutes or so, the head lifeguard blew his whistle and we were told to team up with our partners and go to the side of the pool. Boys started to move to the edge of the water and soon I was alone in the shallow end, turning around looking for my partner. Where was he?

"Where's your partner"

"I don't know."

I was scared. No one could see the bottom of the pool. The water was too dark.

"What's his name?"

"Phillip."

"Phillip who?"

"I don't know." I kept turning in the water, looking, hoping he'd magically reappear and this feeling would leave my stomach and all would be fine and we could go back to our game. "I don't know his last name. I just met him."

Mr. Claudina, the Troop Master for the New Orleans District, was suddenly there, taking charge, asking me the same questions from the edge of the pool.

He ordered all the boys out of the pool until I was alone in the dark water. Mr. Claudina stood above me looking down. His face was hard.

"Are you sure you had a partner."

"Yes, we jumped in together."

"Why didn't you stay together? That's what partners are supposed to do." I was nine years old and under the circumstances I couldn't explain or try to defend myself. He climbed the lifeguard stand and told me to come up with him. We watched as older boys and men formed a line at one end of the pool and walked until they had to swim along the bottom, looking for my partner. I watched with increasing fear as they repeated the search over and over. He was dead and I had caused it. From the top of the lifeguard stand I saw the boy walking to the pool from the car lot.

I pointed and said, "There he is."

Eyes that had been studying the pool and me turned now to the approaching boy.

Mr. Claudina called him over.

"Are you this boy's partner?"

"Yes."

"Where were you?"

"I went to tell my mother I had found a partner."

"Did you tell him that?"

"Yes."

Before I could speak out, before I could say he jumped in with me, Mr. Claudina said loudly so all the boys could hear, "Do you see what you've done? We thought this boy was dead. Don't get back in the pool. You're finished for the day."

I climbed down the stairs feeling the nearness of tears. I felt overwhelming guilt and at the same time anger because I could not speak up. I had not only been accused and stood mute, I actually felt I had done some terrible wrong even though I knew the boy had lied.

Walking way from the pool I heard the shouts of the boys yelling and splashing again and I saw my mother. Surely she had to have seen the entire episode but hadn't moved. She was chatting and laughing with the heavyset woman. I walked up to her needing something. She stopped talking, looked at me and asked, "What's wrong Buz?"

I was sobbing and I coughed out my words, "That . . . rat . . . Claudina."

A look of shock came over my mother's face. Shock and something I recognized as embarrassment. I looked at the large Italian woman. She was looking at me. I saw in her eyes and heard in the silence that followed my words that she was Mrs. Claudina.

I turned and walked away. There was no pampering and no one called after me or followed. I cried near the edge of the woods where no one could see me.

Some two years later my brother tired of the scouts. He quit because of sports and my mother gave up her position in the troop. For my final year of cubing, I was with my friends in my mother's den. When I became a Boy Scout, she joined my brother's high school PTA and eventually became its treasurer. The possibilities for Nat were boundless. We both were offered scholarships to high school. He turned down his offer as he wanted to play for a different school. I would turn down mine because I wanted to be in the same school as my brother.

Nat started his freshman year of high school at Holy Cross. He didn't take to living on campus during the week and being home only on weekends. After several weeks or a month he refused to return to school. He caught a Greyhound bus to meet my father in a small town in north Louisiana. He rode home with him but refused to return to the school. The parish priest, in fact the pastor, was consulted. He spoke with Nat, got him to agree to return to school, phoned the principal of the high school and assured the brother that Nat was sincere. Our pastor had built our church and grammar school, St. James, into the most successful in the Archdiocese. His word carried weight and my brother was allowed to return to Holy Cross. A week later he left again, this time for good, and our pastor never forgave him. It meant Nat would miss a full year of school and I was instructed by my mother not to tell anyone. We pretended that Nat had a private tutor (name and location unknown) but the world knew well that he had dropped out. The irony of the pretense was lost on my mother who had drilled another of her homilies into us in our formative years, "If you lie, you'll steal. I hate liars."

Awareness of the contradiction came too late for me and, thanks to her, I never stole much more than a comic book and I was a pathetically transparent liar. I took her at her word and lying made me far too anxious to be good at it. I didn't want her hatred. I do recall a small early lapse though. I was perhaps seven and went shopping with my father for the family groceries. I stole a small can of orange juice concentrate, putting it inside my jacket. Out of guilt, I think, I showed it to my father when we got into the car.

"Why did you take that son?"

"I've never seen juice like this before. Mom squeezes ours in the morning."

"But it doesn't belong to us; you stole it Buz. Bring it back inside and tell the man you're sorry."

"Come with me."

"No, you have to do this on your own."

From a happy household we drifted that year of my brother's refusal into a darkness that embraced us like another being. No more did nightly laughter emanate from around the TV. From a noisy house full of sound and the bouncing of basketballs it fell into a dark silence and we hardly spoke. I remember none of the discussions on the matter for probably there were none held in my presence but I could feel their impact in the chill of the house and the in few words that were necessary for the routine of living. All attention was focused on Nat and the disappointment he brought my mother. I felt cut off from both of them and I was tense and anxious although I could not say why. I was powerless to lift the despair that claimed us. My days were drifting. I was moving through them with the dread of pointlessness that would last until the family recovered and that wouldn't happen until my brother resumed the life my mother saw for him.

As for the pastor, he took his first public shot at my brother several years later during the summer when he at age sixteen was working construction. Nat had to be on the job at six in the morning and during the week of Catholic Youth Retreat we had to attend a weeklong, nightly session of pointless religious droning. St. James the Major Church, now one of the largest in the city, was filled with teens and young men and women. Nat, seated in the rear of the church, nodded off. The pastor moved to the podium, stopped the rambling priest, took the mike in his hand and shouted, "Kiefer! Wake up and go home." Stifled laughter and snickers were heard.

The congregation watched as Nat rose and walked out of the church. Seated with my friends in the middle, I stood quietly and walked out behind him. It was an uncalled for painful humiliation and my father, who respected the pastor, called him the next day and told him so.

I began weightlifting in the sixth grade when I was eleven and enjoyed the challenge, the self-discipline and the changes it brought on. I was small and if I wanted to play sports, I needed an edge. At that time none of the high schools had a weight program and very few engaged in the sport. In three years I was competing and placing in my weight class. In the beginning the strength gains were rapid.

In grammar school I was neither a leader nor a follower, just an average boy but I was placing in the 98 percentile in the national performance tests. I was a year younger than most of my classmates, having started kindergarten when I was four. Mother said she sent me early because I was bored at home and wanted to go to school with my brother.

The leader of the sixth grade class, the one several boys imitated, was a tall boy with blond hair combed into ducktails. He spoke little, never explained, apologized or became excited. He knew and portrayed the enigmatic elements of cool at an early age. He was a year older than me and could have had any girl in the class, even the early blooming, large breasted Marilou. His name was Aaron.

Before Rock and Roll there was music that blacks were allowed to have for themselves, for a while at least, Rhythm and Blues. It was a music that threatened the status quo when white children began listening to the polyrhythmic tunes with suggestive lyrics. Whites began to sing cover tunes of their songs and from this earthy soil sprang the Rock music of the 60s and today. A local 50s disc jockey, Jiving Jerry by name, began his nightly show with his theme, Big Mamma Thornton's original cut of Hound Dog with her wailing opening line. "Yoooouuu ain't nothing but a hound dog, sneakin' round mah door . . ." blasted out on the airwaves and the white kids went wild. He made appearances at local record shops and he hit ratings gold when he started the Hound Dog clubs. The idea was simple and clever. Groups of friends mailed a letter containing a list of their club members to his station. Each club was given a number and during the show, as each club came into existence, the names of its members were read on air between tunes. With this hook, his audience soared as kids across the city waited to hear their names announced. It was innocent enough but being associated with that threatening music resonated with my burgeoning rebel chord. I started a club in my sixth grade class.

The day after the night our names were read on the radio the kids achieved a sort of overnight popularity in school and I had been the instigator of something for a change. At the same time I was growing stronger from lifting weights and in general I was beginning to seek my own way. Without my realizing, things were headed to the inevitable clash with Aaron. A morning before school he cursed while in a girl's presence and I called him on it. I didn't mean for it to escalate but Aaron apparently thought it was a challenge. As I was to learn afterwards, when his father dropped off his lunch to him that day, Aaron told him, "Buzzy and the Hound Dog are going to get me."

Getting or fighting anyone was not on my horizon and why Aaron thought so can only be assumed: other kids talked and invented things. I wanted him to know nothing more than I had limits.

I was standing beneath the covered wooden shed talking to some classmate when a firm hand grabbed my arm, and turned me around violently. The face of Aaron's father was portrait of anger. Aaron stood at his side, wide-eyed. "Ok, you want to fight him, fight him now, fair and square. None of this gang stuff."

I had no idea what he was talking about and for the second time my ability to think and speak froze in the presence of an angry adult. Before I could choose otherwise, I was in a fight. No one had really hit me before this except Woody and my older and much larger brother who would pummel me with regular and frequent beatings. Aaron struck my face and I was puzzled. What was that? That wasn't a punch. That wasn't even a slap. I fought back, not protecting myself any longer because his hits didn't phase me. I carried the fight to him until I had bested him and his father broke it off. I watched Aaron, much smaller now, walk off with his father as kids gathered around me in an excited mob. "You won! You beat Aaron Burren!" Twain said the worst thing that could happen to a young man was to win his first bet. Winning a first fight, if not the worst thing, could not be too far behind. In years to come, I became a fighter, a street brawler. In all the cuts and stitches that were to follow I never felt pain. The weekly beatings administered at my brother's hand pounded toughness into me or more likely it came from the same bloodline as Mamie and Bunch Gallagher. Regardless of the reason, the unfortunate consequence was that I carried my left too low, due in part to the fact that being hit rarely mattered. I was not going down.

After the year of his refusal Nat went to a newly opened high school, Cor Jesu, on the promise that they would have sports the next year. Mother joined the PTA and when it was learned that there would be no sports for several years, he switched to St. Aloysius High. Mother followed him and became an officer in the St. Aloysius Parents' Club. I continued to lift and my Biddy Basketball team was undefeated. I was offered a basketball scholarship to Holy Cross but chose instead to go to Aloysius. Nat was a junior in my freshman year. Before I started my freshmen year Nat showed me the correct lineman's three-point stance. Feet spread a bit wider than your shoulders, toes and heels squared to the line, weight equally balanced between the fist on the ground and your feet so you could pull out or go forward. This was before facemasks were used and he showed me how, on the snap, to raise my hand from the ground and throw a forearm into the opposing lineman's face. "One the fist play of the game, smash him as hard as you can in the mouth. Hurt him on that play and you'll own him for the rest of the game. You ain't out there to make friends."

He was right about that. I played freshman football and basketball but after the football season of my sophomore year, the head coach asked me to focus on football. Spring training conflicted with the basketball season and I chose football. That second year I was moved up to the varsity and played in some games next to my brother. Our parents were thrilled seeing us on the same field and that year we tied for the city championship.

During my early teens, my father would often surprise me on the weekends bringing home orange tins of cashews and bottles of orange colas. We watched the Giants play Chicago and both eventually lose to Green Bay. The tins are now blue but when I see them, I think of him and those wonderful Saturday afternoons spent quietly watching the games, just he and me. Neither of us were given to yelling although for my mother and brother it was their normal means of communication. I found it annoying. I assumed my father felt the same way for he had told me, "When you raise your voice, you've already lost the argument." Occasionally, we'd go to a neighborhood restaurant before game time and eat plates of bell peppers stuffed with shrimp. Having lived foolishly for a time, having seen the folly of taking too much for granted, the man was, in my lifetime, always at peace with himself. He knew the score when it came to the important things and apparently I was one of the things he felt important enough to hold on to.

In spite of my agility and strength, I remember my mother's words to me as a child, "Of course you can't be as good as your brother. Look at how much bigger he is." He played tackle his senior year at age 18 weighing 225 pounds and won a scholarship to Tulane. My senior year I played inside linebacker weighing 150 pounds. I was captain of the defense but no offers were expected. But in our homecoming game I made seventeen tackles, most of them unassisted. I played my last game when I was 16. Mother was right, I was too small and in her eyes, although I was good, I could never equal my brother. More importantly I had already accepted that without question but not without cause. Nat lettered in football, basketball and track.

Before the beginning of my senior year, we began in August the two-a-day football practices. I was first string guard and inside linebacker. My long-term girlfriend and I had just broken up and I had little besides that on my mind. The adrenaline of heavy contact was gone and I daydreamed my way though practice. At our first scrimmage with a team from up-river, I missed an easy trap block. Coach, who was standing behind the scrimmage line, ran up to me yelling, "Kiefer, what the hell is wrong with you son? The God damn man is right there and you just went by him."

"I didn't see him coach."

"That's bullshit. He was right there in front of you. You turned chicken-shit. Randy get in here an do something for Christ sake."

From first string I was busted to third and in a few days I quit the team.

My father knew how much I loved the game. He also knew how I felt about the girl and understood enough to put the picture together. After a week or so, when we were alone he asked me how I was handling things.

"I can't think of much else Dad. But I'll be all right."

"Are you sure?"

"Yeah."

"What about ball. Do you want to play this year?"

"Sure, but coach won't let be back after I just quit like that."

"Maybe if you can keep your mind on the game instead of this girl he would. Can you do that?"

"Yeah, but hell, there's no sense in even asking him."

"I spoke to him about it and he said if you're ready to play ball, he wants you back."

I still had to practice with the blue jersey of the third string but I felt my anger pumping the adrenaline with each hit. Standing over the first string center I'd shiver him in the head when he tensed his fingers just before the snap. The hit to his head would arrive just as the ball reached the quarterback's hands. No blocker could get to my body. In a three-point stance, I'd forearm linemen lifting them up and move to the ball. Anger and desire had replaced self-pity.

Our season opener was against one of the better teams we would face. Their left guard and center, Negrato and Randall, made All State the year before. I sat on the bench for the first quarter watching them destroy Randy, running up the middle play after play. Finally, the defensive coach looked at me and said, "All right Kiefer. Get in there. 6-oh-8. Stop the middle runs son."

I was the middle linebacker in that defense and stood head on the center. I noticed that the guard, Randall, was pointing his foot, giving away the cross block. I knew the center would close on our right guard and Randall would move behind him to blindside me with the halfback running in the hole between the two blocks. At the snap, instead of cracking the center, I let him move to his block. I slanted to the hole with my knees bent and smashed Randall with a forearm when he appeared. I threw the halfback for a loss.

I couldn't hear the fans cheering. For the rest of the game I knew there were bright stadium lights and a blur of people in the seats, but they weren't there any more, not in my field of awareness. The world collapsed into the space between the left and right tackles and I owned it. Nothing could move between those two points and I beat on Negrato and Randall for the rest of the night. No more runs up the middle worked and they were reduced to running sweeps and passes. In the third quarter, they ran a tandem block on our corner man and their halfback broke clear. He sidestepped our safety. Taking the correct angle, I stopped him thirty yards downfield short of the goal. On an extra point I split their double team and blocked the kick. We won by eight points.

On the bus ride back to school the head coach who had given me the chance to play again asked in a loud voice silencing the team, "Kiefer son, as slow as you are, how did you catch the halfback on that sweep?"

"I don't know coach. I just wanted the bastard."

The team broke into wild cheers, all of us riding the crest of an adrenaline rush and victory. And mine was sweetest of all. I was back, and in large part, it was because of my father.

My ex-girlfriend was in the stands that night and got word to me that she wanted to see me. We got back together; she became homecoming queen, and broke my heart again at the end of the school year. Instead of self-pity this time it ushered in contempt for everything including myself.

Still loving basketball, I played five years in the Catholic Youth Organization league and won the yearly high point award three years running. Nat played in the same league several years as well. The CYO sponsored three divisions grouped by ages. Juniors were fifteen and below, specials were age sixteen and seniors were seventeen and above. One unforgettable night when I was thirteen and Nat was playing on the special team we both won our games and were sitting with a group friends in the crowded gymnasium. We were watching the seniors' game. Nat was seated on the bleacher seat just below me and slightly to the side. I had a whistle in my jacket and we passed it around taking turns whistling the game to a halt. The kids and most of the fans laughed each time. After several game stopping whistles one of the senior players came out of the game and sat beneath us off to the side. No one gave him much thought. It was my turn on the whistle and when I blew it the senior jumped up, pushed his way through the four or five rows separating us, grabbed me by the jacket and pulled me out of my seat. I was prone and being dragged roughly out of the bleachers. I said only one word, "Nat". When my brother's first punch landed he released the grip on my jacket collar immediately. Nat beat him down the length of the gym, each right handed punch knocking him back five or six feet. When they reached the opposite end of the gym the guy was bloody, on his hands and knees and barely conscious. My brother, in a rage, had beaten him savagely. I saw my brother's foot start to pull back to kick him and it flashed instantly in my mind, no, don't, and then I saw his leg relax. The senior player was saying, "Nat, I didn't know. I didn't know." Nat was yelling for him to stand up again.

The pastor burst through the gym door and pushed Nat against the wall. "You again Kiefer! You're always starting trouble around here! Get out! Leave and don't come back!"

And he pushed Nat towards the door.

My brother and I drove home and told our parents what had happened. My father asked calmly, "Are you sure you're both telling me all of it?"

I have never seen my father show anger or, for that matter, excitement except when he was watching Nat or me play ball.

"Yes sir,"

"And that other boy who grabbed your brother is nineteen?"

"Yes sir."

He rose, took his hat off the refrigerator and said, "Boys, I think it's time we spoke with Father Schubert about this."

My mother, addressing her husband, merely said, "Nat?"

Dad said, "Thelma, we have to put an end to this."

We drove to the rectory, knocked on the door and were shown into the pastor's office by the maid. Father Schubert in his white collar and black gown came in and sat behind his desk. My father did not rise when he entered, nor did he offer his hand.

Looking at my father, the pastor asked, "What can I do for you, Nat?"

"The boys told me their side of what happened tonight. I thought I should hear your side of it."

This pastor was known throughout the Archdiocese as a talented businessman who had taken a run down parish and made it into the finest in the city. Since his arriving at St. James the school had all new class buildings, a new gym, and the other parishes envied the size and beauty of the new church. His influence was felt not only in church matters but in politics and business as well. He was highly respected and intimidated most men of the parish.

Father Schubert proceeded to tell my father exactly what we had told him. My father waited until he had finished.

"Buz is thirteen and half the size of that nineteen year old boy who grabbed him. Was his brother to sit there and let him be beaten?"

"No, but—"

"These boys have been taught to stand up for each other and if that boy, a man actually, took a beating from Nat, maybe he's learned not to grab kids."

"Are you approving of what your sons did tonight?"

In flat, unemotional tones my father answered with his eyes locked on the pastor's. "The whistling was boys' play and, no, I don't approve of that but as for the fight, yes I do. Had I been here and saw my young son manhandled like that, I would have done the same thing. But the way you pushed Nat and berated him, that wasn't about this fight. That was about his not returning to Holy Cross and, to your way of thinking, that reflected poorly on you. You've been on this boy's back since that episode. Just this year you humiliated him in front of the whole church for nodding off. You knew he was working a man's job and getting very little sleep. Rather than get that sleep he chose to attend your retreat, something admirable, only to be embarrassed by you in your pettiness."

Father Schubert, a man whose weighty word was never questioned, sat there stunned but dad didn't stop there.

"And I'll tell you something else while we're at it. That janitor you keep around here, that Louis Netton, and maybe one of the other priests . . . I think you're running a queer haven over here and if you embarrass either of my boys again, I'll be back and the next time I won't stop to consider that I'm dealing with a priest."

I was shocked at my father's accusation. How did he know about Netton and how could he say this to Father Schubert? His voice throughout the lashing was measured and never rose in anger but his message was unmistakable. My father then stood and simply said, "Let's go boys."

Father Schubert said not a word. I was bursting with pride.

The 50s were a different time and boys fighting to settle matters was accepted and considered natural. In my freshman year at Aloysius, I was in a fight with an older boy at a high school football game. We fought to a draw and agreed to meet again in two days when Aloysius had the Sunday game. At half time a large part of the stadium emptied out to see the fight. I broke my hand on his jaw before the police broke us up and sent us on our way. The next day, Monday, the school principal, Brother André, was walking down the main hall and saw Nat coming towards him.

"Kiefer, what's this I hear about a fight your brother had at the game."

"The boy was three years older than him brother and he started it at Friday night's game."

"How? How did he start it."

"I'd rather not say brother."

"I'd very much rather that you did. Tell me, how did the fight start."

"He called my brother a mother fucker."

"Did Buz win?"

"Yes."

"Good." Brother André continued his walk and the matter ended there. Nothing like that could happen in today's twisted world. That fight in 1956 was considered honorable by the standards of that day. Today I would be driven from school in disgrace.

In the year of my sixth grade I was kicked on the chin by a horse. I was on a Boy Scout's camping trip going from knot tying to compass reading. Walking in several lines, with me on the end of one, we walked behind a high strung horse. I have no memory of seeing him but I awoke in a clinic, dazed, with several teeth missing and over thirty stitches in my chin. It left an ugly scar. It was then I believe that Sister Monica, my teacher in both the sixth grade and then again in the eighth, took a liking to me. Knowing how I tested and that school bored me, she would, without saying, let me sneak in books from the library to read while she taught the class. She laughed at my jokes and smiled when she saw me.

In my grammar school class there were several boys who had been held back repeatedly. One, Richy Maine, upon reaching his seventeenth birthday in the seventh grade quit school to work on the riverfront. In the eighth grade there were two sixteen-year-old boys with whom I fought for months. I was thirteen and every Friday after school I fought one and the following week I'd fight the other. Sister Monica asked me why I kept fighting them if they kept beating me.

"Because," I said, "One day I'll win."

A year later, as a high school freshman, one had moved and the other refused to fight me.

The night of our eighth-grade graduation dance, one of those sixteen-year-old boys, Kenny, told me he was to fight that night with a boy in a rough gang from across the railroad tracks. Richy Maine belonged to that same gang. For reasons I don't understand, he asked me to be his second to make sure it was a fair fight. I didn't even like this guy; I had no reason to go with him but I did. Honor, chivalry? Stupidity probably.

I knew Kenny's weakness from my fights with him: he couldn't take a hit. If you were able to hurt him, he lost his aggressiveness. But he was strong and fast with good combination punches. The boy he was meeting was Ted Cranston and his second was a snagged-tooth, wiry insect appropriately named Beetle. On the field between the Baptist Seminary and the railroad tracks, under the moss draped cypress trees, they took off their shirts and had at it. Kenny moved to his left trying to connect with his jab. Ted blocked or let most of them slide off. Ted was nineteen and while Kenny was in shape and quick, Ted was ripped with mature muscle and was quicker. Unlike most fights that end up on the ground in a grunting wrestling match, both stood and boxed each other and the punches echoed with a thwacking sound when one or the other connected. Their backs glistened with sweat in the moonlight and they circled and jabbed. Kenny held his own for the first few minutes but a right hook followed by a left upper cut as he tried to close on Ted ended the fight. They shook hands and their difficulties, whatever they were, ended that night. My simply being there was the first step in what would become, within a few months, a gang fight that lasted for years. Beetle and Ted were hoodlums and I didn't want any part of them. But when honor becomes rage and rage becomes sport, honor no longer has much to do with it.

My friends in the neighborhood, who went to Catholic schools, were fairly bright; some were involved in sports and weightlifted at one time or another. Three of us lifted competitively. The bad guys, as we refer to them sarcastically, lived to the south and north of our neighborhood. They were weasels and most could be beaten one-on-one but they did have a share of some very tough guys. Ted belonged to the main group. It was also the oldest and roughest. They lived across the tracks to our southeast and those tracks were the dividing line between two different worlds. Their gang was named after their neighborhood, Forest Park or simply the Park. The others were sort of tangential members of The Park, living as they did in other neighborhoods. They were not as tough or as poor as their brethren in the Park. They drove better cars and wore nicer clothes but they were on the same path. I thought of them as a larval stage of apprentice thugs. I learned later, in my 30's, that many of the guys in the Park were on heroin during those early years of street fights. Several were killed within the decade and one, strung out and alone, killed himself. One or two from the sub-groups also cashed in early as well. They viewed the world in simple terms; you were either in their little club or you were against them. We chose the latter. They thought nothing of beating all hell out of you if they caught you alone or out numbered. At a Saturday night dance I was challenged by a guy not quite my size. The entire dance, boys and girls, spilled outside to see the fight. My friend and I were outnumbered as we were in the wrong neighborhood and things didn't look too bright for the visiting team. I knew the boy was a boxer, and I assumed that they had chosen him as I could take him easily enough, and then I'd have about 20 on my back. While walking to the location of the fight behind the school gym I told my friend that I was just going to pin the guy. It was an obvious set up. We hit each other several times and after a few minutes, we both went down. I was on him pinning his arms with my elbows hoping it looked to the others like something was going on. I felt a terrific, stunning blow to the back of my head. And again. And again. I didn't black out but was dazed. Through a vague awareness, I felt, heard or sensed that the crowd was moving. Moving away from the fight, running. I rolled off the guy I had pinned. There were car lights coming slowly down the street and single bright lights on the sidewalk and on the lawns. It was the police moving forward in a line of squad cars, three wheel motorcycles and on foot with large flashlights. Teenaged kids were running in every direction away from the lights. Two voices came to me simultaneously. The first said that running into the darkness could get me very hurt and the other, my mother's, reminded me that the police were my friends.

I got to my feet and slowly walked to the closest policeman with my hands up. I was still stunned. He kept his flashlight in my eyes and I'm sure he didn't know what to make of me walking to him when half the world was running to beat hell in the opposite direction. I got as far as, "Officer" when, with amazing insight, I learned that mom was not right about all police being friendly. My friend turned his flashlight around, grabbed me by my shoulder, pulled me to him, and jabbed me in the stomach with the narrow end hard enough to bring me to my knees. He then proceeded to take me to the corner where the three wheelers had converged, pushing me in front. He held my arm twisted behind my back. There was excitement at the corner where the police converged but they caught no one except me. I guess they figured those shadows would be none too friendly to them either. Police officers and motorcycles surrounded me. My captor was doing a lot of talking when one of the motorcycle policemen said, "Hey, have you seen this kids head?" I began to hear welcomed words, encouraging words like "holy shit", and "damn". But the phrase that really caught my ear was, "The back of his shirt is covered with blood down to his waist." With that I turned to look at my hip on the side where I felt those powerful hits. He was right. Blood was definitely down to my hip. "Better let him go so he can get to a hospital." How could I get from here to a hospital? I thought now is the time to confront my friend with the flashlight. "No, take me in. This guy beat me with his flash light and I want to be arrested." So the juvenile police took me in. Disturbing the peace by fighting. Suspected of gang activity. Gang? Myself and a friend who was now nowhere to be found? My parents were called and I was released to their custody. No charges were filed and they took me to the hospital. My head was stitched and my stomach ached for days where the flashlight was jammed into me. I later learned I had been hit three times with a pipe. These were not Happy Days and that wasn't Richy Cunningham swinging that pipe.

My parents and I went to see one of the better attorneys in the city and he summed it up for us with eye-opening frankness. He said it would be my word against every policeman who was there. At most, they would say he was pushing me back into the crowd and without much force at that. So from that night I learned that, for some, the rule of law didn't reach and truth was not always the goal of those who enforce it.

This fight and several others like it led to my contacting a friend from high school who belonged to another gang in another part of the city. My contacting that friend and my meeting with many of his friends led to a gang fight that lasted for several years. I was involved in it for three years before I stopped but continued longer. It was also the beginning of the decline of white gangs in New Orleans. In several years, it was getting so out of hand that they were targeted for break up and they were. I got out while still in high school before they began the crack down but I can still remember the names of some of these groups and some of the more colorful characters. There were ten or twelve gangs across the city.

As for the bad guys to the southeast, one was found tied to a lamppost with wire and shot to death because he held out on someone's dope, I heard. The Beetle, a heroin addict, tried a stint in the Air Force. He came home on leave, sat in a chair in his bedroom, tied a shotgun trigger to his door and waited for a family member to do for him what he lacked the courage to do for himself. I didn't learn for some time who the guy with the pipe was and maybe ten years later I heard he owned a bar half a block away from his house in the same run down neighborhood in which he grew up. Just last year I was told he was recently sentenced to a federal penitentiary.

A close friend of Ted's, Bobby Gavin, was killed by a bartender during an argument. Bobby, loaded and angry, told him he'd be back. When he returned with a pistol the bartender was waiting for him with a shotgun he had placed on the bar pointed to the door. His hand was already on the trigger. The full load of shot hit Bobby in the stomach.

Richy Maine did a couple of terms at Angola for aggravated battery and burglary. In time the boy I pinned that night also did time for a handful of similar crimes and appeared briefly in my court. Many of them either went to prison or died but a few managed by the luck of the toss to escape both jail and death. One holds a Ph. D. in psychology.

One spring morning, as I was asleep in my bed, Ted Cranston was being arrested across the street from my home. My mother, cooking breakfast and looking out the kitchen window, saw him in a shallow grass-lined ditch with a shotgun apparently waiting for me. She phoned the police and he was taken away before she woke me for school. That evening my father told me he wanted a word with me.

"Son what I'm going to ask you is a hard thing to do. I know that. When your friends call you to fight, you can't say no, not after all the fights you've been in together. They'll call you a chicken shit and God knows what else. But that's what I'm asking you to do."

"Dad, I was the one who brought these guys into it. They had no beef with The Park until I went to them for help. How can I back out now?"

"I know that son and that's why it's going to be hard on you but you have to do it. We've been to the juvenile authorities three times, you've come home bloody and cut up so often and, after today, this has to stop. I'm asking when they call the next time that you tell them no. I'm asking you this son because you're killing your mother."

He paused and I raised my head to look into his eyes for confirmation.

"Do you hear what I'm saying Buz? You're killing your mother."

He was right, it was hard for awhile but I got out of it. I continued to fight but the gang fighting was over. In stunned disbelief I had stood next to a boy at the lakefront as he fired a pistol at a fleeing car. For six months I had a baseball bat in my car. One of my friends had a sawed off shotgun in his for a period of time. I sometimes carried a foot of chain running down my leg through a hole cut in my pocket. None of this was ever used but I was becoming what I detested and I wanted out as well. How I managed to have a decent girl friend, play high school football, CYO basketball and maintain my grades with all this going on leaves me without explanation as I look back upon those days. My stars or genes or God or luck got me through it. Because I loved my father deeply, and the way he put it to me, it fell right for all of us. He had told my mother he knew me because I was exactly like him. I know that was wrong in one aspect at least. I would be in my fifties before I found the contentment he knew most of his life.

In my brother's senior year, after he signed his football letter of intent with Tulane, he went to Mississippi and secretly married his high school sweetheart. When she became pregnant, he told the family that they were married. Once again the pulse of the family beat erratically. Once again depression ruled my mother. He would continue his education, they would live with us for a period, and mom would get a job to help them out.

She enjoyed working again, she said, but with my brother's future a large question mark, she was unhappy. Without her saying I knew she blamed his wife, Carol, for the predicament they both were in. She was wrong of course. I liked Carol from the first and I knew no one could control or manipulate my brother for a moment. A nineteen year old, uneducated and married with a child on the way, was not in anyone's plans. Mother's depression was always there, sometimes beneath the surface but at other times in full view.

That summer I came home one night while dad was on the road. I had been with my friends at a lounge near the lake. I had had a couple of beers and it was still well before midnight. Mom was in her bed, lying on her side looking down the hall. She was in her housedress. The light was on.

I called to her, "What's wrong ma?"

"Nothing."

"Why are you in bed so early?"

I walked to her room and sat on the dresser chair next to her bed.

"I didn't feel like watching television any more."

I could tell she had been crying. Over Nat I knew.

"I'm still here Mom and I love you."

"What's wrong with you tonight? Have you been drinking? You must be drunk. Go to bed and leave me alone. I'm all right."

I walked to my room, shut the door and turned on some jazz. Why couldn't I help ease her pain? It was Nat's words, not mine, that she wanted to hear and I felt the tears running down my face. I hadn't cried since the swimming pool episode and after this I didn't cry again until eight years later when I cried for my father. I didn't cry when they buried him or when he died. I cried when the doctor told us he had six weeks to live. And then with one exception I didn't shed another tear for almost twenty years. The single exception was when by brother suffered a breakdown.

* * *

With high school and gang fights behind me, I started college and managed to do better than well enough. Nat was playing for Tulane and my neighborhood friends had either joined the Marines or were at LSU. I remained in the city attending a commuter's college. Having again broken up with my girl of three years, I was alone to study without distraction. The anger and emptiness I felt because of that breakup and my particular pathology would result in more than the occasional fistfight. I had three separate fights on each of three different days. There were well over a hundred by the time I quit. They were so frequent I began to forget many of them.

A little over a decade ago I was contacted by my high school. Our coach, Andy Douglas, had passed away and they were honoring him at halftime of the season opener. His old players were being asked to attend and stand with his wife as she was presented with a plaque of appreciation.

Before the ceremony, over a hundred and fifty aging football players were milling around waiting to walk on the field. Many of the others could not be located. I was standing with a group that had played during the late 50s. The conversation turned to one of our halfbacks who had been sentenced to federal prison for dealing in cocaine.

"I hadn't heard that," I said.

The fellow to my right, L.J., who played guard the year before me, continued, "Yeah, he was sentenced about a month ago."

"Never heard about it."

Others said they had and started giving pieces of the story. It was his second offense and had to send him away. L.J. slapped me on my arm and said, "Say, remember when you and he got in that fight at practice?"

"John and I? No way."

"Damn right you did."

A few others joined in saying they remembered it too.

"Bullshit," I said.

He continued, "Yeah, you remember. Douglas just let you two go at it. Man, you and he just slugged it out."

"What happened?"

"Douglas had us stop it before one of you got hurt but while it was going on that was one great fistfight."

I had no recollection of the fight. Not then and not now.

In the meantime I joined a fraternity, drank on weekends and studied. Although Nat was now married, on more than one night, he would wake me to join him in one of his fights. After one of these late night brawls mother told me she asked him why he came to get me instead of his friends who were football players. He told her, she said, "Because Buz will never run." Knowing that he was usually drunk on these nights, I believe he told her that because he knew his answer would reach my ear. I believe the truth was that he knew I'd never say no. But there was a balance to it. When I called him, he was always at my side.

He woke me one night a few hours before sunrise. The night before, at a dance, someone had broken a bottle over his head. He had been stitched up and arranged to meet the guy on the riverside of the levee and needed someone on hand to witness and keep the fight fair. He parked the car and we topped the levee to look down to a broad grassy field separated from the river by a thick stand of willows. Two men were already in the field waiting. The fellow was at least three inches taller and maybe thirty pounds heavier than Nat. His second was larger still and looked as if he could have hid me in his coat pocket. Even with a foot of chain, which I no longer carried, it would have been laughable. Nat and he took off their shirts and began the familiar ritual. They circled, punched and connected. They battled for close to twenty minutes and when one went down, the other waited until the downed man was on his feet again. Their eyes were cut and blood ran from their mouths and when the body blows landed it sounded like a brick being slammed against a side of beef. I would say it was the best bare-knuckled fight I've ever seen. In the end, they were leaning, more or less, against each other, both men reduced to throwing an occasional punch to the ribs. Exhausted and out of earshot, they apparently decided to call it a draw, shook hands and walked off.

"Good fight. I though he was going to kick your ass."

"Next time I'll get some sleep."

"Good thing he kept it clean. I sure as hell wouldn't have been much help with those two."

He looked at me, smiled and said, "You got that right."

He and I were at a piano bar near the lakefront late one summer night. As we were leaving a slightly drunken patron threw an insult at me over a song I had requested. He was trying to impress his friend and the women they were with. Not being in either of our natures to ignore such an affront we ended the matter by the two of us beating two patrons, the owner, the bartender and the piano player. During the melee, I noticed that the fellow who disliked my musical taste was bent over momentarily. Pushing free from the two I was fighting, I closed the few feet between us and hit him with an uppercut that started maybe two feet off the ground and lifted him straight up to his full height.

When it was over Nat and his shaken wife spent the night at our house. At sunup two policemen and the music critic were at our front door. I heard mother, she was standing in the doorway talking to the police. Behind them stood the man I hit. His face had the unmistakable look of having come into contact with something that broke his nose and turned his face into a shaded collage of blues and blacks with touches of red. He was a mess.

My mother was saying, "So you're saying this man was having a fight with my youngest boy and my son did this to him."

"Yes ma'am. And he wants to bring charges against him."

"Did he tell you my son is sixteen? This, what, thirty year old man was fighting with a juvenile and now, because he lost, he wants him charged? I think I want him charged for fighting with my son. And what was the owner of that lounge doing letting a juvenile in there in the first place?"

"Your son who hit this man is sixteen?"

"Yes, here he is. See for yourself."

The policemen looked at me and the three of them stepped off for a brief huddle. Then the first policeman returned.

"He's changed his mind ma'am. No charges will be brought but the owner doesn't want your sons back in his club."

"You won't have a problem with that, I'll see to it. I certainly don't want my young one in a nightclub. You should tell the owner to be more careful in the future. Isn't he supposed to check their identification?"

Nat was up by now and she explained to him what had happened at the door. We were sitting at the kitchen table and she said, "Jesus, you boys . . . When is this going to stop?" Then thinking of the look on the man's face when he heard he was fighting a teenager, and the clown mask he was sporting, she broke out in wild Irish laughter.

Sometimes our fighting was funny in a twisted sort of way. Sometimes it was very, very serious. One winter night years earlier, Nat got me out of a house that was surrounded by thirty or so gang members. He walked through the crowd of thugs with nothing but an empty shotgun. He put his life on the line for me that night and he knew I would do the same.

Tulane in those years did not have a degree program in Phys-Ed as most colleges did. The high academic demand on the student athletes put them at a disadvantage in their division. LSU, on the road to their national championship, beat them 63-0. Nat had been moved from tackle to center, but he did so well in his studies that he was able, after three years of undergraduate school, to secure an academic scholarship to Tulane's School of Law. It was a dramatic shift. Having, until this point, always defined himself in athletic terms, his mind now came to the fore. Other children had been born and when Nat began law school he had three. Working multiple jobs for a time, he was determined to become a lawyer. Law Review Editor, Order of the Coif, and many other lesser but distinguished awards came his way. He joined one of the city's most prestigious law firms.

In my senior year of undergraduate school I married a beautiful young woman from France and we soon had a daughter. After working three years and after the seismic jolt of my father's death, I started law school. I knew with his passing that my drinking and walking daydream had to end. I wished to be more like him, to have his kindness and strength but to achieve that I would have to overcome myself and put aside the suicidal foolishness that held me. His loss began to shape me in ways that eventually pulled me back once again from the edge.

Before dad took sick, Nat had qualified to run for the school board. With our father's illness, he stepped down and put his political plans aside. In a strange bit of irony, dad never approved of politics. He considered it distasteful and dishonest. Distasteful perhaps but he passed away before we could show him that it could be done honestly. The following autumn I began law school and Nat ran for the state house of representatives. He put together a steering committee of a few close friends, perhaps ten of us, only two of whom had brief experiences in politics. We involved other friends, arranged for door knocking three times a week and tried to raise money. Most of it came from Nat himself. I studied diligently, particularly in my freshman year, but I gave him my time for the many nightly meetings and I knocked doors every Tuesday afternoon and all day on Saturdays. He was running against the candidate picked by the local politicians and backed by the governor, Mckeithen. He was also running in the largest house district in the state, the 9th Ward.

During the years of work before law school I played golf at a public course in a black subdivision, usually twice a week. On weekends a friend of ours, Steve Levey, was usually there too. I took lessons from one of the black pros and although my game didn't improve noticeably I enjoyed it enough to play those three years until it was squeezed out by politics and law. On those lazy summer Saturdays when we finished late, Steve and I would hang in the clubhouse drinking beer and meeting a few of the regulars. One was a well known DJ who hosted the best radio jazz show in New Orleans. One of owners of the Louisiana Weekly newspaper, Henry Dejoie, lived just across the street from the clubhouse and was always there. Henry shot a good game. Willie Moten, a long ball hitter with a deep baritone voice and who liked his Dixie as much as I did was there every afternoon.

I became a fixture at these informal Saturday sessions and after most of the white players left for the day, Steve and I were asked to stay for the evening fish fry. Plates of fresh fried fish would pile up along with beer and fried potatoes. When Nat decided to run, I asked Henry, Willie and a few others if they could help. By this time I knew their families and an in-law or two.

Henry asked, "You're brother's running for the house?"

"Yes."

"Against the governor's man?"

"Un huh."

Then Willie asked, "And this is his first race?"

"Yeah. Do you think you could speak to some of your neighbors for him?"

Henry answered, "Well, Willie and I would like to help you but we belong to a little political group out here. We all sort of go along with whoever the majority picks. We'll be to interviewing candidates in a few weeks. What if I call you when we get to the house races? You can bring him over and he can speak to the group. You know Willie and I will vote for him."

Nat spoke before them and received their endorsement. They didn't have a name for their group yet but they were primarily the members of the group Nils Douglas put together when he ran unsuccessfully for the house in 1963. He was now the group's president and in two years they became the dominant players in black politics in the city and the name they chose was SOUL, the Southern Organization for Unified Leadership. Years later Nils and I were magistrates and worked in the same court for ten years before he retired. Nils was a rare breed for a New Orleans politician. He was brilliant, never ruffled and always kept his word even when it was difficult. But what really set him apart was that he was always a gentleman.

In the beginning our group was put together from friends and they remained its core until the end. Friends came from the old neighborhood and from our football teams. They came from law school and playgrounds and none of us had a lot of money. In that first primary of 1967, we were boy scouts, naive political novices. The established political groups had complete control of those precincts and we were lucky Nat made it into the runoff. At that time, each precinct had a leader from the various old-line political organizations and because they were supporting Mckeithen's candidate, those people almost did us in. But we learned in that first primary. Those precinct leaders lived in those neighborhoods, knew all the people and had done political favors for some of them. They would tell them how to vote, often by passing small slips of paper with only numbers printed on them. We had seen how they operated and hit the law books. We knocked on every door before the second primary, a feat that has only been duplicated when Nat ran for the senate two years later. Only in that race we canvassed not only the 9th Ward but also the 8th. And we did it twice. Combined, the two wards had over 80,000 registered voters. But before the senate, we had to win the house seat. We formed sign crews from friends who were uncomfortable on doors. We had our wives phoning the list of voters from our home phones.

If not well seasoned in the art of Louisiana politics, we were younger, more aggressive and smarter. Nat was clearly the better qualified candidate but qualifications in politics can bring you only so far. For election day in the second primary we divided the ward. Nat took half our group to the front precincts near the river and I ran the north half in the city's newer subdivisions. SOUL was in charge of the broad area of black precincts that separated the two sections of white voters. In a highly organized early morning coup, minutes after the polls opened, our friends showed up at over eighty difficult precincts. Each team had been instructed in how to challenge the presence of those self-appointed precinct leaders. If they were not commissioners or legal poll watchers, they had no business being there much less telling people how to vote. We demanded to see some written authorization allowing them to remain. Having none, they ranted, stuttered, and some screamed that they had always been there, for years. The police, one being assigned to each polling place, were summoned, the law read and the gentlemen escorted out. It had never happened to them before. "This is my God damn precinct!"

No, that day it wasn't.

Nat won by over four thousand votes and for awhile, he was the youngest man ever elected to the Louisiana Legislature. That year he was the only candidate on the SOUL ballot to win a race. But there was a flaw in our make up, both of us. The rage and violence that was beginning to subside in me was still in his heart. As brilliant as he was, he could not control his anger, and at times, neither could I. The night after he won, he and I and Mike Roig were driving down the highway visiting bar owners who had helped us in the election. We pulled into a gas station to fill up. On a chance happening, a fellow who had been taking cheap shots at Nat throughout the campaign, the kind that led to a meeting beneath the Dueling Oaks a century before, happened to be there. Not being too bright a fellow, he came out and in a hostile voice started to say something. Nat cracked him with a powerful right hand. I saw Nat's overcoat sail out to the sides like a cloak when he threw the punch and his shoulder continued across his body after he connected. He hit him with his full weight and the punch carried this good-sized man over the tires stacked on the pump island. He landed on his shoulders five feet on the other side without touching the four-foot stack. It was Nat's nature to carry grudges and act on them.

In his first session he rallied other young house members and together they formed the Young Turks. Working together and with Nat's power of persuasion, both head-to-head and on the microphone, they managed to beat back almost all of the governor's tax bills. Additionally, and unusual for a freshmen legislator, he was passing his own bills that directly helped his district and Charity Hospital. The coverage he received in both newspapers could not have been better had he written it himself. The press wrote favorably of him and endorsed him in his three earliest campaigns. They remained favorably inclined until Nat handled a necessary bill that had the potential to impact their financial interests. Being honorable businessmen and protectors of free speech, Nat's coverage became a revengeful hatchet job. His press in the rest of the state was positive throughout his eighteen year political career.

Before the next session Governor Mckeithen called on Nat and asked him to be his floor leader in the house. Nat agreed with one condition. He would not support any tax bill, in fact, he would continue to oppose them. In spite of this unheard of demand which bordered on arrogance, so effective was Nat, that Mckeithen accepted his terms.

Nat's drive to succeed was infectious and demanding but he demanded more of himself. He practiced law with the same energy and he ran his campaigns, full out, driven to win. He worked hard and when he played, he played too hard. One night after leaving a meeting with local legislators he went to the parking lot to get his car. He was more than a little drunk. While he waited for his car to be brought down, a candy truck pulled into the lot and the driver began filling his machines. Nat stepped up, sat in the driver's seat and turned on the key. The driver came over, turned the key off and told him to get away from the truck. Nat said no, put his head on the steering wheel and fell asleep. He was still asleep when the police arrived. The morning paper carried the headline "Kiefer Steals Candy Truck". That very Friday his firm had placed in the mail the announcement that Nat had made partner. The senior partners were not at all pleased with him.

Don Hubbard of SOUL told me a few days later, "Yeah, they asked me about Kiefer stealing the candy truck. I said sure, he took it. He took it and gave all the candy to the kids in the project. The man watches out for his people."

In two years he ran for senate seat in the most bitter and dirtiest campaign we were involved in. A city councilman who planned to run in the mayoral race a few months away openly supported Nat for the senate in exchange for Nat's support in his race. It was a poor call as Nat didn't need his support and it angered every other mayoral candidate. Nat liked the man and that usually carried weight in his decisions. His gut instincts for politics were uncanny but this time he was wrong. He should have remained neutral in the mayor's race at least until his race was over.

We knew we would carry the vote in the 9th Ward where we lived and where his house seat was located. Nat was a moderate/liberal and with our close ties to black politics, we knew the 8th Ward, a very conservative and largely blue collar ward, would be a problem. The 9th had 50,000 voters and the 8th had 30,000. If we held our own or lost the 8th by just a few thousand votes, we had a shot to win in the first primary if we funded SOUL heavily. SOUL's influence in the black community had grown rapidly since Nat won the house seat. Their board of directors now included heads of every organization and agency dealing with community work. Those involved in helping the poor and the jobless were members of SOUL. They would have to take on two old line political groups, the CCIVL, run by a leader of the Longshoremen's Union and the OPPVL, another black group whose strength was mainly uptown.

Nat felt trying to win it in the first primary, against three opponents, was worth the try. SOUL set up their headquarters on the upper end of Caffin Avenue and placed a phone bank upstairs. I stopped by every now and then to see how the calls were being received. They ran the bank every day and the calls weren't just a pitch for Nat. They were holding conversations with the people because they knew them or their aunts or their grandmothers. And more revealing were the yard signs. I drove those black neighborhoods almost daily watching the yard signs appear overnight like blue and white mushrooms. Even on the side streets every third or fourth home had a sign that read "Nat Kiefer Senate". None from the other candidates were seen.

Our group now had a name, NOVA, the New Orleans Voters Association, and we hit the doors again, this time in both wards. We calculated which area we could cover on a given day and mailed a letter to that section timed to arrive a day or two before a doorknocker would call. The letter was from Nat, discussing the race, his qualifications and closed with a line saying he or his associate would be calling at their home within a few days. And then, three times a week, twenty or forty of us would hit the doors. Hello, I'm Nat's law partner and he asked . . . or Nat's cousin or Nat's neighbor or, in my case, Nat's brother. Nat would drive the canvas areas and go to houses in the same block as our canvassers and knock on a few doors. Then he'd drive to the next street making a brief appearance on each block with each group of men. Neighbors would phone or yell to each other and it was not unusual to see people pouring into the street to see Nat Kiefer. There was no middle ground with Nat. People either loved him or hated him and for awhile he strode the eastern part of the city like a rock star. He was tough, smart and direct to a fault. He could tailor his words to match his audience but regardless of his phrasing they resonated with clarity. In his childhood Nat had blonde hair and blue eyes. In later years his hair turned to a light brown that was almost sandy and his eyes became hazel. His collar was always open and his tie pulled slightly to one side. His shoulders were broad, his chest deep and he walked with a loose smiling swagger that projected mixed elements of confidence, humor and excitement. Entering a large ballroom, like static electricity, his presence was sensed and the attention would shift to him. He had an unfailing eye that could see to the bottom and with a few spoken words he could determine a man's fears and strengths. He had a broad face and rugged looks; handsome when he smiled and he smiled often. Like a searchlight his bright eyes would shift and land on one and then the other and in that beam, for that brief moment of contact, you held his complete attention. Talking to another he'd nod or wink to let you know you were important enough to earn his acknowledgement. He'd move though a room gracefully, pausing, laughing and no one was ignored except those who had earned his neglect. In his wake he left trailing eyes that would follow him for several steps before the school of people would regroup and close the opening left by his departure. Laughter came easy to him and for him it was a respite and a refuge. He laughed rarely at prepared jokes but the quick retort, the locker room joustings of men and the daily stumbling of fools delighted him. His laughter drew everyone in until the newcomer felt they were in the company of Robin and his band of men.

We barely missed winning in the first primary but the results from the SOUL precincts were staggering. Nat in a field of four received over 96% of their vote and we knew that would haunt us in the white areas in the runoff. No other white politician ever received that kind of vote. In his prime the last white mayor of New Orleans never received more than 94% of the black vote and that was in a two-man race. One of the candidates in the coming mayoral race, a judge, sent two of his supporters to see Nat. They were political acquaintances of ours who had remained neutral in the first primary. They had much riding on the judge's election. Nothing was personal; it was all business. They told Nat if he agreed not to support the councilman for mayor and supported the judge instead, they would pull the remaining candidate and he would be the senator. Otherwise, the race would become something neither of them wanted to see. Nat knew that those two men were the only ones in the judge's camp who could run such a campaign and they were trying to buy him off. No one bought off Nat and the suggestion angered him. He'd sacrifice much for a friend but wouldn't sell out for anything. It wasn't that the councilman meant that much to Nat, it was his word that they were asking him to break and he told them to fuck off.

In the final week of the election every day a new piece of mail hit the white precincts of both wards. Most showed some of the returns from the black precincts and carried the headline "Nat Kiefer Sold His Soul to SOUL". There were many fliers that carried inflammatory quotes, allegedly from members of SOUL. They were cutting into our white 8th Ward vote badly. We hit back but the damage was done and it lasted for years. These were the days of open racism and in many city barrooms we were spoken of angrily but no one felt the need to say those things to our face.

It was during this time that we developed a reputation for pulling political tricks. Nothing we did was illegal and it was done primarily to break the tension and give our team something to laugh and brag about. Nat inspired loyalty because he was loyal. Those guys, all of us, were walking three days a week in the heat with our coats and ties in place. You couldn't pay someone for that devotion. We did it for Nat and to show that we could not be beaten. "No, leave your ties on. Let them know that you care enough to be in this heat working for a cause. Let them see you sweat. Ask for a glass of water. Drive the point home."

Going over election day activity Nat and I ran down our plan. On election day our phone banks would be reminding voters to go to the poll and vote. Our phone banks had been calling for weeks before the first primary. All the contacted voters were ranked according to how they answered a set of questions and our callers marked them on a scale from one through five. A one indicated very strongly for Nat, a two was a probable for Nat, three was an unsure, four was probable for the opponent and a five was a definite for the opposition. Starting two days before election day and on election day, all the ones and twos would be called again. Not very sophisticated by today's methods but in 1969 it was cutting edge. We had teams who would deliver a dozen doughnuts to each precinct for the poll workers shortly after they opened. Those same teams would return throughout the day the get the number of total votes cast. We kept this turnout information on a chart and if our better precincts had a low turnout, we'd put ten or fifteen canvassers on the doors. This would start at noon and continue, moving from precinct to precinct where the turnout was low, until late in the day. We also had cars ready to drive those who told the phone bank they needed a ride to the polls. We figured our opponent would be doing something on election day besides watching a football game. We knew their plans couldn't be as complex as ours because they simply didn't have the manpower. But whatever it was, Nat decided we had to throw a monkey wrench into it somehow.

I was a senior in law school and was clerking at his firm. During a lull I pulled out the election code. Until the 70s, each precinct provided a small table, usually a card table, located near the door where candidates could place their election day sample ballots. These were a list of candidates selected for each office by the various political organizations. The information that had to be contained on these ballots was very specific, even to the color of ink to be used for certain information. I read the statutes dealing with sample ballots and listed the requirements on a legal sheet. I stared at the sheet and it struck me that there was no limitation on the size of a ballot. I walked to his office and told him what I had found.

"If we print another ballot in addition to our others, making it legal in every way, we can put out a NOVA ballot a foot square with only your picture and name on it. While they're fooling with that, we'll be turning out our voters."

He laughed and said, "That should do it."

"I'll get it printed. You find out which city attorney will be on call election day and tell him he's going to get complaints about a new ballot we'll be using. Tell him not to make a ruling until he hears our side of it. Tell him I can give him the statutes showing that it's legal in every respect."

He smiled. "A foot? No size limitation?"

"No, none."

"Make it as big as a poster."

Before the donut crews arrived, our precinct workers waited for the polls to open and then produced this monster sample ballot that met every legal requirement. They almost covered the tables with Nat's name and face. The other precinct workers went crazy and the phone started ringing at the city attorney's office. Having been told to expect this and having my phone number the attorney called me.

"Buz, Joe. I have a copy of your ballot in my hand. What are you guys doing?" He was laughing.

"Here's the statutes Joe. Check them out. There is no size limit."

"No size limit? You're kidding me."

He was laughing again at hearing this.

"No, there's none at all."

"I'll read the statutes and if you're right, I'll rule that they can stay and they can go to court to enjoin it. No limit. Hot damn."

There was more laughter.

"Joe one more thing. I expect they will get their leftover posters and try to put them in the precincts. When they try that, I'll call you and tell you why it's illegal. Ok?"

"Hahahaha, ok."

Throughout the morning I was interrupted when our guys would bring in one of their posters converted to a sample ballot.

"Joe the one they're using is invalid. It doesn't have the name of the organization causing it to be distributed printed on it. See statute such-and-such."

Pause.

"Ok, I'll call their headquarters and tell them to remove them from the precincts."

"Fine. Our guys can help them with that."

"Joe this time it's illegal because the name of the organization isn't in black ink. See statute so-and-so."

"Ok, I'll tell them."

"Joe, they have the ink right but it doesn't appear diagonally across the bottom of the ballot."

It went on until well past noon and then it must have occurred to them that while they wasted time with foolishness, we were beating them in the turnout.

They carried the conservative 8th Ward but in the 9th Ward we improved on our vote enough to put Nat ahead by a wide margin. And NOVA had put out its first in a long line of ballots. During the beginning days of this campaign, one of the members of SOUL took Nat through the Florida-Desire Housing Projects. One of their many stops was at a woman's apartment. She had a child who was about ten years old. He was completely deranged. She had him chained to the radiator so he couldn't leave, hurt himself or her. Because of overcrowding, Charity Hospital would not take him. I was not on this tour nor did I know of the child until election night. The Governor called to congratulate Nat and asked if there was anything he could do for him. Rather than ask for a good committee assignment or something that could further his career, I heard Nat ask Mckeithen if he could cut through the red tape and have the child admitted to Charity. The child was in the hospital within days.

Most found it perplexing to see this ex-football player-street fighter display such a streak of selflessness. He could be mean and cold but capable of amazing acts of unexpected kindness. He was chivalrous in an age that rarely recognized chivalry. And among politicians, it was almost unheard of.

In the mayor's race a few months later we worked for the councilman who lost, but we worked harder to beat the judge. He ran fifth with our help. The last time Nat had serious opposition for his senate seat was when the new mayor ran his chief of police against him. We carried every precinct in both wards except one.

When Nat wasn't running, we were involved in other races. The essence for him, the stuff of his existence, was competition; he was absolutely driven. He had to win but as soon as he did, his head was turned to the call of the next contest. He was alive in battle and his confidence drove the rest of us onward. Over a few years we developed proficiency at polling, running phone banks, organizing canvasses, designing fliers and writing radio and TV ads. We used various PR people but much of it in the early days we did ourselves. More importantly, we had reliable people who could do any of several jobs and we duplicated everything. We could run several phone banks at the same time and for several different races. We had two people who could pull a sample and run a poll, citywide or in any political subdivision within the city. We could run four or five sign crews if need be. We also had sign wrecking crews. Opponent's signs stayed up as long as they remained within our definition of reasonable. The minute they took down a few of our signs, not a sign of theirs was allowed to stand for more than a day or so. We had four different print shops we kept busy during campaign season cranking out fliers, letters, newspapers, posters and the various organizations' ballots. Organizing a rally was done with a phone call or two. Eventually we kept a permanent head quarters in the 9th Ward but moved to others as the particular race demanded. We chartered a political organization for our wives and their endorsements were mailed to females between the ages of twenty-one and forty-five. In later years, when it became apparent that we needed new troops and younger legs to maintain the killer pace of our activities, we helped set up a group of young college students, The Young Progressive Democrats, who worked the voters between eighteen and twenty-five. NOVA members' parents formed their group, The Senior Citizens. They and their friends would vote on their recommendations and their ballot and letters were mailed to the head of households over age fifty-five. We could split our group, NOVA, in any direction and fully run three or four campaigns at the same time. And we did that quite often, dovetailing where we could and operating independantly when we could not. A candidate needing help would have his operation sized up in a few hours and we'd plug in our guys in the areas that were weakest. By the late 70s we had over a hundred men in NOVA and could turn out at least 50 on any given day for a house to house canvass.

Outsiders did not know completely how we operated and how fast we could change focus. A member of NOVA was running for a municipal judgeship. His brother was a criminal judge with high name recognition. John was well liked and he was running against a political newcomer who was financed primarily by his father, a well-known doctor. We took the race for granted. No door knocking, a minimal amount of TV and radio ads and support from other political organizations in the city made up the extent of a campaign we thought necessary. Two weeks before the election a friend who was in the other camp ran into me at lunch. We spoke of politics and he mentioned that their polls showed their candidate beating John by a good margin. He wasn't bragging. I think he thought it was too late for us to do anything about it. I returned to my office, called one of our regular pollsters and told him to poll the race without bothering with issues. Nat was in Baton Rouge for the legislative session. I had a sergeant-at-arms, a man from NOVA, bring him to his phone.

"Got word from a good source that John is trailing in their polls."

"How good is the source?"

"Friend in a leadership position in their camp. You know him."

"Call Joe and run a poll."

"Already talked to him. We'll have the raw figures in four days."

"Call John, clue him and tell him to start raising money. I'll do what I can from here. Set a meeting for Friday with our leadership. Get the word around to the guys that we have to get off our asses starting Saturday."

The poll confirmed what I had been told and we were already gearing up for a real race. Other organizations were funded, TV ad time was tripled and signs appeared overnight on lawns. Radio ads were put together and aired immediately. As with all of our races, there had to be time for fun. None of the guys in NOVA were paid; we were doing this because we were too old for football. We just loved showing them repeatedly who had the better team. Ridiculing the opposition was part of the games we played but its importance as a stress reducer and morale builder gave it a high priority. One of our members had something of an artistic flare. He drew a twenty-page comic book lampooning the inexperienced young boy who wanted to make "big descissors" and whose father was buying a judgeship for him. It was drawn cleverly, very funny and the perfect finger in the eye move. We had a few thousand printed up and had them dropped off at neighborhood barrooms and house to house in the precincts near the homes of the candidate and his father. The first copy was placed in the candidate's mailbox and the second in his father's. Let them figure how widespread the actual circulation was. John won easily.

In the state elections of 1972 Nat had no real opposition and he had a free hand to influence other elections. He was one of the first elected officials to endorse Edwin Edwards and we were involved in other every statewide and local race. We won all of them from the Governorship on down except the Attorney General's race. In the 9th Ward Nat was re-elected to his senate seat, three winners of the four 9th ward house seats were on the NOVA ticket and one of our members won Nat's old house seat. A member of SOUL won one of the other house seats. Of the four central committeemen for the democrat party, three were in NOVA, and the fourth was in SOUL. But these wins came at too high a cost. Nat was not satisfied to be excellent, he had to be first and he had to be the best. Whether from his biology, his upbringing or from his own faulty wiring, anything less he saw as failure. Pushing himself twenty hours a day for months brought Nat to his physical and mental limits. At a meeting for Charity Hospital he had a spontaneous nosebleed. He collapsed on the floor of the senate. Eventually he suffered a complete nervous breakdown and was hospitalized for almost two weeks. The rumors, while based in truth, were rampant and his political enemies made it their business to keep them circulating.

Don Hubbard told me during his hospital stay Nat had phoned him to talk about cutting into a rival's growing political strength. "God damn." he said. "The man's in the hospital and he's still trying to kick people in the ass."

He rose again, became Edwin Edwards's floor leader and introduced hundreds of pieces of legislation each year. Except for a four-year period, when we lost a governor's race, Nat was senate floor leader from 1972 until he died in 1985. Nothing, it was said, got out of the senate without Nat's approval.

In 1977, when Nat ran for mayor, our organization had been involved in close to thirty campaigns during the previous ten years. If someone did something innovative in a campaign and it worked well, I learned how it was done and we incorporated it into our existing range of programs.

We opened the main headquarters fourteen months before the election and held strategy sessions and many private conversations while we put the campaign together. Overcoming Nat's breakdown five years earlier in the voters' eyes would be difficult to overcome if not impossible. This was the 70s and to run for mayor with such a stigma was a long shot at best. From a lesser man, it would have been laughable.

In our own campaigns the poll results were always kept between four of us: Nat, Bob Cole, our most trusted PR guy, our pollster and myself. We ran a very early poll well before the candidates announced and Nat was in the worst possible position. He had the highest name recognition among the candidates but he was running a distant third. In private, not even shared with Bob, I told Nat to wait, not to run at this time. With him out of the race the conservative would win. With the shifting demographics we could pick him off in four years. Four years further away from his breakdown. The idea, while sound, was just not Nat. His instinct told him the time was now and so he ran.

Bob, in one of those early private meetings, suggested that if the breakdown was to come out, and it would, it would be better for Nat to tell the story himself. He suggested a documentary of Nat's life, the struggle to success. The football, the street fights, the academic scholarship, editor of the law review while holding three jobs, raising three kids, his success in law and politics and his legislation which saved the port and capped the Dome costs, all of it told by the people who saw these things. Then finally Nat, speaking directly to the people, told about his breakdown. In the years we had been together, it was Bob's best idea and it was followed by his most noble gesture. He told us the scope of the project was beyond his abilities. Nat asked Bob for his suggestions and Bob said we'd have to interview the whole range of political PR firms in the state.

I asked, "Bob, who did the Dave Dixon spots? That guy's great."

"Rusty Cantelli."

"That's who we need."

Bob said he'd put him on the list.

I began breaking down the campaign into its logistic parts and we designed the campaign during those early months. While the pieces were being put in place, we began to look for the right person to handle the documentary and the campaign ads. We interviewed a few firms and the most memorable was three hucksters from a well-known Baton Rouge company. The point man was shucking and jiving, giddy with his pitch.

"Now this is just something I had the art department put together to give you an idea of what we have in mind."

He slid out a heavy board of artwork covered with a flap of translucent paper and placed it in front of Nat. It was the name Kiefer in balloon letters the color changing from bright red at the bottom to yellow at the top. The color change was gradual running through the shades in between, including a middle section of orange. It was hideous. I picked up the board, looked at it and then to the fellow seated across from us and his two cronies who were smiling proudly.

"It's exciting, bold," he said.

It was time for the hit man to speak up.

I said, "Does it occur to you that we have here a candidate that's going to be portrayed as a street fighting, candy truck stealing psycho case and you come up with this? Not exactly the calming image we're trying to portray is it?"

That night thumbing through a magazine at home, I saw the exact same colored lettering. They had lifted it directly from a Datsun print ad.

We spoke to several others firms and I told Nat, without meeting with him, we needed Cantelli. This time Bob agreed. In the years that would follow Rusty and I became friends. He was a self-educated, independent man and had one of the best minds I've encountered. Until Rusty passed away, he could not speak to me of Nat without crying. He told me of their first meeting.

"I had heard all the stories about Nat, how he was a street fighting tough and a bull in the china shop. I had met informally with another candidate before Nat and was ready to sign on with him. I went to see your brother to show him respect but I had no intention of doing his work. I sat down and the first words he said were, 'I'm cut up pretty badly and they tell me I need you.' We spoke for an hour and I was floored. The guy completely captivated me. All the stories were wrong. This guy had substance and I liked him immediately. I knew then if we could get every voter to talk to him across a desk the whole damn city would vote for him."

We ran the main headquarters from a building in the central business district and staffed four area headquarters where the legwork of the campaign would take place. The luxury of having so many people who could run independent programs paid off in this multiple headquarters arrangement. Sign crews operated out of them along with the canvassing and the major election day activities.

Again when Nat and I were speaking at the beginning of the campaign he told me he wanted me as campaign manager.

"No, that's a mistake."

"No it's not."

Four years earlier, when I stopped drinking, I was hospitalized with DTs for several days.

"Yes, it is. Guy should be the manager. He lives uptown, he's a lawyer and has excellent credentials."

"No", he said, "I thought about it. Everyone in politics has some enemies. Anyone I put in that spot will have some of their own baggage. You and I have been through all this for so long we have the same enemies and the same friends."

"You're not thinking it through. Campaign managers usually become the chief administrative officer and I don't want that."

"Why not? All you need is smarts and honesty."

"Look, you're running against your hospitalization. Almost everyone knows about my DTs. How is that going to play out? You, with your breakdown, and my DTs? They'll play it up that two nut cases will be running the city."

He sat there looking at the desk for a moment.

"Ok you're right. Guy gets the title but you run the show."

"Good. Guy will do a lot better at the glad-handing and fund raising. He'll put a good face on the campaign and I get to wear jeans. But about the CAO, forget it. I'm going on a long hike after this."

"You're going to help me win this thing and then not help me run it?"

"I'll be on the AT for a few months. Save me a spot somewhere."

Over the years NOVA and our other groups had become more proficient. We had three or four women, usually wives of members, who could set up and run a phone bank just by being told to set up a twenty-person phone bank at such and such address. I'd get them the phone lists for the specific precincts to be called. They knew to contact our treasurer for the money, contact the phone company to have the phones installed, arrange to have our tables and chairs delivered, and run the ads for the workers. We had timed the average number of calls to be made in an hour and how many of those should be a contact resulting in a conversation. If a person fell below a certain number, they were let go. Our ladies reviewed the figures each night and weeded out the slackers. In addition to the noting of voters as one through five, if the conversation sounded positive, the callers would ask if the person would put up a yard sign. If they said yes, their name was taken, placed on a 3" X 5" carbon set. This was before personal computers so one of the pages from the carbon set went to the sign crew who would put up the sign. Once the sign was up, the sheet was turned in so a thank you letter from Nat could be sent along with a bumper sticker. The hard copy from the carbon set was kept in a 3 x 5 file and contacted for each election we were involved in. Naturally we started calling back the ones and twos three days before election day.

A college fraternity brother, a lawyer and jack-of-all-trades Tom Ford designed a silk screen process that silk screeners said was impossible until they saw it. Tom and another attorney friend could turn out pressboard signs cheaper and faster than the commercial shops. These white serif gothic black letters on a maroon background were repeated on billboards, in TV ads, on the sides of buses and on letterheads. They all read simply "Kiefer Mayor". There were made by the thousands for lawn signs and we could replace them as soon as they were taken down. It had been one of my jobs, while working with Nat in those other campaigns, to note as much as I could about each politician's strengths and weaknesses. And primarily to see if they were doing something with technology that we weren't. I kept files for that purpose but we weren't just conforming to standards, we were creating them.

We also did issue polling and when the results were tabulated, our guys were door knocking the neighborhoods that had the highest undecided and the pitch they made was tailor-made for that neighborhood based on the poll results. For months we had Nat himself door knocking in the high-undecided neighborhoods. Someone donated a mobile home for this purpose and his wife, Carol, was walking with him.

There were the usual fund raising banquets, coffee parties, beer and hot dog rallies and the debates. We ran a different program for each of the then sixty-eight identifiable neighborhoods in New Orleans. The intricacies of these operations were such that it was never done before nor would cost permit something of this scale to be done again. It involved running multiple polls of over 5,000 samples instead of the usual 600. We knew exactly where our vote was.

Nat was a moderate liberal in a field that contained another moderate liberal, a right wing conservative and a well-known black judge. Rusty finished writing the documentary and began on the one minute ads. For the documentary they filmed spontaneous comments interspersed with Rusty's text delivered by the narrator. They filmed one of Nat's friends since grammar school, his teachers, our high school coach, his coach at Tulane, law school friends, partners, other lawyers, elected officials and his wife, Carol. I spoke briefly of our father and the memory of his loss made those few lines unbelievably difficult to get out. Nat and his physician spoke frankly about the breakdown. They filmed our mother sitting at her dining room table. They asked her a question, her Irish rose up and she was off. The film began and ended with her voice speaking while photos of Nat's life appeared on the screen. The photos faded out and mother was shown seated in her home still speaking. "It was storming the night he was born," and laughing in reflection she added, "and my life's been a little stormy ever since." In the closing her strong voice rising in determination was heard to say as the same photos faded in, "Football, Law Review, all those honors and all the while having three children. And how did it do it? I'll tell you how he did it. By working three jobs, getting little or no sleep, that's how he did it. This boy exceeded my wildest expectations, beyond my wildest dreams. This boy is an extraordinary man. He never ceases to amaze me."

The documentary hit like a thunderclap. Nothing like it had ever been done. From the barrooms to the boardrooms the city was talking about it and the published reviews were remarkable.

" . . . simply the finest political film ever produced in New Orleans."

" . . . a rather remarkable film . . . the most ruthlessly candid portrayal of a candidate by his own team this writer has ever seen."

"A 40-carat documentary profile."

But perhaps political columnist Iris Kelso said it best. "I would have been fascinated with it even if I hadn't known Nat Kiefer, or if he weren't running for mayor. It's a brilliant film, one that captures the drama of one life, one struggle for success. It's brilliant in its honesty and its realism."

Rusty Cantelli won three national awards for the campaign. The brilliance of the film was without question and the credit for that goes to Bob Cole and the genius of Rusty Cantelli. Rusty wrote his last ad for a Kiefer in my 1992 judgeship race. I miss his keen and curious mind, his warm laughter and mostly I miss him. His passing a few years ago hit me hard and was one of the deepest felt curtains to fall on that year and that unforgettable campaign.

We had so many different programs in the field at the same time it was necessary, in order to control the confusion, that we run the campaign on a need to know basis. Our workers were told there were multiple ongoing programs but to focus on what there group was doing. We could be door knocking, phone banking for signs, and holding coffee parties, mailing printed material all in the same neighborhood and filming an ad at the same time. We had two different polling companies in the field and a back up check being run by a black phone bank all at the same time and none knew of the existence of the other.

There were 442 precincts in Orleans Parish in 1977. I stared at my handmade, color coded overlays on the precinct maps for so long, that I knew the approximate racial composition and average income of most of them just by being given the ward and precinct number. And I knew who was responsible for that precinct and which voices we were against.

Nat and I worked for fourteen months in the mayor's race, twelve to eighteen hours a day, and to make sure we had a program for every aspect of a campaign, I called in a national concern to look over our operation. One of their field men spent a few weeks with me and said he was amazed at what we were doing. We were running ideas no one else in the country had thought of doing. He said he didn't have a program that we weren't running and had no suggestions. I hired his firm anyway for push polling in the black neighborhoods. If the black judge's vote started to grow, it could cut into our black vote knocking us out of the runoff.

When the first primary was a few weeks off, all the polls were showing the same thing; Nat was in the lead and, more importantly, he was everyone's second choice. If he made the runoff, the mayor's office would be his. His support was too wide-based to lose to either the black judge or the white conservative. This was repeated in the independent polls and discussed widely by political commentators. The final week of the campaign our programs reached a crescendo and over a million pieces of mail, each designed for a specific purpose, often to a specific demographic group, began to hit. A small example of this was a program designed for married females between the ages of 25 and 45. They each received handwritten letter from Nat's wife telling them what a wonderful husband and father Nat was along with a black and white formal photograph of their family with the four children.

Election Day we were running turnout figures and at 3:00 PM Nat, having been in the mobile home and in shopping centers all day, came to the central headquarters. I could see he was drained. We all were. I told him to get the mobile home, take 30 guys and spend the rest of the day door knocking and hitting the shopping centers across the river. Our polls showed it to be our strongest ward but the turnout was too low. He said, "I'm beat. I can't go any more. If I haven't won this thing by now, I'm not going to win." He didn't go but I sent the canvassers there anyway.

That night at the celebration hotel we went to sleep running second by 107 votes. Our supporters were celebrating late into the night. When the machines were opened, counted and recounted, Nat ran third. According to our last polls, Nat peaked 3 or 4 days before election day. The black judge gained believability in the black community and ran too far ahead of us. Nat ran first in the ward I asked him to canvass and the turnout there finished 10% below the rest of the city. He lost by 242 votes or about half a vote per precinct.

After Nat's concession speech, I borrowed a friend's mobile home and drove to a small lake for three days. I didn't see or speak to anyone. On the evening of the second day, I pulled out the returns and studied them for a few hours. When I had what became the answers for me, I put the race away. We had given it our best shot, everything we had, and for me, there was no remorse or looking back except to see later how deeply it impacted Nat. He never recovered from that loss.

We began to mark time differently after that. Events in our lives happened not in terms of years but either before or after the mayor's race.

Nat was living in his new home, a 12,000 square foot beautiful fortress that sat on the shore of a lake in East New Orleans where he continued to hold the senate seat. He left his firm after the mayor's race and we opened our own offices, merging attorneys who worked for him and the firm I started with friends from law school. Business was better than good and Nat began drinking much too often. In the next governor's race our candidate lost and we also lost an important race for clerk of court but our batting average was still above .800. A year later, with Nat's assistance, I became a magistrate in criminal court. The mumblings of nepotism were largely silenced by my having been an indigent defender, law review editor and graduated seventh in my class. I had been third until my senior year, the year of his senate race and the mayoral race that made evening a score more important.

We continued to run campaigns, my role now greatly reduced, and it didn't have the same urgency or adrenaline rush as before. But all of us managed to laugh just as frequently. For the citywide elections in the early 80s, ten or fifteen of us were in our headquarters while the rest were out in the street. It was in the afternoon and I needed the latest turnout figures. One of four brothers, Joe Borrello, was among those who were there. Joe and his brothers Charles, Vincent and Peter were like brothers to Nat and me. They had been there from the beginning and for years we were inseparable. Joe was a giant: broad shoulders, deep chest, large arms and strong as a bull. I had been screaming at our crews to get me the turnout figures so I could tell the phone bank where to move. One of the black candidates on our NOVA ballot, a member of SOUL who held a house seat and was now running for councilman, chose that moment to stop by. Traveling with him on his election day rounds was Muhammad Ali. Every one in the headquarters was caught up in the magnetism of this magnificent athlete but I needed my turnout figures. He laughed and joked with our guys and people who came off the street to see him for an hour or longer. On another day I too would have been caught in the moment but not on election day. When Ali left, I lit into the guys.

"God damn we have work to do. Ali comes by and you guys act like you're fucking three years old. I needed those figures an hour ago."

Joe was standing in front of me and my words, while meant for all of them, were fired directly at him. He grabbed my face between his two massive hands, pulling me forward and kissed me full on the lips.

Every man was laughing so hard they nearly fell to the floor, me along with them. Joe was smiling broadly looking at me through his squinty eyes. He shook his head and said, "You crazy bastard."

Nat held parties at his home twice a year. At Christmas hundreds of people, mostly NOVA members and their families, would flow in and out of his house. A thirty-foot tree stood in the glass walled den covered with bows and framed by the swimming pool and the lights reflecting off the lake beyond. Carolers from parish prison lined the red-ribboned inside balcony and sang Christmas carols to the guests below. It was a night of laughter, the cheer of the season and the spirit of a warm brotherhood that was profound enough to be felt even by strangers.

On the Fourth of July we'd all get together again but the party would be outside around the pool. This party was usually exclusively for NOVA members and their families and we had a strange array of characters: two judges, a senator, members of the state central committee, contractors, lawyers, court reporters, a union business agent and more than a handful of drunks. In our earliest days, during the first house race, a sweet old timer from the river section of the ward saw something in Nat he thought good. He helped us for three years and when he passed away his son joined our group. He was genuine, just like his father and every bit as lovable. He worked at American Can Co. until that plant closed its doors. Drinking as he did, he went through a series of jobs and he couldn't stand being in an office. Every job we would find for him, he would turn down. When not campaigning he would paint houses and do odd jobs usually for the people in our group. He preferred to work with his hands rather than go door to door and he became one of our sign men. His name was Gene and in the early 70's Gene found his niche. He became a sergeant-at-arms in the Senate and Nat's driver. He idolized Nat and was his shadow when the legislature was in session. He was with Nat so often, people in the capitol and in our group started calling him senator. Edwin Edwards while he was still governor continued to call him senator even after Nat died.

We usually ran three or four two-man sign crews for our campaigns but Gene was the best and worked alone. He knew most of our locations by heart and found pride in being the best with his crew of one. In the late 70's he began to hang with an alcoholic; a weathered and beaten down older guy named Teddy Bear. They were drinking buddies. When the next few campaigns started, Gene had his own helper: Teddy Bear. He was there with the senator, putting up signs even in the worst weather. He was a nice enough guy though and quiet to the point of appearing shy. Gene began bringing him to those parties. He was still quiet but began warming to us over a few years. It was at one of the July parties, during my separation in 1980 or so, that a few of us stayed after most of the others had left. We were in Nat's kitchen talking nothing more than foolishness and I asked Teddy Bear. "Teddy Bear, how did you get that nickname?"

He smiled and asked in return, "You don't recognize me, do you Buz?"

"No, man, where do I know you from?"

"I'm Ted Cranston."

Things sometimes come full circle. Ted Cranston once waited in a small ditch across from my house with a shotgun meant for me. I was stunned. Not from fear but from what I saw. This had been one of the fastest, strongest street fighters I had seen and now he was a dried up, broken man I could snap like a dry twig. Without editing my thoughts I blurted out, "Ted? From the Park? What the hell happened to you?" Catching myself, I added quickly, "where have you been all these years?"

Not wanting others to hear what could embarrass the both of us we walked outside by the pool.

"How did you make it out Ted? How did you get out of it? I thought for sure you had to be dead by now."

There was no anger in either of us. I was sure we both recognized how lucky we were to be alive.

"Do you remember Bobby Galvin," he asked.

"Sure, he was killed."

"I was with him that night."

"I heard a bartender killed him."

"Yeah." His love for his dead hoodlum friend even after more than twenty years was apparent. I could see it in his face and in his movements and hear it in the shaking of his voice. "He got into it at the bar and told the guy he'd be back."

"I heard he told the guy he was getting his gun."

"Yeah." After a reflective pause he continued, "I told him not to go back, that we didn't need any shit over nothing but he wouldn't listen. We went back to the car, he got the pistol and I drove back to the front of the place to wait for him. Bobby went in and I heard the shotgun go off and I knew he was dead. He came running back to the car and just fell in across the seat. His head was in my lap and blood was all over everything. He looked at me and said, 'I'm dead. Get out of this. Get out Ted before you're killed too.' And then he just died."

What do you say when you hear this kind of horrible story? Do you say, I'm damn glad he bought it before the two of you managed to take off my head? But time had passed for all that. I just felt sorry for both of them. Genuine sorrow. Wasted life.

Remembering the difficulty I had in breaking off my street ties, and realizing he was in it far, far deeper than I could imagine, I asked him, "How did you manage to get out Ted? How did you stay alive?"

"After they held the grand jury on it, I joined the Army and kicked everything."

I'm sure I heard a different story than the DA. I didn't ask him how he got off the drugs but it was fairly obvious that booze had eased the transition and now demanded control.

Some died, some like Ted were shattered internally and some, like my friends and I, were very lucky. My scars were there and except for my family and a few breaks, the difference might have been one of degree only.

* * *

Mother's arthritis was progressing but her nature was untouched. My oldest daughter, Kyna, and her mother Michele, my ex-wife, were living a few doors from her home and the three of them were close. When Kyna was hospitalized for fourteen months Thelma's fire began to flicker a bit. She slipped into a familiar moroseness that disappeared when Kyna recovered. Within a few months mom was hospitalized with an irregular pulse. The doctors assured her and her sons that it was not life threatening and the condition could be controlled with medication. I believe mother caught a glimpse of something in that hospital for when she was discharged she began to refuse to leave the house. No matter what scheme Nat or I tried she had an excuse for missing parties and holiday dinners. Thelma was changing and Nat was becoming angry with her. We spoke of it at the office.

"Damn it, she went into that hospital as Thelma Kiefer and came out a little old lady. She quit on herself for no damn reason."

I began to talk with him about his drinking, tried to get him to pull up. After a few months of my trying one day while we were walking in a park near his home he told me he couldn't stop.

"I've tried it. If I go to bed sober I just stare at the ceiling all night. I have to get loaded to go to sleep."

History is colored by those who record it and there are many histories of Nat for one saw exactly what he allowed you to see. So I learned to look not where his light shined brightest but in the shadows. I remember a night at one of our favorite after work lounges. There were fifteen or twenty of us sitting around a few tables we had pulled together. Having been sober for years, I was laughing with them and watching them all get a little drunk. Nat as usual was master of ceremonies. Peggy Lee was on the jukebox singing. The place was crowded and while the loud noise and laughter continued I happened to look at him. He was staring at nothing. The party momentarily moved away from him and he was mouthing the words of her song, "If that's all there is my friends, then let's keep dancing". I thought then that he was beginning to see he had missed something essential in his insatiable pursuit of what . . . recognition, power? Maybe he was beginning to see that after a point most of it was of no importance. Regardless of how fervently we wish they would, no season of life lasts forever and I felt he was turning homeward, returning to the indispensable. I learned later that this embodiment of toughness and detachment had planted a row of rose bushes and cared for them.

* * *

Nat and I practiced law together, invested in real estate and continued to politic together. Being brothers it was natural that we would clash and usually over nothing that really mattered. We could call each other a son-of-a-bitch but no one else could. We had done it all our lives often to the confusion and amusement of our friends.

In 1984 we argued over some office furniture and didn't speak again for six months. Day after day we'd pass each other in the hall not saying a word or even making eye contact. In December of that year, shortly before Christmas, one of his sons called me.

"Uncle Buz, I know you and my dad aren't talking but I think you'd want to know he's in the hospital and he's pretty sick."

I saw him that night. It was the beginning of a long battle. He had cirrhosis. Early the following month he flew to Georgia to see specialists. I was outside working in the yard on a Saturday and my wife called to me. I walked to the sound of her voice. She held the phone in her hands covering the mouthpiece.

"It's Nat. He's calling from the hospital."

"Hey Nat. What's up?"

I expected the stoicism but not his words; "I bought the farm Buz. I'm not going to make it."

"What do you mean?"

"They say it's terminal."

We talked a bit longer. I asked if he needed help getting home. He said no.

He returned to the city, was hospitalized and began his months long struggle with the unalterable. In an impeccable display of willpower, for an important bill, he flew to the capitol in a helicopter to cast his vote and took the microphone for the last time. He said a few words about the importance of the matter but the remainder was addressed to his colleagues, telling them of his pride in having been among such men.

I watched him become smaller, his eyes lost their smile and became hollow. His features drew in and became gaunt. His chest and arms withered beneath his hospital gown. I went to the airport the morning he was placed into a jet for medical transport. Before I stepped off the plane we spoke our last words, whispering in unison that we loved the other. At age 46 he died in California awaiting a liver transplant. Thousands jammed the church at St. James to attend the funeral. The governor and Nat's close ally, Sammy Nunez, president of the senate, eulogized him. The night before Sammy called me and read the remarks he would make the following day. This hardened politician from a blue-collar district wept as he read to me of his admiration and love and some of the things that Nat had done to win them. In due course the legislature named a building after him; an arena he fought for years to build for UNO. The structure is now the Kiefer-UNO Lakefront Arena.

For years the guys in our group and even our wives lived with an uncanny expectation that he would walk through the door any minute, look around and ask, "You guys didn't really believe all that did you?" It was a lingering impression we shared. This just couldn't happen to Nat. He was too tough, too strong to die. There is only so much the mind retains but the heart remembers much more. In laughter, in the changing seasons, his memory still haunts us.

* * *

Throughout his illness I saw my mother almost daily and called her on the days I could not get to her. I tried to prepare her but she held to the hope that somehow he'd surprise us again. Perhaps from a lifelong premonition, she had always voiced her greatest fear was to outlive either of her sons. We were sitting on her side porch a few weeks after he died. She was so badly crippled with arthritis and distraught that she could not attend his funeral.

"Buz you know I can't get past this."

"What do you mean?"

"I . . . I just can't do it Buz." And Thelma Davis Kiefer, with her hard Irish Channel toughness, broke down and cried with a tormented silent scream that cut into me. What would dad say to give her purpose?

"Ma, that's bullshit. I need you. We both need each other."

She tried to throw her head back, face the world and the bitterness it held, but she could only say, "I'll try son . . . I'll try to be here for you as long as I can . . . but . . . I just don't . . ."

I leaned over and took her in my arms. Her once heavy shoulders were bony and frail. "We'll make it ma. We don't have a choice, do we?"

She died a month later.

*   *   *

I miss the magic of those moments when we were young and the world was still dew covered and tomorrow always held the promise of a sunrise. I miss those who are no longer here: Joe Borrello, Mr. Pete, Jose Meceria, Joe Poolich, Guy Wootan, Willie Moten, Mike Grosz, Mike, Don and Edgar Roig, Nils Douglas, Emile Schneider, Skip Tessier, Rusty Cantelli and most of all Nat and my parents. I miss the laughter of the men with whom we fought and played and their brotherhood, for while it still remains, the fire of it lies in the past. It came to me that we had more in common with our political enemies than with those who never climbed into the arena at all.

Now when I see Nat he's always piloting his twin-diesel Lafayette skiff in the blue-green waters of Lake Pontchatrain. His white polo shirt is tight across his broad chest and the sleeves strain against his biceps. He looks over his shoulder to see his wake kicking up high and broad and turns to smile at me. His light hair is blowing wildly in the wind, his sunglasses are dark and his skin is suntanned. He's away from the city running flat out and I know he's free.

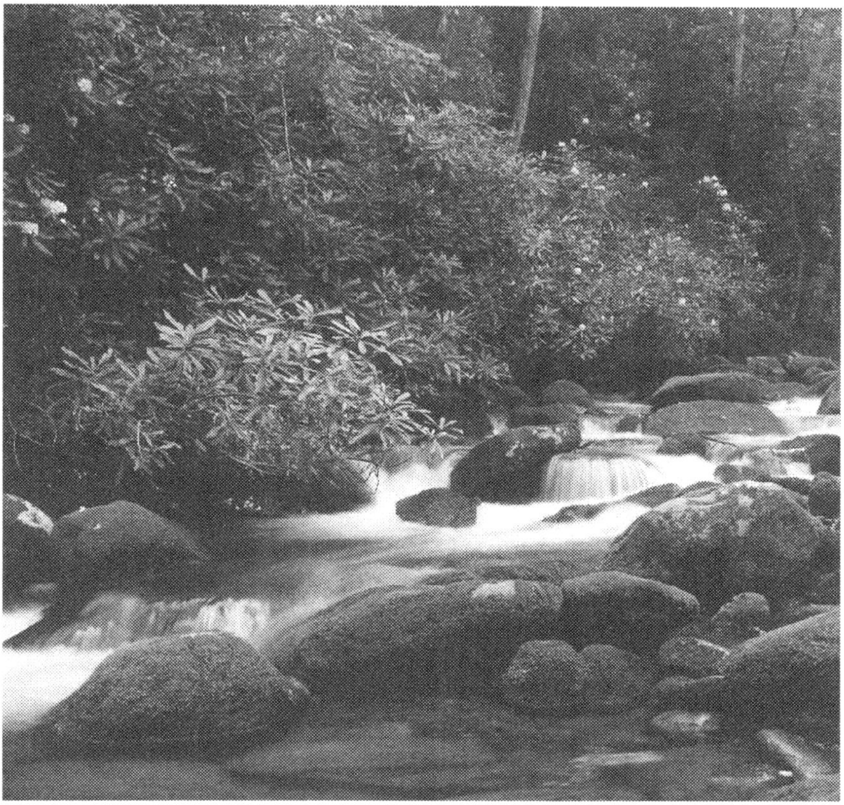

Evergreen

Gossamer night clouds
spread softly through needle leaves.
Of what do trees dream?

The old man swung the large pack in one motion from the ground to his back and slipped his arms through the supporting straps. He exhaled from the strain of lifting, walked without sound to the far wall and grabbed his walking stick. He slipped his hand through the leather thong at the top, grasped the shaft firmly and pushed the gate open. He was the last of the hikers to leave the shelter. He stepped sideways so the pack and his body could squeeze through the opening and he felt a stab of pain in his knee. He turned to the northeast and pushed off. Again the knee pained him.

It was an overcast morning and the forest canopy blocked what little sunlight managed to fall through the clouds. In spite of the coolness of the morning he would soon be sweating. The knee would bother him a while longer, then fade and be replaced by another ache. At his age hiking required not only acceptance of pain but indifference to it. He walked for hours and for much of that time only his thoughts occupied him. If he became preoccupied with pain or allowed it to be first in his mind it would consume all else until it became the hike. Pain was just another part of back packing like the rain that sometimes caught him or the uphills that seemed to go on without end.

In truth, he was not a strong hiker. His body was too damaged, too used up, but his nature drew him to both the physical and reflection, and so, in spite of the difficulties, he hiked. Among tress and along streams he sensed a purpose. The city, his work; that, he believed, was the pretense. He was a professional with a responsible position and did well enough as he prepared and knew the field better than most. But occasionally he would lay awake, wondering if the rules should apply when they brought about the wrong result. The answers given before subordinates were often rechecked in private, convinced there was reason enough for his concern. Straightening his tie or brushing his hair before he took to the stage, he would occasionally stop, let his arms slowly move to his sides and he would study the reflected face of a stranger. How did he arrive here and could others see the lie of it? Whatever he did, whatever small recognition he earned, it was not enough to convince him. He didn't belong here and nothing here defined him. It was the routine that fit him, not the role. We sell our lives for so much the hour and yet, at the end, we would trade it all for a few breaths, for a kiss, to smile into a lover's eyes one time more before the shadow passes. He did not intend for that shadow to choose either the place or the time. When the city's voices momentarily fell silent, he felt the pull of wild places. Between the words of business he could hear the wind rushing up a remote peak, bending and straining the tall trees as they swayed in its grip and a hawk calling as it slipped a thermal and glided sideways in a sudden descent. In mountains and forest he sensed something fundamental and alive. He hiked for the quiet passion wilderness brought him, for the sanctuary of a stream somewhere, always flowing, filled with life and always distant.

The previous afternoon he started from Clingman's Dome and spent the evening at the trail shelter lying just north of Mt. Collin's peak. Located on a short side spur off the Appalachian Trail, the shelter was a three-sided stone hut, fashioned from fieldstone and covered with corrugated tin. On most evenings, these shelters provided refuge to hikers and most of the mice from the nearby woods. Eating whatever they can find, mice scamper throughout the night from pack to pack while their benefactors, the hikers, slept. Occasionally they would chew into a pack, nest in spare clothes, shred a hole or two in a shirt or pair of shorts, and in the process impart a certain character to an otherwise useless garment. Because he could do nothing about them, he had learned that mice too were less bothersome once they were accepted.

His route today would be difficult. He had a pounding downhill to a low gap a few miles distant and then, turning north, a longer downhill to a parking lot. From there he would hitch a ride to the trailhead of Alum Cave and then climb to the crest of Mt. Leconte. But he had an early start and yesterday's short trail to the shelter had acclimated him to both the elevation and the rhythm of hiking again. He was pleased to be on the trail and his enthusiasm would carry him over the harder pulls. It would be a long day, yes, but not an altogether frustrating struggle. Regardless of how slow he walked, he would eventually get to the next shelter by simply placing one foot in front of the other.

Mt. Collins was the northeastern shoulder of Clingman's Dome and, like the Dome, was mantled in spruce and fir. In the high country, these northern trees found a home during the last ice age. As the ice sheets retreated, pockets of these evergreens remained along the spine of the Smokys. The cool summers and the high humidity allowed them to survive for thousands of years. Hiking in these high woods as a young man he found a serenity in them he no longer found in church. Dark and single canopied, the treetops were so thick and tightly woven that only a few shrubs managed to grow in the deep moist shade below. Wood sorrel and ferns were everywhere and rose only slightly above the thick carpet of moss. Here he found enchantment, a mingling of the mystical and the uplifting. Through the woods ran the ribbon of trail, yellow-orange from the ferrous compounds in the underlying stone, leading one not merely to points on a compass, but if one were so inclined, inwardly as well. Resins from the conifers, clean and rich, and beneath that, the subtle aroma of the organic soil and the decaying needles filled the woods with its distinct scent. The clean feel of the chill, moist air on his skin and the freshness of it in his lungs filled him with energy he rarely felt elsewhere. Elsewhere the air was oppressive and brought him remorse.

He was no longer young and this forest was changing quickly. Aphids carelessly brought into the country caused widespread destruction, sucked the fir trees dry and left their corpses behind like crosses in a graveyard. Even in death these massive trees stood for years supported by others whose grip on life was tenuous and slipping.

But there were other causes for the decline. Rain soaked the trees in a bath of acid, percolated down through the soil and attacked the forest in ways not fully understood. Ozone leached minerals from their leaves and caused branches to die. Years of declining rain and snowfall destroyed much of the forest and, in widespread patches, the carpet of mosses was gone. Snails, frogs, salamanders, centipedes—all were failing and increasingly their offspring were found deformed. Death was spreading its tentacles and the flow of energy slowed. Large holes appeared in the canopy and sunlight now struck the forest floor. Tender vegetation unable to survive in direct sunlight was dying. Large unsightly brambles replaced them and spread as the forest succumbed to multiple attacks. Was this merely a cycle whose huge interval precluded prior recording? Or was it a harbinger of a more destructive and permanent shift?

John Knowles had written, "Nothing endures, not a tree, not love, not even death by violence." That compelling observation haunted him and his love for this place was due largely to the counterpoint it offered that unending hopeless isolation. These trees, this holy soil, this panorama of shifting energy had persevered. Everything is in transition, nothing is immutable but he did not want to see the changes coming here. In a life of seemingly endless change it had been a singular constant.

It was still early morning when he reached the gap and several cars were in the small parking lot. A young family had spread a blanket on the grass and were enjoying the morning sun, the trees, and each other. Husband and wife were on the blanket; he sitting up watching the children while she lay with her head propped against his leg. They smiled at him. There were two small children running in a circle of laughter and the old man remembered his family and the loneliness that replaced them.

"Good morning," the young man said to him.

"Hello," he said and asked, "Enjoying the morning?"

"Sure are. How about you? Been hiking long?"

"Nah. Just long enough to loosen the cobwebs."

"How far are you going?" the young man asked.

"Over to Mt. Leconte—about eight miles I figure."

"Where are you coming from?"

The old man turned to the south and saw the endless ridges and valleys extending beyond North Carolina into Georgia. He could see Fontana Lake, and further still, the Nantahalas. Beyond that he knew for certain that Standing Indian and Mount Springer lay further south. His memories of them were vivid. Not only could he see them, he could feel them, smell them and hold them. He knew their winds, their sudden storms and their cathedral-like silence. They were his. They would always be his.

Where was he coming from? From the south, from the north, from this morning, from noon. Forever. I am from here. This is my home.

"Left Mt. Collins a little while ago," he replied. "Left my car at Clingman's last evening."

"How are you going to get back from Leconte to get your car?"

The old man chuckled. "Sure as hell haven't figured it out yet. I suppose I could hitch a ride. You do any hiking?"

"Nah. We used to camp, the wife and I, before the kids, but now . . . it's just too hard. Maybe when they're older."

"Don't wait too long. It's easier to get the message when you're young."

"Message? What message?"

"You see," the old man laughed, "you're already too late."

They both smiled and the old man started down the trail and disappeared beyond a turn. Behind him the couple and their children were left in the patch of sunlight near the parking lot.

"Good luck," the young man called after him.

Get out, he thought to himself. Get out and walk these woods, you and your family. Take them with you and walk through these mountains before you become a ghost man with half a will or before you lock your heart in a deposit box. Get out and see something of the real world. Get out while you still remember your name.

For the next three miles, he descended rapidly, dropping over fifteen hundred feet. The trail followed one of the tributaries of a major stream and had been the earliest road to cross the backbone of the Smokys. Wagons and teams strained against the mountain inching their way up these peaks and paid a modest toll for the privilege. Then, as now, the trail was always in sight or sound of the tumbling, cascading stream. His pace quickened and he dropped below the line of spruce and fir and the yellow birches and maples slowly replaced them. Occasionally, he would see one of the birches perched on stilt-like roots two or three feet high. Seeds had landed on fallen logs and put roots into the soft decaying wood. For years it received nourishment from its ancestor and eventually was left standing on elevated supports as the old tree vanished beneath it.

Near the midpoint of his descent, he stopped to photograph a small group of yellow orchids. The delicate flowers stood on spikes and nodded slightly in the nearly still mountain breeze. He adjusted his shutter speed to allow for this movement and tripped the release. As he stood he felt a stiff, dull pain in his back. The long downhills were easy on his lungs but the pounding they caused increased the pain in his back. He stood up straighter and stretched his back while letting out a loud grunt. It was a fine morning and he filled his lungs with the sweet mountain air. He let out a loud yell and started down the trail again.

He came to a pool lit by a sliver of sunlight at the base of a small fall. Rhododendrons grew to the water's edge on the other side. He dropped his pack, took off his boots and waded into the stream. A salamander, sunning itself on a moss-covered rock took slight notice as he entered. The man gathered a handful of pebbles from the streambed, pebbles that were worn flat and striated with a lighter material. Sedimentary rock, he thought. Laid down on the floor of a sea. A sea bed. And bulldozed up here by plates slamming together millions of years ago. Bulldozed here to cover the inland sea that was here before the plates came together. Here, another sea, long before the mountains were. He studied the pebbles briefly and then lifted his head skyward looking at but not seeing the slow-moving clouds.

Laughter floated down the trail and in a moment he saw two young girls giggling their way uphill. They slowed upon seeing the old man standing in the stream and his worn pack lying on the bank.

"Hello," he said.

"Hi," they replied as they eased past the pool and then quickened their pace. As they disappeared from sight, he again heard giggles.

"I have heard the mermaids singing each to each. I do not think they shall sing to me," he said softly. How he wished to be young again. To discover this land all over. To roam these mountains for another forty or fifty years. To feel the wild freedom of this place with its picture-book beauty at every turn in the trail. To make love in the quiet shade. To hear the birds, feel the brook, breathe the air and to lie in the very heart of these mountains and feel its peace dropping slowly, covering him like a blanket of autumn leaves.

He lowered his head, slowly opened his hand and dropped the pebbles back into the pond. He turned to locate the sun and knew he must hurry; the day was moving on and the uphill to Leconte was still before him.

As he planned, and without too long a wait, he managed a ride from the parking lot to the Alum Cave trailhead. Although the shortest trail to the top of Leconte, it was for him the finest in the park. He had hiked it in snow and in the flames of autumn. He had hiked it in spring's patchwork greening and in the deep shade of summer. He had taken some of his better photographs along this trail. The scene changed not only with the seasons, but by the hour or minute. Each shifting latitude and changing degree in the sun's western flight produced a kaleidoscope of shadows and color and patterns. With his camera he had tried to preserve his understanding of it on film; through his senses he kept it for himself in a special place.

The trail was a garden walk for the first few miles. It meandered on either side of a gentle stream and passed through a virgin hardwood forest. Rhododendron, now in bloom, lined the trail and a small Junco played hide-and-seek as he approached. The bird would fly a short distance up the trail and fly again as the old man drew near. Calling as he went, he dared him to follow.

He came to a large mass of black stone whose center was slowly eaten out by water stealing a grain of it at a time. Now hollow, it now enclosed a stone stairway that was part of the trail. A mile beyond this rock, a large heath bald overlooked the valley he descended that morning. No trees grew here; only stunted shrubs of rhododendron, azalea and mountain laurel. Were it not for the trail, this area would be an impenetrable mass of tightly woven vegetation locked together against the winds that race up the face of the cliff below. On a ledge near the end of the bald he took off his pack and stretched out in the sun, resting. Above this point the trail became more difficult and his body ached. Across the valley he saw Mount Collins where he spent the previous night. He fished out his canteen and a painkiller. After taking a long drink he noticed clouds forming in the valley below and pushing their way up the hollows. He was running out of time.

He rolled to his right onto his side and beyond the bald he saw the rocky stone outcropping that gave the trail its name: Alum Cave Bluff. While he studied the familiar stone wall, memories of years now distant washed over him. A golden red sunset from an alpine meadow in autumn; holding his daughter's tiny hand as she slept, afraid of thunder; a lightning storm beneath a summit on a spring night; countless days of making and sharing love. All these moments, are they lost forever or are they out there, suspended in time, waiting to be lived and relived again and again?

He rolled again onto his back. He poured canteen water on his forehead and let it find its way into his closed eyes. He let it stay there awhile, cooling his face. He sat up, shook his head from side to side, shaking off the water. He got to his feet and swung his pack onto his back. Once again he felt the pain in his knee and a sharp pain in his hip. "Soon," he said to himself while looking uphill.

The pull up the bald is steep and beyond that the trail remains steep. At the base of the bluff he trudged uphill and kept climbing until his wind gave out. Gasping for breath, he bent over from the waist placing his hands on his knees to support his upper body. Sweat ran from his forehead into his eyes and burned. He rubbed his eyes with his balled up fist and turned to his rear to see the full view of the bluff. In a land where everything was green and moss covered, this huge exposed rock was beautiful. Eons of erosion gave the bluff a concave face more than a hundred yards across. From this angle it was stark and powerful.

He wiped the sweat from his forehead, and breathing normally again, he turned and continued uphill. The steepness of the trail increased and soon his breathing was in spasms. The pain in his back and hips became intense. Twenty steps, thirty, fifty and he would stop and gasp for air before starting again. Like a modern day Sisyphus, boulder strapped to his back, the process was repeated.

The arriving would take care of itself provided he kept moving; going was the important thing. What mattered to him internally was that he did not stand where he stood the day before. So by the yard, and bent over, he made his way inexorably up the mountain.

His slow climb eventually brought him again to the spruce-fir forest and near his stop for the night. It was late in the afternoon and already the air had a chill to it. Soon the clouds would catch him. Again he studied the canopy and noticed the hole left by the death of a large softwood. Where do warriors go when war has left their hearts?

He should have quit these uphills years ago. No longer could he escape the pain even while asleep. He would toss throughout the night as painkillers and muscle relaxants failed to bring relief. But this was his last trip and it had been planned for too long. One last race, he thought; one last time up Leconte.

Within the hour, he came to the flat of the mountaintop and could breathe easier. With far less effort he covered the last quarter mile to the trail shelter and walked in. Two young men were already there cooking dinner. His legs were shaking from fatigue.

"Hello," they both said.

"Hey," he replied. "How's it going?"

"Fine, how about you?" asked the one settled on the bunk.

"Rough. Leconte is about two thousand feet higher this year," said the old man.

"Where are you coming from?" asked the one near the stove.

"Mt. Collins this morning," he replied as he slipped out of his pack.

"Pretty hike?" asked the younger of the two.

"Yes, very. How about yourselves?" the old man asked.

"Three shelters north. Started from Davenport three days ago. It's an easy hike once you get past Guyot," he said.

"Been that way a few times," the older man said. "They had a plane crash up on Guyot a year or so ago. Could you see anything?"

"Yeah," the younger one replied. "Looked like it exploded. Small parts of the plane were scattered all over the trail for more than a hundred yards."

"Damn shame that someone should die in a place like this," the other young man said.

"I don't know," said the old man. "Death is all around us here, but so is birth. Look at that log out there. It died just a few years ago, but look at it now. All along the length of it spruce seedlings are sprouting. And look at the mosses and ferns. I'll bet there are hundreds of bugs and millions of bacteria living in there.

"All those bugs eat the plants and each other. One big ecosystem right in that log. The energy going from one organism to another so it can live while the other dies. Atoms and molecules that were locked in that log are scattered throughout the forest up here—in those plants, in all these insects and undoubtedly a deer or two by now. In a way, that tree still is still living. Life and death is a constant cycle here."

"Well, I'm going to `cycle' some of this rice. Would you care for some?" the young man by the stove asked.

* * *

Sunlight filtered through the grove of fir trees in front of the shelter and woke the old man before the other two. He could smell the smoldering embers of the campfire that had managed to glow dimly through the night. Quietly and with an efficiency that came with years of routine, he slipped out of his bag, warmed water over his small stove and made coffee. The odor of the coffee mingled with the smoke of the campfire and cued up memories of countless similar mornings. The metal canteen cup warmed his hands and the coffee was pleasantly warm going down. He sat on the edge of the bunk watching the early morning movements of the woods. A wren hopped from a log onto the ground just in front of the shelter floor and announced the sun in a thin, brave voice.

Soon the young men were up and moving and, mindful of the quiet, fixed breakfast and washed their gear making barely a sound. They were low on food, they said, and the older man, his hike nearly over, gave them the extra ration he always carried. Good-byes were said and the old man was left alone in the shelter. He was in no hurry. The hike to the Jump Off was only six miles and most of that was downhill or gentle. He smelled the spruce trees that told of distant Christmases. His memories of Leconte rushed through the years and filled him with the warmth of contentment. His oldest child's birthday celebrated here by a shelter full of back packers one cool evening in July; a late summer night sky shared with a young girl who wanted to be held but did not ask; a winter storm that raged for two days as the food ran low. He was drawn to this mountain with its needle tree crown; its summit with its harsh windswept southern face creating a natural bonsai garden, the trails leading to the top, each more lovely than the other, and finally, the eastern most peak with its grand sunrises. Leconte was the beating, pulsating heart of the park and stood almost at its center.

He picked up a twig, twirled it slowly in his fingers, studying the needles. "Endure," he said quietly. To himself, after a moment had passed, he whispered, "Ah, Zarathustra, your golden ball passes to me." He folded a bit of paper on which he had written a brief note and placed it and his drivers license into his waterproof film bag and closed his pack. He rose and slipping it on, he turned sideways, and eased himself through the gate. Toward the east he climbed a small rise to a trail junction. To the left and downhill he followed the trail to the Jump Off. Descending steeply for the first mile or so, he came to a series of undulating ridgeline that brought him below the indistinct line separating the spruce-fir forest from the hardwoods. On his third hiking day the pain was constant. He trudged along the trail reaching a hairpin which dropped off abruptly to his left. Halfway, he thought. He slipped out of the sweaty pack and sat on the stone trail, feet stretched in front of him, his back against a tree. He found a candy bar in one of the outer pockets of his pack and took out his canteen. He rarely ate much of a lunch on the trail. He preferred to eat a quick bite and continue on before he cooled off too much. Today he took his time and made iced tea with the water in the canteen. Overhead a hawk gliding on a thermal made a graceful arch, and having located its prey, fell quickly from sight. The loneliness and grace of the hawks' flight in these mountains he understood; he had seen them on his earliest hikes. Where was its mate, he wondered.

The sun was bright and bold shafts of light cut through openings in the shading canopy like hundreds of small spotlights. The morning was quiet and damp and still cool. Growing just off the trail, he found a patch of Monkshood in bloom and he photographed them for the simple joy of doing the familiar. Side lit and solemn, speckled with dew and isolated in a dark background, he was sure the exposures would sell. After taking several frames, he repacked his gear and started out once more. Soon the downhill and flats brought him to the uphill of his last ascent. He stopped at the base, looked up the trail, took several long, deep breaths and began. After fifty steps, he had to stop and breathe. When the gasping stopped he moved again. Over and over the scene repeated itself, until finally, after more than an hour, he reached the summit. Bent over and gasping, the old man raised his head—he was back in the spruce-fir forest.

"It's all downhill from now on, you bastard," he smiled to himself.

The junction with the Jump Off trail was just a short distance ahead. Along the razorback which leads to the overview witch hobble, Clintonia and plantain grew in the shade of the spruce and fir. The view is of the valley separating the Jump Off from Charlie's Bunion to the east. Although each can be seen from the other, they are separated by more than a mile and a plunge of fifteen hundred feet.

He arrived at the rock outcropping at the end of the spur and slipped the shoulder strap of his camera over his head and then eased his pack to the ground. Fishing through his pockets he found two rolls of exposed film and placed these and his camera inside the waterproof film bag along with the rest. Opening his pack, he took out his canteen and some trail food. He then placed the film sack in a protected location in the pack and secured it again. He leaned the pack in plain view against a tree where it was sure to be found. Sitting on the ground he now allowed his eyes to study the view of the valley a few feet to his front and then finally raising his eyes he gazed north to the fertile farmlands beyond the park. To the east and northeast, the entire backbone of the Appalachian crest lay exposed. He studied the majestic line of it until he drank from his canteen.

It was a fine day. Blue skies were accentuated by an occasional cloud. Two hawks slowly riding an updraft slid past his view playing out the ritual of a hunting pair. He smiled at a thought and watched them disappear from view over a ridge to his left. A breeze stirred. He inhaled deeply and held the breath for a moment, savoring it. He looked across the valley and saw the Bunion. How many times had he hiked there? Who was with him? How many years ago?

In time the sun would set, but he would stay there until the fading light of dusk. For now, he was content to rest his back against the stone with his legs stretched out before him. There would be no gesture or ceremony other than that provided by the setting sun. This sunset, on this day, he would not photograph; it would be shared with no one. He judged that today's close would be spectacular. In fact, he was positive.

CPSIA information can be obtained
at www.ICGtesting.com
Printed in the USA
LVHW091603290520
656820LV00001B/15